THE

POMEGRANATE

LADY

AND HER SONS

THE

℘OMEGRANATE

ℒADY

AND HER ℐONS

 SELECTED STORIES

GOLI TARAGHI

Translated from the Persian by Sara Khalili

W. W. NORTON & COMPANY

New York • London

For my brother, Bijan.

CONTENTS

THE

POMEGRANATE

LADY

AND HER SONS

GENTLEMAN THIEF

*M*y mother, my grandmother, and I lived a comfortable and peaceful life in three adjacent rooms and three separate worlds in a two-story house with a garden, a reflecting pool, and an old weeping willow tree.

I was a second-year student of philosophy at the university and I thought about anything and everything except a revolution, a war, the closing down of the universities, and becoming a rootless drifter.

Grandmother was eighty-four. She thought she would live for many years to come and would continue to command and to rule over us.

Mother was a gentle and fragile woman. She loved doing embroidery, making floral arrangements, and cultivating fragrant flowers in our greenhouse. She liked plants more than she liked people.

We had a cook named Ali Agha and a maid named Nanny Henna-Hair. As soon as the revolution broke out, they left us without any notice. Without any explanation. Still, we were grateful that they didn't report us to the authorities; otherwise we would have ended up in prison. At the time, my father was in Canada on a mission for the Shah's government. He had close ties with all the ministers, ambassadors, and government bigwigs. His head was certainly destined for the noose. We thanked God that he was out of the country and we encouraged him to stay away and wait for the revolution to end and for the Shah to return to Iran. Sadly, a few months later he died in a car accident on an icy mountain road. And the revolution didn't end and the Shah didn't return to Iran either.

My mother screamed and cried so much that she not only drove herself crazy, but she drove us crazy, too. She never recovered from my father's death and she lost a bit of her sanity. She took dozens of sedatives every day, spent much of the time half-asleep, and often forgot where she was and what was going on around her. Grandmother grew quiet—the sort of dangerous silence that could suddenly erupt, like a sleeping volcano. She was seething inside and rumbling quietly. At the time, I was in love with a classmate who was pro-revolution and it was this tentative love affair that saved me from going mad like Mother. I would cry for hours, but then with the first telephone call from the young man, I would forget all about my father's death and go running around the streets, raising a ruckus with him. I was oblivious to the treachery and deceit of politics.

My love affair was short-lived. My revolutionary friend was arrested and his family moved away from our neighborhood. I was young and my broken heart healed quickly. Soon I was day-dreaming about another love. I believed the revolution would not touch us and I was content in this delusion. That is, until the Revolutionary Court issued a warrant for our house to be confiscated. We received a notice saying, more or less, The good days are over, please take your leave.

"Take our leave to where?" Grandmother said.

The court's server who had delivered the notice said, "That's not our concern. You can take your leave to hell for all we care."

Grandmother was ready to pounce on him. Mother was watching from a distance. Her eyes were half-closed. She looked like she was dreaming. I threw myself at Grandmother and covered her mouth with my hand. I was no match for her. She weighed ninety kilos. Perhaps more. It was a blessing that she was an invalid and couldn't stand up. Instead, all her strength was concentrated in her sharp tongue.

Grandmother would not be bullied. She wasn't afraid of anyone.

She held her head high and said, "I will not go. This is my house" (it wasn't) "and the deed is in my pocket" (she was fibbing), "and I will shoot whoever sets foot here."

Shoot?

Grandmother produced a rickety rifle from under her pillow and laid it on the ground next to her. It was the old rifle my grandfather used when he hunted wild goats and ducks. It had no trigger and no pellets. Grandmother kept it under her pillow in case she needed to scare away burglars. Thank God the court's server had left.

Mother fainted the moment she saw the rifle and we had to call Auntie Badri and her husband. Grandmother was all fired up and kept aiming the rifle at anyone who came near her.

I thought Auntie Badri would rush over to our house. But she called three times, at one-hour intervals, to say that she was on her way. It was strange, but strange things had become normal. The world, our world, had turned upside down and we couldn't grasp the meaning and logic of events and incidents.

It was close to dusk when Auntie finally arrived. She was worried and upset, but she was trying hard to hide it from Grandmother. She kept smiling for no reason and constantly showered us with flowery terms of endearment. My aunt's husband was standing in the entrance hall and refused to come in. He looked very pale. At first I thought he was sick, but then I realized that he was terrified of being in our house. It was as if he thought they would confiscate him, too. He kept looking at his watch and wanted to leave as soon as possible. I had always had a different image of him—that of a witty and confident man. He was talkative and had an opinion about everything. He wore Western suits and silk ties and his watchband was white gold. Now, everything about him had changed. He hadn't shaved, he wasn't wearing a tie, and he had an old leather watchband. He looked like a faded and altered photograph. It was hard to recognize him.

I could hear Auntie and her husband arguing. Auntie started out by whispering, but gradually her voice grew louder and louder and then she suddenly screamed, "What would you have me do? Leave my mother out on the street?"

Her husband kept repeating, "It's dangerous. They'll come after us."

"Why would they come after us?" Auntie asked. "Are we breaking any laws? I just want to bring my old mother to live with me."

Again, he said, "It's dangerous. They are watching us."

Finally, Auntie told her husband, "Go sit in the car and don't interfere."

Grandmother loved Auntie Badri. She put down her rifle next to her pillow and said, "We will stay right here. We won't trouble you."

Auntie Badri laughed and said, "Dearest Mom, where in the world did you find this dilapidated rifle? Put it away. People will laugh at you. And don't worry about the house. We will file a lawsuit with the court. But it will take a couple of weeks. Come and stay with me until then."

"With me" was a phrase that delighted Grandmother.

"My dear," she said, "I'd give my life for you." She looked like she was going to cry, but she went on to say, "No, I'm more comfortable here. Your house is too big. I won't come."

Mother had taken her sedatives and was dozing off, but she could hear everything. She mumbled, "Here. There. What difference does it make? The sky is the same color no matter where we go."

Auntie Badri insisted. She sat next to Grandmother and kissed her face and hands. "Everything will be all right. I promise. Things won't stay like this. This is all temporary."

Mother moaned and muttered, "Everything is temporary. Everything." And then she started calling for Ali Agha.

Grandmother shook her head sadly and said, "There is no Ali Agha, my dear. That double-crossing louse got up and left the minute things changed."

"He is gone, too," Mother said. "A temporary cook."

Arguing was useless. Grandmother knew we had no choice but to leave. Yet she wanted to at least put up a fight and not surrender too easily.

"I've prayed and fasted all my life," she said. "What the heck do they want from me? As a matter of fact, they should reward me with a second house."

Who were we? Three lone women. We were no match for the Revolutionary Court and the Foundation of Martyrs. We were no match for anyone. We were scared of our own shadow. Grandmother's huff-and-puff was just a big bubble in the air.

Where would we go? For now, to Auntie Badri's house. But what would we do with our belongings and all the household furnishings?

"Don't make it hard on yourselves," Auntie said. "We'll call secondhand dealers and sell everything—from the tables and chairs to the refrigerator and the stove."

Grandmother shouted. Balked. She clawed at her hair and at Mother's hair.

"You want to put my life up for sale?" she screamed. "You want to leave me bare-assed and living in other people's homes? You want to sell the carpet from under me?"

"No," Auntie said. "We'll put the carpets in a bank vault for safekeeping."

The next day, the secondhand dealers came to the house and got busy appraising everything and buying the tables and chairs and the silverware. My heart was breaking for Grandmother. She had lived a lifetime with these things. She felt her pride and honor were being auctioned off and her past put up for sale.

"Mr. Secondhand Dealer," she said, "excuse me, would you please come over here?"

Auntie looked at Grandmother in alarm and stopped haggling with one of the dealers.

The other was holding a large frying pan under his arm. His face was flushed with excitement and he kept running around, asking for the price of this and that item. He walked over to Grandmother.

Grandmother was sitting in her wheelchair, smiling. Her good humor was cause for concern.

"Hello," she said. "How much did you pay for the frying pan?"

Auntie took a few steps forward and said, "Mother, please don't tire yourself." She meant, Please don't interfere.

"Let me see the frying pan," Grandmother said.

The dealer obeyed and handed it to her. He was in a hurry. The other dealer was picking out the better pieces.

Grandmother grabbed the frying pan by the handle and shouted, "You unscrupulous scamp. Aren't you ashamed of yourself? You've raided someone's home like a vulture and you're robbing the dead? But I'm still alive. I'll teach you a lesson, you scoundrel." And before Auntie and I could make a move, she raised the frying pan and slammed it on the dealer's head. Auntie screamed, "Oh!" The dealer yelled, "Ouch!" And he leapt back and groaned. The other dealer laughed and Grandmother, proud and satisfied, laid the frying pan on her lap.

Auntie ran and fetched a glass of water for the man. She apologized a thousand times and whispered to him that Grandmother wasn't well, that recent events had made her emotionally unstable.

Grandmother heard her and shouted, "Not at all! My brain works better than ever. You're the ones who have lost your mind."

Auntie put one of Mother's sedative pills in Grandmother's tea and made her drink it in one gulp. Barely ten minutes later, Grandmother's head dropped down on her chest and she fell asleep. I pushed her wheelchair and took her to her bedroom.

The dealers hastily bought our past for a pittance and left.

The next day, we stuffed our clothes into suitcases and got ready to move to Auntie Badri's house. As we were leaving,

Grandmother paused at the door. Sitting in her wheelchair, she turned and looked back at the house and suddenly burst into tears. She wanted to go back. She wanted her home.

AUNTIE BADRI'S HOUSE wasn't like it used to be—happy and with lots of people coming and going. The sofas in the living room were covered with bedsheets. They had taken the antique paintings off the walls and rolled up the carpets and stacked them next to the wall. It looked as if the homeowner was away or getting ready to go away. They had even taken down the chandeliers from the ceilings. Instead, there were a few small lamps on the side tables and they weren't all that bright. The house was almost dark.

Grandmother looked around and frowned.

"Oh, it's so depressing here. It makes you feel like it's the end of the world," she said. "Let's go back to our own house. Otherwise, tomorrow they'll pack us up, too, and God knows where they will send us."

Mother was tired. She dropped her handbag on the floor right next to the living room door and lay down on a sofa. One of her shoes fell off and in a bristly voice she said, "We don't have a house anymore. It's finished."

Auntie Badri assigned each of us a separate bedroom. Mother slept in her own room, but in the middle of the night she came over to mine. She had had a bad dream. And then she started imagining that there were people walking around in my room.

"Do you see them, too?" she asked.

"Yes," I answered.

Grandmother was in her own room, fast asleep and snoring. She was neither scared of burglars, nor of ghosts and spirits.

Life at Auntie Badri's house wasn't easy. Our clothes remained in suitcases and we felt as if we were living day by day, as if it was all temporary, just as Mother had said. We changed our rooms a few times. The house was noisy and doors were constantly being slammed shut.

"This is a ghost house," Mother said. "I can see them. They roam around the rooms."

Grandmother took a few folded sheets of paper with prayers written on them and tucked them under her prayer rug.

Every night, a group of people came to Auntie Badri's house. They would all sit around the radio and listen to the BBC and Radio Israel. We watched them from a distance. Auntie's husband constantly looked out the window and kept an eye on the garden. He was afraid the Revolutionary Guards would show up. Listening to Radio Israel was a crime. He kept turning down the volume on the radio.

"Gathering in groups is dangerous," he said. "It creates suspicion. They may think we are plotting something."

"Who can see us? Have they put cameras in the rooms?" Auntie asked.

"Yes," he said. "They have equipment that allows them to see through walls."

"They can read our thoughts," Mother said. "They go inside our head. Inside our dreams."

I HAD SPENT the better part of my life in that house and with Auntie Badri. I used to spend the weekends and most of my summers there. No one was closer to me than Auntie. She always took me along when she went on her summer holidays. But this was all before fear, like a dark shadow, became part of our existence. Fear of the unknown, fear of an uncertain future. Auntie Badri was worried for me, but she was more worried for herself and for her old antiques that could end up in the hands of strangers.

Two weeks later, she told us that her husband had decided they should leave the country as soon as possible. They had received visas for Canada.

Mother sighed and said, "I wish we could leave, too."

Grandmother got angry and snapped, "No! This is where we belong. We have to go back to our own house and to our own life."

"What life?" Mother said. "It was just a fleeting moment in a dream." And tears rolled down her face.

Auntie was rushing back and forth, overseeing the packing of their belongings. She had hundreds of bowls and pitchers and plates and statues of Buddha from ancient times. She couldn't take them with her. It was illegal to take antiques out of the country. She put them all on the dining room table and looked at them with profound angst.

"What are you going to do with these?" Grandmother asked.

Auntie sighed. It was as if the antiques were part of her being.

"I will die if one of them breaks or gets lost," she said.

"So what if they get lost," Mother retorted. "If I were you, I'd throw them all in the trash."

"Every one of them has great value—sentimental value, artistic and historical value," Auntie explained. "This statue of Vishnu is three thousand years old. He is the god of existence and life."

Grandmother looked at the statue with contempt and said, "This black guy with four arms and four legs is a god?"

I wondered why, instead of bickering with Auntie Badri, they weren't asking her what we were supposed to do after she left. Where were we to go?

Auntie Badri had the answer. A few days later when Grandmother posed the question, Auntie said, "There is no place better for you than Homayoun's house."

Uncle Homayoun! What a choice. Of course, I loved Uncle, but he was a special sort of person and his door wasn't open to everyone. He had spent many years living in India and he had his own beliefs and way of life. I thought, When he finds out what Auntie Badri has in store for him, he will pack up, go back to India, and pitch his tent on the banks of the Ganges River.

Grandmother, who had grown tired of Auntie's house, clapped her hands and said, "Let's go today. I would give my life for my son. A son is a mother's crown."

"Homayoun won't take us in," Mother said. "He is used to being alone."

Grandmother chided her. "What are you saying? Hadn't we, too, grown accustomed to our comfort? Now look what has become of us. People get used to everything and Homayoun will get used to us."

"Poor Homayoun. His life is going to be turned upside down," Mother said.

"Didn't ours turn upside down?" Grandmother flared. "The world is upside down. Its head is down and its feet are up in the air."

Uncle Homayoun didn't know that Auntie was getting ready to leave the country and he wasn't aware of our circumstances. He lived his own life. He never listened to the news on the radio, he didn't have a telephone or a television, and he didn't read the newspaper. We sent someone to deliver a short note to his house. We were worried that he might not even read the note. Fortunately, he did. And as soon as he learned that we were going to be homeless, he rushed over to Auntie's house. He kissed Grandmother's hand and my face and happily agreed to us living with him. But when Auntie Badri insisted that he also take her antiques, the color drained from his face. Auntie cried. Pleaded. Begged.

Uncle was confused and didn't know what to do. He said, "It's better if you sell them or give them away. What good are they to you now that you're leaving?"

"They are tokens of the past, of my life," Auntie said. "One day the page in the book of times will turn and I will come back."

Mother was mumbling to herself. It was obvious she was thinking of my father. Grandmother couldn't bear Mother moaning and groaning. She couldn't bear anyone moaning and groaning. "Get up and go take a nap," she snapped. And then she took Auntie's side, and the mother and daughter argued and pleaded with Uncle until he gave in. He just wanted to put an end to Grandmother's grousing and Auntie's entreaties. Still, he knew that moving all those precious objects was not going to be easy. If the Revolutionary Guards saw them, they would immediately confiscate them and our lives would be in danger.

We had to be as careful as possible. One by one, we would load the ancient pots and pans and silver trays and Indian statues and Russian candelabras and a hundred other odds and ends into the trunk of the car and under the cover of night we took them to Uncle Homayoun's house. The items that were smaller and lighter, we packed in a variety of bags, and walked out of the house with them, pretending we were going about our daily life. Mother was thin as a rail and because of the sedatives she took she kept staggering. But we would tuck a tennis racket under her arm and send her out carrying a sports bag filled with the smaller pieces. Sometimes she would lose her way and she would sit in front of someone's house and doze off.

We didn't trust anyone. A neighbor's simple glance made us shudder. But finally, with plenty of fear and trepidation, we moved all the antiques to Uncle Homayoun's house and lined them up on the dining room table. We wanted to store them in the cellar, but Grandmother wouldn't allow it. She wanted them right where she could see them, lest one of them went missing, and she counted them every day—how many hand-painted Persian plates, how many old Chinese bowls, how many Indian silver trays, how many Russian candelabras, etc. She didn't trust Haji, uncle's male housekeeper, and she watched him like a hawk.

Auntie Badri cried the day she left. She hugged me and held me tight against her chest. I looked at her. Something had changed in her eyes, in her voice. Perhaps it was anger or dread of exile and life in a cold, unfamiliar land.

UNCLE HOMAYOUN ANNOUNCED that there were two conditions to life in his house. "First, bring nothing with you other than your clothes and necessities. Second, cooking meat is forbidden in my house." We had to eat simple foods—vegetables, fruits, bread, cheese, and walnuts.

Grandmother objected. "Absolutely not! You think we are fakirs? Why don't you just tell us to sleep on nails? I won't have it. I'm used to sleeping in a warm and cozy bed. I have a bad back. I have to eat meat and fish for lunch. Its doctor's orders."

Uncle was kind and soft-spoken. Again, he said, "There will be no meat in this house."

"Is this the army barracks?" Grandmother retorted. "If it is, I am the commander in chief and you, my dear son, are a lowly soldier."

Uncle Homayoun and Haji lived upstairs. Uncle's room was full of books and smelled of incense. He wore white Indian pants and shirts and his long salt-and-pepper hair was always in a pony-tail. He had given Haji a few sets of Indian clothes, too. Haji wore his Indian shirt with a pair of Kurdish pants and went from room to room all day long dusting the furniture with a grimy rag. He was hard of hearing. He misheard everything we said and replied with a bunch of nonsense. The only creature who understood him was Jimmy—Uncle's huge, hairy dog who communicated with Haji by wagging his tail and the expression in his eyes.

We had put Grandmother's mattress in the living room. She didn't like it there and every night she would shout, "Haji, you idiot, come prepare my bedding."

Grandmother was paralyzed on the left side of her body and couldn't stand properly. She had to lean on a wall or grab the edge of a table. The first night we spent at Uncle's house, she behaved worse than a two-year-old. Uncle and I took her under the arms and with great difficulty made her sit down on the mattress.

She thrashed about and screamed, "Leave me alone!" Uncle Homayoun was thin as a reed and could barely keep his balance.

"Damn it, Homayoun!" Grandmother shouted. "Who can I turn to? Why the heck did you turn into an Indian fakir? The hell with India. Your father died of a broken heart. He wanted you to study law and become an attorney. Instead, you went and lived in India and turned into a weed-eater. Can't you see what you look like? You look like a scrawny goat."

Haji put Grandmother's cane next to her and he received the first strike of the cane on his ankle. It caught him off guard. He was writhing in pain and staring at Uncle with his jaw hanging and his eyes wide with surprise.

"You deserved it," Grandmother growled.

From the moment she opened her eyes in the morning, Grandmother bossed Haji around and screamed if Uncle's dog stepped into the living room. She had ordered Haji to supply her with some stones which she kept close at hand. Jimmy, clueless and happy and wagging his tail, would trot into the living room and a big stone would hit him in the head and he would run away howling.

Grandmother's temper was fouler than ever before. Anyone who walked past her would get whacked on the ankle with her cane. She wanted to be the absolute ruler of the household and she couldn't. She was immobile and her legs ached. A burly nurse came every day to take care of her. But Grandmother fought with her, too.

LIFE WENT ON somewhere between sleep and wakefulness. The Iran-Iraq war was still raging. At night, we had to live with the lights turned off. Uncle Homayoun would read by candlelight and we used paraffin lamps. Grandmother spent the evenings listening to the small battery-operated radio she kept next to her pillow.

Mother had stashed all her valuables in her handbag. We spent her money with great prudence. Uncle was generous. Even though he didn't have all that much, he made sure that we lacked for nothing. I would go to the corner grocery store and buy chicken or meat cutlet sandwiches for myself, Mother, and Grandmother, and Uncle would put a large bowl of salad and a basket of fruit on the dinner table. Haji only ate white rice with yogurt or tomatoes and he shared whatever was on his plate with Jimmy.

Life had become one long wait. I was waiting for the universities to reopen. Grandmother was waiting for Auntie Badri to
come back. Mother was waiting for a miracle and for the mullahs to leave. Among us, Uncle Homayoun was the only one who
didn't talk about the past and didn't think about the future. For
him, time was always today. But we three women were like mute,
motionless beings in a deep coma. We were waiting for something to happen or for someone to seek us out. Our prayers went
answered.

One night, I was getting ready for bed when I heard someone
knocking on the glass door in the living room that opened to the
garden. It was dark and all I could see was a shadow outside. I
looked more carefully and saw a tall man wearing a brimmed hat.
Without thinking, I automatically opened the door a little. But
before I could ask who he was, the man pushed his way in and
said hello. Grandmother stared at me and the stranger.

"Who are you?" she asked.

The man took off his hat and said, "Please stay calm. I have no
intention of harming you. I will just take something small and leave."

"Speak up," Grandmother chided. "What did you say?"

The man repeated himself a bit louder. Then he blushed, looked
down, and took a handkerchief from his pocket and wiped the
sweat off his forehead.

"Excuse me," he said. "With your permission, I will take this
bowl and clock and I will leave."

Grandmother half rose, clutched her cane, and shouted, "Con-
gratulations! I've seen all sorts of burglars, but never a polite one.
Theft with permission! Are you crazy? Get lost or you'll end up
in a black hole in prison." And she took one of her stones and

hurled it at the polite burglar. The man grabbed his nose and groaned.

"I didn't think you would be this rude and impudent," he said.

"Wait, I'll show you," Grandmother retorted.

Then she pulled the decrepit rifle out from under her pillow and aimed it at the burglar. The man froze in his place.

"My dear woman," he said, "please put the gun down. It's unbecoming."

Grandmother raised the rifle up higher in front of her. "Put your hands on your head."

The burglar obeyed.

I had never seen a thief and I was so terrified that I couldn't move. Grandmother, on the other hand, was in top form. She said, "I will call the police immediately."

The burglar lowered his arms and said, "Please don't waste my time with empty threats. I'm in a hurry."

Grandmother turned to me and said, "Did you hear that? The gentleman thief is in a hurry. He has two other houses to rob."

"Please don't make snide remarks," the burglar said. "I don't like it." All the while, his eyes were glued to a porcelain bowl.

Grandmother took note. "If you so much as touch that bowl, I will shoot. The bowl belongs to my daughter and it is in my safekeeping." Then she turned to me—still frozen in place—and she yelled, "Wake up! Why are you just standing there? Call the police. Call Haji. Scream 'Thief!' Call the neighbors."

The burglar took a few steps forward and said, "Please don't scream, or I will lose my temper."

Grandmother took advantage of the man's proximity and whacked him on the ankle with the butt of the rifle and started to scream, "Haji! You moron! Wake up! There's a burglar in the house!"

The burglar was in severe pain. By now, his nose was swollen, too. He howled and leapt back, but he noticed that the nozzle of the rifle was broken and he started to laugh.

"You miserable creature, what are you laughing at?" Grandmother snapped.

"At you," the burglar replied. "You're a feisty old woman."

"Go laugh at your mother's grave!" Grandmother said.

The burglar turned red in the face. "My dear lady, please watch your mouth. I don't want to be rude to you."

Grandmother raised her cane. "I would smash your head in if I could reach you. Step forward, if you dare."

I had to do something, but I was shaking from head to toe and stuttering. The thief noticed and it seemed to distress him. "Young lady, I'm not going to hurt you," he said. "Just keep the old lady calm. I will take that bowl and lamp and I will leave."

"The hell you will, you contemptuous son of a bitch!" Grandmother shouted.

The burglar was suddenly furious. He barked, "Don't insult me. I told you to watch your mouth."

Grandmother burst into laughter. "Heh! The gentleman thief is insulted! What nerve. Excuse me, you idiot, if you were half-decent you wouldn't be robbing people. You've broken into our house in the middle of the night and now you're acting all uppity?"

The burglar didn't seem to be a dangerous man and my fear somewhat subsided. I said, "Look here, mister, these things belong to my aunt and she's left them here in our care. You can take that carpet instead."

Grandmother lost her temper. "You're giving charity? You have legs. Kick the louse in the butt and throw him out!"

Again, the man turned red. "First of all, I'm not a thief. I'm a math teacher. And I will not allow anyone to insult me."

Grandmother was about to scream, but I stopped her. I turned to the burglar and said, "Yes, of course, Mister Teacher. Take this carpet and go."

"The school you teach at should burn to the ground," Grandmother said. "A thieving teacher!"

The burglar hung his head and his expression changed. Looking visibly troubled, he said, "Please call me a temporary thief. I was let go from my job."

Grandmother cut him short. "You probably stole the kids' notebooks."

The man raised his voice and said, "I told you, I'm not your run-of-the-mill burglar. And if I take something from your house, I will return it when my circumstances change."

Grandmother wasn't convinced. "I will be dead by then. And you don't have much life left in you either. Your circumstances aren't going to get any better."

The honorable thief's pride was injured. He held his head high and said, "I can't take any more of your insults and accusations." And he picked up the Russian clock.

"Haji! Get over here!" Grandmother shouted.

The door opened and Mother walked in, dazed and confused and with her hair disheveled. She looked at the burglar, she looked at me, and she just stood there looking lost. For an instant, she dozed off and was about to topple over when she came to. She turned to the burglar and said, "Fetch me a glass of water."

I took Mother's arm and helped her lie down on the sofa. Grandmother said, "How wonderful! The gentleman is a thief, a teacher, and a servant."

"I'll go bring some water," I said.

The burglar carefully put the gold-colored clock back on the table and followed me. "If you don't mind, I'd like a glass of water, too."

"A glass of water?" Grandmother roared. "Never in my life have I seen a cheekier thief!"

The burglar and I quickly returned with a bottle of water and two glasses. Mother gulped down half a glass and became more alert. She looked at the burglar and asked, "And who are you?"

"The gentleman is a thief," Grandmother explained.

Mother didn't understand. She smiled and muttered, "Thief." And then she suddenly understood. She recoiled and screamed, "Thief?" And she fainted.

The burglar was more rattled than me. He splashed some water on Mother's face and started to shake her. Just then, Haji walked in, looked at the burglar, and said hello.

All we were missing was Jimmy, and he, too, showed up. The instant the burglar saw the dog, he yelled, leapt to the other side of the living room, and took shelter behind the dining room chairs.

Grandmother laughed and said, "Jimmy, you good-for-nothing mutt, he's a burglar. Attack, you useless dog!"

The burglar, looking utterly pale, turned to Haji and said, "My good man, I'm begging you, I'm terrified of dogs. A dog bit my leg when I was a child. Take this beast away."

Mother opened her eyes. She couldn't remember where she

was and what was going on. She thought it was morning. She said, "Haji, did you buy bread? Have you brewed some tea?"

Jimmy liked strangers. He wagged his tail and ran toward the burglar. He wanted to sniff the man's shoes and jacket. The burglar yelled, picked up a chair and held it in front of him as a shield, and started walking backwards.

I was worried about Mother. I was afraid she would faint again. Grandmother, on the other hand, was excited. She kept shouting, "Jimmy! Attack! Bark, you stupid dog!"

I took Mother to her room and put her in bed. I told her she had had a nightmare and that there was no burglar in the house. Then I went back to the living room.

Just then, we heard Uncle's voice coming from upstairs. He was calling Jimmy. The burglar became even more agitated. He said, "I'm leaving. I don't want your belongings. But I warn you, be careful, real burglars show no mercy. They're not like me."

The man saw Uncle coming down the stairs and he dashed out of the living room and into my bedroom, and closed the door behind him. Jimmy started jumping up and down. Grandmother threw a stone at the dog and shouted to Uncle, "There's a burglar in the house!" But Uncle didn't grasp what was going on.

"He must have grabbed something," Grandmother said. "Haji, go after him."

Haji looked at her and said, "Were you talking to me?"

Grandmother hit him on the leg with her cane and shouted, "You ass! Run and catch the thief."

Haji groaned. Jimmy howled. "What is going on?" Uncle asked. "All of you, be quiet and explain."

Mother had woken up again. She walked into the living room,

sat next to Grandmother, and started to cry. She had had a bad dream. Jimmy ran over to her and rubbed his nose on her shoulder.

Grandmother whacked Jimmy on the back with her cane and said, "Get this filthy dog out of here. Get lost, dog! Don't come near me." Then she yelled, "Where the hell did the burglar go?"

Still confused, Uncle asked, "What burglar?" I quickly explained what had happened. Grandmother pointed to my bedroom and said, "He's in there. He's hiding."

Uncle checked my room. The window was open and there was no one there. Uncle was calm and composed. He shook his head and said, "The poor man. A math teacher has had to turn to burglary! You should have given him some money and helped him out. Why didn't any of you call me?"

"Instead of all this nonsense, go find him," Grandmother said. "He's hiding in the bedroom. He's probably under the bed."

"If I were you, I would sell all this stuff and give the money to charity," Uncle said.

I dragged Mother back to her bedroom. I put her in bed and closed the door.

"All of you, go to bed," Uncle said. And he turned around and went back upstairs. Haji and Jimmy followed him.

It was a strange night, but it had ended well. I went to bed and reached over to turn off the bedside lamp when I noticed that Mother's handbag wasn't in its usual place, next to my bed. My heart sank. I leapt out of bed. Damn him. The burglar finally got what he wanted. I looked under the bed and behind the bedside table. No, it wasn't there. I dashed out like a madwoman and ran barefoot up the stairs, two at a time. I was in the middle of the staircase when the doorbell rang.

I thought, They've caught him! And I called up to Uncle.

Grandmother was still awake. "They caught the thief," she shouted. "Good! He'll get what he deserves."

Fed up with the evening's commotion, Uncle Homayoun came downstairs with Jimmy following him. "What is going on now?" he groaned. Just then, before anyone could stop him, Haji opened the front door and three Revolutionary Guards walked in.

One of them said, "Your neighbor reported that he saw a man jump out of a window in your house. We've come to see what is going on."

"As you can see, there is nothing going on," Uncle said. "We haven't seen anyone."

All three guards looked at Jimmy in disgust. One of them said, "This dog is impure. Kick him out. Aren't you Muslims?"

Uncle quickly pushed Jimmy out into the garden. The Revolutionary Guards searched all the rooms and the kitchen and came into the living room and saw the antiques hoarded on the dining room table. Grandmother turned pale and her chin started to quiver.

One of the guards walked up to the table. Grandmother couldn't bear it. "Sir," she said, "these are all old. Please don't touch them. They belong to someone else."

The guards became even more curious. "Where is their owner?"

"They're traveling," Uncle said. "They'll be back soon."

The guard who was the shortest said, "These are antiques. According to the law, all antiques belong to the government. We have to confiscate them until their owner returns."

"I'm the owner!" Grandmother screamed. "Don't touch them! Are you deaf? I said don't touch them."

Uncle stepped in. "Excuse me, but my mother is ill. If you would please leave."

"If you talk too much, we'll take you, too," the guard threatened.

"Who are you?" Mother asked. "What do you want? Why are you here?"

"Don't be scared, my dear," Grandmother said. "They are Revolutionary Guards. They're from the committee. They're the real thieves."

Jimmy was barking and clawing at the glass door.

"Insulting a guard is punishable by fifty lashes," the guard said.

"Lashes?" Mother screamed. Uncle and I took her under the arms and led her to her room. This time, we locked the door.

The guards started gathering up the antiques. Grandmother was distraught. She wanted to get up, but she couldn't. She kept screaming, "Don't touch them. They belong to my daughter." She looked like she was about to have a heart attack. Suddenly, she grabbed the broken rifle and aimed it at the guards. One of them kicked it out of her hand and it landed next to the wall.

Grandmother roared, "I will curse you in my prayers tonight. And tomorrow you will suffer something terrible. You will turn into stone."

Uncle put his arm around Grandmother and said, "Mother, don't worry. We will get them back. It's not as if we have stolen them."

But Grandmother kept screaming and the guards, ignoring her shouts, my pleas, and Uncle's polite requests, piled everything in their car and drove away.

GRANDMOTHER WAS QUIET and wallowing in grief. The antiques were as dear to her as Auntie Badri. She constantly moaned and every night she cursed the guards in her prayers. Haji and Jimmy had grown quiet, too, and spent most of the day upstairs. Uncle, who was secretly happy that he was finally free of the antiques, was now doing all the cooking and household shopping. He cooked soups and rice without meat and Grandmother refused to touch them. Every time I left the house, my eyes kept searching for the gentleman thief. A few times I saw a man wearing a brimmed hat. I ran after him, but he wasn't the burglar.

It was a month after the incident that Grandmother came down with a fever and no longer recognized any of us. She was hallucinating and talking to an invisible person. A few times she spoke Auntie Badri's name and sighed. And one cold winter night, she closed her eyes and her heart stopped. Her cane and rifle were next to her. Auntie Badri called and cried for an hour on the telephone. We didn't tell her about her antiques. She said she didn't like living in Canada and wanted to come back. She was lonely.

The universities reopened, but it was chaos. Most of the professors had either been arrested or had left the country. Uncle Homayoun was worried about my education and he was encouraging Mother and me to leave Iran. Mother used to keep her passport and documents in her handbag. We couldn't leave the country.

A month passed and again something strange happened. Grandmother had been right. To understand our new life, we needed a different logic.

One day the doorbell rang. By then, its chime always frightened us.

"Haji," Uncle called out, "don't open the door. First, ask who it is."

Haji, being half-deaf, didn't hear Uncle's order. He warily opened the door, but there was no one there. There was just a package behind the door.

"Don't touch it! It could be a bomb," Mother warned.

Haji brought the package in and put it on the table. Uncle ripped it open. Inside was mother's handbag. All her documents were there, as well as two-thirds of her money and a brief letter. Uncle read it out loud. "Dear Sir and Madam, you cannot know how ashamed I am. I did tell you that I am not a thief. Sometimes, life forces you to do things against your desire and beliefs. I have taken two hundred thousand tumans of your money. But I will repay you. Please forgive me."

A few months later, Mother and I prepared to leave for Istanbul. We had an acquaintance there who said he knew the Canadian ambassador and could get us visas to go to Canada. Leaving Uncle was difficult for me, but staying in Tehran was no longer feasible.

"Don't worry about me," Uncle said. "Haji and I have grown old together. We'll take care of each other."

I hugged him and held him tight. His shirt smelled of incense and Indian spices. It smelled of his travels.

FIFTEEN YEARS HAVE passed at the speed of lightning. I'm in my third year preparing for a doctorate degree in Indian religions and mythology at McGill University. Perhaps it was Uncle's love of India that has taken me down this road. I have to go on a short trip to India. My plan is to stop in Iran for a few days to see Uncle Homayoun.

Returning to Iran isn't easy for me. I try not to give in to melancholy. I take sleeping pills and sleep through the entire flight. I wake up and see the passengers standing in the aisle even though the plane is still taxiing on the runway and the flight attendants are constantly asking them to return to their seats.

Imam Khomeini Airport is new to me. I run and follow everyone else. Most of the women are wearing long black coveralls. I'm nervous that something unexpected might happen. What if they take away my passport? What if they ban me from leaving the country? I'm afraid my family name will get me into trouble—it is still associated with the old regime.

Frightened and trembling, I go through passport control. All goes well. I pick up my suitcase and rush out of the terminal. I take a taxi. I've decided to stay at Sheraton Hotel. I don't know what its new name is. The driver says, "Esteghlal Hotel."

I have a restless night. I wake up a hundred times and think about seeing Uncle Homayoun. I regret that I haven't been able to come back sooner. But I had to take care of Mother. I had no other choice.

It is eight in the morning. I'm in a taxi. I have written down Uncle's new address. A few years ago, before he had a stroke, he wrote that he had sold his house, he needed the money, and had rented a two-bedroom apartment. And after Haji passed away, he hired a man who now takes care of him.

We pass Vanak Circle and turn onto a narrow road. Number 16. It is an old cement building. Each apartment has a balcony and they are all crammed with odds and ends, except for one where there are a few pots of geraniums. I am sure it is Uncle's balcony. I know they tore down his old house and built a high-rise there, and I've heard Auntie Badri's house has been turned into a museum. I guess her collection is there. I'm going to go there after I visit Uncle Homayoun.

His apartment is on the second floor. I ring the doorbell. A distinguished-looking man, with gray hair and beard, opens the door. My eyes are brimming with tears and I can't see the details of his face. Uncle's bed is set up in the living room. His arms are resting on top of the sheets. His long white hair is gathered on top of his head. His beard is also long and completely white.

The distinguished man offers me the chair next to the bed. Then he goes and stands a little farther away. I sit down. I take Uncle's hand and quietly call him. I stroke his hair and kiss his face. He moves his head ever so slightly.

"Uncle, can you hear me?"

He looks as serene as a Zen master in deep meditation. There is a faint smile on his lips. I look around. The room is half-empty. There is a small table with a bowl of apples and a cluster of grapes, and an ironing board next to the wall with a pile of clothes and sheets on it.

The distinguished gentleman asks, "Can I offer you something?" I thank him. I don't want anything. "How did you meet Uncle?" I ask. Now, I can see his face more clearly. He looks familiar. He notices my gaze and looks down.

"It is a long and strange story," he says.

"I'm used to strange stories. Please tell me."

"It's difficult for me to talk about it. If you remember, I once broke into your house."

He is so overwhelmed that he breaks into a sweat and starts to cough. He pours himself a glass of water. I suddenly remember. I am shocked. I shift in my chair and put my hand over Uncle's hand.

The dignified gentleman says, "I stole your mother's handbag and I took the amount of money I needed from it."

"Yes, I remember."

"My wife was pregnant and had to have a cesarean, otherwise she would have lost the child. I always intended to return the rest of the money. The next day, I set out looking for work. All doors were closed to me. Believe me, I wasn't a real burglar. A month passed. I had given up hope. One day I was walking down Pahlavi Avenue and I saw a sign for the Antiques Museum. It reminded me of the things I had seen in your house and I decided to go to the museum. I remembered the things you had. How your grandmother, God rest her soul, wrangled with me. At the museum I asked them why there were no guards or custodians. They said they did have a guard, but he stole one of the antiques and they fired him. You see? It's such a strange world. I went to the administration office and applied for the job. It was as if they were waiting for me. They asked me a few questions and took my identity card and told me to come back the next day. I didn't have much hope that they would actually hire me. But they did, and I ended up guarding yours and other people's antiques."

"How did you meet Uncle Homayoun?"

Looking less nervous, the gentleman thief says, "One day I saw Haji walking down the street. He was holding on to the wall, trying to keep himself steady. He kept calling Jimmy. An Afghan worker told me that Haji wandered around there every day looking for his dog. I struck up a conversation with him. He kept asking, 'Sir, have you seen my dog?' There was a piece of paper pinned to his collar with your uncle's address on it. They knew he would wander off and get lost. I walked him home, and on the way, he told me that the old lady had passed away and that you and your mother had moved to Canada. When we arrived, I went in with him. Mr. Homayoun was reading. He immediately recognized me. He looked at me with kindness and invited me to sit. I told him my life story. We agreed that every night, after the museum closed, I would go and work for him. He wanted to write his memoir, but his hand shook badly. My job was to write. He said the work was in repayment of what I owed him."

"You're a guard at the museum and you take care of Uncle? How?" I ask. "Where do you find the time?"

"After Haji died, my wife started taking care of him during the day, and I'd come over after six o'clock and spend the night here. Sometimes my niece or nephew helps us out. Everyone in my family loves Mr. Homayoun. He wasn't feeling well today and I came over earlier than usual. I have to go back to the museum in an hour. My nephew is going to come. Don't worry. We've all become one family."

One family! I think to myself, I wish I were a member of this family. "Do you iron these clothes and bedsheets?" I ask.

"Sometimes I do it, other times my wife takes care of it."

It is time for Uncle's lunch. The distinguished gentleman, the former thief—I don't know what to call him—explains that Uncle is fed through a tube in his stomach. Apple or carrot juice.

"A nurse at the hospital taught me how to do it," he says.

I can't watch. I rest my cheek on Uncle's hand and gaze at his face. I don't want to leave. I know that soon a door will close behind me and remain closed forever.

My next stop is Auntie Badri's old house. The taxi driver knows where the museum is. Pahlavi Avenue looks just like it used to. The sycamore trees are green and thriving. The only thing that is different is the crush of pedestrians and the abundance of cars. Traffic is heavy; it takes a while for us to arrive. When I get out of the taxi, my heart is pounding and there is a lump in my throat. Near the front door there is a sign hanging from a massive tree, "Gateway to History." Older women clad in chadors, young women wearing colorful headscarves, children of all ages, old men and idle young men, walk into the museum out of curiosity or simply to kill time. Entrance is free for the families of those martyred at war. A profound sadness drifts through me; it is almost a physical pain. These people, these curious strangers, don't know that the best years of my childhood were spent in this house. I know every single tree in the garden; especially the weeping willow next to the swimming pool. If I wrap my arms around it as I used to, I am sure it will recognize me.

I walk into the house. Wherever I look, I see Auntie Badri. Her liveliness used to waft through the rooms like a pleasant fragrance and the sound of her laughter resonated all the way to the far end of the garden. Her sewing room was to the left of the hallway. The downstairs hallway, right where I am standing. The door has been secured with a chain and a padlock. The sewing machine was a gift her husband brought for her from Istanbul.

Together with the other visitors, I go upstairs. I know the way. The living room has been divided into two by a wooden partition. One side is dedicated to antiques from the Safavid period to the Qajar period, and on the other side silk carpets are spread out on wooden platforms. The large mirror above the fireplace is still there.

People look at the items on display with indifferent expressions on their faces. I am the only one who can see the hidden world behind every piece, who can hear the sound of Auntie Badri and her guests' laughter coming from the other side of the wall. Time and history weigh on my shoulders. I'm gasping for air.

Outside, the sun is shining and the new guard, or the old burglar, is standing at the museum door. His shift has started. I want to say goodbye.

"Rest easy, I will never leave your uncle alone," he says. "I owe him my life. You see, life is like mathematics. All its events are connected."

Although in the Islamic Republic it is a sin and a crime to kiss a man who is not your immediate kin, I take the museum guard's hand in mine and I kiss his cheek. His white shirt smells like Uncle Homayoun—the scent of incense and his trips to India.

IN ANOTHER PLACE

*T*he quiet and untroubled life of Amir-Ali was turned upside down one night for some unknown reason—perhaps it was because of the onslaught of a mysterious disease or psychological disorder (even though Amir-Ali possessed a fully sound mind). A bout of consecutive yawns and vomiting. The date and even the exact time of this incident can be determined: Friday, October 9, 1998, eleven minutes after midnight.

His diaries, letters, and miscellaneous writings are in my safekeeping. The reason for this confidence and trust is simple. Amir-Ali and I grew up together and were always in each other's company. Ever since the start of our friendship—that of two young classmates—Amir-Ali was someone important to me, someone unique, different from everyone else.

Life made a gentle and docile being of him, an obedient husband and vice president of an important company. Yet I, who had known him from long ago, knew that another Amir-Ali lurked beneath that respectable and conservative façade, imprisoned in the silent depths of his being, waiting to escape. I have had no news of him for years, but I am sure wherever he is (and God knows where that might be—at the end of the world, in the North Pole, on a turbulent sea, in some faraway jungle, or in a small village hereabouts)—near or far, he is well and happy and will one day turn up.

What I mean by "happy" is a certain kind of contentment that pertains to Amir-Ali's temperament and the world he lived in. It is not our kind of happiness, yours and mine. I mean you and me and all the rest of us, the domesticated and docile lot. I have laid out his writings, his letters, and his notes, and I am trying to sort out my memories of him: the childhood days, the summers he spent with me and my family in the countryside, his sayings, his desires, his peculiar fantasies, his love of celestial happenings and cosmic mysteries (the little astronomer), and his secret war against his father, his teachers, and all those who wanted to mold him into a perfect son and student. I am putting all these moments together in an attempt to reconstruct his life. I want to know the real Amir-Ali. I want to discover something new about him, by examining him, his relationship with others, his hit-and-run tactics, his buried angers, his obstinate silences, the mask he wore for the world, and the way he deceived himself and others, by taking apart the nuts and bolts of his personality and his past. There is much for me to learn. The "whys" are many.

I will start from that particular evening, from that party and the emergence of that mysterious and hard-to-describe being. That second Amir-Ali.

Let us pretend we are watching a movie, sequence by sequence: Amir-Ali is asleep. He goes to bed early and is a sound sleeper. He is among that rare group of men who don't snore. He doesn't get thirsty in the middle of the night and he doesn't go to the bathroom at the crack of dawn. He is lazy in the morning and likes to doze off, or lie half-awake with his head under the sheet and think of things he is fond of—imaginary expeditions in vast deserts, snow-covered steppes in the Arctic, cosmic occurrences and the off chance of discovering life in another form, in a better place. But where? He doesn't know. Perhaps right here, in this very city, in his ancestral land, somewhere in harmony with his thoughts and beliefs, in proximity to the things he loves and in tune with his emotional ebbs and flows, somewhere closer to his true self. But he doesn't allow himself the luxury of daydreaming. He knows he must be at his desk by eight o'clock. At his wife's behest, he exercises before breakfast, and at her resolve, he watches his weight and his figure. He is a handsome man and looks at least twenty years younger than he really is. Women flutter around him. His wife (Malak-Azar) has her little jealousies, but her mind is at ease. She knows that this man is hers, just like her children, her identity card, her house, and all her belongings and antiques, and she knows that without her he is incapable of asserting himself. This is more or less what everyone believes. Everyone except me.

MALAK-AZAR IS SLEEPING next to him like a bouquet of flowers—delicate, beautiful, and fragrant. She breathes gently and smiles even as she sleeps. She is probably dreaming of her husband and her children. She is happy. Sometimes, as she lies half-awake and half-asleep, she reaches out and touches Amir-Ali's shoulder or the side of his neck with her fingertips, as though she wants to reassure herself of his presence. During the night, she often snuggles up to him and in a tiny voice whispers sweet little nothings in his ear. Sometimes she wakes him up to hear his voice, to make sure that he is well, that he is happy, that he is satisfied with their conjugal life, and that he loves her as much as he did when they first met and fell in love. Perhaps even more.

Amir-Ali is a sound sleeper. He wakes up, rolls over, mutters something incomprehensible, caresses his wife's bare shoulder, and falls asleep again. He doesn't like to be woken up in the middle of the night to listen to sweet nothings. He could say, "Leave me alone, darling, let me sleep. Can't it wait until morning?" But he doesn't. Perhaps he is too kind or he simply can't be bothered. He knows that opening his mouth and saying something like, "Let me be, dear. I want to sleep," is too dangerous. His words could be interpreted in a thousand and one ways. It isn't worth the trouble.

Malak-Azar loves this man more than the entire world. This is what she says—to everyone, to me, even to strangers—and she enjoys this confession. Her pleasure is laced with anxiety and apprehension, with a muted tension hidden behind her triumphant smile and confident voice. She is bent on convincing me that she loves Amir-Ali more than ever, more than the first day they met. I don't mind. No contest. But she will not give up. She must plunge her invisible dagger deep into my heart and with feminine cruelty reopen my old wounds. She avoids looking at my face, because she is afraid of seeing the smallest flicker of doubt in my eyes. She knows that I can see through the multiple layers of her countenance and that I am well acquainted with all the different faces hidden behind her many masks, like the progression of an oil painting from a faint pencil sketch to the final layers of paint, apparently complete, but never quite finished.

AMIR-ALI HAS SURRENDERED his will to her. His life and destiny are in her hands and he shows no initiative of his own. Others believe that Amir-Ali's absolute submission to his wife is rooted in his fervent love for her. But I know him like the back of my hand. I know that his birth coincided with the appearance of a comet in the sky and that he is in fact an elusive and unattainable creature. He does not belong to anyone. No one. He has a secret world of his own that he never reveals. I was able to peer into this inner world because we were childhood friends and grew up together. Amir-Ali gives in easily because he wants to be left alone. For instance, his job was chosen for him by Malak-Azar. Sitting behind a desk at a commercial company must be deadly dull for a man like Amir-Ali. But he quietly puts up with it. Malak-Azar is a sensible and farsighted woman. She has a good sense for the right measure and limit of things. She appears cold and conservative and cannot laugh wholeheartedly, nor does she know how to make others laugh. She controls herself and does not dare give in to her desires, or to what her body needs— simple needs such as stretching a leg that feels numb for lack of movement, or relaxing and leaning back in a chair, or closing her eyes when she is sleepy or tired. Her body and her mind are restrained by two thousand rules, two thousand considerations and precautions. An inherited pride binds her hands and feet and restricts her movements.

On the other hand, contrary to his well-groomed and immaculate appearance, Amir-Ali is not a fastidious man. There is a wild side to him, and if left alone, he will end up on top of a mountain or in the middle of a desert, or in some obscure far-flung town or primitive tribe. It will come as no surprise to me if one day his bones are found somewhere in an African jungle or near the North Pole. This outwardly calm and quiet man is capable of anything, any act of madness. He has to be constantly poked and pried to be controlled. Malak-Azar knows how to rein him in. In her hands, Amir-Ali has turned into a sensible and docile man who appears to be satisfied with his life.

WHERE WERE WE? Oh yes, we were observing the husband and wife sleeping next to each other. For the first time, Amir-Ali tosses and turns freely in their king-size bed. He is restless. He is thirsty. He feels hot and the soles of his feet burn, as if he has a fever. A pesky mosquito flies around his face and goes away. Half-asleep, Amir-Ali waits for the mosquito's return and its vicious attack. There is no sign of the insect and he sighs with relief. He pushes the sheet away from his face and at that very moment the mosquito's horrible buzz explodes in his ear and he is bitten on the forehead and neck. Amir-Ali is so angry that he wants to hurl something to the floor and smash it; for example, that enormous, ornate chandelier hanging from the ceiling with all its crystals and prisms and umpteen pendants, or that expensive porcelain bowl sitting on the bedside table. He hates this ancient bowl that reeks of old age and bygone days. There is one similar to it at his grandmother's house. It always reminds him of death and mourning.

Amir-Ali loves the open air, the sky, and vast horizons. He loves to sleep on the rooftop or in the garden. He hates over-crowded rooms with low ceilings. He wishes he could remove all the antiques—all those expensive jars and bowls and paintings and unearthed prehistoric objects—from the tables and walls and replace them with flowers and plants. He wishes he could open the curtains, move his bed next to the window, and fall asleep gazing up at the moon and the stars.

But Malak-Azar is, well, a princess. She was brought up with silk rugs and velvet curtains and she is afraid of empty spaces and austere rooms. The intimidating portrait hanging from the bedroom wall—the one facing the bed—is that of Malak-Azar's great-grandfather. All through the night, he glares down at Amir-Ali with his piercing eyes. Malak-Azar feels safe in the midst of the old chinaware which is part of her ancestral heritage. The presence of these centuries-old objects is comforting to her. She maintains an affectionate relationship with them and considers them to be her property. Her very own.

IN THE MIDDLE of that night, Amir-Ali has forgotten everything that brings him joy; his only concern is that damned mosquito. He slaps himself hard on the forehead and neck. He feels something slimy under his fingers and a big smile spreads across his face. He stretches. He yawns and presses his face against the cool edge of the pillow. Sleep hovers behind his thoughts and in between his eyelids. One half of his brain is switched off, but his body is alert and anxious. His hands are restless and cannot find a comfortable position. His eyes are closed, but he can see the chandelier overhead and feel the weight of all those shades and bulbs and crystal pendants on his chest. He thinks of the sky beyond that thick plaster ceiling, of open spaces, of wide horizons, and of the possibility of life in another form. In another place.

Malak-Azar rolls over. The tips of her icy toes touch her husband's leg and make him shiver. The neighborhood cats shriek and start to fight and a she-cat calls out to her mate, caterwauling painfully. Amir-Ali sits up. His heart is pounding. He can't breathe. He thinks he has eaten something unsuitable and that the strange tension in his body is due to overeating and fatigue. That night, they had had a dinner party and Amir-Ali had started yawning from early in the evening. One yawn after another, until the guests were called in to dinner. His yawns were unusual, deep and seemingly endless, originating in his gut and making him arch his back and stretch his neck. These yawns, akin to those of a monster, were hardly expected from a polite and civilized person such as him, and not one but ten, in quick succession and while the guests were talking. They were watching him from the corner of their eyes and Amir-Ali, embarrassed, had covered his mouth with his hand and was trying hard to keep it closed. If he were alone, he would have laid his head on the table and slept. But how could the host justify dozing off right in front of his guests?

Amir-Ali could sense his wife's concern and her reprimanding look and he struggled to control himself. Once or twice, he forced himself to laugh—an awkward, lifeless laugh—and at one point he made an irrelevant remark in the middle of a serious discussion. In spite of his efforts to look sober and alert, his eyes kept closing. He stared at people (meaning, I am awake. I am with you) and nodded in agreement to whatever was being said. He was in a strange state. It seemed as though the objects around him, the plates on the table, the barbecued chicken on the platters, the chandelier's crystal pendants, were all multiplying and he felt a strange angst in his heart. The guest sitting next to him was busy eating, but his plate remained full. Every time Amir-Ali glanced at the plate, everything—the potato chips, the chicken leg, the lettuce, the rice, and the radishes—were all still there. And worse yet was the morsel in the man's mouth that he would not swallow, but continued to chew while shifting it from one side of his mouth to the other.

Amir-Ali felt like someone who has drunk bad wine or taken the wrong medication. He closed his eyes and dozed off for a second. His head fell forward on his chest and his body leaned to one

side. He was about to fall off his chair when he suddenly woke
up and gazed around with a blank look in his eyes. A lady gasped,
"My God!" and someone laughed. Malak-Azar's angry glare shot
toward Amir-Ali like a poisoned arrow; it flew in between the
crystal glasses and over the heads of the assembled company,
and it hit him in the chest and pierced his heart. This was the
first time her well-mannered and refined husband was behaving irrationally and contrary to the rules of etiquette. To cover
up the incident, the guests attacked the barbecued chickens and
someone started to tell long, inane jokes that everyone had heard
a hundred times. The storyteller, holding his sides, laughed out
loud at his own jokes while the others forced themselves to smile.

Amir-Ali was fighting off sleep and the profound lethargy
that held him in its grip like an octopus. He felt an even deeper
yawn rising up his throat and toward his mouth. He pressed
his lips together. His nostrils flared and his cheeks puffed out
like balloons. Suddenly he snatched the dinner napkin from the
lady sitting next to him and stuffed it in his mouth. And still, a
strange sound, like the bleating of a sheep, escaped his throat
and cut his wife short. Silence spread around the room. Malak-Azar faked a laugh and sent the salad bowl on yet another
journey around the table.

The doorbell rang. A young woman rushed in, agitated and
distressed, shouting and complaining as she made her entrance.
She threw her headscarf and long overcoat to the side and started
blaming her spineless, incompetent husband for anything and
everything that was wrong with the world. It turned out that
the Revolutionary Guards had stopped the lady right in front
of her house just as she was getting into her car, because she
had failed to observe the proper Islamic dress code—a common

occurrence. She rang the doorbell to her house several times, but no one answered. Her husband, who was busy washing a crate of grapes to make wine, refused to open the door. The lady resorted to her neighbors. The neighbor to the right opened the door a crack and gestured that he had company and that his guest was busy smoking opium and he quickly closed the door. The neighbor to the left (God knows what he was up to) pretended he had not heard the doorbell at all. Luckily an acquaintance arrived at the scene and talked to the Revolutionary Guards. He gave them his own ID card and the title to his car as bond and the case against the lady was deferred to a later date.

The male guests sided with the wise and farsighted husband. They said, "Anyone else would have done the same thing." This further angered and infuriated the lady.

"I would have opened the door, even if it meant my own arrest," she retorted. "This revolution has forced a lot of people to show their true colors, especially you yellow-bellied, chicken-hearted men."

The yellow-bellied, chicken-hearted men laughed, winked at each other, and continued eating. The women seized the opportunity to attack their husbands, and this led to a host of accusations and complaints.

"We are the ones who work," the wives argued. (They were right. One of them sewed children's clothes, another baked homemade pastries, translated books, and wrote film reviews, and the third one gave private English lessons and offered a bridal hair and makeup service.) "We are the ones who run the household and bear the responsibility of raising our children. You honorable gentlemen chickened out from day one. You've suffered a thousand psychological disorders and found comfort in the golden pipe."

The men smiled without defending themselves and nodded to each other as a sign of union and sympathy.

Amir-Ali used this opportunity to leave the room. He went to the bathroom and held his face under a stream of cold water. He unbuttoned his collar and took several deep breaths. He felt better. His yawns were gradually subsiding. He waited a while and then quietly opened the door and peeped out. There was no one around. Without making a sound, he snuck out into the courtyard and stood behind a tree. The grogginess that had numbed his body like an anesthetic evaporated and gave way to a sweet and gentle buzz. A humid breeze touched his face and a pleasant quiver crept under his skin. He breathed freely.

It was a bright night and the Big Dipper's seven stars dazzled his eyes. Someone hummed an old tune inside his head and someone gazed at the distant skies from behind his eyelids. He smelled pleasant aromas coming from the far side of the courtyard, from the neighboring garden.

When he was a child, Amir-Ali used to sleep outdoors, on the rooftop, and he would count the stars until he got dizzy and forgot how many he had counted. Then he would start counting all over again from the other side of the sky. Having his head in the clouds, so to speak, was a result of his love for the galaxy and for closely observing cosmic phenomena. The vastness of the universe would not fit into his head, and he longed to solve impossible mysteries. He was no more than thirteen or fourteen, but he was already something of a philosopher. He was head and shoulders above other children his age in maturity and ran a thousand

miles ahead of them in intelligence and knowledge. He had the
look of an adult, an adult capable of thinking things through. His
head was always buried in books, history books—the history of
ancient Egypt, the history of early civilizations, the history of the
genesis of the universe and the emergence of human life.

He was one year younger than me. Only one year. And yet
he behaved as though we, the older boys on our street and the
soccer champions of our neighborhood, were not capable of
comprehending his important pronouncements and were not
endowed with much brainpower. But he didn't put on airs. That
was Amir-Ali—reticent and reclusive—and we accepted him for
who he was. Amir-Ali was immersed in his own world and in that
world he traveled to the farthest reaches of the earth.

AMIR-ALI COULD hear a concoction of sounds coming from
inside the house: loud peals of laughter, the clatter of silverware,
the sound of a door being repeatedly opened and closed, and the
sound of a sentence being spoken that seemed to go on forever.
He couldn't bear the thought of returning to the living room and
rejoining that crowd. He was sure the moment he set foot in the
room he would start yawning and feeling sleepy again. But he
had to go back. He knew that Malak-Azar was impatiently waiting for him and that his behavior was unacceptable. He waited a
while longer. Then he walked around the courtyard, stood behind
a window, and looked in through the lace curtains. He gathered
his scattered thoughts and went back inside and forced himself
to smile at the guests—with his lips tightly pressed together.
He feigned interest in the topic being discussed and nodded in
agreement or shook his head in disagreement (meaning, I have
heard all your arguments. I have been right here all along). The

guests realized that Amir-Ali was not feeling well and did not argue with him. They accepted his contradictory remarks and agreed with him on every point.

LET US GO back to where we started. Malak-Azar is sleeping and her sweet slumber pains her husband. Amir-Ali tosses and turns. He feels terrible and doesn't know how to interpret this sudden illness. Never before has he experienced such nausea and anxiety. This insomnia, too, is a novel experience that worries him; especially when his wife is sound asleep and unaware of his condition. He wants to open the window. He needs fresh air and he loves to sleep in a room bathed in light. But Malak-Azar wakes up with the slightest noise and the faintest ray of light, despite the soft wax she puts in her ears and the black scarf she uses as an eye mask. Amir-Ali grows more irritable by the minute. A small wound gnaws at him from the inside. The heat, the mosquito, and that evening's overindulgence are all mere pretexts. He knows in his heart that the reason he feels ill is the letter he wrote the previous morning—in spite of himself and under coercion—to an influential government official. It was a letter full of false flattery, containing a pack of lies, subtly offering a bribe, and conveying his obedience. The company's state of affairs is not stellar and such letters are necessary.

Even worse was his hypocritical participation in Friday prayers. Malak-Azar's brothers had insisted that he make an appearance. It was irrelevant that he didn't know the prayers by heart. It would be enough for him to get up and down on his knees in sync with the rest of the worshippers. This was what so-and-so and such-and-such did.

Malak-Azar's brothers wore black, fingered their prayer beads, and went up and down on their knees together with everyone else. It was obvious that they had plenty of practice. They glared at Amir-Ali and with their angry looks asked what the hell he thought he was doing. Why was he standing motionless as though in a daze? Bend down, you idiot! Kneel! Say your prayers. Move your lips. Now stand up. Why are you frozen in that pose of prostration with your head stuck to the prayer stone? What the hell are you doing? Are you asleep? Face the crowd! Why do you have your back to them? People are staring at you. They have noticed, you fool. Move!

Looking deathly pale and drenched in sweat, Amir-Ali was squirming and fighting his body. His actions were not deliberate. He simply couldn't force his limbs to move in time with the other worshipers. His back, his legs, and his head did not respond to his will. It was as if invisible strings were tied to his limbs and an unseen puppeteer was maneuvering him. Had he panicked? Had he gone mad?

At the end of the prayers, his angry brothers-in-law had cornered Amir-Ali and subjected him to a barrage of questions. Why did you behave that way? Did you want to get yourself arrested and dragged off to jail? Did you want to put your life and our reputation at risk? Amir-Ali was overcome and exhausted and his head was spinning. He didn't know how to defend himself. A heavy cloud shrouded his mind and he couldn't remember what had happened. From the moment he entered the crowd of worshippers to the time he left, Amir-Ali had felt that everything—all the words, sounds, movements, and genuflections—was part of a timeless and surreal dream and far from the reality of that morning. He was in a strange state of mind (Amir-Ali's notes at this point are very confused. It is clear that he was not able to explain his actions). The only thing he could remember and kept repeating was: "I couldn't help it." And this is the explanation he offered Malak-Azar. But I am sure that the painful significance of this apparently simple statement, which nobody took seriously at the time, marked the beginning of later episodes.

THE WORST THING to do is to think in the dark. Amir-Ali breathes gently. He lies still. He is sure he will fall asleep in a few seconds. Malak-Azar's hand is resting on his shoulder, but unlike other times it feels cold and obtrusive. The sounds of that evening—all those people talking and laughing and their glasses clinking and clanking—are fresh in his mind. God, how he hates these boring parties. Always the same people, the same talk of politics, the same dishes, the same stale anecdotes—like the needle of an old gramophone stuck at the end of a record and making its final obnoxious noise.

Unlike her husband, Malak-Azar loves parties. She cannot bear the idea of being alone at home. The frightening weight of the minutes and the tangible presence of time torment her. When she thinks of the future, her heart aches. Old age terrifies her more than death. She likes to wear heavy makeup and hide her real face. She wants people to admire her eternal beauty. Their flattering lies warm her heart.

Once again, Amir-Ali hears the persistent drone of a mosquito and seethes with anger. Where is it? His hand is ready to strike. With his eyes closed, he listens for the bloodsucking insect in the dark. He has pulled the sheet up over his face and is about to fall asleep when he feels a sharp sting in the heel of his foot. His feet have been exposed and the enemy has attacked him in that sensitive spot. It is nothing important, just the bite of a miserable mosquito. But trivial incidents are sometimes the beginning of major events. And Amir-Ali, in that darkness, in that state of confusion, feels that an invisible enemy has assaulted him from behind.

The itch in his foot soon becomes a burning sensation that spreads under his skin. He sits up. He is drenched in sweat. The ray of white light that has penetrated the heavy velvet curtains falls across the bed and Malak-Azar's face. He looks at his wife and his heart sinks. He doesn't like her gaping mouth. Another face, a much older one, has replaced her face, and this new appearance is unfamiliar to him. Everyone looks different when they sleep, in darkness or in moonlight. It is simple and natural. But that night, the simplest things seemed absurd and unnatural to Amir-Ali. He feels pangs of anxiety in his heart and is inexplicably distraught. And then, something strange happens. Suddenly his right arm begins to rise, all by itself and seemingly under the command of someone other than him, until it stands erect above his head like a dead branch. What does this mean? He doesn't understand. He is confused. He tries to return the arm to its original position. It's no use. The arm seems to no longer be a part of his body. The hand is clenched into a tight fist and a throbbing vein has appeared on one side of it. Again, he uses all his strength to force the arm back down to his side, and again he fails. Then, as he watches helplessly and in utter amazement, he sees this dubious arm, this foreign body, make a strange move. It reaches up even higher, moves back, pauses, turns, and then, against Amir-Ali's will and free of all control, it descends like a heap of rubble on his wife's delicate and beloved head.

Malak-Azar jolts awake and leaps out of bed with a scream.

She switches on the bedside lamp and calls her husband. Amir-Ali is even more frightened than she is. He is panic-stricken and cannot understand what has happened. Dazed, he looks at his wife. He is unable to speak and his body temperature has suddenly dropped. Malak-Azar has had a terrible fright, her vision is blurred and she feels faint. She thinks perhaps a piece of plaster from the ceiling fell on her head, or an earthquake shook the house and a book fell off the bookshelf and struck her. Or maybe a wild cat pounced on her, or her own hand somehow struck her face as she slept. With her heart still pounding, she imagines a thousand and one implausible explanations.

She looks at Amir-Ali and becomes even more terrified. He has turned deathly pale, his mouth is gaping, and his eyes are about to pop out of their sockets. Her questions turn to anguish for her husband. She holds his hand (the same damned hand) and shakes it. She calls his name. She realizes that he cannot speak and that his hand is as cold as that of a corpse. She tells herself, Oh God, he has had a stroke. And she gently lays his head back on the pillow. She feels his forehead. Takes his pulse. Listens to his heart.

Trembling like a leaf, she thinks, He has suffered a stroke. He is dead. She is about to call a doctor who is an acquaintance when Amir-Ali regains his speech. He reaches out and takes the telephone receiver from her hand. He mutters something incomprehensible and only manages to speak a confused and incoherent jumble of words. He racks his brain for a convincing lie. His confusion is no less than his wife's. He is too frightened to think. He must explain. He must calm her down and stop her from creating havoc. He must cover up the incident.

He hesitantly starts a sentence, but gives up. He looks at his hands. He is afraid of himself. He is afraid that his limbs might

begin to move on their own or that his face might become distorted. He touches his teeth. For a moment, he thinks his two
upper incisors have grown into fangs, like Count Dracula. He
looks at his wife's white neck and he covers his face with his
hands. He must look at himself. He must make sure. He may have
a fever. He may be delirious. He gets up and runs to the mirror on
the wall. He fumbles for his glasses. Malak-Azar can't understand
what he is doing. Amir-Ali looks intently in the mirror. His face
has undergone no particular change. His teeth are where they
should be, in their normal shape and size. He calms down.

He takes his wife's trembling hands and kisses them. All the
while, his brain is churning like a machine. He must make up
a story and cover up the incident. At last, with utmost embarrassment he explains that as he was about to swat a mosquito, a
pesky one that had bitten him all over his body, the idiot that he
is, sleepy and exhausted, he mistook her lovely head for his own.
And now he doesn't know how to apologize to her nor what to
say. In short, he doesn't know what the hell to do.

Malak-Azar looks at him. She can't understand what he is saying. She can't think. She feels dizzy. Amir-Ali is utterly ashamed
and confused. For a moment he thinks he should tell her the
truth, but he doesn't have the courage. The whole thing is too
incredible. Even for him. Malak-Azar rubs her temples and forehead. She is in pain and her vision is still blurry. She takes two
pills from the bottle of sedatives she keeps handy. She leans her
head against Amir-Ali's shoulder and waits for her heart palpita-
tion to subside.

Malak-Azar is a sensible woman. She never acts hastily and
doesn't start a quarrel over nothing. There is no reason why she
should not accept her husband's explanation. She looks at him

from the corner of her eyes and feels sorry for him. She thinks, Oh God, how helpless he looks. What will he do without me? And she strokes his neck with the affection of a forgiving mother. He has taken my head for his own. And to her this mistake has an amorous connotation. She repeats to herself, He has taken my head for his own. She laughs silently. To her this phrase bears a romantic significance. It even has a mystical meaning—the notion of losing one's self in another being. It is with this sweet and captivating thought that Malak-Azar closes her eyes and falls asleep.

Amir-Ali was relieved that the horrifying episode had ended well. With goodwill and smiles—more forced than genuine— Malak-Azar, too, attributed the incident to her husband's natural lassitude and romantic absentmindedness and she tried not to think of the symptoms (his yawns and his dozing off at the dinner table) that had preceded it. Such things happen. There are people who do strange things in their sleep. They sleepwalk on top of narrow walls and they even commit crimes.

The one who couldn't forget the events of that night was Amir-Ali himself. He would recall those suspenseful moments and shudder. Malak-Azar trusted her husband. But not completely. She watched him like a hawk. She would not allow him to be alone even for one second. Domesticating Amir-Ali had not been easy. It had taken a long time for him to understand that he was the son-in-law of a respectable, wealthy family and that this was a status he could not take for granted. It had its own rules, like the rules of grammar and idiom in a foreign language. He could not haphazardly throw some words together and make up meaningless sentences. With this new language he needed to have new ideas, new sentiments, a new outlook, a new voice, new dreams, and new aspirations. He could not simply enter an unknown territory and take the seat of honor. To enter this world, he had to observe special etiquettes, follow certain customs, and engage in a thousand forms of give-and-take.

I didn't believe Amir-Ali could manage all this. God knows how he struggled and how tolerant he was to put up with the vice presidency of the Yarn and Spool Imports Company. Everyone considered him a lucky man. In the uncertain days of the revolution, many had lost their lives and others their livelihood, but he, thanks to a successful marriage, had acquired an affluent life and an enviable social status.

A MONTH OR TWO passed peacefully. It seemed that the worst was over and that life had returned to normal. But that invisible being, that obtrusive shadow, was lurking in the wings, waiting for the right time to make an appearance.

Amir-Ali and his mother-in-law were born on the same day of the same month, twenty years apart. Malak-Azar attributed this coincidence to Nature's wisdom and regarded it as a sign of the enduring union between the two families. And every year she celebrated that happy occasion by inviting all her family and friends. Deep in his heart, Amir-Ali was unhappy that he was born on the same day of the same month as his mother-in-law. But he pretended to be pleased and proud. His mother-in-law was not all that fond of her son-in-law either. Deep in her heart, she mistrusted him. But she, too, concealed her feelings and feigned love for him. They both knew that they were deceiving each other and understood that deceit was the only course of action.

The mother-in-law's seventy-fifth birthday and the son-in-law's fifty-fifth was a more important occasion than the previous ones and it called for a special celebration. Even though a large and noisy party could attract too much attention in the neighborhood and alert the Revolutionary Guards at the nearby committee, Malak-Azar went ahead with her plans. For the first time, she was throwing caution to the wind. For her, Amir-Ali's birthday was as important an event as the discovery of America.

Uncle General, or Uncle G. as everyone called him, was Malak-Azar's oldest paternal uncle. He was a retired military officer who lived alone, had lost most of his friends in the early days of the revolution, and now to pass his time and forget his sorrows, he had nothing better to do than to socialize. He loved parties, weddings, social pastimes, and gambling. He attended every funeral service, every celebration of a new birth, and every circumcision. On Friday mornings, he panted his way up to the top of the mountain ahead of all the other hikers. And in the winter, he geared up for skiing—goggles, gloves, boots, the lot—and sat in a café at the foot of the mountain, basking in the sun, a cigarette dangling from his lips. He would not move for fear of slipping on the icy slope. He was happy to just be there, looking perfect.

Uncle G. was afraid of being left out by the others—the younger happy-go-lucky generation. Early each morning, he called all his acquaintances to remind them, with much ado, of his continued presence in the world. If he heard of a party to which he had not been invited, he would take to bed with grief. He would think a thousand suspicious thoughts and attribute the incident to a major conspiracy. And if he was invited, he would get all excited and couldn't control his dizzying verboseness. He would talk and talk until everyone felt queasy.

On the day of the party, he would wake up at the crack of dawn and start counting the hours. Late in the afternoon, he would lay out his formal evening clothes. He would polish his shoes. He would glance at the clock on the wall and at himself in the mirror a hundred times. He would comb his silvery hair and his dyed mustache. He would tie a silk scarf around his neck and show up a full hour before the other guests. Sometimes, he would get emotional over nothing and a lump would rise in his throat. Sad movies and sorrowful poems affected him so deeply that all alone he would cry for hours on end. Sometimes he would become mean and vengeful and could not control his sharp tongue. He would direct a barb or two at one person or another and alienate them.

That evening he had shown up really early, when the hosts were not yet expecting any guests. Malak-Azar had just showered and was in her dressing gown. She swore under her breath at her silly, pestering uncle and rushed to get ready. She tied her husband's necktie for him, objected to the plain shirt he had chosen, asked him to change it, and told him which trousers to wear with which jacket.

Uncle G. was not too fond of this niece. Her intellectual airs and smug smile irritated him. And yet he leaned toward her and opened his arms. "My dearest darling doll! How nice to see you. You will have to forgive my barging in so early. You know . . ." And he was about to go on with his phony pleasantries when Malak-Azar cut him short. She coldly offered Uncle G. her cheek, and keeping her mouth away from his freshly moisturized face, she kissed the air and felt nauseated by the pungent scent of his aftershave. "You did well," she said. "You are most welcome at any hour."

Tired and miserable, Amir-Ali was watching the scene from a distance. The thought of having to put up with these foolish guests and phony compliments for at least ten hours made him feel lethargic. He swallowed his yawn, cleared his throat, and heard Malak-Azar call him. He planted a strained smile on his lips and went to greet Uncle G.

The next guests to arrive were the company's other shareholders and their wives. Uncle G. adored beautiful women and would in advance prepare a routine of charming anecdotes and scientific speeches to pour into their delicate ears. The retired general liked to portray himself as a worldly man knowledgeable about the latest scientific developments. His information came from European magazines and foreign radio broadcasts, to which he added his own embellishments and then presented the mix to his audience. That evening he had decided to talk about the origin of the universe. But no one was in the mood for a discussion about planets and stars. The hot topic of the day was the trial of the mayor of Tehran and the fate of the city's construction companies.

Uncle G. was trying hard to redirect the discussion to the heavens and stars, but each time he opened his mouth someone interrupted him. At the dinner table, the conversation turned to other subjects. Those who had recently traveled to Europe talked about the latest news in the world of film. A gentleman attacked American movies and defended Third World cinema. The ladies objected. Malak-Azar's mother had a special way of not listening to what was being said and then asking, "When? Where?" And the discussion would have to start all over again, and again the dear lady would not pay attention and she would ask the person sitting next to her, "What are they talking about?" That evening, too, she kept asking her silly questions until everyone got fed up. Amir-Ali turned to her and said, "Was your ladyship sleeping?"

Malak-Azar frowned. There was a moment of silence and Uncle G. seized the opportunity to ask, "Has anyone seen the film about the origin of the universe?" No one had. "Then let me tell you all about it," he said.

Uncle G. was about to start delivering his lecture when the lights went out. There was a power outage. It was the best time to bring the birthday cake. Someone's glass fell and broke and Amir-Ali used the opportunity to yawn—a deep drawn-out yawn. A lady proposed that they eat the birthday cake with Beethoven's Ninth Symphony playing in the background. They all agreed and drank to the health of their hosts. The cook came with the news that the water had also been cut off. Someone shared the news about the burglars who had broken into his neighbor's house and decapitated two women and a man. Uncle G., who shuddered whenever he heard bad news, pleaded, "Please, no talk of such things." And in a chorus of small oohs and aahs the ladies agreed.

"The world outside is a dark ocean," Malak-Azar said. "But in the midst of all this darkness, here we sit, thank God, on an island of light, heedless of what goes on around us. We are still ourselves." A gentleman replied, "We think we are ourselves. But we—you, me, and all these dear friends—are out of the loop. Totally out. We count for nothing. Nothing!" He gnashed this last word between his teeth and spat it out with venom.

Amir-Ali's left leg was numb. He moved it around and sat up straight. Two minutes later, he had that usual sensation of pins and needles in the sole of his foot. It felt funny. His foot had swollen and his shoe felt terribly tight. He shifted his chair slightly back and away from the edge of the dining room table.

Uncle G. was saying, "Let us imagine that we are at the start of creation. Total darkness reigns everywhere." Amir-Ali's left foot was hovering above the floor. It had lifted up and was swaying left and right. It was shaking and refused to obey its terrified master's command to remain still. In its black leather shoe, the tip of his foot was like the nozzle of a concealed pistol seeking a target. Horrified, Amir-Ali looked at his arms. His rogue arm was not moving from its position. He was relieved, but at the same time he was dreadfully worried about his foot. The heel itched and felt ticklish. Suddenly a piercing pain shot through the tip of his big toe and he felt queasiness in the pit of his stomach. Hard as he tried, he could not force his foot down. That sly mastermind, that hidden alter ego, had taken control and it was not clear what it intended to do.

Malak-Azar was sitting a safe distance away, at the other end of the table. But his esteemed mother-in-law and Uncle G. were sitting to his left and right, with their legs not too far away. Confused and nervous, gripped by fear and on the alert by an instinctive warning, Amir-Ali felt that something unpleasant was about to happen and decided to get up and make his escape before it was too late. He put his obedient hands on the arms of his chair and was about to get up, but remained half-stooped. His left foot was now riveted to the floor and would not move. In the dark, Amir-Ali could feel Malak-Azar's eyes watching him. He sat back in his chair.

The lights came back on. The birthday cake was brought in accompanied by Beethoven's Ninth Symphony being played on the gramophone. Amir-Ali's left foot was again as restless as a wild boar and it was tearing at the carpet.

"The birth of man and that of the cosmos should be celebrated together," Uncle G. said. Malak-Azar served him the first slice of cake.

Just then, Amir-Ali's left foot decided to do something strange. It moved back, paused, and then with great force it kicked the retired general's ankle. Uncle G. dropped his loaded dessert fork that was heading for his mouth and yelped in pain. Mother-in-law leapt up, Malak-Azar half rose in her chair, and the confused guests started to babble. Chaos ensued. Uncle G. was rubbing his ankle and groaning. Amir-Ali was in a sweat. What was he going to say? How was he going to explain his dreadful action? How was he going to exonerate himself? There was only one course of action open to him: to escape.

Uncle G. bent down and looked under the table. Someone had kicked him. Who was it and why had they assaulted him? Under the table, the sight of his sister-in-law's small feet brought back memories of old love. He rolled up his trouser leg and massaged his ankle. At his age, his bones must be brittle and there was risk of a fracture. One of the servants brought him a glass of water. Malak-Azar turned to her husband and her heart sank when she saw him hurrying out of the dining room. Uncle G. turned and stared at his sister-in-law with an astonished look in his eyes. Clearly, the kick had come from her. The reason for it went back many years and to a lovers' quarrel. And now, on the eve of the lady's seventy-fifth birthday, the old wound (so Uncle G. thought) seemed to have reopened. That unconscious kick hinted at a secret love and masked a painful and delicious significance.

Still moaning and groaning, the wounded general stared at Malak-Azar's mother with languorous eyes that seemed to say the kick had been sweeter than any caress. He even whispered, loud enough for the lady to hear, a line from the poet Hafez.

"Old as I am, embrace me tightly one night . . ."

He couldn't remember the rest of the verse. He sighed and

laughed, a laughter tinged with sorrow and regret. Someone laid a comforting hand on his shoulder and this unexpected gesture of kindness moved him to tears. He pressed his cheek to that manly hand and started to sob.

Uncle G.'s laughter, followed by his loud crying, led the guests to believe that the good general was in a grave state of mind, what with the revolution and the war and some of his comrades having fallen prey to the firing squads. That languorous look and his poetic murmurings were clearly an indication that he was suffering from momentary insanity, and it was easy to conclude that the story about having been kicked under the table was nothing more than a cry for attention and affection. A gentleman who knew something of Uncle G.'s past and had been privy to some of his secrets, smiled knowingly, and a young lady mumbled, with much sorrow and regret mind you, that old people became childlike, and then she shook her head.

Uncle G. was helped up from his chair and led to the drawing room limping—for the benefit of the guests, most of them thought—and there he was eased into an armchair. He sighed with satisfaction and turned and gazed amorously at Malak-Azar's mother. He blew her a small kiss with his fingertips and closed his teary eyes.

Malak-Azar went running after her husband and told him that her foolish uncle had totally lost his mind and was acting bizarre—he had winked at her mother, blown kisses at her, and whispered a love poem. It now appeared that the story about him being kicked in the ankle was a mere fantasy, invented by the poor man. All through the evening he had wanted to talk, to show off his knowledge, but no one had taken him seriously. The poor wretch! Yet one point remained a mystery. If he had not been kicked, then why was his ankle swollen and red? Malak-Azar was not an idiot. She had seen Uncle G.'s inflamed and bruised ankle with her own eyes.

Amir-Ali turned red and broke out in a sweat. And this, too, did not escape his curious wife's eyes. "I don't know," he said. "Why, yes. You are right. Poor Uncle G.!" And he shook his head and chuckled. Then he turned and stood with his back to her. He scratched his head, pointed to a hairline crack on the wall, and said, "It's high time we repainted the house."

Malak-Azar was too clever to be fooled this easily. If she decided to hush up the incident, she had good reason to. She didn't want her guests to know anything about what had happened (which she herself did not quite understand) and she decided not to pester Uncle G. or her husband with too many questions that evening. But she was determined to get to the bottom of it later, in good time.

Pale and shaky, Amir-Ali returned to the drawing room and offered a few lame excuses for his absence. Then he went to the kitchen and opened the refrigerator door. He didn't know what he wanted. The cook was watching him. He picked up a radish and bit off its root. Then he walked out and went to the bathroom. He looked at himself in the mirror. He pinched himself above the left knee and punched his ankle. It was his leg all right. It was susceptible to pain. He moved it. He lifted it off the ground and put it back down. He gave the leg a few commands. There was nothing wrong with it. It was his old obedient limb.

The birthday cake was cut and served. The happy general was offered a second slice. And as they had not listened to Beethoven's Ninth Symphony, everyone agreed to listen to it in silence and then to call it a night. Amir-Ali's loony leg was now quiet, but his heart was racing and a strange confusion was swirling around in his head. He knew that Malak-Azar would not leave him alone and that she would pursue the matter more persistently than any clever detective. Perhaps the best thing to do was to come clean and ask her for help. He could confess that his body had gone mad and that an invisible creature, an evil spirit, had taken possession of it. But no, she would not believe him. She would think he had lost his mind and that would only lead to scandal. The best thing to do was to wait and, for the time being, to cover up the incident.

Uncle G.'s happy ankle throbbed with sweet, passionate pain. His house was at the end of the street and Amir-Ali volunteered to walk him home. Malak-Azar looked at her husband quizzically, her eyes full of suspicion. She wanted to prevent him from going, but she stopped herself.

Uncle G. clung to Amir-Ali's arm and limped along, quietly mumbling to himself. He was in heaven, tipsy and jolly without having had a drop to drink. He wanted to tell Amir-Ali about his old love which had been fanned back to life, but he couldn't bring himself to do it. He made some vague references to Leyli and Majnoon, the legendary lovers, and to Romeo and Juliet, and he sighed. Once or twice he stopped, rubbed his ankle, and groaned and laughed at the same time.

Out on the street, it was another world. The streetlamps were out and black mourning banners were hanging from the rooftops of a few houses. No one knew about Amir-Ali and his mother-in-law's birthday; no one was celebrating his birth into this world. On a nearby rooftop, a man was busy camouflaging a satellite dish. When he saw Amir-Ali, he stepped back and disappeared into the dark. A patrol car drove by. It slowed down. The Revolutionary Guards sized him up and drove off. A man was pacing the sidewalk in front of his house. He asked Amir-Ali for the time. It was two in the morning. The man was clearly worried and desperate to talk to someone.

"Do you have children?" he asked.

Amir-Ali shook his head and thought of his sons who were abroad. He missed them.

"Lucky you!" the anxious man said. "I have a son and a daughter and every night I pace the sidewalk until the wee hours of the morning, waiting for them to come home from a party. I can't lock them up in the house, can I? But I'm afraid they will get arrested and flogged."

Amir-Ali thought to himself, I'm a happy man. I must appreciate my comfortable life. And that night's elaborate banquet flashed before his eyes—food-laden tables, shiny silverware, crystal glasses, old china, precious antiques, fine carpets, European paintings, and velvet drapes—and he felt depressed. He felt the weight of all those objects on his shoulders. He was exhausted, but he didn't want to go back home. And yet there was no place for him on those dark half-paved streets, in that big boisterous city, amid those brick towers, in that world of lies, contradictions, and conflicts. He only pottered around on the sidelines. Nothing depended on him and there was no one to congratulate him on his existence or to offer condolences on his demise.

That night and on nights that followed, the husband and wife went to bed in silence. They lay with their backs to each other and neither one slept a wink. They both thought about the incident, the incident that remained as elusive and vague as a shadow on water. They didn't know where to start or what to say, and so they preferred not to speak about it at all. But each, in their mind, reviewed what had happened, moving from one night to the next, from here to there, from what he had said to what she had said, only to arrive at a dead end. Malak-Azar looked to the distant past. She started from the day they first met and then moved forward, pausing on small differences, on potential misunderstandings, on forgotten quarrels and reconciliations, taking shortcuts, going back, opening the dossier on some incident, analyzing it, speculating, only to reach a wrong conclusion that led nowhere.

Fearing an interrogation and a confession (to what sin?), Amir-Ali used every excuse to stay away from his wife. He was sure that any explanation he offered, to himself or to her, would be premature and unfounded. Time eventually unveiled the secrets of unexplained occurrences, things that at first appeared mysterious and hard to fathom. And Amir-Ali preferred to wait for things to take their natural course and for the reason behind the incident to reveal itself to him.

In contrast, Malak-Azar was angry and restless and could not understand her husband's stubborn withdrawal and strange behavior. Silence had built an invisible wall between them and their conversations and smiles had become forced and phony. They both feared that something terrible was going to happen and neither one of them wanted to face the bitter reality. With concealed uneasiness, they kept their distance. They didn't want to accept the fact that something disturbing had entered their ordinary and peaceful life. They didn't talk about it, and this refusal to talk became a wound that spread through their bodies and souls, causing them pain.

Malak-Azar expected her husband to open up his heart to her like a sensible boy, to talk about his problems, and to ask her, as always, for guidance and help. But to her chagrin, Amir-Ali, with the doggedness of a stubborn child, was doing his utmost to blur the subject and avoid telling her what was going on in his heart. The thought of Amir-Ali keeping something secret from her was killing Malak-Azar. How could it be? Were they not, the two of them, like one soul in two bodies? Amir-Ali's silence was unforgivable. Unimaginable. Malak-Azar felt humiliated. She felt that by covering up his ailment, Amir-Ali was insulting her. This man was hers inside and out and he had no right to hide anything from her. This was something he had never done before. Never.

Insomnia was Amir-Ali's latest affliction. As soon as he closed his eyes, his brain would set to work and a series of confused images would appear behind his eyelids. He had become conscious of his body and constantly watched his arms and legs. His hands, which until recently had served him like a faithful nursemaid, combing his hair, feeding him, buttoning his shirt, washing his body, and tying his shoelaces, the hand that wrote, caressed, and was ready to serve him obediently, had for some unknown reason become a nefarious enemy that obeyed someone else, some unknown and invisible being, and God only knew what lay in store for him. Anything could happen. What if he, without wanting to, took Malak-Azar's delicate neck in his hands and strangled her? What if he picked up the metal vase on the table and smashed it on her head? The agony, the sorrow, and the shame of such acts were bad enough, but worse yet was the explanation. How on earth was he going to explain his actions? Could he say, "My limbs were out of my control and my brain was receiving orders from someone else?" No one would believe him. They would put him in a lunatic asylum.

All night long, he struggled with these horrifying thoughts

and tossed and turned under the sheets, rolling from side to side, sleepless, troubled. Often he would tuck his hands under him and jolt awake with the slightest movement of his body. One night, two nights, two weeks, two months, how long could he allow this to go on? The most sensible thing to do was to put distance between himself and Malak-Azar—of course, temporarily—and to sleep in a separate room. In the boys' room, or in the spare bedroom. Anywhere.

Malak-Azar listened to her husband's proposal and thought she had misheard or misunderstood him. She laughed. She touched his cheek affectionately and fastened one of his shirt buttons that had come undone. Amir-Ali's eyes were glued to the floor and he kept repeating his brief justification—with much stammering, coughing, and half-finished sentences. For reasons he could not discuss at that time, his suggestion was in the best interest of both of them. And he could not say more, because there was no more to say.

Both of them? Which two did he mean? Were they now going to be two separate entities? A separate you and I?

Amir-Ali could not explain himself. He repeated what he had already said and uttered those final words—"in the best interest of both of us"—in a tone that left no room for argument. Malak-Azar died and came back to life. She felt dizzy and a thousand conflicting thoughts rushed through her mind. Each of them in a separate room? One of them upstairs and the other one downstairs? For twenty years they had slept together like Siamese twins, joined so tightly that separating them would not be easy. It was unthinkable. News of it would spread. What would people say? There would be rumors that they had had a fight, that their relationship had soured. Other rumors would follow with

gross exaggerations. Their life story would become a subject for
gossip and scandal would follow. Never. She argued that this kind
of separation would lead to a true separation. And she listed the
couples who had mutually consented to sleep in separate rooms
and had ended up getting divorced.

Amir-Ali laughed affectionately at his wife's unfounded fears.
He held Malak-Azar in his arms and pressed her to his chest. He
nearly succumbed to her wishes and said, Very well, I accept. But
just then his eyes fell on a pair of scissors on the table and his
heart sank. It was the same thoughts all over again, the same hal-
lucinations, the same fears. What if I pick up the scissors and . . .
No, no. He had to get away from her. There was no alternative.
He had to sit alone and collect his thoughts and find the cause of
this affliction, this confusion, these sudden attacks of madness, a
madness that had nestled in his body, in his bones, in the chemistry of his blood.

Without allowing the argument to continue and without waiting for anything else to be said, he pushed Malak-Azar aside, picked
up his pajamas and slippers, and took refuge in the guest bedroom.
It was large, comfortable, and well lit. The curtains were sheer lace
and the room was bare of antiques, paintings, and chandeliers.

The first night was difficult for both of them. After much toss-
ing and turning and feeling guilty and lonesome, Amir-Ali finally
fell asleep. He liked the cool air in the room and the uncluttered
space gave him a sense of tranquillity. This was the only room in
the house where a plant, a living one, had been placed next to the
window. (Malak-Azar was allergic to plants. All the flowers in the
house were artificial.) The bed was large and he could comfortably stretch out. On the second night, he lit the bedside lamp and

read before going to sleep. He drew the curtains aside, flung open the wooden shutters, and slept under a bright moonlight. And contrary to his usual habit, he stayed in bed until late morning.

Malak-Azar struggled. She would push away the sheets and flip her pillow over, again and again. She would curl up in a corner of the bed and try to sleep. But she couldn't. Every night, she tossed and turned until dawn.

One night, she got up and climbed the stairs barefoot. Her heart was pounding. She held her breath and stopped behind Amir-Ali's door. She put her hand on the doorknob and stood motionless. She wanted to open the door with one flip of the wrist, go in, slip into bed, and snuggle up to him, so close that he would feel compelled to admit to his mistake. It was a good idea and yet she couldn't bring herself to turn the doorknob. Her pride wouldn't let her. They were not on speaking terms. She could not belittle herself. She expected Amir-Ali to come to her, humiliated and sorry, caress her, kiss her hands and feet, and beg her forgiveness. Perhaps, in need of love and attention, he was waiting for her to go to him. Men were like that. They made an apparent fuss, but in truth they were just like lost children in need of a mother.

Encouraged by this reasoning, Malak-Azar drew in a deep breath and turned the doorknob. The door was locked. No, it couldn't be. By what right had he locked her out? By whose permission and why? She didn't know what to do—knock, shout, or break down the door? She went back downstairs, making every possible noise as she went and stomping her feet out of spite. Meaning, I am awake, I am here. Do you get it? She opened a door and slammed it shut. Once, twice, three times. Do you hear?

Wake up. Come on! She turned on all the lights in the house. She put a tape in the tape recorder and pressed the play button. The voice of a black jazz singer filled the room. She turned up the volume. The house was shaking with earsplitting noise. Amir-Ali was asleep. Asleep and deaf. Perhaps he had died? Perhaps something awful had happened to him?

Distraught and panic-stricken, she ran up the stairs and banged on Amir-Ali's door with her fists and feet. He opened the door, sleepy and yawning and startled by the loud noise coming from the tape player downstairs. He was in a foul mood. Malak-Azar was not used to his scowling and angry face. She saw that he was safe and sound and that nothing had happened to him, and she blushed. She turned away, muttered something, hesitated a moment, and ran down the stairs two steps at a time. She turned off the tape recorder and switched off the lights. She ran into her room, closed the door, lay on the bed, and stared at the ceiling, wide awake. She was hurt and humiliated and couldn't understand what was happening. If they had had a fight, one of those fights over nothing so common between husbands and wives, if they had had a serious disagreement, okay, it would be understandable. They could talk about it. One of them could give in and compromise. They could reach an agreement or they could go on with their quarrel. All these were possible if only Amir-Ali would offer a clear and logical explanation for his actions. But he wouldn't. He was as slippery as an eel. He played the fool. He talked nonsense. He put on an act. He mumbled. He would kill you with his foolishness, but he wouldn't talk.

Everything passed in darkness, in the painful ambiguity of conjecture and uncertainty. "It is in the best interest of both of us." What do you mean by that? Explain. Why are you silent? We

have shared the same bed for twenty years. Now, all of a sudden, it
is in our best interest to sleep apart? Why? And then that absurd
behavior. If you have gone mad, then fine, we will go to a neurolo-
gist, to an ENT specialist, to . . . oh, I don't know. We will go away,
we will go abroad and visit the children, we will do something.
There is no illness that can't be cured.

Malak-Azar's private monologue went on and on. She was
troubled by this distance Amir-Ali had created between them.
She was addicted to this man's presence, addicted to the scent of
his skin, to the gentle rhythm of his breathing, to his cautious and
deliberate movements in bed, to the rustling of the newspaper
he read before going to sleep, and to the slurping sound he made
as he drank water when he woke up in the middle of the night.
She pictured him sleeping soundly (which was not far from the
truth) and it made her more agitated. She wanted to break something. She wanted to claw at Amir-Ali's face and torture him. She
wanted to make him jealous and miserable. She wanted to rob
him of his sleep.

She told herself that her best weapon was indifference; to act
as if nothing had happened. Good morning, dear! Did you sleep
well? Fine. What a lovely day! What beautiful sunshine! What a
sumptuous smell of freshly toasted bread! She told herself, You
could even whistle or hum to express your happiness. You could
stretch your arms and legs and sigh contentedly. You could lie
back in an easy chair and laugh for no good reason at all. You
could dress up, carefully put on your makeup, wave goodbye,
and go out. You could come back late at night and offer no explanation as to where you have been. You could say, I have already
had dinner, but not reveal where and with whom. You could even
pretend that you have had a good night's sleep, better than ever

before, and express your appreciation for your husband's decision. And if all this doesn't work or proves to be too difficult and
painful, if all these games fail to make Amir-Ali jealous and don't
stir him into action, if he turns deaf and dumb and blind without
giving any indication of what the hell is wrong with him, then
you could take that porcelain bowl from the bedside table and
smash it on his head.

Amir-Ali came to the breakfast table, still sleepy and absent-
minded and completely unaware of his wife's deliberations and
plans. He looked at her from the corner of his eyes and sighed with
relief. He had expected to find her sad and sulking, but here she
was, vibrant and smiling, smartly dressed and made-up, and in good
humor. He thanked his lucky stars for not having gotten engaged in
an ugly scene of accusations and counteraccusations. His conscience
was relieved. He had a hearty breakfast and failed to notice the
anger that seethed behind his wife's seemingly joyful eyes.

The nights that followed were the same. Malak-Azar would
struggle with herself. She would get up and walk about, smoke
a cigarette, sit up in bed and stare at the melancholy shadows
around her. She couldn't sleep, and if she did catch a wink, it
was just a wink. Sometimes she would wake up with a start and
think that someone was behind the door and her heart would
race. She would imagine that it was Amir-Ali and she would feign
sleep. She would wait. Two minutes, three minutes. She would lie
still. Five minutes. She would open her eyes ever so slightly. What
happened? Where did he go? She would jump out of bed and look
everywhere and she would find no trace of him.

This went on for several nights. Once again she thought Amir
Ali had come to her, and again she realized she was mistaken. At
last, she realized she couldn't go on with all that buffoonery. She

could no longer deceive herself and bury her head in the sand. Reality, however bitter, was better than that sham. She wanted to find out everything right then. She wanted to hear the truth from her husband's own lips. What was going on in his head? What was the truth of it all? She cornered Amir-Ali in his room before he could leave the house. She closed the door and forced him to sit down. She put her hands on his shoulders to hold him there and sat down in front of him.

Amir-Ali glanced at his watch. He said he had an appointment. An important one. It had to do with the company's state of affairs. "Let's leave it for this evening when we can sit and talk things over at leisure," he said. And he got up to leave. But Malak-Azar was determined. She grabbed his jacket with both hands and made him sit down again. "On the night of the birthday party," she said, "when the lights went out, what really happened? Who kicked Uncle G.?" Had it really been her mother, the venerable lady? If so, why did Amir-Ali run out of the room, his face ashen and drained of all color? Why?

Like a snared gazelle, Amir-Ali made a desperate struggle to free himself and remained silent.

"Why?"

Silence.

Malak-Azar noticed him looking around, waiting for a chance to escape. She moved her chair closer to his, pressed her knees against his shaky legs, put her hand under his chin, and forced his face up toward hers. It was as if she was encouraging a naughty boy to speak up. Her voice was gentle, with no trace of anger or reproach. "What is it, my love, my sweetie pie. Speak to me. I'm your wife, I'm you, your love. Do you remember?"

Apparently Sweetie Pie didn't remember. Suddenly, in an

unexpectedly firm and confident voice, Amir-Ali blurted out that everyone has a secret and everyone is entitled to keeping a corner of their life private. He had put his foot in his mouth. What did he mean by "private"? Which part and which corner of his life? Did Amir-Ali have another life, independent of his wife's? It was a tactless statement that had popped out of his mouth. He himself didn't understand how his tongue had turned and how those words had taken shape.

Malak-Azar, who had not expected this reply, snapped, "I'm a stranger in your eyes, am I? You don't trust me, do you?"

Amir-Ali couldn't trust his tongue and his voice. He realized he had no control over what he said and he was afraid that more unintended words would pour out of his mouth. He picked up the water bottle from the bedside table, and unlike his usual well-mannered self, he started to drink straight from the bottle. Malak-Azar objected to his rude behavior. But the water was refreshing and he raised the bottle to his mouth again and gulp, gulp, gulp, drank to the last drop. He felt calmer. Malak-Azar was irate, but she held her tongue. This was not the time for reproach. This man was like a child, obstinate and stubborn. He had to be tricked. She started to praise and compliment him. Men just love being admired. Even a hard nut like Amir-Ali could be cracked with a slick tongue. She softened her voice (perhaps too soft) and laughed. A bitter sorrow lined her laughter and falsehood fluttered in her excessively gentle voice. She took Amir-Ali's hand (the same unkind hand that had come down on her head) and caressed it. She lowered her head and kissed his fingertips. She sensed hardly any feelings in his hands and was offended. She could tolerate anything, as long as her pride was intact, and yet she swallowed her anger.

"Amir-Ali," she said, "we were once intimate, you and I. We
didn't hide anything from each other. We were like one soul in
two bodies. Have you forgotten? There is nothing in the world
that I haven't done for you. "(She wanted to say, You owe everything you have in life to me, but she checked herself.) "You have
to talk to me. You have to tell me the truth. Why did you move to
a separate bedroom? Why are you shying away from me? Why?"

Her voice had grown louder as she spoke and her last "why"
rang with menace. Amir-Ali had run out of cigarettes. He crumpled the empty pack and tossed it on the table. He picked up
the matchbox and began to twirl it between his fingers. He lit
a match, blew it out, and put the burnt matchstick back in the
box. He lit another one and held it until it burned his fingertips.
Malak-Azar hated it when people put burnt matchsticks back in
the box. This was exactly what Uncle G. did and it always irritated her. She took the matchbox from him and removed the
burnt matchsticks. She noticed that he was not feeling well. A
throbbing blue vein had appeared on the side of his forehead.
Why was he so distraught? She didn't know this man. This was
not her beloved gazelle. He was a stranger bent on deceiving her.
It was obvious. He didn't want to talk.

Malak-Azar hated illogical and ambiguous events that were
outside the realm of proof and evidence. Every incident had a
reason and it could be explained rationally and scientifically. Life
was a collection of choices. To succeed in life, you have to hold up
your head, watch where you are going, determine your interests,
put things in their proper place, and take responsibility for your
destiny. Amir-Ali didn't know the proper place for things and he
wouldn't learn. For example, he would forget that he should hang
up his clothes in the closet instead of piling them up on a chair

or on the bed. He would often forget that the proper place for books was not on the kitchen table or in the bathroom. Or that he shouldn't take off his shoes in the middle of the hallway and leave them there. Or that he should not be searching, from dawn until dusk, for his eyeglasses, his lighter, his telephone book, and for this or that important document.

Sometimes, Malak-Azar wondered why she loved this man, and the first thought that occurred to her was that he belonged to her, that he was in love with her, that he could not survive without her. Perhaps choosing Amir-Ali had been the only hasty decision in her life. Had she really fallen in love with him or had she married him to spite me? Whatever the reason, she would not submit to defeat and admit she had made a mistake. Never! She would continue on the course she had chosen to the very end. She would do anything and everything to prove she had been right.

She had made up her mind to turn Amir-Ali into a creature after her own heart, and she had succeeded. A success that had lasted all of two decades. It was no joke. She had managed to stay high and dry in spite of all the adversities, the revolution, and the war. Her house was confiscated and twice the doors of the Yarn and Spool Company had been padlocked. She had spent four years going from one citizens' committee to the next and from one district attorney's office to a higher one until she finally managed to get her house back, revive the semi-bankrupt company, and reinstate Amir-Ali as its vice president. And now that she wanted to sit back, put her feet up, and celebrate her victory and her husband's birthday, Amir-Ali was disrupting the orderly pattern of life. He was rebelling for no good reason. Perhaps he was afraid of getting old? Perhaps he feared death? She had heard that men suddenly act up when they approach sixty. That instead of continuing with their growth and transcendence, they suddenly panic and become rapacious. They realize that they have very little time left and that they must seize the day and scrub the bottom of every pot and pan they can lay their hands on. If this was the case, then Amir-Ali's condition was only temporary and it would pass. She just had to bite her fingernails and be patient. For Malak-Azar the greatest humiliation was to give in. She would never admit defeat. She would go on fighting.

It had taken her a long time to corner Amir-Ali and she was not going to let him go. She wanted an answer, a clear and candid one. "What is the meaning of all this?" she persisted. "Answer me. Have you gone mad? Are you sick?" The word "sick" came to Amir-Ali's rescue. "Yes, you are right. You should know that, yes, I am sick. Are you satisfied? I am sick, mentally sick. I am capable of anything. I have no control over my actions. Do you hear me? Do you understand?"

If left to himself, he would go on and on for hours. An unprecedented anger had surfaced from the depths of his soul, a faceless and sweeping rage directed at invisible men, at one person in particular who represented all the rest and who had no recognizable face; a rage directed at everything around him, at the newspaper on the table, at the distorted lines of objects, at all the vexing noise that came from the outside, at all the glaring lies, at himself, at Malak-Azar, at the boring ugliness that swirled in the air like gray dust.

Malak-Azar was staring at him, bewildered and terrified. She had never seen him so agitated. She was not used to his panting and the beads of sweat that lined his upper lip. She thought he was acting, trying to fool her, wanting to silence her. What a lousy actor! A mental patient? My foot! Dangerous? No way. The truth lay somewhere else. It was what he was hiding from her and did not dare express. For a few moments, they remained silent. Then they both started to talk at once, interrupting each other. Neither one heard or understood what was said. Like two confused souls, they sat there, staring at each other. Something had broken. They couldn't believe it. Accepting it was painful. Amir-Ali turned away, and Malak-Azar, involuntarily and for the first time in their married life, shouted at her husband. Her voice reverberated throughout the house. The cook heard the shout and dropped his spatula and the cat sprang off the windowsill and ran away.

THE YARN AND SPOOL Imports Company was in a bad way. The shareholders were up in arms and the municipality refused to pay the money it owed the company. Despite his reluctance, Amir-Ali was compelled to go to the office and call for a board meeting. At the meeting, Malak-Azar's brother, the company chairman, blamed their woes on Amir-Ali's incompetence and accused a veteran accountant of embezzlement. The old accountant defended himself and became so emotional that he nearly had a heart attack. The shareholders intervened and helped the old man, who was having difficulty breathing, out of the room. Amir-Ali told the board members that he would ask for a meeting with the mayor or his deputy and that he would single-handedly solve the company's problems.

The next day he came over to my place and we went to see one of my uncles who had considerable seniority and influence among the merchant community and in the local government.

My uncle was a fair-minded man, and although he had been at loggerheads with Amir-Ali's late father, he promised, for my sake, to help. He said the deceased had made many grave mistakes and had committed many sins, but his children should not have to suffer for their father's misdeeds. He said everyone was responsible for their own destiny, and he went on and on. I can hardly remember any more of what he said.

Three days later, a high-ranking official at the municipality received Amir-Ali in his office. Two other men were also present. Whenever Amir-Ali was to meet with government officials, he would let his beard grow into stubble and he would wear an old suit to the meeting. He had also memorized a few lines from the Quran and would come up with an Arabic quotation or two whenever necessary.

The high-ranking official started to speak and Amir-Ali, for his part, praised the gentleman's intelligence, humanity, and piety. The other two lower-ranking officials also spoke for about an hour. From time to time, Amir-Ali nodded in agreement. Everything was going well when suddenly Amir-Ali's stomach started to growl. It sounded as if two thousand frogs were croaking in his intestines and their sound was being broadcast over loudspeakers. His guts were about to explode. The high-ranking official was flabbergasted and involuntarily moved away from Amir-Ali, and the other two men stared at him in alarm. Finally, the rumbling subsided and there was a moment of silence. A semblance of order returned to the meeting. But the high-ranking official had barely opened his mouth when Amir-Ali's stomach-growling gave way to long hiccups. Hiccups so unnatural and loud that everyone in the room, himself included, was startled. Amir-Ali was breathless and struggling to control himself. He felt his stomach churning and thought he would throw up on the dossiers on the table at any moment. Something like a wild beast was in his belly and it was fighting to break loose and leap out. The men frowned and glowered at him. Their voices echoed in his ears and their glares pierced his body. He signed a document and was still holding the pen when suddenly his body emitted a dreadful noise that jolted everyone. The high-ranking official leapt up in anger and his minions picked up their dossiers and headed for the door. They were still in the doorway when Amir-Ali vomited on the documents in front of him.

He returned home broken and exhausted. He went straight to his room, locked the door, and lay down on his bed. His bowels were no longer churning and growling. It was as if nothing had happened, as if they had not been on the verge of explosion a mere sixty minutes ago. Yet his body was no longer that old lovable organism he so cherished. Every part of it, every limb, had rebelled and was at war with him. His brain was being disloyal to him, it had joined forces with an evil power and God only knew what sort of plot it was hatching against him.

Amir-Ali was relieved that his wife was not home. He didn't have to explain anything to anyone and he didn't have to pretend he was well and happy. No one would understand his illness. Once or twice he had thought of seeing a psychiatrist, but he had given up on the idea. He didn't believe in psychology and psychiatry. He had no time or patience for such things. His cure was not in sedatives and sleeping potions. He knew that the root of his ailment—if it qualified as such—lay somewhere in his past. It was an old virus that had nestled in his heart and soul. His body had not run amok without cause and it was not acting up for no reason. He had to find out. But how far back did he have to go?

AMIR-ALI'S CHILDHOOD memories are disjointed and vague. In his mind he has preserved certain days, incidents, and a few handpicked fragments of the past (those that were agreeable to him), and he has consigned to oblivion certain other, older memories. His recollections are full of black holes, full of lapses in time and silences. I can still picture the young Amir-Ali. He was tall and handsome, reclusive and reticent. He was not one for playing soccer or running races or ganging up with the neighborhood boys. His greatest pastime was going to the movies. It would take him a long time to disengage from the plot and events of a film he had seen. He loved seafaring movies, the story of some lonely captain and his sailors casting anchor at every port and calling no place home. He traveled with these films and lived their adventures, and one could tell from his absent gaze that he was in another world.

When he was younger he would break things, utensils, bowls, porcelain vases, anything he could lay his hands on, especially things that belonged to his father. No matter how many times he was asked, "Why are you doing this, you jackass?" he would not answer. He couldn't help it, he was incorrigible. His father was a tyrant and a disciplinarian. He had Amir-Ali locked up, first in an upstairs room and then in the dark cellar. His mother was worried to death for him. She would say, "My son will die of fright. I will lose him." She didn't know that her son was quite happy all alone in the dark. The cellar had a window set high in the wall, near the ceiling, and images of the moon and the sky reflected on it. Amir-Ali would sit and stare at the stars, oblivious to the world. He would make up stories. He would go on imaginary journeys and fly from one planet to another.

When he was older, he stopped breaking things, but he gave his family another cause for concern. He stopped talking to his father and wouldn't look him in the eye. His father spent most of his time traveling, but whenever he came back, once a week or twice a month, he wanted to assert himself and make his presence known to his sons. But Amir-Ali would make himself scarce, and no matter how many times he was called, refused to answer. He had a dual relationship with his mother. As a young boy, he would cling to her. Perhaps too closely. He would even sleep in her bed. Then at one point he broke away from her and grew more and more distant.

I carefully go over Amir-Ali's diaries. Nowhere does he refer to the cause of this breakup with his mother. His references to her are like a half-solved crossword puzzle. I have to fill in the blanks. And still, I get nowhere. There is always a word that remains incomplete and I can't identify the missing letters. His mother's image remains concealed, like a sacred icon, behind a veil of vague words and cautious references. Each time he writes about her, his handwriting and even his prose change. He writes a sentence and then he crosses it out. It is clear that he is fighting with himself. He wants to say something, divulge a secret, but he can't. I remember his mother when she was young. She was thin and fragile and beautiful in a subtle way. A beauty that at first glance went unnoticed. She didn't stand out. It was only after a second or third look that her clear, bright eyes and her sweet smile revealed themselves. From then on, whenever you looked at her, you saw her as being beautiful.

As a young boy of four or five, Amir-Ali slept in his mother's bedroom. He knew and understood even then that despite her gentle smile and kind hands, his mother was utterly miserable. At night, she wept quietly with her face buried in the pillow. And the only thing Amir-Ali could do with his small hands was to break things. His mother's crying fits were a nocturnal exercise. In the morning, she turned a new leaf and put on a different face. She put rouge to her lips and cheeks, but the effect was temporary. Ten minutes later the artificial redness had been wiped off and replaced by a ubiquitous gray, the color of swallowed words and unspoken sorrow. The only lasting redness in that tired and sapless face was that of her eyes and eyelids.

Why did she pretend to be happy? Was she ashamed? Was she afraid? Perhaps this was how grownups behaved. They had two faces, one for the day and one for the night. Amir-Ali didn't like two-faced people. His young mind couldn't grasp the notion of duality and contradiction. It confused and frightened him. Everything seemed unreal to him, like one shadow on top of another. He would stand in front of the mirror and look at himself. He saw that he was no different from the night before and the day preceding it and he would feel relieved. He promised himself that he would have only one face when he grew up, his real face, just as he was.

His father had four, six, ten faces. Cardboard faces. And none of them was for his mother. When it came to her, he was faceless. Just an empty circle with two pointed ears, like a flat caricature drawn by a child. When it came to the maid, he had two pairs of eyes, a big watery mouth, and moving lips. At times, this face would grow long and narrow, with a pronounced frown and sparks flying from its eyes. This was his ugliest face—mean, jealous, and dangerous. It was with this face that he had drawn a gun on his oldest son. Amir-Ali's brother was crawling on all fours, trying to get up on his feet, wanting to get away, but his father kicked him in the back and made him fall down again. With the gun aimed at his face, the young man's mouth was gaping in fright and he could barely utter a sound. His father watched him in this helpless and terrified state and gnashed his teeth in pleasure. The bone of contention was the neighbor's comely wife. Amir-Ali's mother was watching the fight from behind the window and her sad and happy faces had merged, like a pair of ink drawings on wet paper. Amir-Ali was standing next to her, shaking. He couldn't understand why his mother did nothing. Why wasn't she screaming? Why had she put her hand in front of her mouth? Amir-Ali wanted to scream for help. He wanted to save his brother by calling out to the neighbors or the servants. He wanted to pick up a vase and smash it on his father's head. But his mother wouldn't let him. She was pressing his face to her skirt to stop him from watching the scene. But he had already seen too much. Boys his age should not witness such scenes. And then she put her finger on his lips to indicate that he should keep quiet. And this finger stayed on his lips for years to come; even after his brother's death.

Amir-Ali kept his head down, pressed his lips together, and a big silence settled in his small body. And as he grew up, this silence turned into some sort of lethargy and passivity. People attributed Amir-Ali's indifference, which bordered on resignation, to his wisdom, and they whispered to each other that he had a sharp and calculating mind.

DEEPLY HURT AND troubled, Malak-Azar sat down and thought things through. She put two and two together and concluded that

Amir-Ali had fallen out of love with her. A husband who ran away from his wife and slept in a separate bedroom (making sure the door was locked from the inside), who struck his wife on the head (she was now sure it was Amir-Ali's own doing), and who deliberately and premeditatedly vomited on the municipality's dossiers with the intention of bankrupting his wife's family company, did not love her; not only that, he was most certainly in love with some other woman.

Why had this not occurred to her sooner? Amir-Ali and another woman. But who? For a moment, the vague image of a young, beautiful woman flashed before her eyes. This was the first time she was considering such a possibility, and that invisible "other woman" suddenly became more real than any other reality, more real than the glass of water on the table, than the breeze caressing her cheeks, than the shoes on her feet, more real than she herself. In all likelihood, others already knew, but had kept it from her. Uncle G. was a nosy busybody and often put his foot in his mouth. Malak-Azar reasoned that her meddling uncle must have wanted to tell a story about Amir-Ali. He had intended, out of malice, to hint at Amir-Ali's relationship with a certain lady and Amir-Ali had shut him up by kicking him under the table. Yes, that must have been it. Plain and simple.

A new window opened on Malak-Azar's fantasies and a black curtain lifted from before her eyes. She accepted without a moment's hesitation what her feminine logic dictated. That was it. Another woman! Her first feeling was that of fear. The fear of finding herself abandoned and unprotected in a dark maze, all alone. She felt she had lost her grip and the ground was shaking beneath her feet. It was a feeling similar to death, similar to watching her own funeral. She clawed at her long hair. She felt pain. The feeling was real, that of an unhappy and exasperated living being. The chill of death gave way to the heat of unbridled anger. Her heart valves were opening and closing in a frenzy and with each pulse love was giving way to hate.

At that moment, she was capable of setting the house on fire, killing herself and Amir-Ali. She had not believed a word of what he had said about his mental illness. She told herself that all his theatrics were part of a grand scheme, orchestrated for a reason, for a precise and calculated intention. Amir-Ali was a cheat and a liar and unfaithful, like all other men, like so-and-so and so-and-so, and she, the gullible Malak-Azar, had been fooled by his innocent act. What a mistake! Not even once had she tried to find out what he was up to, and only now did she understand why he came home late on certain evenings and why he quickly hung up the telephone whenever she walked in the door.

Where did he go and with whom was he spending time? All his words and deeds now seemed suspicious. Even his face looked ugly and monstrous. She had no doubt that another woman, a younger one, was involved. The word "younger" reverberated in her brain like an earsplitting blast. She wanted to know everything: when they had met and where, her name, her age, her address, her telephone number, and most important, her looks. Malak-Azar was determined to find out. Not knowing was driving her crazy. A hundred times a day, she asked herself, Who is she? And she wallowed in jealousy over an imaginary woman.

Irrational fantasies and destructive nightmares drove the plain reality of life out of Malak-Azar's mind. She felt disoriented. She could not come to grips with being in a specific time and place. And yet, life went on, as did her daily routine— waking up, saying a cheerful "good morning," getting dressed, working out, chatting with friends on the telephone, seeing to household matters, and going to parties. She rearranged things around the house. The old porcelain bowl, the tall crystal lamp, and the cut-glass vase were moved from one room to another. Curtains were drawn aside. A crumpled newspaper was tossed in the wastebasket. Windows were opened and closed. And all this was done by a stranger, by an absent Malak-Azar who had become a pale shadow of her old self, of the proud and success-ful woman who believed in everlasting happiness. Now, without warning and unprepared, she had stumbled, as though an invisi-ble hand had suddenly pushed her from behind. She had slipped, lost her balance, and had plunged into the chaos of blind urges and the abyss of disorientation.

For Amir-Ali, the days passed at a slow and monotonous pace, void of color and fragrance. Life was a photocopy of events past, a mechanical reproduction of things that had lost their original form. He felt it was impossible to carry on like this and decided to sit down and write a letter to his wife and explain everything— from the events of that first night to their latest argument. The first draft turned out to be too short and he tore it up. The sec-ond and third attempts were too long. The fourth and fifth drafts were incoherent and confused. He ran out of paper. He called the servant to ask for more paper. When the servant walked in, he sniffed and said, "Master, there is a funny smell in this room." And he asked if he could open the window. Amir-Ali also noticed an unpleasant odor. He thought there might be a dead mouse some-where and he looked for it everywhere. But he found nothing. Then he realized that the stench was coming from his own body. It was the smell of putrid flesh.

He took a bath and washed himself thoroughly from head to

toe. He soaped himself. He stood under a hot shower until his skin started to burn. Then he smelled himself and felt nauseated. Some part of his body was rotting. He stood in front of the mirror and carefully examined his teeth one by one. He thought perhaps an abscess had opened in some hidden part of his body, perhaps between his toes, or in his armpit. He checked himself from head to toe. He was intact. No scratches. No wounds. No abscess. And yet there was a horrible odor emanating from his pores. What would happen if Malak-Azar saw him in this condition? What if this foul smell, the smell of rotting flesh, reached his sons? All doors were closed to him, the world was up in arms against him, and he didn't have it in him to fight destiny.

The only course of action was to go away. He packed a suitcase and took his checkbook and all the cash he had in the house. He wrote a two-sentence note to his wife explaining that he was ill, that he was going away for a few days, that one day he would explain everything to her, but for now the only thing he could do was to leave and put distance between himself and his loved ones.

AMIR-ALI SET OFF with no particular destination in mind. His car was large and comfortable and he was enjoying being on the open road. He felt free; it was a novel experience for him. His body's foul smell had subsided a little and he could breathe more easily. He pushed down on the gas pedal and drove on, not knowing where he would end up. He drove past Karaj. He drove past Hamadan. Then he stopped at a small roadside restaurant and had lunch. He felt drowsy. He lay down in the shade of some trees and watched the afternoon sky and the patient passage of the clouds, and he catnapped. His eyelids drooped and lifted again.

His tranquil body felt void of all temptations. Playful, carefree birds chirped noisily in the trees and prudent, wise ants scurried around on the ground.

A little farther away, a woman was washing dishes in the stream while her menfolk sat reclining on soft cushions, finishing off a watermelon, their eyes full of afternoon slumber. A brass samovar was simmering next to them. A boy carrying a tray walked over to Amir-Ali and offered him tea. The men nodded invitingly, urging him to accept. The woman dried the dishes with the corner of her chador. Then she got up, put her hands on her pregnant belly, and yawned. She glanced at Amir-Ali with the intoxicating languor of a woman expecting a child.

He spent the night at a roadside inn. He got out of bed several times to look out at the crescent moon and the twinkling stars, and he slept with his eyes full of images of the galaxy and cosmic rays. He set off again at the crack of dawn. There lay before him, as far as the eye could see, bare and barren land, and then suddenly, in the midst of that parched emptiness, a row of green poplars stood in line like neat schoolboys. Farther on, in the heart of the desert, a small oasis appeared.

The sun was setting. The horizon was lined with a world of colors and a mass of orange light was descending from the sky. Driving on that dirt road wasn't easy. Once or twice the wheels sank in the soft, muddy soil and the car stalled, labored forward a few yards, and got stuck again. It was getting dark. Amir-Ali got out of the car, took off his jacket, spread it on the ground, and lay down on it. The earth was silent and the nearby mountains were still. The breadth of the desert gradually seeped into his body, carrying him forward like a light-headed kite. No one was watching him, no one was judging him. He could metamorphose into any shape. He could die, and opting for death was a choice he could make.

He thought of Malak-Azar. Her chiming voice tinkled softly in his ear and the memory of her perfumed body tickled the back of his throat. Some fragments of this woman lingered in him, and her absent presence hung from the edges of his thoughts like a cobweb spun by an old spider. When he was away from Malak-Azar, he missed her, he missed an imaginary Malak-Azar who had the hypnotic voice of a mermaid and a comforting embrace as vast as an eternal plain. He longed for this unreachable woman.

Amir-Ali traveled for two months. His body's repugnant smell had completely disappeared and his limbs were no longer acting up. Several times he thought of calling his mother, or one of his friends, but he gave up on the idea. He did call Malak-Azar, but before he had a chance to speak, she slammed down the receiver. The second time he called, a servant told him that the lady of the house was not home.

He told himself, It is still too early to go back. This isn't the right time. My wife is still angry. I must wait longer. I must be sure of myself.

He spent another month traveling, going from one village to another, from one satellite town to the next, from one teahouse to the other, driving aimlessly, dreamy and euphoric, oblivious to time, unaware of specific people and places, mindless of the Yarn and Spool Company and of duplicate and triplicate accounts. During the day he drove along the edge of sprawling deserts, and at night he lay down and gazed at the sky and the sweeping landscapes. He felt he was part of that silent universe, and his solitary being gradually atrophied because of its contact with the blazing sun, with those endless plains, and with the clear and cloudless sky. And yet he was still tied to the past. Clearly, the reasonable thing to do was to contact his family and end their worries. It was hard for him to say goodbye to the mountains and the plains and the tranquillity of the desert, but he had to go back. His mother's life was hanging by no more than a thread and was as fragile as a soap bubble in the air. He had to see her. He had to see her off.

The front door to his house was locked and the lock had been changed. Long as he rang the doorbell, no one answered. He realized he couldn't go to his office looking like he did, completely unkempt. He decided to go to Uncle G.'s house, which was just around the corner. The old man was shocked to see him. He took a step back and his jaw dropped. His mother-in-law was there, too. Amir-Ali saw her peeking out from behind the upstairs bedroom window, but she quickly moved away. Amir-Ali asked about his wife. But Uncle G. just kept staring at him.

"Where have you been all this time?" he finally asked.

Amir-Ali was in no mood to explain and again asked about Malak-Azar. Uncle G. sighed, put his hand on Amir-Ali's shoulder, and cleared his throat. He was preparing for a long lecture. Then he extended his right arm (clearly he had rehearsed this pose in front of the mirror), stretched his neck, and in a quivering voice he said, "Life is a strange enigma. It has its ups and downs. Sometimes you are up, sometimes you are down."

Amir-Ali laughed. He didn't know why. Uncle G. looked down and once again became a small and sad old man. With the voice of a retired actor, void of any resonance or excitement, he explained that Malak-Azar had gone abroad. She had put the house up for sale and given the key to so-and-so (meaning me).

Amir-Ali was neither surprised nor upset. He seemed to have expected this all along. He said a hasty goodbye and was about to leave when Uncle G. called him back. He had another piece of news for him. Bad news. This time, with a voice that had regained its dramatic tone, he said, "I'm sorry. I don't know how to put it. It's not easy."

Amir-Ali's heart sank. Uncle G. was mumbling. He wanted to prolong Amir-Ali's misery as much as possible. He took a hand-kerchief from his pocket and blew his nose, once, twice, all for theatrical effect. He coughed. Amir-Ali's eyes were glued to his mouth. Turning deathly pale, Amir-Ali asked, "My mother?"

The doorbell rang. "Please, let me open the door," Uncle G. said. Amir-Ali felt like kicking Uncle G. in the ankle again. "Please tell me what has happened," he said. Standing at the door, Uncle G. replied, "You have been gone for three months and during all this time you never contacted your wife or your children or your mother. What did you expect?"

Malak-Azar's brother and I had arrived on the scene together. When Amir-Ali saw me walk in, he heaved a sigh of relief and stepped away from Uncle G. He knew that I knew everything. I got straight to the point. I gave him the key to his house and told him that it had been placed in my trust and now I was return-ing it. Then I told him calmly and coolly (I knew how much he detested excitement) that his mother was in the hospital, that it was hopeless, and that she could pass away at any moment.

My car was parked right outside the house. I offered to drive him to the hospital. He accepted and ran out ahead of me.

"When was the last time you spoke with her?" he asked.

For a moment I thought he was talking about Malak-Azar and my heart sank. I wanted to tell him that I was going to join

Malak-Azar, but it wasn't the right time. I had to wait. Amir-Ali's thoughts were with his mother.

Again, he asked, "When was the last time you spoke with my mother?"

"Two days ago."

"How was she? Please tell me."

I couldn't drive and talk about this at the same time. We were in front of a school. Children were running around. A truck was unloading bricks at the end of the road and it had blocked our way. Amir-Ali was going out of his mind. He was sweating. He got out of the car and said, "I'll get there faster if I walk." And he started to run.

The hospital was crowded. There were lines everywhere, in front of the elevator, in front of the pharmacy, in front of the restrooms. And there was a disorderly line in front of the information booth. His mother's name was not on the patient list. Amir-Ali stopped a passing doctor and with a lump in his throat asked for help. The doctor was a good man. He was in a hurry, but he asked what Amir-Ali's mother was suffering from. "Such patients are usually sent up to the fifth floor. Inquire at the upstairs information desk."

The elevator went up to the third floor and then went back down to the second floor and stayed there. Amir-Ali got out and ran up the stairs two at a time. A framed photograph of a nurse holding her finger to her lips was hanging on the wall. A nurse was walking by with a tray of medications. Amir-Ali stopped her and gave her his mother's name. The nurse nodded toward the room across the hall. Room 503.

She was still alive. Never mind that an IV was connected to her arm, that a tube was inserted in her nose, that she looked like a plucked chicken, that her face was drained of all color, and that the line on the heart monitor was almost flat. She was still alive.

Shocked and trembling, Amir-Ali stood by the door. He couldn't bring himself to go in. A nurse came and checked the patient, took her pulse, and tidied the sheets. Amir-Ali was about to collapse. Did his mother remember him? Perhaps she was looking at him with her soul, with a third eye, with a mind that existed outside her body. His mother's white hands, lined with spidery blue veins, lay on the sheets. Her fingertips quivered. She was aware of his presence. He gently turned her face toward him. He gazed at her and saw two translucent circles shining deep in her eyes, two windows to another life. And he saw himself, from the moment of his conception, an embryo floating in a warm and humid space, until the moment of his birth, in various shapes, in a thousand images scattered in his mother's silent memories that were coming to an end and like shiny specks were slowly being absorbed by a much larger memory. That one moment had been enough. It was as though the old lady, sitting on the brink of death, had been waiting for that last encounter.

Amir-Ali tucked his mother's cold hands under the sheets. He closed her eyes and shut the door to the past. A major chapter in his life had come to an end. He felt he no longer belonged to anything or anyone and that all the sunny shores and clear, bright skies and all the green fields and vast deserts were waiting for him.

Malak-Azar had moved most of the valuables—the carpets and the antique objets d'art—and everything else that belonged to her, out of the house. Only the drapes and the beds, stripped of their mattresses and sheets, remained. The cabinet doors were left ajar, their interiors emptied out. The drawers had been pulled open and left in a state of disarray. The floors were littered with old newspapers and torn papers and photographs—Amir-Ali's photographs. His clothes—pressed trousers, clean white shirts, double-breasted jackets, neckties, imported scarves—all lay in a heap at the foot of a wall, like corpses on a battlefield. Malak-Azar had left him a note on the kitchen table, cold and concise. There was no greeting, no "Dear so-and-so," nothing. In very few words she informed him that she had no intention of coming back and that she never wanted to see him again, ever. This last word she had underlined twice for emphasis. (She had sent me a short letter, too. With a temporary address and a telephone number that I was not to give to anyone else.)

Amir-Ali lay down on the empty bed in the master bedroom and stared at the low ceiling. Scenes from his life passed piecemeal before his eyes, like an experimental film shot with a cast of strangers. Perhaps it had all been a dream. Perhaps he himself was just an obscure character, a stranger, in someone else's dream. The sensation of the vast desert still crawled under his skin and the sound of a murmuring brook still hummed in his ears. The walls, the doors and windows, and even the smell of that house were unfamiliar to him. He got up, packed his things, and took the money and dollar bills he had hidden in the back of a closet (instinctive farsightedness) and shoved them in his pocket. He also took the half-dead plant that was in the guest bedroom and he left.

ONE NIGHT AT a roadside teahouse, he looked at himself in the mirror and was startled to see a sixty-year-old man looking back at him. Until then, he had fought the onslaught of age. He had looked twenty years younger than he really was, and by hook or by crook he had hidden those twenty years somewhere

behind his face. He had obsessively watched his figure and his
good looks. He would not touch fatty foods or sweets. And the
clothes that Malak-Azar carefully picked out for him presented
him as a youngish man of good taste. Now he had become someone else: a middle-aged man with a small double chin, sunburnt
cheeks, a deeply furrowed forehead, crow's feet around his eyes,
a graying stubble, and strands of white here and there in his hair
and eyebrows. He was wearing a pair of loose Kurdish pants he
had bought at a bazaar in a small village. He didn't mind letting
out his paunch and he didn't worry about people's judgments and
inquisitive looks.

Amir-Ali stared at the image in the mirror with growing
amazement. He realized that he knew that face, that he had seen
it before. He moved closer. He had imagined a different reflection
of himself, and this man in the mirror was quite someone else.
He and that other man stood staring at each other, and Amir-Ali
realized that this other man was the one who had ruled over his
limbs and made his bowels rumble, he was the invisible being
who he thought had followed him like a shadow and was at war
with him. But perhaps this shadow had not been at war with
him after all. He had been a friend, abandoned and forgotten
and hence wounded and vengeful. The image in the mirror was
looking at him with friendly, inviting eyes. The two approached
each other until they merged, and only a memory remained of
the old Amir-Ali, the respectable vice president of the Yarn and
Spool Company.

AMIR-ALI IS in his car, driving along mountain roads. He has no
destination in mind. He enjoys this aimlessness, this trip toward
unknown and unexplored deserts. He is happy that no one knows

him and that he is not confined in a mold. He can be anyone he pleases. His body is relaxed and his limbs are at peace with him. He has rolled down the driver's side window and the autumn sun is shining on his face and bare arm. He feels he can drive on forever.

He spends the night in a small village and gazes at the sky and the stars, and once again that vastness seeps into his body and absorbs him. A gaunt cat walks over and sits next to him. Amir-Ali reaches out and strokes the cat on the head. His hand is full of kindness. He has had a light supper and he is in a good mood. His eyes look deep into the sky, at the bright crescent moon and the galaxies spread out in the universe. He thinks of somewhere beyond the farthest celestial bodies, of a world parallel with another, of a past that is renewed and of a time that is yet to come, and he returns to his beginning. For a moment he envisions himself in that rich cosmos, transformed into a tiny speck, floating in space. An indescribable pleasure creeps into every cell of his body. For a moment he thinks he has disintegrated, been pulverized and absorbed into the Milky Way. Perhaps he is dreaming. In whatever state he is, asleep or awake, he is happy. His happiness is not that of an affluent or successful man. It is the happiness of a speck floating in space. It is not easy to understand and it may sound like nonsense. But nonsense or not, this is how Amir-Ali feels and it cannot be expressed in any other way.

LET US OBSERVE him: He has been awakened by the crow of a rooster. Dawn is breaking. He is at a roadside teahouse, sleeping outside on a wooden bed, under a satin quilt, and he feels cold. He hugs his knees. A cool breeze brushes over his face. The smell of freshly baked bread is wafting in the air. He feels hungry. He opens his eyes a little and watches the fragments of his dream fly away. His gaze slides over the tousled leaves and the drooping branches of a young weeping willow tree and a translucent green hue spreads across his thoughts like a sheer silk veil. He falls asleep again. The sun is shining on his face when he wakes up. The air has warmed up to a pleasant temperature. He gets up and washes his hands and face in a stream flowing under the trees. The teahouse keeper brings him bread with feta cheese and hot tea and Amir-Ali allows himself, after many years, to eat two soft-boiled eggs. He pays his bill, gets into his car, and pushes down on the gas pedal. Where is he going? He doesn't know and he doesn't care. His body and the image of that bearded middle-aged man he had seen in the mirror—the Amir-Ali of yesterday and today—are at peace with him. At some point along the way, he stops and buys a watermelon from a roadside stand. Sometime later, he pulls over and stops. Two poplars stand side by side in the middle of the wilderness. He takes a mat from the car trunk and spreads it in the shade of the trees. The watermelon is red inside. It is a bit warm, but refreshing. He lies down with his hands tucked under his head. He can smell the fragrances of his childhood summers. The scent of the wet mud-and-straw orchard walls and the smell of the sticky resin oozing out of the pine trees. He can fly with his memories. He can roll over. He can shout. He can talk and pour out the unspoken words that have remained imprisoned in his chest. He can make choices, protest, make decisions, or do nothing. No one can tell him that he has to be for something or against someone, that he has to be a freedom fighter or a political activist or the Iranian ambassador to the Court of St. James's or the president of the Yarn and Spool Company. He can lie down under the trees and listen to the crickets.

He can realize his old dream and become an astronomer. Or he can water his plot of cucumbers and plow his land. He wants to start from the beginning, from his own beginning.

UNCLE G. HAD READ somewhere that all the occurrences in the world are somehow connected. He had wanted to pontificate on this, but he had not been given the chance. Yet, for once in his life he had been right, and those who were eating dinner around the table that night never learned how a series of thin threads hang from every word, every random encounter, and every minor incident, and how these threads are woven together like the colorful fabric of a celestial carpet. If on that fateful night a pesky mosquito had not bitten Amir-Ali's foot, in all likelihood nothing would have happened, and the destinies of Amir-Ali and Malak-Azar and her mother and Uncle G. and the Yarn and Spool Company would not have changed course. Likewise, my destiny.

—originally translated in collaboration with Karim Emami

THE GREAT LADY OF MY SOUL

*K*ashan. The city of poets and pomegranates. What a blessing to get away from noisy, polluted Tehran. I head out. I am unfamiliar with the city and end up taking a side road. The air is pure and imbued with refreshing, invisible particles. The wind smells of wet weeds and early-blooming flowers.

"MR. HEYDARI, WHAT is your share in this revolution?" I asked.

He was trembling. His fear of famine and lootings had robbed him of sleep. He had locked the door to his house and kept a vigilant eye on the street from the corner of a window.

"I'm suspicious of the landlord," my wife said. "I think he has links to the antirevolutionaries."

The city is tense and alert. Doors and windows open and close. There is the sound of random gunshots and turmoil. Somewhere a building is burning and strangers are chasing each other in dark alleys.

"This, too, shall pass," says my father, while looking for premium-quality raisins for his homemade wine.

. . .

FAR FROM HUMAN commotion, the sky above Kashan glistens like a clear spring. The meadow is abounding with wild rue and red poppies all the way to the hillsides. The mountains, naked and sober, resemble the body of a mythical woman and the desert has a nurturing presence.

In the distance, at the bend of the dirt road, a woman is sitting on the ground, and here, near me, a man is praying in the shadow of a pomegranate tree. The smallest flower in the world has blossomed right next to my feet.

"MISTER POET, WHERE is your historical conscience?" I asked.

"I am still in awe of this flower," he said.

They have shut down the university and professors are being put on trial in absentia.

My students shout, "Down with philosophy. Down with reactionaries." They beat their young fists against the walls and run along the university corridors searching for the meaning of freedom.

"Sir, what does 'unity in words' mean?" they ask. "Which is more valid, matter or idea? Which bears the truth, God or history?"

My wife believes in the jihad for reconstruction. She has donated her silver bangles to the nearby mosque and on Clean City Day she swept the dirt road in our neighborhood.

"In Islam, revenge is permissible," she says. And with fear and awe she looks at the pictures of those who have been executed. At night, she rushes off to the Women's Guidance and Religious Education classes. She believes in the dictates of good and evil.

She has cleaned and cut her long red nails and wiped off her green eye shadow. She covers her hair with a black headscarf and she is especially careful that people don't see her earlobes. She is restless and excited and her newfound faith makes her heart race. She sits next to me, looks at me, and tells me all about blasphemy and sin, about the devil's temptations and the need for punishment.

"Don't you believe in heaven and hell?" she asks.

"No, I don't."

She often stays up at night and quietly prays. Her breath is cool and her skin smells of rose water. Every time I look at her, she is smiling and gazing up at the sky outside the window.

"Listen," she says. "Can you hear the angels singing?"

"No, I can't."

I bury my head under the pillow and search for sleep. I can hear shots being fired and people shouting "God is great" on the rooftops in the neighborhood.

Friends say, "We should leave."

Friends say, "We should stay and fight."

Friends are in a frenzy to start a newspaper and to organize a political party.

Mr. Heydari has stocked his basement with flour, rice, and kerosene, and he has brought his silk carpets over to our house for safekeeping. He has taken his money out of the bank and he has put his gold coins in a pouch he wears around his neck.

Mr. Heydari is afraid of the enemies of the revolution and has decided to leave the country, but he is also afraid of loneliness in exile.

There is unrest at the university. Someone is giving a speech and the crowd salutes the Prophet and his family. Outside the university walls there are pictures of Imam Khomeini hanging from tree branches and peddlers are selling roasted beets and potatoes. An old woman stops me and shows me a photograph of her martyred son. She cries. The sidewalk is crowded with street vendors selling religious books, jeans, and sneakers. A little farther away, a guerrilla fighter is teaching people how to use an Uzi machine gun, and in the shadow of a tree, a man with his wife and children are sitting on a blanket eating lunch.

A student stops me and asks how I have been. I don't recognize him. He has wrapped a checkered scarf around his head and neck. I think he is a young Arab from Palestine. He is carrying a machine gun and shoots a few bullets in the air. The women scream and throw themselves down on the ground behind the trees.

Someone is knocking at the door. It is late at night. My wife leaps up from the sofa. My father quickly hides his bottle of arak. It is Mr. Heydari. He has brought us milk powder, canned foods, cheese, and Indian fish oil. He is out of breath.

"There is no gasoline," he says. "There is no flour. There is cholera and smallpox. Soon people will start eating each other."

My wife laughs at him. She believes pious people will bring us food. My son angrily pounds his fist on the sack of flour and says that the true revolution has yet to come. He believes that in the end the proletariat will triumph. He goes to the factory every day and he doesn't know how to make friends with the laborers. He wears dirty clothes and is proud of his dusty shoes. My son loves poverty and is obsessed with the idea of belonging to the working class.

My artist friend is from Kashan. He invited me to visit him there. I was delighted. I set off immediately. My wife was praying. She had just learned how to pray and didn't know the verses by heart. She read them from a piece of paper she had pinned to the wall.

The landlord was in the courtyard. He jumped up the minute he saw me. He was shaking. He was waiting for someone. He looked at my bag.

"Are you running away?" he asked.

"No."

"Is your name on the list, too?"

I shook my head.

"They will arrest me," he said. "Today or tomorrow. They will arrest you, too. They will arrest everyone."

My father was awake. He was sitting by the window, tuning his sitar. Until recently, he was a sitar teacher, but his students have stopped coming. They are busy singing revolutionary songs. Monsieur Ardavaz is Father's old friend. Once in a while he comes to visit him and they talk about the past. Monsieur Ardavaz has closed his liquor shop. He has turned a corner of his courtyard into a store and he sells crispy bread and pear preserves. Monsieur Ardavaz is terrified of imperialism and has voted for the Islamic Republic.

They have flogged the landlord; twenty lashes.

My son is against capitalism and says that the landlord should have been hanged.

OH, HOW DISTANT this green meadow is from the hysteria of history. How silent and sober. Far away, on the mountainside, a silent hamlet is sleeping in the shelter of trees, and somewhere in the distance a bird is singing. I feel light, I feel like a dandelion floating in the air. I sing to myself:

I have come searching for a dream
Or a ray of light
Perhaps for a pebble or a smile.

Up ahead, on the elevation, there is a water reservoir next to a mud and straw hut. It is a still body of water full of floating algae. An old man and his donkey walk by. He says hello. His bag smells of fresh bread and his clothes of burnt firewood.

THOUSANDS UPON THOUSANDS of people are standing in congregational prayer. The streets are milling with women clad in black chadors. There is a young man next to me. He is leaning against the wall. He is shaking with emotion. His eyes are closed and tears are streaming down his face.

My poet friend is bedridden. They say he has gone mad. I go to visit him. My heart is heavy. He is sleeping, half-unconscious.

His wife doesn't understand what is wrong with him. She is distraught, confused. She bursts into tears the minute she sees me.

"Wait until he wakes up," she says. "Perhaps he will talk to you. He talks to imaginary people. He prays twenty times a day and he is constantly repenting. At night, he goes up on the roof and shouts, 'God is great.' He cries and can't sleep for fear of God's presence."

I can't believe it. He was a quiet and timid man. He rarely said what was on his mind and in his heart. He wrote poems. Lovely, simple poems. When the revolution broke out, he started coming to our house in the evenings. He would sit and not say anything. We would sit in silence and listen to the shouts of "God is great," to the strange pandemonium in the city, and to the sound of bullets being fired. I would think some building was burning. We could hear the fire trucks and ambulances. My poet friend remained silent the entire time.

My hand still smells of fresh blood, warm blood, the blood of a youth who was the same age as my son. He was restless and excited. He was panting. He was shaking his small fist in the air and threatening the soldiers. I lost him at the bend of the street. There was a fire somewhere. The street was filled with suffocating smoke. Women were running and men were hastily closing their shops. The shooting had started. My poet friend was next to me. He was trembling. He was talking to himself. Death had a familiar face and it was sauntering around the city like an alluring seductress. I caught sight of the young boy. I didn't know him. He had crouched down and wrapped his arms around a tree. I picked him up. He wasn't breathing. The bullet had struck him in the chest. I called to a passerby. I stopped a man. I pounded on the door to a house. My poet friend didn't speak. He was standing next to me, spellbound, staring at death.

THE SKY IS GROWING dark. Where am I? There are no people around. I'm lost. Before me, a silent road creeps toward dark, unknown lands. The wind is my only companion. My heart is pounding. I keep going, aimlessly, with no destination. It will soon be night. A vague fear whirls inside me and strokes the back of my neck. I walk faster. My shoes are hurting my feet. I look around for a tree, a village, a human being. I turn left. The desert glares at me. There is an amorphous cacophony in the air. I see a narrow path that like a magical sign beckons me to an unknown place. I am tired. Thirsty. Stumbling, I drag myself forward. Now and then, the path ends and starts again a short distance away. I think to myself, I will never arrive. My only hope is this rugged path.

I stop. My heart skips a beat. Am I dreaming?

In front of me, in the middle of the desert, in that silent wasteland, there is a secluded garden sheltered by white walls. A half-open door summons me. I peek in. There is no sign of a human being. There are two rows of tall poplars flanking the surrounding walls and four aged cypress trees in the middle of four flower beds thick with wild red poppies and desert flowers. In the middle of the garden there is a pool brimming with crystalline water and the blue of the sky. The cobblestone walkways are coated with a thin layer of dust. No footprints, no signs of disturbance, no remnants of an intrusion. On the north side of the garden, at the top of a stone staircase, there is a sprawling veranda. Above it sits a white, celestial house. It is so dazzling, so pure. Perhaps it is a vision. Perhaps a dream.

Slowly, with cautious steps, I move forward. I am afraid the house might disappear if I take my eyes off of it, or it may crumble if I breathe too hard.

I sit on the edge of the pool and wash my face. What pleasure! The reflection of the house shimmers deep in the water and the green of the trees floats on its marble-like surface.

The water's cool scent is tempting. I take off my clothes and slide deep into the pool. I open my eyes. The blue sky has spread in the depths of the water. I feel as though I am floating among the galaxies. The water's breath blows away the thousand-year-old dust from my soul. My spirit quivers with pleasure. It is as if invisible hands are giving me ablution in the spring of eternal life. I lie floating on the surface. The sun has climbed halfway down the wall and in the fading light the cypress trees have grown taller. Again, I turn my eyes toward the house. How simple and unassuming, how noble and immaculate. It reminds me of someone close but forgotten, someone at the tip of ancient memories. At the edge of a sweet dream.

I climb out of the pool. I shiver. Dusk in the desert is cool and refreshing. I get dressed. I pick up my shoes and set off barefoot. I count twelve stairs. Someone had been praying on the veranda and has left behind a prayer stone. I step onto the veranda. It is an empty space with plain, unadorned walls. The windows are framed with modest cut-mirror designs. On either side of the veranda there are two half-open doors that lead into a room that is adjacent to a hidden alcove. Dim, labyrinthine hallways and spiral staircases draw me to themselves.

I am breathless by the time I reach the top floor. From here, I can see the four corners of the world. The sky is only a step away and the desert stretches as far as the horizon. I sit. For a long time. What point in time is this? Where am I? A sweet slumber hovers behind my eyelids, but it doesn't reach my brain. The stars have one by one appeared. My gaze floats in space and my thoughts, like runaway ripples on water, have no constant or defined shape.

I cannot feel my arms and legs. My body has lost its physical bounds and boundaries. I feel like I am an extension of the house, of the garden, of the desert, and that my eyes are suspended from the stars. I float in space. Weightless. Empty. How removed I feel from everyone and everything, from the geometric relationship of objects and the logical symmetry of things, from the tyranny of time and the exactitude of numbers, from the massive slate of law and the heavy tome of ethics. How far away I am from the validity of matter and the authenticity of history, from the invariable legitimacy of ideas and the conflict between the haves and have-nots, from the rituals of purification and the ceremonies of shrouding and burial.

I wake up. It is dawn. Bewildered, I look around. I get up. I am hungry, yet I feel well. I feel light and rested. There is a pleasant breeze. A rooster is crowing in the distance. A small village, down there, at the foot of the mountain, is awake. I put on my shoes. I hear footsteps. I climb down the stairs. An old man is sitting on the edge of the pool, performing his morning ablutions. His long, bushy beard is white. I say hello. He nods. He is praying.

When I reach the garden door, I stop and look back. In the half-light of dawn, the house looks like a vision, a luminous manifestation of a divine presence. It says something to me, something unspoken. I understand, and a sense of calm and confidence settles under my skin.

The way back is no longer unknown to me. The desert is quiet and still and void of daunting temptations. When I reach the green meadow, I take a shortcut and walk through the fields. Back on the road, a truck stops and the driver offers me a ride. He is a young man with a black beard and sunburnt skin.

There are dozens of pictures of ayatollahs taped to the windshield. I get out at a teahouse near town. Only now I realize how hungry I am. It is morning—a bright, warm summer morning.

I go back to the city and to my room at the inn. There have been several telephone calls from Tehran and from my friend with whom I was supposed to meet last night. He has left a message. Something important has come up. I must return to Tehran as soon as possible. My students have gone on strike and the professors are planning a sit-in. I pack my odds and ends and head out. The circle at the city center is crowded. Trucks are loaded with people going from one village to another. They are shouting slogans and chanting verses from the Quran. They have sacrificed a sheep and they are smearing its blood on the back of the trucks. The young men are wearing black shirts and shaking their fists in the air.

The stores are closed. Half the city is shut down. The thoroughfare is congested and chaotic. It is full of cars and carts and donkeys. Outside Qum, I get caught in a traffic jam. There is a funeral procession. I wait. The crowd is shouting prayers. Women dressed in black are moving in a tight cluster. A beggar boy is hanging from the fender of my car. The air is full of dust and smoke and the smell of gasoline. I'm hot. I'm sweating. I can barely breathe. I pull over and wait for the road to open up.

In front of the mosque, the Revolutionary Guards stop me and ask to see the registration card for my car. They search the car. There is a newspaper on the backseat. They leaf through it. They confiscate it and they let me go. I feel light-headed. I bite into the cigarette butt. I spit. I blow the horn. I yell. A woman beats her fist on the windshield of my car and curses. Her child is crying.

I reach the main road and speed up. The oncoming trucks are driving at breakneck speed. They have no mercy. It will be a miracle if I reach Tehran alive. My throat burns. My mouth is dry. I roll down the window. I need air, a drop of rain. There is nothing but desert and dust and rocky mountains and brick kilns as far as the eye can see.

I have a meeting early tomorrow morning. The article I had promised to write is not finished and as soon as I arrive I have to go to the funeral services for my friend's uncle.

A car honks behind me. The driver wants to pass. He doesn't

understand that I'm locked in traffic and can't move aside. He honks again. Consecutively, intermittently, loudly, together with threats and obscenities. I want to get out and slap him in the face. I want to grab him by the collar and shake him. The smell of gasoline and smoke has permeated the air. Heavy, cement-like clouds hover above me. The air is thick and it burns my eyes. I am thinking about the chaotic days to come when suddenly, from deep inside the hazy horizon, the image of the house appears before me like a heavenly gift. It slowly moves toward me. I see it and know that its celestial spirit is hidden behind everything, and I realize that from that moment on, it will occasionally come to me unannounced; that on gloomy, sweltering evenings, on turbulent days and hopeless nights, and at the time of my death, it will be with me, this immortal beauty, this great lady of my soul.

THE FLOWERS OF SHIRAZ

*M*adam Yelena is a dance instructor. Her studio is on Naderi Avenue, next to Khosravi pirozhky shop where they make the best Russian rolls. With Madam Yelena, you can learn all the dances in the world—classical ballet with special pointe shoes, Lezgi, Armenian, Iranian, Arab, modern American in the Fred Astaire style, African, Indian, and Spanish dances with castanets and fans. The Flowers of Shiraz is the name of the dance group that will perform onstage at the Culture Hall—first at the Culture Hall and then, on Fridays, at Rex Cinema. My friends and I are the Flowers of Shiraz. Fat, thin, lanky, short, frizzy-haired, and olive-skinned. Flowers of every color, gaudy and gay. Taking dance classes is just for fun. We are in eighth grade and it is 1953. The city is in turmoil—demonstrations, arrests, shootings. They say Dr. Mossadeq has come to certain agreements with the communist Tudeh Party. They say the Shah is prisoner in his palace. They say Queen Soraya has left the country. True or false, every day a new rumor spreads and all these events, in the 104-degree heat of the summer, have increased the fervor and excitement of the Flowers of Shiraz to a frenzy. Our parents are worried. They

have forbidden us from riding our bicycles on the hills in Elahieh
and from hanging out on Istanbul Street. But they are no match
for us and we don't listen to them. We are grownups and have a
thousand pretensions.

I have managed to rid myself of the piano lessons and I'm
happy. They sent the old, half-dead piano to I-don't-know-where
like an ailing elephant and saved my life; my life and the life of
the piano instructors and the world of music. Going to Madam
Yelena's school is a good excuse to get out of the house. Istanbul and Lalehzar Streets are two heavenly avenues that cross our
dreams and feed our imagination. They are filled with amazing
promises and magical events. The clothing stores (women's lin-
gerie, see-through, sequined, lacy, and tasseled), the cinemas, the
posters of foreign actors, Berlin Street and its hustle and bustle,
the hoodlums, the wisecracks, the pinches, the Marefat bookstore at the end of Lalehzar Street, to us the center of world
poetry and literature, all those books, all those words, all those
ideas, all those fleeting moments of happiness, they all stun and
mesmerize us. We are restless, confused, and impatient. We are
in a hurry to become adults.

An hour before the dance class, we meet at the intersection
of Pahlavi Avenue and run all the way to Andre sandwich shop.
The Flowers of Shiraz have an amazing appetite and each of us
devour two, perhaps three, bologna sandwiches in a heartbeat.
We hurry from Shah Street to Naderi Avenue and burst into
Khosravi pirozhky shop. We can't pass up on pirozhkies. We swallow the last bite without bothering to chew it and we make it to
class panting. We are late and Madam Yelena is angry. We quickly
change our clothes and, reeking of garlic, pickles, and bologna,
walk into the dance hall. Madam Yelena says the Flowers of Shiraz

should smell nice and we stink. Other than us, there are other flowers. They are seriously interested in dance and in physical exercise. They can lift their leg up all the way to their head. They can bend backwards and touch their head to the back of their knees. They can pirouette on their toes while flailing their arms. My friends and I can't do any of this. Our stomachs are full and we are short of breath. We can neither bend nor lift our legs that high. Mitra starts hiccupping loudly and Madam Yelena angrily stomps her foot. She wipes her nose with a lace handkerchief and stuffs it in the cleavage of her dress. Then, together with the Armenian song her daughter is playing on the piano, she sings:

"Sway your hips and swing your legs."

And we, the Flowers of Shiraz, our bellies stuffed with food, strut, wiggle, and twirl.

Madam Yelena has sewn outfits made of satin and cardboard for us according to the flower we represent. I am a tulip. My skirt is knee-length and there are cardboard tulip petals sewn around my waist. My head barely peeks out from above the petals. It's a lousy dress. I feel trapped in it and I can't breathe. Mitra, with her long neck and her hair in a ponytail, is a carnation. The petals on her dress are short and only come up to her neck. She looks like a goose popping out of its egg. Madam Yelena has decided that the performance of the Flowers of Shiraz should be accompanied by the poetry of Mr. Rahi Moayeri. The minute we hear Rahi Moayeri's name, we break into a sweat with excitement. The day he comes to our class, we blush and sigh a thousand times. Parivash pretends to swoon and Mitra bursts into tears. I have brought two thick books to class. I tuck them under my arm and parade in front of Mr. Moayeri. He is tall and has green eyes and he looks at us as if he is in love with every one of us. At least that's what we think. The Flowers of Shiraz are writhing with jealousy and rivalry, and they furiously bite into their bologna sandwiches. There is another gentleman who is supposed to recite Mr. Moayeri's poetry behind the microphone. He has round black eyes and every time he walks by, he pinches our arm or our waist. The Flowers of Shiraz steer clear of him at all cost.

In addition to dance, Madam Yelena has started a fencing course. The instructor is a young man who wears white shoes and socks and his pants are so tight he can't sit down. We forget Mr. Moayeri and we all fall in love with him.

The Flowers of Shiraz are also interested in politics and political debates. Two other girls and I are supporters of Dr. Mossadeq. Three others support the Shah. Jena M. is a member of the Tudeh Party and a phony defender of the poor. She says her father is a mineworker and her mother has been arrested for distributing antigovernment leaflets. She is lying. She thinks we're stupid. She has made a hole in the sole of her shoes and has torn the hem of her skirt. She wants to go to Russia and join the Russian Ballet. Madam Yelena has forbidden any talk of politics in her class. We keep quiet, but at the first opportunity, we go at each other. Those who love the Shah stand back and kick us in the butt from behind.

There is a sullen girl in class who talks very little. Her name is Gol-Maryam. Before starting to dance, we stretch and exercise for half an hour. Gol-Maryam participates in this part of the session, but she's not interested in dancing or being told to "sway your hips."

She stands in a corner and watches us. Madam Yelena leaves her alone. The girl is into books and newspapers. Her bag is full of papers and magazines. I want to figure her out, but she won't open up. She comes to class with a private car and chauffeur and doesn't join in our debates. She doesn't eat pirozhkies either. The Flowers of Shiraz don't like her and don't look at her. Someone who comes and goes with a private car and chauffeur, someone who isn't interested in debating, screaming, shouting, laughing, and giggling is cut from a different cloth and belongs to a different clan.

Every half hour we have a ten-minute recess. Gol-Maryam sits in a corner and reads. All the while, she blinks rapidly and bites her fingernails. She is thin and pale and has large black eyes with long eyelashes. She is beautiful. A special kind of beautiful. She looks half-European—half-French, half-Russian. She has a nice name. Her skin is as white as a tuberose and, unlike the Flowers of Shiraz, she smells nice. Madam Yelena loves her and doesn't understand why she won't join the dance performance. I want to figure her out. She's much too quiet and far too lonely.

I tell myself, I have to make friends with this girl, and I try to come up with a thousand and one excuses to strike up a conversation with her. But how? She comes on time and leaves on time. No one has her telephone number or her address. But I've noticed that she is not indifferent to my jokes and pranks. She swallows her laughter and hides behind her book. I have a feeling she will soon show me a green light. My prediction is right.

At the intersection of Pahlavi Street, I'm waiting for the bus to Shemiran when a car stops in front of me. Gol-Maryam is sitting next to the window. She nods to me (this girl doesn't know how to smile) and offers to give me a ride. That's great. We are going in the same direction. We both live in the Mahmoudieh neighborhood. Her home is on the incline of Baghe Ferdows. I have ridden my bike up and down that incline a thousand times, but I have never seen her. I guess she never steps out of her house. I am friends with the girls and boys of both our neighborhoods. Homayoun and Parviz are the famous, handsome boys of Baghe Ferdows. I describe them to her.

"No," she says, "I don't know them."

"Me, my cousins, and a few of the Flowers of Shiraz go for bike rides in the afternoon," I say. "We start off at Baghe Ferdows and take a shortcut over the Elahieh hills and the plains around them and we go as far as the Rumi Bridge and then we turn back."

She is quiet. She is searching for something in her dress pocket. The car next to us honks. It is filled with ugly, thin boys. They look at Gol-Maryam and me and they laugh. Gol-Maryam taps on the chauffeur's shoulder and asks him to drive faster. The boys whistle and wave to us. They speed up and go after the next car.

"Do you want to come bike riding with us?" I ask her.

"No," she says. "My father won't let me." And she blushes.

"How about the movies? Bahar Cinema, near Tajrish Bridge, is showing an American film."

She shakes her head. She doesn't know where Bahar Cinema is and knows nothing about what goes on in the world.

"It's simple," I say. "Don't tell your father."

She is taken aback and gapes at me as if I have said the worst thing in the world. She explains that her father is the best father in the world and that he is right to be strict. She has never lied to him and she never will. She doesn't have a bicycle and she doesn't want one either. The guys in the neighborhood are impudent and stupid. The Elahieh hills are deserted and dangerous, and full of crazy people and vicious men. She likes the word "vicious" and repeats it twice.

I shrug and say, "As you wish. We go anyway, and we do have a good time."

Our house is just before the Mahmoudieh bus stop on Pahlavi Avenue. I point it out to her. She looks at it from the corner of her eyes. Perhaps she expects me to invite her in. No, I don't feel like it. This girl is of a different breed. She is too cautious and reserved. The Flowers of Shiraz climb up walls and wreak havoc, they love to live and they have great dreams.

THE CITY IS IN turmoil. People are shouting and yelling. The deafening sound of car horns is overwhelming. A group is shouting slogans in defense of Mossadeq. Madam Yelena closes the front door and doesn't allow anyone to leave. The parents call and ask about their daughters. None of them are happy that we go to dance classes and hang out on the streets, especially on turbulent days like these. Long lectures and threats are useless. The dance performance of the Flowers of Shiraz is an important event and we must practice.

Gol-Maryam is waiting, but there is no sign of her car and chauffeur. She calls her father and learns that the roads from Shemiran to downtown have been closed. The only thing she can do is wait. She's scared. She's worried and moves closer to me and the other girls. Whatever we do, she will do, too. Madam Yelena turns on the radio. We hear that bullets have been fired in Baharestan Circle and several people have been wounded, or perhaps killed. The supporters of the Shah spit at us and we're about to get into a scuffle. Mitra (the Carnation) pulls a newspaper out of her bag. It is filled with pictures of Dr. Mossadeq. She rolls it up and beats Parivash on the head with it. Parivash is a supporter of the Shah. She takes advantage of the opportunity and kicks Gol-Maryam in the ankle. In defense of Gol-Maryam, I grab her by the collar and shove her back. Madam Yelena claps her hands loudly and waves her lace handkerchief in the air. "Quiet!" she shouts. She is so angry she starts to cough.

Someone is banging on the door downstairs. It's Gol-Maryam's chauffeur, Javad Agha. He had to park the car some distance away and walk. Gol-Maryam tells Madam Yelena that she will take me home. I call my mother and tell her that I'm not alone and that she shouldn't worry. My mother speaks to Javad Agha and gives him a thousand instructions. The pandemonium has died down and Istanbul Street is calm. We have a long way to walk to reach Gol-Maryam's car. We set off. Khosravi pirozhky shop is closed. Most of the shops have pulled down their shutters. We walk faster. Near the Lalehzar intersection, again a crowd of people wielding clubs and sticks, on foot or piled on the back of pickup trucks, have blocked the street. We're in front of Mayak Cinema. "Run inside," Javad Agha says. He shoves me and Gol-Maryam into the cinema and quickly buys three tickets and follows us in. The cinema is crowded and there are no empty seats. The film has started. We feel our way up the aisle and stand behind the last row, against the wall. Most of the people are standing up and shouting anti-British slogans. It's a political film. It's about Churchill's life. The actor playing Churchill looks like a pig. He's sitting at a table eating. He cuts large chunks of meat and throws them to his dog; and this is at a time when the people of England are hungry. The audience shake their fists in the air and their shouts of "Either death or Mossadeq" shake the theater. Gol-Maryam is trembling. She grabs my hand. She sees that Javad Agha and I are shouting, too. She doesn't know what to do. She is cowardly and shy and doesn't have the nerve to participate in these sorts of demonstrations. Policemen rush into the theater and start blowing their whistles. The lights go on and they stop the film.

People start complaining. There's going to be a clash. Javad Agha grabs Gol-Maryam and me by the hand and we scurry out. Gol-Maryam's cheeks are flushed and her face is drenched in sweat. She is worried about her father and is in a hurry to get home. She doesn't mention her mother. She looks at the posters of actors, at the crowd, and at everything around her with astonishment and fear. Women knock into her and kids step on her toes. She doesn't know how to protect herself. She doesn't know how to push and shove her way through and how to counter the pinches and the wisecracks of the hooligans. The Flowers of Shiraz always carry a long needle, and if a man dares touch their arm or their waist, they stab him with it.

It has been an eventful afternoon. It's growing dark and I'm thinking about my evening plans to go to Tajrish Bridge. My friends and I go there and hang out in front of Villa Ice Cream shop. I tell Gol-Maryam she can come with us. Where? With whom? She shakes her head. "No, my father is alone."

When we reach the car, she explains that her father doesn't like her to socialize with strangers, he doesn't like anyone disrupting their quiet life, he doesn't like her to waste her time . . . and, and, and . . . The entire way, from downtown to Shemiran, she talks about her father. She is all excited. Her hands are hot and she is panting. She has finally opened up and wants to tell me her entire life story before we reach the Mahmoudieh bus stop. But she doesn't have much to say about herself. Her father is her hero—a perfect father, the best in the world. He is a medical doctor, but he stopped practicing many years ago. He never wanted to be a doctor. He wanted to study philosophy, but his father didn't allow it. He lived in France, Switzerland, and Belgium for many years. He speaks several languages and has read thousands of books.

When he returned from Paris, Gol-Maryam's father turned the second floor of their house into a medical office. But something bad happened. Really horrible. One of his patients was a young, mentally disturbed girl who refused to eat. She couldn't sleep and screamed day and night. It just so happened that one night she swallowed all her antidepressants and died.

Gol-Maryam is suddenly overwhelmed by a profound sadness. She stops talking. We are both silent for a few minutes. I take her hand and squeeze it tenderly. I want to know what happened next. Finally, she composes herself and picks up the story where she left off. Her dear, kindhearted father blamed himself and mourned the girl's death. He closed his medical office and sat at home. Every night, he dreamt of the girl. He thought he heard her voice and was in contact with her spirit. One of their relatives knew a medium who invoked spirits. Gol-Maryam's father brought the medium to their house to communicate with the girl. The girl sent a message saying that she was well and in a wonderful place.

No. I don't believe it. No one speaks of such things in our house. Hassan Agha, our cook, believes in fairies and jinns, but we make fun of him and don't take his stories seriously.

"Do spirits talk?" I ask.

"Of course they do. They signal. You ask a question and they answer."

I'm confused. "How?" I ask.

"The table moves, or the light goes on and off, or a door slams shut. A thousand things happen."

I can't hold my tongue or curb my curiosity. All this girl talks about is her father. Where is her mother?

"My mother is dead. She died in a car accident."

She is quiet and a deep sadness spreads across her face. My heart aches. I am happy that we will arrive in a few minutes and I will get out of the car.

Two weeks later, Gol-Maryam invites me to her house. Should I go, or should I not? I take the plunge. I'm curious. I want to see this "best father in the world."

That evening, Gol-Maryam comes to pick me up with the car and chauffeur. They have bought a new car. A black Cadillac that looks like a car the Shah or some other important, mysterious person would own. Its windows are tinted gray and you can't see inside. I don't know who the doctor is scared of and why he wants to hide behind gray windows. Gol-Maryam has told me that her father hardly ever leaves the house. Javad Agha does everything for him. His life changed after that young girl's suicide and her mother's car accident.

"My father is a doctor," she says. "He has lived most of his life abroad, in Europe. He always thought logically and scientifically. Like Westerners. Until my mother's spirit appeared and moved the table."

We arrive. Homayoun and Parviz, the handsome boys of Baghe Ferdows, are standing at the foot of the incline. They are Gol-Maryam's neighbors. They know me and say hello from a distance.

"Do you know them?" I ask Gol-Maryam.

She shakes her head. She doesn't look at them.

"They live right here," I say. "Two houses down. They're members of our bicycle group."

Gol-Maryam gets out of the car. Javad Agha opens the front door for her and she goes in without looking back.

The boys hurry over to me. They know Gol-Maryam and they

know she pays absolutely no attention to anyone. Especially not to them.

"What are you doing here?" they ask. "Are you friends with her? With the ice queen?"

"I don't dislike her," Homayoun says. "I just want to rub her nose in the dirt and snub her."

"Tell her to come bike riding with us," Parviz says.

Javad Agha is waiting by the door. I walk in. Unlike our house, Gol-Maryam's house is quiet and dim. There are tall pine trees flanking the garden walls that are covered with half-dry ivies. The water in the pool has turned an awful color. It looks like it hasn't been changed in years. The pool is filled with large gray fish; the kind they sell in the bazaar.

Gol-Maryam calls me. She is standing in the entrance hall. To the left are the living room and the dining room. The sofas are covered with white sheets. It looks as if the owner of the house is traveling or has put the house up for sale. I want to turn the lights on or open the curtains. I tell myself, This is a ghost house. If a door slams shut, or if the lights start flickering on and off, I will run away.

Gol-Maryam is in a hurry to go see her father. We climb up the stairs. The door to her father's room is closed. She knocks softly. There is no sound. She puts her finger on her lips and signals for me to be quiet.

I whisper in her ear, "He's sleeping."

We are about to leave when we hear a cough and a sleepy voice says, "Come in, my dear."

My dear! A phrase I have never heard from my father's lips. I want to turn back. These words and relationships are foreign to me. I'm uncomfortable. I feel awkward and miserable. I'm wearing a boyish shirt and pants and my shoes are dusty. I am sure the doctor won't like me. Gol-Maryam is happy. She wraps her arms around her father's neck and sits on his lap.

"Here's my friend. Tulip!" she says. And she laughs.

The doctor has a kind face and puffy eyes. He is wearing house clothes—navy blue silk pajamas with a yellow collar. His room smells of cologne and cigars. His glass of whisky is half-full and he looks half-sleepy and half-drunk. There are books and magazines everywhere, from floor to ceiling. Bookshelves, bookshelves, bookshelves, against all four walls. There is a large photograph of Dr. Mossadeq on the bedside table, together with a few small- and medium-sized silver frames with photographs of a young woman who looks just like Gol-Maryam; the same eyes, the same delicate nose, and the same cold, serious gaze.

"Come see this other room," Gol-Maryam says.

"This other room" looks like a museum. There are no books, but as far as the eye can see, on the tables and in the glass display cabinets, there are all sorts of old clocks, small and large rocks, colorful crystals, perfume bottles, foreign coins, and a hundred different kinds of pipes, calumets, and cigarette holders. And there is one cabinet full of old LP records.

"My father loves detective novels and music," Gol-Maryam says. "That's why he rarely leaves the house."

"What about you?" I ask. "Do you like staying at home, too?"

She shrugs and says, "You saw what's going on outside. A bunch of hoodlums almost beat us up. I don't want to leave my father alone. I love him. We read together. We talk and have a good time."

"Come bike riding with us," I say. "Or come to the movies. Cinema Iran, on Lalehzar Street, and Cinema Rex show the best films. And you have no idea how fun Tajrish Bridge is on Friday nights."

She looks at me and says nothing. She won't leave her father alone. Never. This, I read in her cold gaze and solemn look.

We eat dinner with her father, in his room. There is a small table and three chairs in the corner. The doctor is a vegetarian. He eats salads and cooked vegetables. Gol-Maryam and I have fish and boiled potatoes. (I think the fish came from the pool.) No salt. No taste.

An old housemaid brings the dishes, takes them away, and grumbles. The doctor tells sweet stories about his youth and his years studying in France. Gol-Maryam, who I am certain has heard it all a hundred times, listens intently and laughs louder than me. The program for the evening is to look at photo albums: photos of the doctor in different cities around the world, holding an umbrella and dressed in a hat and raincoat in front of a church, in swimming trunks on a beach, wearing formal black tie and tailcoat, on the arm of a blond woman, on a bicycle, on a horse, in a park, at a zoo, in a museum, sleeping, standing, sitting, etc. Gol-Maryam goes on a journey with these photographs. She knows the people standing next to her father. This is Professor Jean-Michel Latour, the mayor of the sixth arrondissement, this is Madame Jacqueline Mercier, chemistry professor, this one is Jacques, this one is dead, this other one is half-dead, this one has disappeared, this one has been married three times, this one has eight children, this one, this one, this one . . .

From time to time, Gol-Maryam pauses. She makes a mistake with the name of a person or a place and the doctor takes over. They talk to each other, look at each other, unaware that my head is throbbing and that the life stories of people I don't know—especially people who mostly died fifty years ago—are not interesting for me. I'm hungry and thirsty. Our dinner was barely two mouthfuls and it was cold and bland. My stomach is growling, my head is aching, I'm not listening. The doctor's eyes never leave his daughter's face. Now and then he strokes her hair or caresses her cheek or pats her on the shoulder. I yawn. I'm bored. I'm tired of all these photographs and old memories. The Flowers of Shiraz are now on Tajrish Bridge, eating grilled corn and ice cream. Or perhaps they have gone to see an adventure movie, or they have fallen in love for the hundredth time and they are happy. Outside this house, there is war and gunfire, Mrs. Shokat's daughter is getting married, and my cousin Sima has given birth to a girl. There is Madam Yelena's dance class and Mr. Moayeri's love poems. There is the world of real people, living people. I stand up. I look at my watch. I say it's getting late and that I have to go. Gol-Maryam still has dozens of photos to show and thousands of stories to tell—stories about her father. She notices that I'm cranky and fed up and concludes that looking at all those photographs was enough for that night—just that night.

"Next week we are having a séance to invoke spirits," she says. "You can talk to your grandfather, or to anyone you want."

I'm in a hurry to leave—to escape. Javad Agha drives me home. Shemiran Street is crowded. There is a traffic jam. It's a hot night and the drivers are all honking their horns for no good reason. A beggar woman shoves her hand in through the open car window. She won't give up. Javad Agha smacks her hand away and the woman mumbles a curse and moves to the next car.

I arrive home and I tell myself I will never go to Gol-Maryam's house again. It's a halfhearted decision, though, as I'm tempted by the spirit-invoking sessions.

Two days later, I call her. I tell her that I will go, but with one condition: she has to join me and my friends when we go out and play games. She mumbles. She thinks. She's not sure. What games? Where? First she says no. Then she says maybe. She's not sure. She has to ask her father. Finally, with fear and foreboding, she agrees. She says she will come early and leave early.

"Maybe I'll come with my father," she says.

"Forget it! Are you nuts? Your dad on a bicycle? With us?"

She laughs and hangs up.

Wednesday afternoon, right on time, she arrives at Zafaranieh Street with Javad Agha. She doesn't have a bicycle. She dismisses Javad Agha and stands next to me like someone who has never seen a street, a car, or creatures with two legs. She is afraid of crossing the street, she screams and grabs hold of the back of my bicycle. Our group consists of a few classmates, two of the Flowers of Shiraz (so far, all girls), two of my cousins (boys), and two of the neighborhood guys (Homayoun and Parviz). Gol-Maryam feels out of place. She regrets having come, but she has no way back. She is happier with her father, the photographs, and the spirits. The jokes, the pranks, the screaming and shouting, and everything we talk about is new to her. She doesn't understand our language. Worst of all, she doesn't have a bicycle. She climbs up behind me. She fidgets. She's scared and wants to get off. At the corner, she jumps off before I have time to stop. She loses her balance and falls. We stop. The cousins start grumbling. Gol-Maryam has scratches on her hands and her knee and she is limping. Parviz holds her under the arm. He takes out his handkerchief and ties it around her knee. The Flowers of Shiraz smirk and snicker out of spite and jealousy. Parviz's bicycle is large. We put Gol-Maryam behind him. She is clumsy and shy and doesn't know what to do with her hands. She is holding her legs out and away from the back wheel and she won't sit tight against Parviz. I'm sure they will fall. We set off. I hear Gol-Maryam scream, but I don't look back. We speed down the incline of Baghe Ferdows. Parviz overtakes everyone. Gol-Maryam, her eyes wide with fear and her mouth open and ready to scream, is staring straight ahead. She has wrapped her arms tight around Parviz's waist. The wind is blowing through her hair and under her skirt. The Flowers of Shiraz are still smirking. The narrow alley and back roads of Elahieh are filled with pleasant shadows. We stop in front of Amini Garden. There is a wide stream that flows at the foot of the garden walls and under the trees. The water is cool and clear. It comes from Mrs. Fakhrodolleh's reservoir. We take off our shoes, put our feet in the stream, and wash our face and hands. Gol-Maryam's face is flushed and she's panting. She pats some water on her face and then she, too, takes off her shoes and dips her feet in the stream. The Flowers of Shiraz splash water on each other and chase after one another. It is a pleasant game on such a hot day. Gol-Maryam hides behind a huge tree. I think she will start crying any minute now. But no. She hops from behind one tree to the next and splashes water on Parviz and laughs.

We ride out to Rumi Bridge and turn back. We make plans to go to Tajrish Bridge on Friday night.

"Will you come?" I ask Gol-Maryam.

She doesn't know. She looks at Parviz and blushes. She's late. Javad Agha is waiting and it's her father's dinnertime. She rushes off.

PARVIZ IS PROUD of his dashing hairstyle and sparse mustache. He walks tall and thinks that all the girls in Shemiran are in love with him. He considers himself the leader of the neighborhood band and regularly gives political speeches. His parents are modern and think like Westerners. They let him throw parties and he is allowed to invite anyone he wants and he can dance with girls his own age or older. Every Friday afternoon we gather at his house and talk about politics and literature. Parviz lends us his books and says things that are too complicated for us to understand. There is a picture of Lenin hanging on the wall in his bedroom and he wants to change the world. His parents are members of the People's Party and they smoke cigarettes. They love Parviz and they tell us that one day he will be someone important. Parviz is infatuated with Gol-Maryam. He has called her house three times and Javad Agha has answered the phone. Parviz didn't dare speak and just hung up.

I have no news of Gol-Maryam until the day we have dance class. She whispers to me that they are having a séance tonight, and she reminds me that I had promised to go.

Oh dear. Going to the house of spirits. But I am curious. Does the table really move? Do spirits actually exist? I take the risk and agree to go. Three nights a week I'm allowed to have dinner with my friends and stay out until ten-thirty. I tell Gol-Maryam it's not necessary for Javad Agha to pick me up. I will take the bus. I tell Parviz and immediately regret my own stupidity. He is determined to come with me.

"Gol-Maryam won't let you in," I say. "It's impossible."

He won't give up. "Let me handle it," he says. "I'll talk to her."

We quarrel all the way to Gol-Maryam's house. Javad Agha opens the door. He is surprised to see Parviz. Gol-Maryam is in the front yard. She comes to the gate and the minute she lays eyes on Parviz she turns pale and starts to blink rapidly.

"I had nothing to do with it," I say. "He followed me. Talk to him. There's no reason to be embarrassed. Just tell him he can't come in, that your father won't allow it."

"We have guests tonight," Javad Agha says. "Perhaps some other time."

Gol-Maryam is squirming. She looks at Parviz and blushes.

"Yes, tonight we have guests," she stammers. "Some other night."

I close the door on Parviz and I tell Gol-Maryam that she shouldn't give boys the upper hand. Parviz is a good guy, but he is too arrogant.

Gol-Maryam knows that Parviz has been calling her and hanging up the telephone. She knows that he walks past her house every day and looks up at her bedroom window. She stops at the foot of the staircase in the hallway and says, "This is awful. I should have invited him in. He was embarrassed. This is awful."

We see the doctor coming down the stairs. He is wearing a black suit and he is waiting for his guests.

"You young ladies stay in a different room. The guests are strangers and I don't want you mixing with them."

Gol-Maryam listens to her father and whispers to me, "We'll keep the door open a little so we can watch."

The telephone rings. Gol-Maryam grabs the receiver. She turns and stands with her back to me. She listens, but she doesn't say a word. I tell myself, I shouldn't have given Parviz her telephone number. It's my fault. He is not going to give up until the girl falls in love with him. He wants all the girls, the ugly ones, the pretty ones, even the ones who are ten or twenty years older than him, to fall in love with him. We call him the Don Juan of Baghe Ferdows. God knows what he's whispering to Gol-Maryam. He has his ways. He's not into flirting and necking in secret. He likes girls to fall in love with him, to write love letters to him, to pull their hair and cry in jealousy.

"Was it Parviz?" I ask. "What did he say?"

She doesn't answer. The doorbell rings and we run and hide in a dark corner in the hall. The first guest is a man who stutters and enunciates his words.

"He's the medium," Gol-Maryam explains. "He has powers."

The next guests are two women. Gol-Maryam whispers to herself, "Who are they?"

The fourth guest is an old, fat man with a limp. He walks in leaning on his cane, and having barely arrived, he lights a cigarette and starts to cough. Gol-Maryam knows him. She shakes her head and says, "The poor thing. His daughter drowned in the sea. He comes every Wednesday. He cries the entire time. The medium says he shouldn't, because the spirit will suffer. It will sulk. It won't come."

The doctor closes the living room door. Gol-Maryam motions to me to keep quiet. We tiptoe into another room. There is a door here that leads to the living room. We can see the medium and the table through the keyhole. We stand with our ears to the door.

"Recite a prayer in your heart and salute the Prophet and his family seven times," the medium says. "Small, mean spirits are floating around in the room. They can harm you. Please don't talk. Concentrate on the spirit you want to summon."

"Last time, my mother's spirit didn't come," Gol-Maryam whispers. "She was sulking. My father cried and begged, but it was no use. The medium said her spirit is troubled. It's not free. Sadness and tears are like a prison for spirits. They can't fly. The medium called me to join them. The minute I sat at the table my mother's spirit appeared and the table moved."

I shudder. I feel cold. This is all strange and unbelievable. But Gol-Maryam is used to this kind of life and these rituals. She talks about her mother as if she were still alive. If I tell Parviz, he'll laugh. He won't believe me. I wish he was here to see it with his own eyes. But for now, he is smitten with Gol-Maryam and can't be bothered with ghosts and death.

We push the door open an inch. The guests are sitting around the table. The medium is standing to the side. One of the ladies says, "I would like to communicate with the spirit of the Prophet Zoroaster."

"It's very difficult. The great spirits won't appear easily," says the medium.

"I'm a Zoroastrian. If I ask, he will grant us his presence."

The medium hesitates. "I'm not sure. We should first use a lighter spirit to send a message to his holiness."

They all put their hands on the table and no one makes a sound.

"I think the great spirit is with us," the medium announces.

"Yes," the doctor says. "The table feels warm."

The Zoroastrian woman moans and her head drops down on the table. Another lady takes advantage of the opportunity and talks to the great spirit. "Prophet Zoroaster, please tell me, who stole my carpets?" she asks. "If it's a man, move the table to the left. If it's a woman—"

The medium cuts her off. He's angry. He waves his hand and warns, "Private questions are not allowed. The question has to be important, it should concern everyone."

The doctor reports that the table is now cold. The spirit has left. They pick up the Zoroastrian lady and carry her to the sofa and bring her a glass of water.

The doctor is worried about Dr. Mossadeq. He asks that they invoke Reza Shah's spirit.

Gol-Maryam is bored. "Who are these weird people, these stupid women?" she says. "Let's go out. My father is busy and being entertained."

"You stay home," she instructs Javad Agha. "I won't go far and I don't need a guard."

It is one of those pleasant summer nights. The streetlamps are lit and a long line of cars are heading toward Tajrish Bridge. Gol-Maryam looks around. She can't stand it anymore and asks, "So, your friends, the guys, where are they?"

I know she means Parviz.

"They are probably at the bridge. We can walk there. It's not far."

My guess is right. Parviz and a few others are in front of Villa Ice Cream shop. There's a large crowd at Tajrish Bridge. Women dressed in colorful dresses and high heels are leaning against their cars eating grilled corn and fresh walnuts. Men wearing four-button jackets and shiny shoes are strolling up and down Sadabad Street. They all know each other. They all look at each other and smile. It's as if they've come to the biggest party in town. The area at the head of the bridge is divided into two sections. The side closer to the entrance of the bazaar and the steep road to Darband is half-dark and less crowded. This is where taxi and bus drivers and women in chadors gather. There are stands that sell lamb and liver kebab. Sometimes, people get into fights and scuffles. Men with thick mustaches and tattooed arms get drunk and start hollering. My friends and I aren't allowed to go to that side. We hang out in front of Villa Ice Cream. Fruit-flavored ice cream is something new that has come from the West. It is the first time sour cherry ice cream has been introduced in Tehran and at Tajrish Bridge. It has a different taste and a hint of French perfume.

Parviz has bought a sour cherry ice cream for Gol-Maryam. She licks it slowly, with her eyes closed. She is in heaven and oblivious to the fact that the ice cream is dripping from the bottom of the cone and staining her clean white dress.

She opens her eyes, looks at Parviz, tastes her ice cream, and closes her eyes again. I tell her that it's time for her to go back. Her father's guests will soon leave. Gol-Maryam's concern for her sad father has infected me, too. But she doesn't want to leave. Her eyes follow Parviz wherever he goes and she is reluctant to return to that quiet house. She has grown distant from the paper people in the photo albums and from her father's memories. Finally, she leaves, but comes back an hour later. This is not the same shy and reclusive Gol-Maryam. She has learned to laugh, to talk fast and loud. She has learned to scheme, to lie, and to sneak out of the house. She has also learned to stand in front of Parviz, to stare into his eyes, and to sit next to him in the cinema or on the bus.

IT IS THE END of August. The Flowers of Shiraz are to perform onstage in mid-September. Madam Yelena has decided to add a Spanish dance to the program. We are international flowers. We pop up in Spain and in Africa and we easily grow wherever they plant us. Madam Yelena's special seamstress has sewn our Spanish costumes. We try them on. Our hats are tall cardboard crowns with a piece of black lace draped over them. Our skirts have three pleated layers. The top layer is long and drags on the floor. It gets caught underfoot and it's very irritating. Each dress costs a hundred tumans. Our parents are fed up and complain about the extra costs. Madam Yelena has also bought castanets. We put them on our fingers and shake them and make hideous clanking sounds; it's as if we're banging a pestle on the bottom of a pot. Gol-Maryam is dying of laughter.

We are stomping around in our costumes when we hear people shouting and running in the street. We rush out to the balcony. A group of club-wielding roughnecks are smashing store windows. Truckloads of people armed with shovels and sticks are heading toward Shah Street. Some people on the sidewalk notice us and are stunned by our getup. God knows what they are thinking. They point us out to each other and laugh. Madam Yelena frantically pushes us back inside. She draws the curtains and locks the front door. We quickly change our clothes and sit waiting. Gol-Maryam calls her father. He tells her that people are fighting on the streets, the army has fired bullets at members of the Tudeh Party, and a group of the Shah's supporters are beating up Mossadeq's followers. Gol-Maryam knows that her father loves Mossadeq and she is very upset by the news. A few hours later, the commotion on Istanbul Street dies down. My grandmother's house is on Si-Metri Avenue. My mother is there. There is no sign of Javad Agha. I later learn that he has been injured in the demonstrations and his leg is broken. Gol-Maryam comes with me and we run all the way to my grandmother's house. There are people on the street carrying tables, chairs, and chandeliers on their heads. We hear that Dr. Mossadeq's house has been ransacked.

My mother, Gol-Maryam, and I take a taxi. When we reach Baghe Ferdows, I see Parviz standing at the corner waiting for Gol-Maryam. We ask the driver to stop. My mother waits for me to go in with Gol-Maryam and see how her father is.

The doctor is lying on his bed and the bedside lamp is turned off. He has been listening to the news on the radio and knows about the looting at Dr. Mossadeq's house. I wonder what this reclusive man who deals with spirits and is drowned in the past has to do with Dr. Mossadeq. Gol-Maryam sits next to his bed and turns on the lamp. The doctor looks at his daughter with tearful eyes and then turns away. There is no point in my staying there. I walk out and I see Parviz still standing at the corner.

THE DON JUAN of Baghe Ferdows roams around the neighborhood like a peacock, with no end to his dreams and fantasies. He is sixteen and has sixteen thousand plans for the future. In two years, he will graduate from high school and go to America. He wants to become a university professor. In what field? In physics, or economy, or maybe philosophy, or astronomy, or . . . He hasn't decided yet. He likes cinema and theater, too. Gol-Maryam laughs. She asks, "Hollywood films?" And he sees himself as the future champion of swimming, tennis, and of course, hiking, sailing, and mountain climbing. He will marry Gol-Maryam and they will have three children. And, and, and . . . His dreams have spread to the rest of us, too. Every night before we fall asleep, we fly from one tree to another and circle the earth. The future has a thousand doors and the key to every door is in our pocket. We hear them jingle and we wonder which door to open, when and where.

THERE ARE ONLY ten days left before school starts. We are anxious and desperately holding on to the last days of summer. We have planned to go bicycle riding. It will probably be our last get-together. Soon it will be autumn, and then winter, and nothing but studying, studying, studying.

All the kids—the Flowers of Shiraz, the two cousins, Gol-Maryam and Javad Agha on crutches, Parviz with his mass of wavy hair and wearing his white shirt—have gathered at the head of Zafaranieh Street. Homayoun and Sohrab are here, too. We're a larger group than ever.

Parviz has suggested a race. The plan is for Gol-Maryam to ride behind him as far as the Mahmoudieh hills. Then she will get off and watch the race from there. Carnation and Violet say they don't want to participate in the race. Everyone sees Gol-Maryam take off her chain necklace and put it in Parviz's hand. The boys whistle and Carnation, jealous and heartbroken, rides her bicycle into a ditch, takes a tumble, and her eyeglasses break.

We set out. Parviz and Homayoun have let go of the handle-bars and are pedaling fast. Gol-Maryam is scared. She screams and shouts. They veer to the side a couple of times and almost fall. Madam Yelena has told us that we have to take very good care of our health and our looks. We shouldn't catch a cold. We shouldn't get cuts and scratches on our face. The Flowers of Shiraz must be as fresh as a flower. The cousins have fallen behind and I am out of breath. Going uphill is difficult. It needs strong lungs, which I don't have. Gol-Maryam is the luckiest one. With her cheek resting on Parviz's back and her arms wrapped around him, she is glowing with happiness. We change direction. We turn left and ride to the far side of the Mahmoudieh hills. From here to the start of Amanieh there is an open plain with no pits and potholes. It's the perfect place for a race. The champions line up. Gol-Maryam has borrowed her father's camera. She takes a group photo of us. Parviz is standing in the middle, making silly faces. Then she takes a picture of me and Parviz. And then, a solo picture of the Don Juan of Baghe Ferdows. Finally, Gol-Maryam gives the camera to me and she goes and stands next to Parviz and holds his hand.

We agree to ride all the way behind the hill in front of us and then turn around and ride back. Gol-Maryam has the starting whistle.

Ready. Whistle. Go. I know I will lose. It's impossible to beat these big, tall guys. Of course, anything could happen. Homayoun could get a flat tire. Sohrab could fall. Parviz's bicycle chain could break. But no, Parviz will definitely be the champion, and he knows it. Gol-Maryam's necklace is in his pocket. It is for her that he is pedaling and overtaking everyone. He doesn't even look back. He has no intention of stopping. He reaches the spot we had agreed on and he keeps going. We call out to him. He is oblivious. He has ruined the race and annoyed us all.

The second part of the competition is a running race. We determine the starting line and decide that the finish line will be behind the third hill ahead. Gol-Maryam is joining the race. She is a fast runner. She is slim and agile and overtakes Parviz, too. The cousins and I give up halfway. Homayoun, Parviz, and Gol-Maryam are in the lead. They run up the first hill and course down the other side. Gol-Maryam is in the lead with Homayoun right behind her. There is no sign of Parviz. I can't explain it. I was watching him from a distance. He had almost caught up to Gol-Maryam and then he suddenly vanished. Gol-Maryam stops and looks back. The cousins run toward her and call Parviz. Homayoun turns around and starts running back and then he suddenly comes to a dead stop. Gol-Maryam catches up with him and starts to scream.

In the middle of the plain, right at our feet, there is a large well. Its opening had been covered, but it wasn't a sturdy cover. It has

broken and Parviz has fallen in the well. Gol-Maryam bursts into
tears and starts running back and forth. Confused and terrified,
we are all standing around the well, unable to make a decision. We
can hear Parviz at the bottom of the well calling out for his mother.
We have to get help. A workman is passing by. He hears us scream
and shout. He comes over. He says we need a rope and a lamp. We
run to the houses nearby and knock on every door. People rush to
the well. They lower a man down with a rope. The well has caved
in. We can't hear Parviz's voice anymore. Gol-Maryam has moved
away from the crowd and is watching from a distance. Her eyes are
closed and her lips are moving. She looks like she's praying.

Time passes. Uncle Colonel's house is not far. He has heard
the news and shows up. Another man goes down the well with a
shovel and a burlap sack. He fills the sack with dirt and sends it
up. There is commotion. Parviz's parents have arrived. They push
their way through the crowd. His mother faints and his father
stares at everyone like a crazy person. Time passes. Gol-Maryam
is sitting on the ground, clawing at the dirt with her delicate
fingers. I try to calm her. I am certain that Parviz, the swimming
champion, the running champion, the fencing champion, Parviz
the astronaut, the mountain climber, the ship captain, will survive. He is sitting under the dirt, waiting for them to pull him
out. Nothing bad is going to happen to him. He is only sixteen.
He is in love with Gol-Maryam. It is impossible for him to die.
It's impossible for him to even have a scratch on him. I give voice
to all these thoughts with hurried, broken words. Gol-Maryam
shakes her head. She makes no sound. She doesn't believe a word
I say. Sack after sack full of dirt is sent up from inside the well.
Parviz's mother calls down to him. He doesn't answer. It's getting
dark. They have brought lanterns and paraffin lamps. The crowd

suddenly shouts. They have brought out Parviz's body. Uncle Colonel stops me and the cousins. He doesn't let us see him. The Flowers of Shiraz are weeping. No one dares look. No one dares say that Parviz is dead.

GOL-MARYAM CLOSES the door to everyone and doesn't return my phone calls. High school starts and new lessons and new teachers fill the void Parviz has left behind. Carnation and I tell Madam Yelena that we will not participate in the dance performance by the Flowers of Shiraz. We let the dance classes slip from our memory, but we remain faithful to Khosravi pirozhky shop. I miss Gol-Maryam and often think about her. One day I take the plunge and decide to go and see her.

I stand in front of her house. My heart is racing. Memories of her short-lived love with Parviz are choking me. Finally, I ring the doorbell. Javad Agha opens the door. He is happy to see me. I ask about Gol-Maryam.

"The doctor has a meeting," he says. "Come in. But don't make any noise."

The living room door is closed. I go to the room in the back. There is no sign of Gol-Maryam. I peek through the keyhole. I see her sitting at the table. Her eyes are closed.

"The spirit is ready," the medium says. "It is a light, young spirit. He has a message."

I hear Gol-Maryam's trembling voice, "If you are here, move the table toward me."

I open the door a crack to see better. The table shifts toward Gol-Maryam and she moans. I run out into the street and I keep running until I reach our house. I lean against a tree and cry.

AMINA'S GREAT JOURNEY

*B*efore the Islamic Revolution, having a foreign maid—whether Filipino, Indian, Afghani, or European—was a new phenomenon that was inconsistent with our old customs and traditions. It was a change that both pleased and perplexed us.

Amina was from southern Bangladesh. With her long black hair, white teeth, and dreamy eyes, she looked like the actresses in popular Indian movies. She knew that people's eyes followed her and their gaze lingered on her eighteen-year-old body clad in those colorful saris—yellow or lime green chiffon with tiny gold flowers. She had been in Tehran for two years and spoke Farsi fluently. She was happy and comfortable in our house. When left alone, she either slept or dove deep into her world of fantasies. Her husband, Mr. Raja, was thirty years older than her and had another wife and two grownup sons. According to Amina, their house had eight rooms and all the carpets in the rooms belonged to the first wife. The pots and pans, curtains, and velvet cushions also belonged to the first wife, as did the skinny, dark-skinned Mr. Raja with greasy hair and dark lips.

Amina showed me a photograph of her daughter. Six or seven

years old, scrawny, with disheveled hair, a thin neck, a wide mouth, and dazed eyes. Her name was Shalima. She looked like an Indian child beggar; barefoot and hungry.

Amina loved to sleep, ten-hour-long coma-like slumbers. In the morning, she always woke up dazed and disoriented, as if returning from another world. She would drag her sluggish body from room to room and it took hours for her to organize her wandering thoughts. We had to get her busy doing something tangible, such as hanging the laundry out to dry or sweeping the carpets, so that she would find herself in a real place at a real time and remember who and where she was. She had a few movie magazines filled with pictures of Indian actors and singers. She used to sit in the garden, in the shade of a tree, and stare at the pictures in utter fascination. She wouldn't hear us if we called her and she wouldn't notice the comings and goings around her. She was somewhere else, somewhere beyond the reach of Mr. Raja, the beggar Shalima, and us.

Amina the dreamer, barefoot and sleepy, is sitting on the lawn, in the shade of a weeping willow tree. A green rhinestone shines on the side of her nose like a crystalline mole and her young arms are laden with colorful glass bangles. She hasn't washed the lunch dishes and she hasn't taken down the clothes from the clothes-line. Her gaze is fixed on the pictures in a magazine, photo shots of a sentimental film, a love story full of tear-jerking scenes and edifying adventures.

She has forgotten that she has to sweep the rooms and put the children to bed. She has forgotten that she is a foreign maid and on the first of every month she has to send her pay to her husband, Mr. Raja. She has even forgotten scrawny Shalima. In her fantasy world, Amina is an actress. Her picture is in the magazines. She is standing with her back to Mr. Raja and her beggar father and dark-skinned Shalima.

Whenever I unexpectedly opened the door to her room, I would see her standing in front of the mirror talking to herself. Coquetting, acting, laughing. Or I would find her sitting on the floor rubbing coconut oil in her hair and putting nail polish on her tiny fingernails and toenails. The neighbor's servant was an Afghan man and he was friends with an Indian woman. On Amina's days off, they would come to our house and sit in Amina's small room. They would play music and sing and Amina would dance for them. But for Amina, there was no escape from Mr. Raja. His invisible presence weighed on her chest and his far-reaching shadow hovered over her head.

"Amina," I said, "why don't you keep your money for yourself?"

"Why" was one of those strange words that had no place in Amina's world. Mr. Raja determined the whys and devised the answers.

"Missus, my husband tricked me," she said.

And she said it as though it was only natural for a husband to trick his wife. There was no anger in her voice, nor was there any surprise or regret.

"He had a wife and kids—two grown boys. I didn't know and I hadn't asked around. He said he was Muslim, that a Muslim man's heart and words are pure, that he doesn't lie, and if he does, it is only out of kindness. I was Hindu. He said I had to convert to Islam. I agreed. By the time I found out he had another wife, it was too late. He beat me. He said a wife doesn't need to know everything. A good wife closes her eyes and ears. His first wife was fat and lazy. She lived in the rooms upstairs and I lived in a small room at the end of the courtyard. His first wife was in charge. She ordered me around and pulled my hair. My husband said, 'Amina, you have to work and give me your pay.' He said, 'I'm the master. I'm everything.' He sent me to Jeddah and I worked there for two years. My Arab boss sent my salary to my husband. Shalima was two months old. My Arab boss wanted to marry me and asked my husband to divorce me, but Mr. Raja didn't agree. He said, 'Amina has to work and send me her pay.' The Arab boss wanted to get back at him and didn't pay me for six months. He had four wives; they were all old and couldn't stand the sight of me. They decided to do me in and constantly put poison in my food and tarantulas and scorpions in my bed. Whenever the Arab boss went on a trip, they locked me in the cellar and gave me only stale bread to eat. When the boss found out, he took pity on me. He was a good man and he was afraid his jealous wives would kill me. He gave me a gold bangle and a few dresses and sent me back to Bangladesh. My husband's first wife took them from me. She was rich. She had a house and property, but she was stingy and wouldn't give Mr. Raja even a rupee. She ate and slept and wallowed in sorrow because she was away from her parents. She would sit on the veranda and weep like a lost child. She didn't like Mr. Raja. Her sons were addicts and gamblers. They used to beat her and take her jewelry. From the moment she opened her eyes in the morning until she went to bed at night, all she did was eat. Bowl after bowl of rice and curry, lamb's meat and bread. She would eat so much that her stomach would bulge and then she'd start moaning. She was getting fatter by the day. She would sit in front of the mirror and put kohl on her eyes, paint her eyebrows black, put a mole on her face, and curl her hair. Then she'd see that she was still old and fat and she'd start screaming. She would beat herself and claw at her face and throw the mirror at the wall and break it. I was thin and young and this made her sick. She was scared that she would die before Mr. Raja and me. Her father used to visit her once a month and she would put her head on his knees and weep like a child, like Shalima."

Amina knew that Mr. Raja had cheated and double-crossed her. She knew that he used her and took her money. She knew that he beat Shalima. But this knowledge prompted no reaction in her. Mr. Raja was the absolute master and the reality of his existence—with all his faults—was as natural as the monsoon rains and the flood that had washed away her mother and brothers. And life went on.

"Missus," she said, "my husband heard that Iranians are rich. An Indian lady was coming to Bangladesh and recruiting maids to bring them to Iran. Mr. Raja arranged my papers and handed me over to her. I left Shalima with my father. He was happy. He said a beggar makes more money when he has a child with him. Mr. Raja's first wife was jealous, despite all her comfort. She said, 'You're free and I'm captive.' She used to get sick the minute she smelled Mr. Raja's scent. I felt sorry for her. My husband said, 'Amina, Tehrani men are corrupt. They don't pray. If I find out they've so much as looked at you, I'll skin you alive.' He was lying. I'm comfortable here. I wish Shalima were here, too."

Shalima occasionally sent two-sentence letters to her mother and signed her name and her grandfather's name under them.

"My father isn't one of those disreputable beggars," Amina said. "His vocation is begging. He has a permit. After he dies, his permit will go either to me or to Shalima. His workplace is three streets and a square. Just like Mr. Engineer who has an office. My father has lice in his hair. If the lice die, Shalima will borrow some from the other beggars and she'll put them in his hair. A beggar without lice is like a king without a crown. I'm a maid. Being a maid is worse than being a beggar. A maid lives in other people's homes."

"Does your father have a home?" I asked.

"Yes. A cardboard shack. Cardboard and tin. That's what the beggars' homes are like. But whatever it is, it's a private home."

As a child, Amina lived in a village. Her mother baked bread and her brothers worked in the field. In the evening, they would sit together and eat and then, with their stomachs full and their fingers greasy, they would sleep happy and satisfied. But the monsoon season came and the rain didn't stop. The fields lay underwater. There was no rice left and nothing to eat. Her father found an unripe watermelon and divided it among the children. Her mother gave her share to Amina. Her brothers ate what was left of the weeds and tree leaves. Then came the big flood that swept away her mother and brothers, their mud-brick home, their cow, and their goat. Everything they had. Her father carried Amina in his arms and tied her to a tree. Her head was underwater and her mouth was full of mud. She knew she was dying, but she wasn't afraid. In a way, death was like sleeping and Amina loved to sleep. Her body went numb and her brain no longer functioned. She shivered under the water and entrusted her freezing body to the law of the sea.

Amina is still underwater and she likes it. She is still unable to think and part of her mind is still numb.

"Amina, keep your money for yourself," I said. "Save it for your daughter."

She gaped at me. She didn't understand. Or if she did, she found it unbelievable.

"Missus, Mr. Raja keeps my money. He buys me gold and saves it for me."

There was no arguing with her. Her husband was the master and her father a beggar. Her mother had been swept away by a flood and Shalima had no one else. Amina was condemned to working in other people's homes, condemned to scrubbing floors, doing laundry, and washing dishes. For the rest of her life, she had to go from one town to another and send her money to her husband. That's the way it was. Even if she were to be born a hundred times, everything would always be the same. But perhaps something could be done for Shalima. Perhaps.

"Missus, help me bring Shalima to live with me," she pleaded. "She won't bother you. I will put her in school and I will pay for her food and clothes. She will sleep in my room. In a house this big, she won't bother anyone."

I had no objections, but we had to convince Mr. Raja. Amina wrote to him and the man replied that Shalima would stay right where she was. We wrote longer letters and explained that I wanted to increase Amina's salary and that the master would have more money, more than little Shalima was making as a beggar. Finally, the Indian louse agreed. Of course, he let it be known that he was in complete control and that he could change his mind at any time.

Amina couldn't believe it. She cried. She quickly stuffed the movie magazines under her mattress and with the little money she had saved she bought clothes and shoes for Shalima. And then she packed her bags and rushed off.

It was the early days of the Islamic revolution. There was chaos in the city. Arrests and imprisonments. Martial law. The Shah left.

The Imam came. All foreigners had to leave the country. The Filipino, Afghan, and Indian maids quickly left. There was a shortage of gas and the price of meat soared. And amid all that turmoil, Amina and Shalima vanished from our thoughts.

Three years went by. Many people died, many fell into misery, many others stomped their feet and clapped their hands and their lives improved. I ended up in Paris, all alone with two frustrated children who climbed the walls and couldn't understand why they were sent into exile, from that big house to this small apartment.

Hiring a French maid was impossible. They were too expensive. The Filipino maids were bad-tempered and beat the children. I decided I didn't need anyone. I had forgotten all about Amina. But Mr. Raja hadn't forgotten about me. He found my address and sent me a groveling letter replete with empty compliments, feigned expressions of friendship, and fake cordiality. Three pages, back and front, and written in poor English. In short: Amina is out of work, she misses you and your dear children, and she dreams of coming to Paris to kiss your hand, your mother's hand, your late father's hand, and the hand of your uncles and aunts and the neighbors to the left and the neighbors to the right and Mr. Mitran, and, and, and.

Amina in Paris? With her getup, those sheer Indian saris? Never.

I didn't write back.

The second letter arrived. Again the same supplications. But this time, Mr. Raja had added that he, Amina's sacrificing husband, would pay for the round-trip airfare, that there was nothing he wouldn't do for the Tehrani lady, that it couldn't be any better or easier than this, and that if by some impossible chance I were dissatisfied, which I certainly wouldn't be, I could put Amina on a plane and send her back. And then he had written two pages saying that Amina was half-foreign, half-Western, spoke Farsi, knew me well, was trustworthy and kind, had a thousand and one merits, and, and, and.

I didn't write back. But I hesitated. I argued with myself. I was half-convinced.

The third letter was from Amina herself. She had written in English. In fluent and correct English. She had asked someone to write it for her, but the words were hers—sweet, simple, and familiar. Her sleepy eyes and velvety voice (when she sang under the trees) and the coconut scent of her hair oozed from between the lines. Her warm body appeared before me and I was duped.

I knew Mr. Raja was plotting to take advantage of the situation and that Amina was his cash machine. Consequently, I offered a low salary. Mr. Raja haggled. He filled three pages listing Amina's virtues and capabilities—cooking, sewing, housekeeping, carpet weaving . . . Talent simply dripped from her fingertips. Lie after lie. I knew Amina and I remembered that she was lazy and good at nothing. Her only merits were her kindness and simplicity, her beauty and her sweet laughter. I knew she was mild-mannered and wouldn't mistreat the children. But I had to set Mr. Raja straight from the start. He was a con man and a cheat. I told myself I would open a bank account for Amina and I wouldn't let her send a single dollar to him.

Mr. Raja asked for four hundred dollars a month.

I wrote back, "Two hundred."

He wrote that he would settle for three hundred fifty.

I wrote, "Two hundred." End of story.

He wouldn't give up. He begged and pleaded, "Three hundred."

"Two hundred." Shut up! It's this or nothing.

He groused and griped. He wrote that Amina was a gem, that she was worth more than a thousand dollars, that he wouldn't send her. Fine. Goodbye. Don't send her. The hell with you. Again, another letter. More bickering. Finally, he agreed. We wrote up a contract.

The month and day of Amina's arrival was determined— December 17. Two in the afternoon. Air France.

The children were happy. Someone new was entering their life, someone who used to live with them, who used to sleep at the foot of their bed.

They used to constantly ask me, "Who is going to take care of us if you die?"

Now I could answer, Beautiful Amina with black eyes, luxuriant hair, and colorful clothes. In my absence, eternal absence, she will take you to Bangladesh and she will get a begging permit for you.

December 17 was a cold and rainy day. All the passengers were wearing coats and scarves, and carrying umbrellas. Everyone except half-naked Amina, who entered Paris wearing strappy sandals and an old, lime green sari. Her shirt was skintight and short-sleeved and her midriff was bare. Looking lost and shaken, she was clasping her bag to her chest and looking around for me. She wasn't the old Amina. She seemed broken, crushed. She had lost her youthfulness. She was dragging her feet and her gaze was filled with fear and reticence. She was a stranger. I suddenly felt sad and my instincts warned me that I had been too hasty. Still, I tried not to let doubt into my heart. I waved at her. She didn't see me. As usual, her mind was wandering and she was aimlessly following other people around.

I realized Amina was a different person in Paris. She had no razzle-dazzle. Here, she was a third-rate actress in a shoddy movie. There were many like her and they weren't in demand. In Tehran she was somebody. She turned heads. Now, she looked like she hadn't slept all night and Shalima's absence was written all over her face.

"My dear Amina," I said, "this isn't India or Saudi Arabia. It's bitter cold outside." And I draped my coat over her shoulders. She didn't have a suitcase, just an old bag filled with red pepper and other dizzyingly hot spices.

She cowered in the corner of the taxi like an orphan. Her eyes were brimming with tears and her nostrils were trembling. I took her hand and said, "Wait until we get home. The kids are waiting for you. Think about it. You're in Paris. Few people have such good fortune."

She said nothing. I asked about Shalima. She lifted her head and perked her ears. Shalima was in her eyes.

"I wanted to bring her with me," she said, "but Mr. Raja wouldn't let me. I have a two-year-old son, too. His name is Mohsen." She laughed. Her face blossomed and her eyes gleamed. "Mohsen is playful. He eats a lot and he's chubby." She puffed out her cheeks, shook her head, and giggled.

"He has just started to talk," she said, and she mimicked him. For a moment, she forgot where she was. Then, she looked around and wiped the foggy car window with the back of her hand and grew quiet.

Amina wanted her children. Her heart was with Mohsen and Shalima. It didn't even take a day—the moment she laid eyes on my children, her tears started to flow. She sat on the kitchen floor, put her head on her knees, and wept.

"I miss Mohsen so very much," she said. "What should I do?"

What a mistake. I was fooled by that Indian scoundrel's sweet talk. Stupid, gullible me. Greedy for porridge, I fell into the pot.

The children watched her with sorrow and surprise.

She took my daughter in her arms and kissed her all over the face. She was kissing Shalima.

"Shalima is taller, but she's as skinny as a corpse," she said. "Mohsen is a good eater. He's chubby. They're with my father. They go out and beg with him."

If I were to let her be, she would talk about her kids until dawn. Shalima, Mohsen, Mohsen, Shalima.

I knew I had made a mistake. Amina didn't belong in Paris. She would die of a broken heart. I told myself, Thank God she has a return ticket, I have to let her go immediately. It's not worth the trouble. I'll put her on a plane tomorrow and send her back. But Amina wasn't thinking of leaving. She had other plans.

"Missus, help me," she said. "You have children, too. You understand. Mohsen is only two. He is used to sleeping in my arms every night. I was still breast-feeding him. Help me bring Mohsen and Shalima to be with me."

Mohsen? Shalima? In Paris? That's all I needed.

"The first wife is my children's enemy. When she found out Mr. Raja was sending me to Paris, she went crazy. She screamed and yelled and threw herself on the ground. She said, 'You're a maid but you're free. I'm in a cage, in prison.' She hit me. She hit Shalima. She went around screaming for her father. The upstairs rooms are hers, the carpets are hers, but all she does is cry. She sits in the dark or sleeps and pulls the sheet up over her face. She doesn't want anyone to see the wrinkles on her face. She wanted to throw boiling oil on my face. I'm scared she'll hurt my children."

"Amina, my life is different now," I explained. "Paris isn't like Tehran. It's me and two children in a small apartment. There is hardly room even for you. You have to sleep in the living room. And you want to bring your kids?"

She was clever. She had her answers ready.

"I'll rent a room somewhere," she said. "Shalima is ten and she'll go to school and I will work for you during the day." You see? It's that simple.

"What room? Where? Do you think you're in Bangladesh? Do you want to build a cardboard shack on the side of the street?"

"I'll work and pay the rent."

"First, you have to get a residence permit and for that you need a sponsor. And to get a room, you have to pay two months' rent up front. It's not a joke."

She stuck to her words. Shalima, Mohsen, Mohsen, Shalima.

"No!" I shouted. And I checked her airline ticket. I wanted to put her on the first flight out. Her place wasn't in Europe. Mr. Raja had to make other plans for his wife.

Oh!

Amina's ticket was one-way. Bangladesh-Paris. No return. I had been hoodwinked.

I held the ticket in front of her. I was shaking with anger.

"Didn't your husband say he was buying a round-trip ticket?"

"Yes, that's what he said."

"Then where is it?"

She shook her head and looked down.

"Your husband promised. He put it in writing. What happened?"

She repeated the lines Mr. Raja had taught her. It was obvious. Two days before she left Bangladesh, a big fire burned down half the town (which town?). Mr. Raja's house was destroyed and he lost all his worldly belongings. The first wife and the elder sons had been homeless ever since. The fortunate Mr. Raja had become quite unfortunate (who cares?). The dear missus, the Tehrani lady, being a generous angel (thank you), would help them. Despite being burdened with debts and misery, the bankrupt Mr. Raja had managed to buy a ticket for Amina so that he could keep his promise to the Tehrani lady. The kind Mr. Raja spent every waking and sleeping moment thinking about the Tehrani lady and her children. Despite all the ills that had befallen him, he had kept his word. The Tehrani lady, the munificent lady, would pay for Amina's ticket and everyone would live happily ever after.

As simple as that!

Amina knew there was no hint of emotion or sincerity in her voice. She had memorized the lines and repeated them like a parrot. She was a terrible actress. She tried hard to bring tears to her eyes, but she couldn't. She had promised Mr. Raja to convince the Tehrani lady and she kept repeating the story like a sleep-talker. There was a fire, the entire town burned down, Mr. Raja and his wife were burned (I think Amina added this herself. It was the only sentence that came from her heart). The Tehrani lady was an angel. She would help.

I screamed that the Tehrani lady was no angel, that she was a wolf, and she was going to show them.

Again, she said, "The Tehrani lady can understand."

I had really fallen into a trap.

Amina was asking for the money for her plane ticket, but her tone was cold and indifferent. She was listless. She was reaching out to Mohsen. Her yearning for her children wasn't an act.

"For now, go and sleep," I said. "We will talk about it tomorrow."

I wanted time to think. I had no doubt that Amina had to go

back and she had to go back soon. But who was going to pay for her ticket? A thousand dollars. She didn't have it, neither did I, nor did that bankrupt swindler Mr. Raja.

Early the next morning, I sat across from a drowsy Amina and told her that bringing her children to Paris was out of the question. There was no room in my apartment. If she wanted to leave and not work for me, then farewell. But, getting back to the issue of the airline ticket, I bluntly told her that I didn't believe a word she had said and that I knew the story about the fire was a ridiculous lie from beginning to end.

Amina blushed and started to laugh sheepishly.

"If you want to go back, then go back," I said. "But I don't have the money to pay for your ticket. Ask Mr. Raja to send it to you."

My words were stern. Amina grew quiet. She had played her game and now she quickly confessed that Mr. Raja had ordered her to tell all those lies.

"Now, what do you want to do?" I asked.

She thought for a moment and then she said, "I'll stay."

"Without the kids?"

She said nothing.

And so, Amina stayed. Her salary was three hundred dollars a month. I told her she shouldn't send all her money to her husband and that I would keep and save one hundred dollars a month for her.

"Oh, missus!" she said. "If he finds out, he will kill me. He will kill Shalima."

"He wouldn't dare. Write to him that the Tehrani lady only pays you two hundred dollars a month. If he has the guts, he can come and deal with me himself."

Amina was afraid. Mr. Raja was a dangerous man. He could come to Paris and kill the Tehrani lady. He could abuse her children. He could burn her father's begging permit. He could turn the town upside down. Mr. Raja could go up against the entire world. She wanted to go on, but I stopped her.

"When? Where? Hold it! Nothing bad is going to happen. The hell with him. He wouldn't dare."

I had to make Amina understand that Mr. Raja was not the almighty, but getting this into her dense head wasn't easy.

"My dear, open your ears and listen to me. Lesson one: You work and your salary is yours. It belongs to you."

"Yours" was a word that had an unfamiliar ring to it. She looked at me. There was primal fear in her eyes.

"He will come and kill me."

"No he wouldn't. If he so much as raises a hand to you, you will call the police. They will deal with him really well and then they will kick him out of the country."

Call the police? Ha! Amina calling the police to report Mr. Raja? Amina the maid filing a complaint against the almighty master? The Tehrani lady had lost her mind. She was talking nonsense. Lesson one was complicated, it was difficult to grasp, and Amina was a slow student. Still, she didn't mind listening to the strange things I said. There was a childlike glint in her eyes, the glint of a sweet dread. She stared at the wall (God knows what was going through her mind) and then, with cautious pleasure, she smiled—a strange smile induced by fear.

She had barely stopped grinning when again she felt heartsick for her children. It was a constant longing; silent, but present and palpable every minute of the day.

Through Amina's sad eyes, Shalima and Mohsen quietly entered our lives and found a permanent place among the people and objects around us. Every time Amina looked at a youngster or jumped at the sound of a child out on the street, every time she had tears in her eyes, every time she received a letter from her father, every time she curled up in a corner or lay down facing the wall and muttered to herself, every time she sat in front of the mirror and hummed a heartrending song, Shalima and Mohsen would appear next to us, sitting in front of the television, or at the foot of the bed, or on the bench in the park.

We often found them in the silent moments between our talks, in the layers of our dreams, in seeing a child beggar on a street corner, in the news about wars and floods and earthquakes, in the scent of the spicy foods Amina cooked, and in the pleasing melody of an Indian sitar. Often when we were warm and cozy and happy, Shalima and Mohsen's sad eyes would peer out from the dark and impose a sense of guilt on us. I would see the barefoot Shalima begging on the street and searching for a few large lice to put in her grandfather's hair. She was responsible for sweeping and washing the floors and caring for her young brother. I knew how much she missed her mother and how lonely and tired she felt. In Amina's silent angst, I saw that Mohsen was sick, that he had a cold, that he had a fever and coughed. When Amina looked in the mirror and sang while combing her hair, I knew that the danger had passed, that little Mohsen had recovered.

Amina never left the apartment. She was afraid. It was too cold outside, or she wanted to sleep. If we let her, she would sleep all day. And when she was awake, she wasn't alert or quite present. We had to push her, nudge her, and tug at her hair for her to come to life and to put the small mirror or the movie magazine under her pillow and to get up, to briefly hide the fantasy of her children under her eyelids, and to stumble through dusting and cleaning the apartment.

One day, I finally dragged Amina out of the apartment and showed her the way to the children's school. The next morning, I sent her out with the kids, but she hurried back only moments later. The following day, she pretended to be sick and stayed in bed. The third day, she said she wouldn't go out and she pleaded and cried. On the fifth day, we got into a fight and argued. On the sixth day, she gave in and went out. And on the days that followed, she learned her way around the nearby streets. Then she walked to the end of the main avenue and, afraid of getting lost, she ran back. Gradually, she found her way around the neighborhood and discovered the square behind the park, the local movie theater, and the less expensive shops. She even learned that bus 87 goes all the way to the Eiffel Tower, and that did her in. It did us in, too.

"Amina."

"Dear Amina."

"Missus Amina."

She was nowhere to be found. The moment I turned my head, she would skip out of the apartment with no notice or explanation. She had gotten over her fear and just like a cat that has discovered the way out, it was difficult to keep her at home. She would take the bus and only God knows where she went. She had made friends with a few Moroccan and Tunisian maids. They were all about the same age as she, but they were savvy and semi-Western in their attitudes. They were obedient but also bold and brassy, housewives and housemaids aware of their limits and their rights. Amina's new teachers.

Sundays were Amina's days off. At first she just stayed home, but didn't work. She slept, read magazines, wrote letters, and dreamt of her children. Or out of sheer loneliness, although she was a Hindu she went to the church across the street. There was a small park in front of our apartment building and once in a while she would go there and feed the pigeons. It was during these outings that she met Jamila, the Tunisian woman who worked as a janitor in the building next door. She communicated with her with the few French words and Arabic phrases she had learned. With every day that passed, a more savvy and hungry Amina—hungry to see and to learn—passed before us, with her curious gaze dashing ahead of her.

Jamila was her teacher. She took Amina around the neighborhood and taught her the ins and outs of living in Paris. Little by little, I started getting worried about Amina. I had to rein her in. Mr. Raja appeared to be concerned, too, and wanted to know what Amina was up to and why she was getting paid so little money. It seemed he had gotten wise to the fact that Amina was keeping part of her salary for herself. He wrote a letter to me in poor, muddled English to inquire about Amina. He threatened that if he found out Amina was cheating him, he would skin her alive. I didn't write back.

Not long after, an excited Amina told me that her dear husband missed her terribly and wanted to come to Paris to see her. It was the first time Mr. Raja had expressed any love for her and Amina was thirsty for affection. She jumped to the conclusion that Mr. Raja had given up his first wife and had rediscovered Amina's youth and beauty. He was going to bring Shalima and Mohsen and he was going to rent a small room, a real room, where they would all live together. Who knows, perhaps her beggar father would join them, too, and he would apply for an official beggar's permit from the French government. And a thousand other hopes and maybes.

No matter what Jamila and I said, it was all useless. Amina's eyes had still not opened and Mr. Raja's magic remained more potent than our rational advice. The Indian louse's chicanery and deceit was obvious, but Amina either didn't see it or didn't want to see it. All of a sudden and for no apparent reason, Mr. Raja had fallen in love with his young wife and he was suffering in her absence! Amina believed in miracles and the almighty master's expressions of love were proof. Letter after letter. Lie after lie. In short, to get a visa, the besotted Mr. Raja needed a formal invitation letter and, with great humility and in a roundabout way, he was asking Amina to send one to him and to pay for his airline ticket as well. In return for all this kindness, Mr. Raja would bring his beautiful wife a gold bangle and ruby earrings, as well as a basketful of love, a crateful of caresses, a world of sincere intention, and of course he would bring the children. He would even pay for their tickets.

"Amina," I shouted, "don't be a fool!"

"Missus, one's husband is one's master," she said. "He's the master. He promised me. He wouldn't lie."

I thought I had misheard. "He wouldn't lie?" I snapped.

She looked down. She couldn't look into my eyes.

"He'll bring Mohsen," she said. "I don't want a gold bangle. He promised he'll bring Mohsen."

The hell with it; people deserve what they get, I told myself.

I GAVE HER the money I had been saving for her. One thousand twenty-five dollars. As quick as the wind, she bought a ticket and sent it to her master, along with the invitation letter, which she asked Jamila to write.

Two months later, Mr. Raja arrived—empty-handed, without the gold bangle and the basketful of love and, of course, without the children. Without Mohsen. Without Shalima.

It was the first time I was seeing him. He was more wretched and more vile and slimy than I had imagined. He was sallow, short and skinny, with thick lips, rotten teeth, and a lecherous look in his eyes. He spoke English and constantly wagged his head and licked his dark lips. Barely having arrived, he set out to establish his social rank and class lest I think Amina's husband was a beggar like her father. He was arrogant.

"Tehrani lady, I'm rich," he said. "I have a large house and I've rented out eight of the rooms."

I wanted to snap at him, but I held my tongue. Amina offered him tea. She looked cross. She knew she had been duped, but she didn't say anything.

"If you're rich, then why does your wife have to work as a maid?" I said. "And why didn't you pay for your own ticket?"

He laughed and pretended he hadn't understood me. He was sitting with his legs crossed and he was smoking and playing with his gold ring.

"How much does Amina earn every month?" he asked.

"Two hundred dollars," I lied. I wasn't going to give Amina's salary to him.

His eyes narrowed and he looked at Amina. She turned away. Her mind was in turmoil. She had realized that all his promises were lies. Exasperated and humiliated, she just stared at the floor.

She deserved it. I was angry at her for being so stupid and I didn't mind her being punished. In any case, there was nothing I could do. Changing Amina would take a long time, perhaps longer than my life would permit.

Mr. Raja's arrival disrupted our lives. The man of authority immediately rented a room in Paris's twentieth arrondissement, where mostly Arab and Indian families lived. Amina was to spend the nights with her husband, spend the days working, and at the end of the month give him all her salary. As simple as that!

It was important for me to have someone stay with the children at night and Amina's leaving was contrary to our agreement. The contract I had signed with Mr. Raja stated that she would be my full-time, live-in employee. I showed her the contract. She looked down and said nothing. There was nothing she could do. Her life was in the hands of the master. He made the rules.

I thought the master had come for a short visit and would soon leave. But no, he had come to have a good time and to beat Amina. He had no intention of leaving.

Amina forgot about the gold bangle and gave up on her salary, but she couldn't forget her children. She had lost her money for the love of Mohsen and Shalima, and this time, Mr. Raja's scam was too big for her to swallow.

"Missus, I will go and bring the children myself," she said.

She sounded determined. I was taken aback. A stranger was speaking to me; an angry woman seething with primal instinct and ready to defend her children like a wildcat.

"I won't let Shalima turn into a beggar," she said. "I won't allow Mohsen to sleep on the street. I will go and bring them."

"How? With what money?"

"I will find a way. The first wife stole my money. I will take it back from her. She owes me. I will file a complaint against her. I will burn down her house. I will steal her rugs."

"Without Mr. Raja's permission?"

She was confused. Something had shifted in her mind. She had learned to look and to see. I was worried about her and I was terrified of the Indian louse's reaction. Rightfully so. Learning that his wife wanted to go bring the children without asking for his permission, Mr. Raja turned red and then black. He locked up Amina in their room, with no food and no water, and he threatened to skin her alive.

The day I saw Amina with bruises on her face, I lost my temper. Her lips were swollen and her arm ached.

She said, "Missus, my husband mocks me. He says, 'Now you've turned into Madame Amina for me?'"

Her eyes were brimming with tears, but she chuckled like a child and said, "My husband told me that every day I have to leave my money on the table for him, that I have to ask the Tehrani lady for more salary, and that if you don't agree, I'll have to go work for a French lady."

"Amina, what do you want?" I asked.

She stared at me with a blank look in her eyes. "You" was an absent audience, a fictional character in a movie, in a dream. What was important was what Mr. Raja said.

"Missus, I can't say no to him."

But in this last sentence, in "I can't say no," I sensed a halting agitation. She had doubts, half of her being was restless, weighing, evaluating. Her protesting half wanted a better life for her children.

"I'll go and bring the kids," she said. "If they stay there, they will end up as beggars. I want Shalima to study, just like your children."

With this hope and this intent, Amina left us. For three months, I had no news of her. And then she showed up—sick, frail, and depressed. She looked pale and there were dark circles under her eyes. She didn't want to talk. Her silence was weightier than her sorrow. I thought something had happened to Shalima. She shook her head. She was writhing with agony. Finally, she opened up and told me what had happened to her. All these months, she had been in Paris, working. She was too embarrassed to come and see me. She got pregnant, but Mr. Raja didn't want the child. He kicked her in the stomach. Now, she had been bleeding for three days and she was in terrible pain.

"Missus, I know the child in my stomach is dead."

"You have to see a doctor," I said. "Let's go to the hospital."

She threw herself at my feet. She was afraid. Mr. Raja wouldn't allow it. He had told her he would kill her if she told a doctor what had happened to her.

"You have to report it to the police," I said.

She shook her head.

"Amina, the law will protect you. You have rights."

Amina had no notion of the law and her rights. What rights? This was the way the world worked. It was the law of nature.

I dragged Amina to the hospital. Two days later, she lost her child. I told the lady doctor what had happened. She was devastated. She immediately called the authorities and made an appointment with a social worker. I kept Amina at my apartment.

Mr. Raja showed up at my door, subservient and scared. He wanted to take Amina with him. I didn't let him in. I had locked the door to Amina's room. He threatened me. I called the police and he ran off as fast as he had come.

The social worker, Jamila, and I spent the entire week talking to Amina. She seemed to have come to her senses, but I didn't trust her. She vacillated between certainty and doubt. She was angry, fraught, thrashing about.

Her eyes had opened and she had discovered rage.

Mr. Raja didn't give up. He knew that if he ended up in the hands of the police his circumstances would be precarious. He was looking for a solution. The Tehrani lady was dangerous. She was brainwashing Amina. At the end of the week, looking meek and remorseful, he again came to see Amina. He had brought her a pair of leather shoes and a length of fabric, along with his tearful eyes and yellow teeth.

He said he wanted to return to Bangladesh. Of course, with Amina. He didn't want her to work anymore. A woman's place was next to her husband and he would support Amina and her beggar father. Amina liked the lies, the sweet lies, the easy lies laced with kindness.

The master knew Amina's weak spots. He promised to give her one of the upstairs rooms, to make her the first wife, and to send Shalima to school. Amina's face blossomed like a flower. It was easy to fool her. The moment he mentioned her children, she turned into putty and forgot that tiny seed of sense we had planted in her head.

"Missus, I'm dying to see my kids," she said. "I have to go. Shalima is all alone. Mohsen cries. I can't stand being away from them anymore."

We were back to square one.

It was raining the day she left. It was exactly nine months from the day she arrived. She had a one-year residence permit.

"Amina," I said, "you have three months. You can come back. The social worker and I will help you."

"If one day I decide to come back," she said, "I will bring my children with me. I won't be separated from them again."

Amina left. I was all by myself, but I decided not to hire another maid. I was happy that I never had to look at Mr. Raja's face again.

Once in a while, Jamila would receive news of Amina and she would share it with me. The first wife had kicked her out of the house and Mr. Raja had rented out the room at the end of the courtyard. Amina and her children were living with her beggar father in his cardboard shack. Under the incessant rain. Underwater.

And then, I lost her. Amina was easy to lose. She would suddenly disappear and then she would unexpectedly show up again.

TWO YEARS WENT BY. It was Labor Day. I was getting ready to take the children to the park when the doorbell rang. I wasn't expecting anyone. I opened the door and saw Amina standing there with a dark-skinned girl and a chubby boy. I couldn't believe it. She laughed. Her eyes were gleaming. She had gained weight, but she had the pleasant plumpness of happy mothers.

Shalima was shy and reserved. Just as I had imagined her. Mohsen was fat and had a big appetite. He was eyeing his surroundings with his bright black eyes. Barely having arrived, he took a banana and started to eat. He wiped his sticky fingers on his mother's skirt, laughed with his mouth full, and took another banana. Shalima shook her head. She didn't want to eat anything.

Amina's eyes were gleaming with joy. She wanted to talk—in that sweet and proper Farsi she had learned and still remembered— but she didn't know where to start.

She started from the very beginning. As soon as they arrived back in Bangladesh, her husband reneged on his promises. The first wife was sick. She was itching. She was scratching herself, rubbing her body against the rattan rug and the bricks in the yard, and she was hitting her head against the walls. At night, they had to tie her hands and feet and lock her up in a dark room. Mr. Raja took to drinking and bringing prostitutes to the house. The elder sons were out of work. They constantly asked Mr. Raja for money and sold the household furnishings. Again, Mr. Raja sent Amina away to work as a maid. This time to Jordan, to the house of a British diplomat. After her contract ended, the diplomat applied for a visa for Amina and took her with him back to England. Then he helped her bring her children, too. Amina was looking at her children and talking fast. Her chest was heaving. Her large breasts looked like the breasts of a pregnant woman, pregnant with the joy of maternal instinct.

"Missus, can you believe it!" she said. "I finally brought my children."

"The English lady was a good woman," she said, "but she had no patience for children. She was right. They didn't have any kids and their life was as organized as a bouquet of flowers. Shalima was quiet, but Mohsen was always at the refrigerator. The English lady would give him three bananas a day, but this greedy kid's eyes were after the box of chocolates. No matter where they hid it, he would find it and eat all the chocolates. The English lady got tired."

Amina looked at her son and laughed from the depths of the happiest nook in her heart.

"My husband wrote that I should ask my English master to apply for a visa for him, too," she said. "He wanted to trick me again. He wrote a letter to the Embassy of Bangladesh and claimed that I had kidnapped his children. He told a thousand lies."

"Oh, so Mr. Raja told lies?"

Amina blushed. She stroked Shalima's cheek and sat on the floor and pulled her children to her side.

"The English lady was very generous," she said. "She paid me three months' salary and asked if I wanted to come to Paris, to the Tehrani lady."

This Amina wasn't the clumsy and meek Amina I knew. The fate of her children was in her hands and she was fighting for them. She knew that raising her children in the West would not be easy, but she had made up her mind. Her eyes were open and her ears could hear. Opinions took shape in her mind, and her thoughts and feelings were real. She still dreamt, she still imagined herself starring in a make-believe movie, but she was the one writing the scenario and producing the film. A film created in partnership with her children.

She was my guest for a week and then she rented a room. During the day, she worked as a maid for a French family—clandestinely, without a work permit. Her income was enough to cover their expenses. She enrolled Shalima in the local school and Mohsen in the kindergarten. Mademoiselle Shalima and Monsieur Mohsen. At night she slept between her children and knew that the monsoon season was over.

On Sundays, Amina would rest during the day and come with her children to visit me in the evening. The scrawny Shalima had gained a little weight and was starting to look healthier. She looked people in the eye, greeted them, and answered simple questions. And all this time, Mr. Raja followed Amina like a shadow and wouldn't leave her alone.

"Amina, be careful," I said. "I'm afraid the master's love for you will rekindle again and drive him crazy."

"Missus, there is no way I would allow Shalima to become a beggar," she said. "I want her to study. I want her to become a doctor. I want Mohsen to work, to go to the university. I will go to the embassy and ask for help. I will do whatever I can."

Her words were the words of a rebel. I had never seen Amina so determined and strong, so awake and alert. She no longer dragged her feet or stumbled around. Her eyes were full of questions and her ears chased after every sound.

Mr. Raja was searching for Amina through me and I was throwing his letters in the trash can without reading them. I had no idea that he had packed his bags and would soon show up. Amina didn't know either. She was busy with work and her new life. Shalima was struggling with the difficulties of living in a new country, but she had seen the ups and downs of life and knew how to get by. Every day, she walked her young brother to kindergarten and back, and in her mother's absence she took care of the housework.

Life was peaceful. Their worries belonged to the past.

I WAS HOME. There was a knock at the door—tap, tap, tap—and then a long doorbell ring. I opened the door and my breath froze in my chest. I wasn't expecting an Indian guest, especially one that looked like that. The pungent and dizzying smell of cologne had flooded the hallway and Mr. Raja's uneven breaths wafted at me from the bottom of a pot of Indian spices. With feigned humility, he said hello. His teeth were yellower than before and his tongue was stained red. He was wearing a tie, a black jacket, and new sneakers, which had undoubtedly been purchased that same day from the shoe store at the corner.

The start of trouble.

I didn't invite him in. Standing in the doorway, he said his greetings and asked where Amina was. I told him I didn't know, I excused him, and closed the door. He wouldn't give up. He knocked again—tap, tap, tap—and then he rang the doorbell. From behind the closed door, I told him that he was intruding and that I was going to call the police immediately. The Indian louse had a particular fear of the police and became flustered the moment he heard the sound of *p* and the hiss of *c*. He tucked his tail between his legs and scurried away.

Sunday came. I was waiting for Amina so that I could tell her about her husband's arrival. It was dusk when she arrived, unawares and cheerful, with Shalima and Mohsen at her side. She was eyeing her surroundings with pride and coquetry. She wanted people to notice her. She had discovered herself and, alert and content, was carrying herself like a precious asset. She was a mother with gentle lines on her face, a sweet double chin, and a few strands of white in her lustrous hair. A new feeling of self-respect gave her energy and made her breathing more intense. She hungered for a thousand things and there were a thousand things she feared.

"Amina, beware," I said. "Your husband is here."

She froze. She grabbed Shalima's hand and stared at her son. She wanted to run away. She was shaking.

"I'll go see the social worker right away," she said. "And I know a lawyer. He has come to take my children away. What should I do?"

Shalima was quiet. She couldn't understand a word of Farsi, but she knew that her mother was suddenly upset and she was certain it had something to do with Mr. Raja. Even Mohsen had sensed that a hidden danger was threatening them and the last bite of banana remained bulging in his cheek.

We were thinking of a solution when the doorbell rang. I heard a rasping cough and knew it was Master Raja. I decided to open the door and let him in so that Amina would once and for all tell him to get lost. I believed she was now ready to do it.

Amina ran and stood behind me and Shalima and Mohsen

clung to their mother. I could hear Amina's heart beating. Mohsen
had a lump in his throat and Shalima was staring at the floor.

A smiling Mr. Raja, with yellow teeth and white sneakers,
walked in and tossed his cigarette butt in the flower pot next
to the door. Then he coughed and spat his mucus into a grimy
handkerchief. He had brought a box of pastries for me. He took
two pieces of candy out of his pocket and gave them to Mohsen.
Amina leapt in front of him and glared into his eyes.

Mr. Raja had brought a gold bangle for Amina—the same one
that his first wife had taken from her by force. Amina recognized
it and started to talk—quietly at first and then louder and louder.
God knows what she was ranting about. I didn't understand their
language, but from the way she was shaking her head and flailing
her arms it was all obvious. Mohsen burst into tears and Shalima
ran off and locked herself in the kitchen.

I stepped in. I calmed Amina and told Mr. Raja to stop harass-
ing her. He started his usual "dear missus, dear missus." Then he
swallowed his anger, took on the look of a devoted father and
husband, and spoke to Amina in a gentle tone. He acted meek,
hung his head down, and let out a heartrending sigh. Then he said
goodbye and left.

"Amina," I said, "don't you for one second believe his lies."

She was rattled. Looking nervous, she took her children by the
hand and left.

A month passed. I had no news of Amina. I guessed she had
again fallen in the clutches of her husband and was too ashamed
to come and see me. I had no idea what had become of her,
until the day I ran into Jamila on the street. She had heard from
Amina. She was still working and, as usual, she was leaving her

salary on the table for her husband. Mr. Raja was working in an Indian restaurant and he had rented a room, bought a TV, and was having a good time.

"Does he have a work permit?" I asked.

No. He didn't. Thank God. I thought, if he was working illegally, he was in for a load of trouble. The authorities could grab him by the scruff of the neck and toss him out with a kick in the rear end. But it all depended on Amina, and Amina, despite her anger, her plans, and her children, was still weak when it came to her husband's power and authority. I wasn't sure whether she had the strength to go up against him.

Jamila believed that Amina was furious inside and that one of these days her rage would erupt. And that is exactly what happened. The dormant volcano started to rumble.

Jamila told me about Amina's eruption.

ONE NIGHT MR. RAJA came home drunk, wasted, singing loudly. Their room was in the attic, on the sixth floor. He plodded his way up the stairs and now and then sat down to rest. One of their neighbors opened the door and yelled at him. Mr. Raja quieted down. Amina heard his footsteps. His shoes had metal heel protectors that clinked as he walked. He took off his shoes, but she could hear him panting on the third floor. The door to their room was ajar. The lightbulb in the hallway had burnt out. The staggering Mr. Raja felt his way in, but the master stumbled over a suitcase and fell on top of Shalima. Thinking he was a burglar, the girl screamed and grabbed the water pitcher next to her bed and smashed it on Mr. Raja's head. Amina rushed to her daughter's aid and the husband and wife got into a scuffle. Mr. Raja clawed at Amina's hair, Mohsen bit his father's leg, and Amina started screaming for help. She opened the door and ran barefoot into the hallway and down the stairs. Mr. Raja chased after her, and the children, wielding a broom and a metal spatula, chased after Mr. Raja. The neighbors poured out of their rooms. Mr. Raja caught up with Amina and she started clawing at his face. Mr. Raja grabbed the metal spatula from Shalima and beat Amina with its edge. With gashes on her head and face and drenched in blood, Amina fainted on the stairs.

The neighbors called the police, but Mr. Raja disappeared before they arrived.

Amina came with her children to see me.

"Missus," she said, "I want to file a complaint against him. Tell me how. Who do I have to call?"

I sighed with satisfaction and said, "You have to call the police, my dear." I felt as if a heavy burden had lifted from my shoulders. We had taken a few steps forward—a few large and fateful steps.

"This man has been cruel to me and my children," Amina said. "I want to divorce him. Should I talk to the police about that, too?"

For the first time, Amina was experiencing remonstration, the law, and the police, and she no longer felt alone in the world.

"Wait," I said. "First, you have to file a complaint. Then we will see about a divorce."

She had no patience. She wanted a divorce, that day, that minute.

Jamila was familiar with social services and the laws that pertained to foreigners. She took Amina to the local town hall and retained a pro bono attorney for her. First, Amina had to renew her residency permit, and to do so she had to prove she could financially support herself and her children. Jamila, the French lady Amina was working for, and I deposited some money in her bank account. It was understood that she would later reimburse us. Fortunately, the leftists were in power and the immigration laws had become less stringent. The authorities renewed Amina's residency permit for another five years.

Mr. Raja was in hiding for a while and had stopped going to work. He was waiting for things to calm down and for Amina to come to her senses. He was counting on her limited common sense and her ability to quickly forget. He was sure he could win her over again with a string of deceitful words and colorful promises. He sent her a letter moaning and groaning about being separated from his children, being lonely, and suffering a sad life in a foreign land.

Amina showed me his letter and said that the man's promises were all lies and that she would not rest until she was divorced from him. To be on the safe side, she rented a different room and didn't give anyone her new address.

Mr. Raja took Amina's silence as a sign of submission, and hoping to take her money—two months' salary—he went to the children's school. Shalima spotted him from a distance and hid among the other students and her half-drunk father didn't see her. But Mohsen got caught—fooled by a handful of candy and a banana—and hand in hand with Mr. Raja he went home. Again, the Indian oaf settled down in Amina's room. But Amina had a plan. She was hoping Mr. Raja would again beat her so that she could inform the police. The neighbors all knew about her plan and had promised to help.

One evening, Mr. Raja went home happy. Amina let him in, kept her eyes down, and didn't speak a word. Mr. Raja was delighted to find her so modest and obedient. He nodded in approval and immediately asked for food and drink. Amina didn't move, so he repeated his request in a louder voice. Amina still didn't react.

Mr. Raja was puzzled. He wasn't used to this kind of behavior. He flared his nostrils and beat his fist on the table. Amina ignored him. Mr. Raja leapt up, grabbed her braid, and kicked her in the side. Terrified, the children ran out into the hallway and started to scream for help.

Mr. Raja was hungry. The master wanted his food and drink and he was deaf to the commotion of the neighbors pouring out of their rooms and blind to the appearance of two policemen at the door. They walked in and asked for Madam Amina. Mr. Raja sensed danger. He tried to leave, but they blocked his way and asked to see his papers, his passport, his residency and work permits. He didn't have them. He was in big trouble; bigger than he could imagine. He was trapped and he had no way to escape.

Mr. Raja was given one week to leave France. Amina took care of everything else. Together with her lawyer, she went to the Embassy of Bangladesh and filed for a divorce. The neighbors testified in her defense and the embassy took her side.

Broken and defeated, Mr. Raja came to see me before he left the country. He had transformed into a whimpering weakling and pretended to cry. Or perhaps he really did cry. He said Amina had brought him shame, that she had a lover, that she was pregnant, that as a Muslim man he had the right to behead his adulterous wife. But because he was a kindhearted man, he was willing to forgive her if she agreed to repent, to be obedient, and to return to Bangladesh with him.

I kept silent. I don't know why, but I suddenly felt sorry for him. I was embarrassed and didn't want to witness his humiliation.

"My first wife was taken to the hospital," he said. "They say she was bitten by a rabid dog and is incurable. She has gone mad.

Amina has gone mad, too. She's become rabid. God has turned his wrath on me. All the women in my life have gone insane. Tehrani lady, what am I to do?"

He was sitting there with no intention of leaving. He was distraught and incapable of analyzing the chain of events.

"Missus," he said, "my father had three wives and he beat them all, but they didn't become rabid. It was customary. Everyone accepted the fact that the man is the master. It's the law of nature. A wife who calls the police on her husband isn't a wife. The West has ruined Amina. It's my own fault. I sent her here. She was a good girl when she was in Iran. She was decent. And when she went to Saudi Arabia, she remained obedient. She didn't become rabid. The West changed her. It ruined her."

THE INDIAN LOUSE doesn't understand that Amina has discovered new values. His first wife is from a wealthy family. Her father is a fabric merchant. So the rooms upstairs belong to her. It is her right. Amina is a Hindu. Her father is a beggar. Her heart isn't Muslim. So her place is downstairs. It's only natural. Everything is based on ancient laws and wisdoms. It is Amina who has raised havoc and stepped beyond her limits. She must be beaten. She must be punished. She must be reined in and tied up. Mr. Raja has acted according to the laws of his tribe, the laws of his ancestors. He doesn't see why he should be held guilty. He complains about the French police, but he is powerless. If only he had not sent Amina to the West. If only.

AMINA HAS HER divorce. She looks around her, she looks at people. She is overwhelmed. She is a stranger to her new self and she is frightened by the naked freedom that now surrounds her. Endless roads and opportunities lie ahead. Which should she choose? From now on, she is responsible for her own and her children's destiny. There is no Mr. Raja to bully her and dictate what her life should be. She runs. She twirls. She knocks into doors and walls and she falls. She is scared. She is alone. Still, she is standing on firm ground and on this firm ground she will build her children's future. She has nailed down her place at the center of this ground. This is where she wants to start, from this stable point and special moment.

Shalima must become a doctor. Mohsen must work and earn his banana money. Amina wants a real house. A house made of stone and cement that can withstand floods and storms.

She comes to see me. She is breathless.

"Missus, I'm very busy," she says. "I have to get a work permit. I have to make money. I have to raise my children. I have to think about getting permanent residency. I have to think about my future."

My future! The phrase sounds strange coming from Amina. She and I always talked about the past, about Tehran and the days when she lived with us. That was the only real world we knew. And now, with one leap, Amina has overtaken me and she has discovered a new dimension of time—tomorrow. She imagines herself and her children in better times and she is running toward it. She has grabbed my hand and she is dragging me with her.

AMINA LEFT. As always, she disappeared. I often thought of her, but I wasn't worried. I knew that she was somewhere busy with life, work, and her children. I ran into Jamila on the street. The last news she had of Amina was from a year ago. She said Amina had left Paris and was living in a different city.

At last, she called. Two years had passed. She was living in a town in southern France.

She sounded warm and cheerful. It was as if she had only left us yesterday. She couldn't grasp the fact that two years (two long years) had passed and much had happened. For those of us who counted the days and took measure of every small joy, two years was as long as Noah's life. But Amina was setting her watch based on a different logic. Her notion of time stemmed from ancient knowledge, from the million-year-long sleep of mythical gods.

"Amina, where have you been all this time?" I asked.

"All this time?"

"Two years is a lifetime. I've grown old."

She laughed. She sounded like her old self when she used to wander under the trees in our garden in Tehran and dream golden dreams.

"Missus, I'm married," she said. "My husband is young. He's a custodian at a park. We live in the park. We have two rooms behind the guard's office. It's as if the park is ours. I wish you would come and join us. God has given me the biggest garden in the world. There is room for you and your children. Missus, I have two more children. Twins. Shalima is in school and she speaks French. Mademoiselle Shalima. That poor Raja has become a beggar. His first wife is in a madhouse. My father gave Mr. Raja his beggar's permit before he died. He gave him his begging territory, too. After all, Mr. Raja was his son-in-law, he is Shalima's father. I want to go back for a visit. Half my heart is still there. The bigger half."

The line was disconnected. I waited. I thought she would call back. She didn't.

TEN YEARS HAVE passed since I last saw Amina. The doorbell rings. It isn't the children's restless and persistent ringing. It is a stranger's hesitant finger on the doorbell. Someone who thinks he or she might be at the wrong address.

"Who is it?"

Silence.

I stand behind the door. In the old days, when someone knocked, I would open the door without fear and without asking who it was (as was our tradition). It took a long time for me to get used to questions and cautions, to latching the door chain, to looking through the peephole.

"Who is it?" I ask again.

An unfamiliar voice says, "It's me."

Whoever "me" is, she has a delicate and shy voice. I think she has come to the wrong apartment. I open the door slightly. A dark-skinned girl, with large, timid eyes, long braided hair, and strappy sandals on her feet, is standing in front of me. She is wearing a sari—a pistachio green sari.

She says hello in fluent French and without a foreign accent. Her name is Shalima. She is looking down and fidgeting.

When I take her in my arms, I smell her mother's scent. But she doesn't have her mother's beauty. She says she is in her last year of medical school. She wants to become a pediatrician. She laughs. She has her mother's white teeth. She says Mohsen is in high school. She shows me a photograph of him. He is wearing sneakers and he's still a little chubby. They have French passports, and a brother and sister, eleven years old. Her stepfather is a good man. He pays for their expenses. She has a scholarship and works in an English bookstore three days a week.

I want her to tell me about Amina, about their home in the park, and about her own plans for the future. She is silent. She looks down and a gentle sorrow settles over her face. My heart sinks.

Shalima's silence is timid and comforting. She opens her handbag and takes out a yellow envelope. "My mother wanted me to give you this photograph," she says. "She wanted me to thank you. She was very ill. We took her to the hospital. She passed away six weeks ago. She twice opened her eyes and spoke your name. I will finish my studies this year. Then I'm going back to Bangladesh. My father is ill. He has lost his eyesight. I have to take care of him."

She talks of her mother's death so serenely that I, too, simply accept this implausible event. I take the photograph out of the envelope. It is a color photograph. Amina is standing in the middle, with her husband and her children around her. She is smiling. She knows that her illness is incurable and that she will soon die, but she doesn't look troubled. Her hair has turned gray and there are beautiful wrinkles under her eyes. She is wearing a white sari; it is wrapped around her thin figure like delicate ivy. All these changes have enhanced her beauty—the beauty of a bird that has given wing to her chicks and is now ready to fly to faraway lands. The twins look like their father—blond and blue-eyed. But they have their mother's smile and playful eyes. Half-French, half-Bangladeshi. Madam Amina's children.

"What about Mohsen?" I ask. "Will he stay or go back?"

Shalima's answer is vague. Perhaps.

"This boy has taken after my mother," she says. "He can't sit still. He wants to work. He has no patience for studying. All he thinks about is traveling. But I'm not worried about him. I know my mother's spirit is watching over him."

Ms. Shalima, the pediatrician, shakes my hand, says goodbye, and leaves. Her gait resembles her mother's saunter when in her fantasies she saw herself starring in a sad, romantic film, or when she hummed and danced in front of the mirror.

Amina's photo sits in front of me like the last chapter of an enchanting book. Her face is alive and her expression changes from one moment to the next. Amina appears before my eyes. She is young, she is beautiful, and then she fades away only to reappear, submerged in muddy waters and thrashing about. The flood has swept away her home, her mother, and her brothers. They pull Amina out of the water. She is alive. She breathes. Her children's destiny is in her womb, in the depths of her soul; an ancient mother worrying for her offspring. Her journey has no end, and her heart, beyond unfamiliar horizons, beats for her children, for her grandsons and granddaughters, for those who will be born in another time, in the never-ending cycle of births and rebirths.

THE NEIGHBOR

*A*ll of us—my children, the friends who occasionally visit us, I myself—are scared stiff of the
downstairs neighbor. Our lives as foreigners in
Paris are full of hidden anxieties. To begin with, we feel guilty for
having taken up space that rightfully belongs to the natives, yet
hidden beneath our apologetic smiles and submissiveness lurks
an anger that stings and lies in wait for revenge. Humiliated, we
painfully swallow our pride—a pride that has been instilled in
us over the past two and a half millennia, a confidence that we
descendants of Cyrus the Great, even in defeat and despair, are
superior to the rest of the world (why, God only knows), and if
we have fallen on hard times, if little is left of our past glory and
splendor, you Western exploiters are to blame.

Even if this accusation is false, one thing is true: the cause
of my current misery is the woman who lives downstairs and
haunts our chaotic life like an evil spirit, omnipresent. We don't
dare walk, talk, or laugh. Having only recently arrived in this city,
unfamiliar with the hows and whys of life in the West, having
been hurled to this side of the world from the bosom of our
family and friends, from a spacious house with a sprawling gar-

den, we roam around like sleepwalkers and wonder how we can live in such tight quarters without disturbing our neighbors and being in anyone's way.

The children have turned into wild beasts. One is five and the other is four. They are nervous and agitated and they express their anxiety through earsplitting screams and by kicking and punching anything and everything in sight. My son hits my daughter, I hit my son, and our neighbor pounds on our door. Sometimes she bangs on her ceiling with a broomstick or a long pole, or shouts out the window, "Be quiet!"

Then, to be sure we have gotten her message, she comes upstairs to lodge a complaint in person. My timid gaze remains glued to the floor, my voice trembles as I awkwardly mumble a few words, my hand lingers outstretched in greeting, while my shaky legs are ready to beat a retreat and my body stays helplessly frozen in place. This is all proof of my guilt. I promise the downstairs lady that those inhuman sounds will never be heard again, that the children, even though they have not yet had dinner (who cares?), will immediately be sent to bed with a kick in the butt and a smack on the head, and that I myself, with my feet never touching the floor, will fly to the end of the hallway like a weightless mosquito and will stay under the mattress or if necessary under the bed for three days and three nights in deathly silence, and that I will make every effort to comply with the laws of the land and to observe the customs of the people of this city.

The downstairs lady does not believe a word I say. She again confronts me, again raises her voice, again glowers at me, again flares her nostrils, and in between her long sentences she huffs and puffs and hoots and howls and with all these sounds that resemble thunder and lightning she makes me understand that the situation is worse than ever and that war will continue to rage.

Our tiny, modest apartment is in the heart of Paris, on the fifth floor of a building that overlooks a church with several trees in its courtyard and a few sparrows and fat pigeons fluttering around under its eaves. The trees and the well-fed birds somehow remind us of our garden in Tehran and temporarily erase from our minds the memory of the woman downstairs. In addition to these superb advantages, our mousehole has a two-meter-long balcony where we entertain guests, relax, and enjoy some fresh air. We have crammed this sprawling garden with as many pots of geraniums and petunias as possible, and in the evenings, weather permitting, we sit in our green space, among the fragrance-free flowers, and leisurely savor large, tasteless cucumbers. If a friend happens to drop by, we invite her to join us in our make-believe garden so that she, too, can share our joy and forget her longing for the motherland.

The lady downstairs, or as the children have nicknamed her, Madame Wolf, disapproves of our use of the balcony and expresses her displeasure by intermittently screaming, "Quiet!" Her command is so forceful and authoritative that our voices choke in our throats and our smiles freeze on our lips. We give up sitting in our garden and sheepishly close the balcony door. I tell myself we have to be patient. Coming from a country ruled by hardline, anti-West mullahs, we are in no position to argue. We have been accused and found guilty of unknown crimes. Perhaps in this country people do not sit outside on their balconies and chuckle and giggle with their friends and they do not waste precious time in idle chitchat and casual folly. If they ever want to see a friend, it is probably to discuss politics or literature or

some other weighty matter, and they do this in a café and settle
the issue over a cup of strong coffee. My reasoning is convincing
to me, but the children are oblivious to it all. From the warm and
loving embrace of their grandmother and aunts and from bound-
less love and affection, they have been exiled to a cold, dreary, and
unemotional place and they cannot understand the reason for
such great injustice. They love the sound of the telephone and the
doorbell ringing. They even prefer the presence of Madame Wolf
to the silence and seclusion of our new home.

People here do not easily open up their homes to others.
First, they carefully look through the peephole to see who is
behind the door. Then they ask who you are and what exactly
you want. When they have made certain that you pose no danger, they undo the door chain, unlock the top and then the
bottom lock, and in the interim again look through the peephole and again ask questions until finally they cautiously open
the door a crack. If you have gone to their home without prior
notice, they will quickly send you away, and if you are there on
an urgent matter, they will deal with it right there at the door
and send you off.

Our front-door has no chain, no bolt, and no peephole. As
quick as the wind, without asking any questions, and excited
to have an unexpected guest, the children fling open the door
and invite whoever it is to come in; even Madame Wolf. I prefer
Madame Wolf to come in, sit, relax, and have a cup of tea, and
even if we have complaints and grievances, I would like us to
find the right moment to bring them up and discuss them. But
the lady downstairs has no time for any of this. She comes. She
knocks. She yells. She leaves. The lady concierge is the same way.
She comes. She knocks. She delivers the package that has come

in the mail. She leaves. Exchanging greetings and pleasantries are not customary.

Our next-door neighbor is a middle-aged woman. She is not foul-tempered, has no complaints against us, and does not pound on our door. In fact, she seems ignorant of our existence and her mind does not register our presence. Once in a while, I run into her in the hallway or we ride together on the elevator. Neither of us speaks. If I say hello, she will respond. If I don't, she says nothing. She leaves early in the morning and comes back late at night looking drained and exhausted. Her solitude troubles me. Imagining someone this isolated and alone in her own country makes my heart ache. The lady downstairs is alive. She is full of vitality. She is set against us and this itself is some sort of a relationship. There is not one second when we are not aware of her presence and there is nothing we can define or describe in our life that is independent of this knowledge.

I have enrolled the children in the local kindergarten and it is a relief to keep them away from Madame Wolf for a few hours every day. I wish the kindergarten were open until late at night and on Sundays, too. Taking the children there is not easy. They don't want to go; they are terrified of the teachers who speak a language they don't understand. The mornings are dark and often rainy. We don't have a car and have to walk the length of one avenue and three side streets, and the children weep most of the way. By the time we get to the second street, my son's daily stomachache starts. He writhes and clings to my leg and wants to go back home. I feel sorry for him, but as soon as I consider taking him back to the apartment, our neighbor's face suddenly appears before me and overrides my maternal compassion. In the mornings, my daughter is sleepy and groggy and practically catnaps all the way to the kindergarten. She sits down on the stairs in front of every single house on our route and yawns. If I let her, she will fall asleep right there. The only way I can get her to continue walking is with the lure of chocolate and candies. As soon as she sits down, I show her a piece of candy with a colorful wrapper. She leaps up and for the love of sweets runs two or three meters. But the instant she devours it, she again sits down and snoozes. Finally, I grab the back of her collar and drag her the rest of the way. The rain is a big nuisance, too. The children refuse to stay under the umbrella and are soaked to the skin by the time we arrive at the kindergarten. I worry that they will catch a cold and that the sound of their coughs and sneezes will reach the sensitive ears of the lady downstairs.

If Iran was not at war, I would go back home. If it weren't for my fear of the bombs and rockets, I would not stay here a single day. But in truth, the real battlefield is here. We are always either retreating or evading and an invisible machine gun is constantly aimed at us. Saddam Hussein is on the other side of the world, but Madame Wolf is only a few steps away, sitting in ambush. And like prisoners of war, we have put our hands on our heads and with humiliation and shame we have surrendered to her. In fact, what makes us so obsequious is our inability to speak or understand the French language. The enemy attacks with a sword of words and we remain defenseless.

The lady downstairs has come up with a new strategy, a lengthy official letter—similar to a writ of execution—in which she has issued seven or eight key directives. Immediately cover the parquet floors with heavy carpeting so that there will be less noise when you walk. Avoid wearing shoes (especially those with high heels) and wooden slippers. Do not sit out on the balcony. Do not talk in the bathroom or the kitchen because the ventilation ducts carry sound. Do not take showers or flush the toilet early in the morning or after nine in the evening. Do not slam the closet doors. Do not make any loud sounds, such as laughing, sneezing, coughing, and hiccupping. And the final directive, underlined in red, emphasizes the need for us to spend less time at home and to go out more often.

It seems I have no choice but to comply. I immediately cover the floors with thick wall-to-wall carpeting. We walk barefoot and our conversations have turned into murmurs and whispers. Friends who come to visit us take off their shoes at the door. Our fear has infected them, too. We have accepted the fact that we must be cautious and silent and deny ourselves the freedom to live as we wish. We have gradually forgotten that we are human beings and that every individual is free within the four walls of his or her home. We have quickly and without argument obeyed the orders dictated to us and we have submissively accepted Madame Wolf's tyranny.

Madame Wolf is aware of her supremacy and with every day that passes she sharpens her fangs even more. Of all the directives she has issued, the last one is the most difficult to obey—"spend less time at home." Where can we go? Most of my friends are artists and writers and don't have spouses and children. They are not wealthy and don't have the means to entertain guests. They live in small rooms crammed with books and papers or easels and canvases. Their homes are not well-suited to children. And the few friends who are married and have children are so fed up with their own kids that they cannot bear to have more of them around. As a result, our only escape is to go to the park. There is a shabby one on our street. It is a haunt for old women and Arab housekeepers, and late at night, drunken beggars gather there to divvy up their day's earnings. I hate this park. It depresses me. The children's only entertainment there is to play in the sandbox or to go up and down a dilapidated slide. The Luxembourg Gardens is beautiful, but it is far away and going long distances in Paris's unpredictable weather is difficult with two small children. By the time we get there, it usually starts to rain. Coming from a sunny country, we are still not accustomed to carrying hats and umbrellas and we are often caught off guard and end up standing for hours under a store awning, waiting for the rain to stop.

My happiest hours are when the children are asleep, the lights downstairs have been turned off, and I have three or four letters from friends and relatives in Tehran or scattered around the world. I don't read the letters as soon as they arrive; I wait to read them in bed, late at night, with a cup of hot coffee and a hearty cigarette. The first one is from Lili who lives in Tehran and is, or pretends to be, happy and content with her life. Her children are going to school, have two thousand friends, play in the garden or roam around the streets and squares of their neighborhood, and they are not scared of the war and the bombings. Lili works, she doesn't mind wearing hijab, and every night she goes to a party or has dozens of guests at her house. The second letter is from Dariush A. It is so sad and bitter that I want to cry. He is out of work and out of money. His son is a fugitive, his friends have fled the country, and he has such a grim view of the future that it terrifies me. The third letter is from Mr. K. It is a precise and concise report of all the bad news. His nephew has been executed by firing squad, his mother has twice tried to commit suicide, inflation is wreaking havoc and soon everyone will die of hunger, and every night Afghani laborers raid people's homes and decapitate women and children, young and old. Moreover, the Russians have come to terms with the Americans and Iran's Balkanization is certain, and his gardener's sons have joined the Revolutionary Guards in the Mahmoudieh district and they want to confiscate all his assets and belongings.

The last letter is from my mother. It is several pages long and reads like the screenplay for a shoddy Iranian movie—it is full of contradictions and inconsistencies. According to her, people are extremely fortunate and extremely miserable. There is no end to the parties, outings, and entertainments. Everyone is always together, eating, drinking, and they are all grateful to the Islamic Republic. Then the page turns and the sentences that follow speak of the intolerable hardships people are suffering. There is no electricity, no water, no meat in the market, there is plague, there are no doctors and no medicine, there is no safety and security, there is no police force . . . inflation, high prices, and famine are ravaging the country, there are two meters of snow on the ground, there is no fuel, the weather is deadly cold, and worse of all, she must endure loneliness and separation from her children. At the end of the letter, she again curses and cusses at the West and boasts that in Iran people have everything, that living in their own city they are their own boss and not indebted to and at the mercy of Westerners, and that all those who went abroad have made a grave mistake. Then she reverts back to the parties and feasts and in the end she suddenly and very true to character announces that she intends to sell the house and everything she owns and that she will find a hole in some corner of the world where she can spend the final days of her life in peace and quiet.

It is late. I can't sleep. My daughter has chickenpox and she is burning with fever. I am worried and I don't know whom to turn to for help. I want to write, but my brain doesn't work. I leaf through the book I am holding. I read one page and realize that I have not registered a single sentence. It has been raining nonstop for two days. I wish someone would stop by.

The children are asleep. They both have a fever. I tell myself I should go back to Iran. At least in my own city I have a mother, an aunt, and an uncle whom I can turn to for help, and there will be no one living above me or below me. There, I am not afraid of my neighbors and I can jump up and down in my own home as much as I like. I can laugh. I can wail and weep. I can dance. Dariush A. is the only person who is urging me to stay in Paris. "My dear," he writes, "who says you will be free in your own home? You will not be able to breathe, talk, think, dress, eat, or even defecate in any manner other than the one prescribed by the government and in accordance with Islamic norms. Even mating and dying are not free of rules and government control. Every moment of your life will be preregulated."

I jump at the sound of someone knocking on the front door. Who could it be? The doorbell doesn't work. The person is now banging on the door. It must be bad news; I am sure of it. My heart is pounding. A thousand thoughts rush through my mind. Something has happened to my mother. My brother has been arrested. It is the police. It is a friend on the run. I drop my book. My foot gets caught in the bedside lamp's wire. I quickly pull a long shirt over my nightgown and run to the door. "Coming! One minute," I say in Persian and in French as I open the door. What? It's Madame Wolf. At this hour of the night? She is usually asleep by now and we have given her no reason to come and knock on the door. I stand there confused. I feel I have turned pale. My heart is still pounding in my chest. I am frustrated by my own awkwardness and the way I am stammering. Madame Wolf bristles as soon as she notices how shaken and nervous I am.

"What is going on?" she roars. "What are you doing?"

"When?"

"What is all this racket?"

"What racket?"

I have been conditioned to believe she is always right. I think the children must have woken up and are jumping up and down. I run toward their room. There is total silence. There is absolutely no noise in the apartment and the downstairs lady is wrong. She is wrong and I can say so to her face. This is a matter of two plus two makes four. It has nothing to do with fluency in the French language or knowledge of the culture and customs of the West. This has to do with simple human logic. This time, I will not give in to her. I am right and being right is a great advantage that gives me power and courage. I hold my head up and raise my voice.

"What noise?" I ask.

Madame Wolf did not expect a rejoinder and is not used to being questioned. She pokes her head inside the apartment and takes a quick look around.

"What noise?" I ask again in a louder voice.

Madame Wolf looks confused and her unprecedented hesitation makes me bolder. An old visceral rage surges in me and spreads through my body like a fever. I feel hot. I start to sweat.

"What noise?" I holler so loudly that Madame Wolf leaps back in shock. She did not expect such anger from me. I become even more daring and take a step forward. This time, I glower at her and stare into her eyes and for the first time I see her for who she really is: an ordinary woman, about my age, approximately the same height and weight as me, with short, brown, greasy hair. Unlike most Frenchwomen, she is not neatly and elegantly dressed. There are two deep lines on either side of her mouth that make her look bitter and surly. She seems tired and tense. She is pregnant. She looks like all sad women who go to work at the crack of dawn and at night pass out in front of the television.

In broken French, I explain that the children are sleeping and that I was in bed. I struggle through a few more muddled sentences in an effort to make myself understood and then, frustrated and self-conscious, it suddenly occurs to me to speak in English, a language I am fluent in. The French mock Americans and with haughty airs refuse to learn English. But their contempt is only superficial; deep inside, they are impressed and infatuated with America and Americans.

I open my mouth and a torrent of words gush out. I feel as if I have grown wings and can fly. No one can stop me. I float in an ocean of words, my thoughts and words become one. I no longer have to trim my phrases and speak in short, simple sentences. I want to pontificate. I am drunk with the power of my speech. I can curse in English, and I do. I don't know if Madame Wolf understands what I am saying, but I don't care. The tone of my voice, my blazing eyes, and my aggressive gestures make the lady downstairs understand that she has to get lost and that if she ever shows up at my door again, the biggest piece left of her will be her ear. The filthy, miserable, stupid piece of shit. I flail my arms and raise one foot as if I am going to kick her. As I roar and soar, Madame Wolf seems to shrink and shrivel. I swell, I become taller, and I grow two sharp teeth like Dracula's fangs.

Madame Wolf looks like a small lamb about to be slaughtered. She lets out a short shriek and runs for the elevator. I will not relent. God only knows what I am ranting. Captivated by my own power, I want to go upstairs, knock on all the doors, and order everyone to shut up. I want to tell all the tenants that they are not allowed to talk or walk or sit outside on their balconies.

Gasping, the lady downstairs jumps into the elevator the second its door opens and she disappears. There is no sign of her the next day and the days that follow and the next month and the months that follow. She seems to have melted and vanished into the ground. Much later, we run into each other in the hallway near the building's entrance. We both quickly look the other way and walk away from each other. The only memory of her that lingers in my mind is her large stomach and her tired eyes. She is in the final days of her pregnancy.

In the absence of Madame Wolf's daunting presence, life becomes normal. We walk in the apartment with our shoes on and we talk comfortably and without dread. On sunny days, we even sit outside on the balcony and we are not afraid to laugh. The children are calmer. We go out when we want to and if we stay out it is by choice and not by force.

Summer arrives. It is almost dawn when an infant's shrieks wake me up. I listen carefully. The noise is coming from downstairs. I smile. Madame Wolf is trapped. Now, it is her turn to shish and shush and to go without sleep.

Years pass and I am still thinking about going back to Iran. The children have grown up and no longer cry and sulk because they have to go to school; they walk there and back on their own. They are less apprehensive and Madame Wolf's presence has become just an old memory.

It is a typical autumn Sunday. The sky is overcast and a biting wind is blowing. The children are home and we have guests coming in the evening. I go out to buy a few things from the Arab grocery store that is open on weekends. I walk past the dreary neighborhood park and I catch sight of Madame Wolf sitting on a bench, staring into the distance. She has raised her coat collar against the cold. There is a half-open book on her lap, a half-extinguished cigarette between her fingers, and her hair is as usual greasy and disheveled. Her right leg is stretched out, her foot is turned inward, and her shoe has slipped off. A little girl is sitting on the ground in front of her. Madame Wolf looks so broken and depressed that I feel sorry for her. Why is she sitting in this miserable park in the cold and wind? Remembering days gone by, I recall her letter of commands. Without a doubt, a neighbor has ordered her to keep her child outside the building as much as possible. Another Madame Wolf has sharpened her teeth for her. Thought of this depresses me. In this modern building overlooking a church and a courtyard, dozens of wolf-like sheep are sitting in ambush, blaming each other for their miseries; tired, hopeless wolves with petty desires and illusory dreams, waiting for better days.

I wonder if things could have been different. Could they?

Two or three drops of rain fall on my face. I walk faster. The lady downstairs is still sitting there, looking dazed and perplexed. A drunken beggar is lying unconscious under a tree. Or perhaps he is dead. No one looks at him. I think about the reception I am hosting and my guests who will be arriving soon. I hurry to the grocery store and in my haste to read my shopping list, I forget the question I had asked myself only a moment ago.

UNFINISHED GAME

Orly Airport, Flight 766, Iran Air.

he Paris-Tehran flight is completely full. The pleas, supplications, pomposities, and pretensions are all to no avail. There are no more seats available for anyone. Not for the rich, not for the poor, not for the elderly, not for the sick, and not for the foreigners. Not even for the French. Yet, for some unknown reason—some sort of hereditary optimism and faith in divine grace—the passengers without seats on the flight are emphatic and won't budge from their place. The impossible does not exist and the door is never completely closed. A man who believes in this magic door quietly recites:

"If God in his wisdom closes a door

In his mercy he opens another door."

The passengers are all waiting for this other door to open. Not only will they not step back from the ticket counter, but while chatting and eyeing their suitcases, they slowly push forward. If the airline were Air France or Lufthansa, they would leave, because those airlines don't have a magic door. Foreign carriers have an electronic door that opens and closes based on scientific principles and it has nothing to do with divine grace. Apparently, last week there was an even larger crowd for even fewer available seats. But at the last moment, the usual miracle happened and everyone boarded the plane. (Did the airplane expand? Did the seats multiply? No one knows.)

Today's passengers, too, are convinced that in the end everything will somehow work out. How? It's hard to say, because it is outside the realm of science and mathematics. Of course, these suddenly available seats don't fall from the sky, they are not free divine blessings. They belong only to the deserving and the capable—the clever and the shrewd who know how the system works. The best approach is to find an acquaintance with behind-the-scenes influence, or to contrive a convenient, heartrending tale. But the first and last rule is to get ahead of the person next to you—with a smile or a jab, it makes no difference. The point is to gain ground, with persistence and perseverance, with agile steps, deft kicks, elbow pressure, or brute force.

A distraught young woman, with peculiarly red lips and excess luggage (two suitcases, three carry-on bags, and two plastic bags stuffed with odds and ends), steps on my toes and shoves herself in front of me. She is nervous and rushed and ignores the passengers' gripes and grumbles.

"The end of the line is over there. The head of the line is over here. Wait your turn. Dear woman, please step back."

The dear woman is deaf to the objections. She stubbornly explains that her mother is sick and could die any minute. They must let her board the plane. She's willing to sit on the floor. She's willing to stand. She's willing to hang from the wing or to sleep in the cargo section. She will do anything they want, as long as they let her get on the plane.

Another passenger also pushes his way forward. He is shaking with anxiety—real or fake. He explains that his father has Alzheimer's disease and that he has been missing for some time. It seems the man walked into a cinema, but he didn't walk out. The cinema only had one exit door. Everyone walked out except his father. They've looked for him everywhere. He must go to Tehran to find his father.

"Please, no matter how, put me on the plane. I'm just one person," he pleads.

Ignoring the other passengers, Just Her and Just Me stand face-to-face, with glaring eyes and bodies ready to pounce.

"My good man," someone says, "you should have come to the airport sooner. Before your father got lost. You should have planned ahead."

People are curious. They are discussing the incident. How can someone get lost in a movie theater?

"Did they look under the seats?" someone asks.

"Yes. Behind the screen, under the stairs . . . they looked everywhere."

A pessimist wearing sunglasses says, "Your father was probably kidnapped." And he says is it as if he has secret information.

The young man is upset. He fidgets. He doesn't like this line of reasoning.

"My father is eighty-six. Why would anyone want to kidnap him?" he says.

The pessimist gravely shakes his head and says, "For a thousand and one reasons."

Once again, the passengers are informed that there are no more seats available.

"Ladies and gentlemen, the flight is full."

Do you understand? Full—with a stress on the *l*. *Fullllll*. Stop insisting. Please leave.

No one moves.

The ladies and gentlemen ignore the announcement. A sleepy-looking woman (probably traveling from far away, perhaps from America) pushes her luggage cart forward. She begs everyone's pardon and makes her way to the front.

My eyes linger on her face, on her mouth, her neck, and with a strange sense of curiosity, my gaze seeks her eyes. I wish she would take off her sunglasses. She looks familiar. I've seen her somewhere. I look at her more carefully and I wonder why I suddenly feel uneasy. A tiny pebble has scraped the membrane of my memory. The woman is poised and confident. She has a seat on the plane and she is holding her boarding pass.

Who is she?

A hazy image crosses my mind. I see a face, faded and fragmented. There is a name at the tip of my tongue; it jiggles my memory. Azadeh Derakhshan? Maybe.

I peek at her, secretly, from the corner of my eyes. A sudden anxiety creeps through my body. A sort of sweet foreboding that belongs to long ago. Long ago, meaning when I was fifteen or sixteen, meaning Anoushiravan Dadgar High School, sports tournaments, André sandwich shop, the neighborhood boys, Lalehzar Avenue, and Cinema Iran. Long ago, meaning Azadeh Derakhshan, unbeatable, the champion of all sports, the heroine of my dreams.

The fortunate passengers who have a seat on the plane have checked in their luggage and like a triumphant troop they pass before us. I push aside the Just Me's (ignoring their objections) and make my way to the front of the crowd.

"Sir . . ."

Sir is busy and doesn't answer.

I have to come up with a story, a moving story, gut-wrenching and deserving of an excellent seat on the plane.

In a soft and innocent tone, I say, "Dear sir . . ."

Dear this and dear that isn't going to work. I have to wait. My name is last on the waiting list.

A woman is looking for a kindhearted and trustworthy passenger who would agree to take some medication to Tehran for her ailing mother. "If my mother doesn't receive this medicine within the next twenty-four hours, she will die," the woman says.

No one volunteers. It seems the old mother is condemned to death.

Finally, the-maybe-Azadeh Derakhshan (I am still not certain it is her) agrees to take the package. She writes down the name and address of the recipient. Whoever this woman is, she is refined and meticulous. She is reliable. My obstinate gaze chases after her and crawls along the trail of time, looking at the fantasy image of Azadeh Derakhshan.

It's her. With one hundred percent certainty.

At last, the woman takes off her sunglasses. The look in her eyes, her figure, and her face resemble Azadeh Derakhshan. Yet it isn't her. Definitely not. Azadeh Derakhshan was beautiful— young, slim, and agile. Of course, there were many who were beautiful, but more than thirty years have passed and most of those beauties have changed. Or died. Now, let's assume this woman is Azadeh Derakhshan. So what? Good for her. I want to say, The hell with her, and get over it. But I can't. What if it is her? Despite the uncertainties, this chance encounter stabs at me like the sudden pain of a bad wisdom tooth.

The general manager of the airline—the big boss—arrives. He is the decision maker. Once again, everyone is pushing, shoving, assailing. Two men get into a polite argument—in Persian, peppered with French, a mishmash of linguistic errors. Persian, peppered with English, an even greater mishmash of linguistic errors. A few passengers intervene. No one knows what the argument is about, nor do they know who is in the right.

"Gentlemen," someone says, "you should be ashamed of yourselves, behaving like this in front of foreigners. It's no surprise that they say we are a backward people."

"The hell with them," someone else retorts. "Two thousand years ago when we slept on silk quilts and ate out of gold plates they didn't even exist."

A woman laughs and says, "For now, it's us who don't exist and they who sleep on silk quilts."

I'm still desperately hoping to get a seat on the plane when I see an airline employee who is an acquaintance. This is what they call the "gates of mercy." I leap and grab the man by the collar. Friendly greetings, pleas and supplications, until finally, the bewildered acquaintance who doesn't remember me and can't recall my name (thinking, Maybe this woman has mistaken me for someone else), out of decency and respect, offers me a half-baked promise. I grab onto his promise—like a tick—and with his help I manage to get a seat on the plane. Others, too, via other "gates of mercy," make their way onto the plane. Drenched in sweat and exhausted, but triumphant, people flop down on the first empty seats they find. No one pays any attention to the seat numbers.

To my left, next to the window, there's a devout man mumbling prayers. His eyes are closed and he is gently nodding his head. He is twisting a long strand of prayer beads around his fingers, untwisting it, retwisting it, and going through the motions again and again. I turn away. The strand of yellow prayer beads twirls in my head. I decide to change my seat.

Azadeh Derakhshan (?) is looking for her assigned seat. She carefully checks the seat numbers and looks at her boarding pass. Her seat is two rows away, next to the window. Some of the passengers are still looking for a place to store their bags. Each time they open the door to an overhead compartment, a bunch of things tumble out.

I ask the flight attendant, "May I change my seat?"

She shakes her head and points at the bright seatbelt light. An elderly woman is looking for the section designated for praying. She stumbles and almost falls.

The plane is ready for takeoff. A heartwarming prayer for mercy and compassion is broadcast over the speaker system.

The Iran Air flight, chaotic and casual, is a world unto itself. It's like Tajrish Bridge in the old days, when people—men, women, children, young and old—gathered there in front of Villa Ice Cream or at the corner of Sadabad Avenue to eat and to socialize. It is bustling and noisy. People are coming and going, they are talking, debating, joking, and gossiping. And all the while, the harried flight attendants are desperately trying to show us the emergency exits in case of a crash, and instructing us on how to use the life vests in case of an explosion, and the pilot is reporting on our altitude and the temperature outside. Yet most of the passengers rely on their faith. They believe in fate and destiny. What must happen will happen. Safety instructions don't change anything.

The open area in front of the first row, next to the exit, is a difficult spot. The two-square-meter space is the gathering spot for men and the hub of political debates. It is also where children play and old women pass through on their way to and from the bathrooms, from the moment the plane takes off to the moment it lands.

The plane is jerking up and down and jolting from side to side. The passengers are unperturbed; no one thinks about the possibility of a crash and the probability of death. Conversations are all about the high price of meat and chicken, the exchange rate for the dollar, the price of real estate, how to pass through customs in Tehran, and where to hide fashion magazines and videotapes of Western films and music (tucked in the jacket, at the bottom of the handbag, inside the shirt, under the girdle).

The passengers sitting behind me are arguing over a blanket. Within minutes of boarding, all the pillows and blankets were seized and many people are left without.

Children are running up and down the aisle, pushing and shoving each other.

I snap at one of them, "You little baboon, if you kick me one more time, I'll teach you a lesson you won't forget."

The child stares at me and walks away backwards. He turns the corner behind the bathroom and then peeks out and makes a face at me.

Impudent brat.

I wish I could fall asleep. I'm tired and my feet have swelled in my shoes. I close my eyes. Azadeh Derakhshan is fluttering around behind my eyelids. She appears and disappears in different guises, she swings on my thoughts and leaps from one memory to another, from one year to the next. I remember waking up every morning eager to see her.

Excited and happy, I quickly get ready, grab my schoolbag, and run to take the Shemiran bus. Azadeh Derakhshan is usually on this bus. She sits in the back and reads. She is two years ahead of me in school. She nods to me and goes back to her book. She is the most important student in high school and she doesn't often acknowledge people this easily. She is the running and jumping champion. She's the champion of all sports. No one can beat her. And to me, she is the most complete human being in the world. I want to catch up with her and, shoulder to shoulder, run past everyone else. I want to get an A+ and hang my report card on all the walls in the world. Everyone dreams of being like her. Tall. Slim. With that chestnut-colored hair and the plaid scarf she ties sideways around her neck, with that sun-kissed skin and those prominent cheekbones. I am light-years away from her. To begin with, I am two years younger and half a meter shorter than her, and I get an F in physical education. I follow her on the street—from Shah Reza Avenue to the intersection of Pahlavi Avenue—at a twenty-meter distance. I stop wherever she stops. I look at whatever she looks at. I step on the same lines, on the same cracks in the asphalt, and in the same potholes. I hold my head high and my shoulders back, one hand swinging free and the other in my pocket, just like her. I am in love with her; an adolescent infatuation that will possess me for years to come.

A flight attendant announces that they will soon serve a warm, delicious meal. At the mention of food, the passengers all hurry back to their seats.

The man sitting next to me jolts up. He's ill. He drops his prayer beads, takes a large handkerchief from his pocket, and holds it in front of his mouth.

The flight attendant is tired and moody, but she is still smiling. She has a plain and pleasant face.

"Chicken and rice or kebab and rice?" she asks.

The passenger next to me buries his face in his handkerchief and shakes his head.

"Chicken and rice," I say. But I realize that my stomach is churning and it is impossible to eat sitting next to this sick man.

The unruly boy is again running up and down the aisle and knocking into everyone. The minute he comes near me, I pinch his ear and twist it. He yelps.

A crew member takes the boy by the hand and walks him down the aisle and row by row shows him to the passengers. No one knows him. There's no mother or father in the picture. Or if there is, they prefer not to speak up.

After dinner, they turn the lights off to show a movie. I think about Azadeh Derakhshan. Could this sad, worn-out woman sitting a few rows away be my childhood heroine? Is it possible?

The man next to me has fallen asleep and he's making a strange noise. I look around. I have to change my seat. I take my handbag and set off. On the left side of the aisle there is an empty seat. I don't know whether it is really available or if its occupant is wandering around somewhere. I ask the flight attendant. She is frustrated and fed up with the passengers.

"Lady," she snaps, "just find a seat and sit down."

Two rows down, there is another empty seat. It's next to the woman who may or may not be Azadeh Derakhshan. She has taken off her sunglasses and she is taking a nap.

Should I or shouldn't I? I'm indecisive. I look around. There are no more empty seats and someone has already taken my original seat. I sit down, fasten my seatbelt, and take a quick peek at the woman. Long eyelashes, deep wrinkles around the eyes, two distinct lines across the forehead. She stretches her legs and opens her eyes.

The seats are small and uncomfortable and her arm gently presses against mine. This simple contact, this slight, passing touch, strings together the scattered beads and connects the dispersed fragments.

Azadeh Derakhshan (I speak her name in my mind with certainty) looks at me from the corner of her sleepy eyes and pulls herself to the side. She closes her book—a book in English—which had remained open on her lap and she stares out of the window.

Nervous, tired hands with protruding blue veins. She is half-asleep. Her book slips on her lap. She leans her head against the window and sighs, a loud, deep sigh mixed with a stifled yawn and a few mumbled words. She takes off her silk headscarf. The same lustrous short hair, with a few strands of white on her temples. She puts her headscarf back on and secures it with a tight knot under her chin. For an instant, her childhood look, fresh and radiant, emerges from deep inside her aging face and then retreats again like a sad expression behind a thin mask.

I don't have the courage to speak. I'm wary. I practice in my mind: Excuse me, are you Azadeh Derakhshan?

No. Are you . . . is a stupid, bookish sentence. It has to be simple and to the point: Azadeh Derakhshan? Simple. Casual.

What if she doesn't answer? What if she says I've mistaken her for someone else?

She takes a postcard out of her handbag and starts to write. She is left-handed. Azadeh Derakhshan used to use her left hand to hold the ping-pong racket. It must be her. But something is missing. She is broken, dusty, faded, like a precious painting abandoned for years in a humid cellar. Nevertheless, a few hints of her simple beauty and proud profile remain, unscathed.

She doesn't know that I, the passenger sitting next to her, know her past and that the memory of her youth (our youth) is still vivid in my mind.

The schoolyard appears before my eyes. Mrs. Banou, the Zoroastrian supervisor, is wielding a long cane and inspecting the students. Wearing ankle socks is forbidden and Azadeh Derakhshan is wearing white ankle socks and sneakers. Mrs. Banou whips her bare legs with the cane. Then she comes after me. She stabs the tip of the cane into my ponytail and walks me around the schoolyard like a bundle hanging from the end of a stick.

Azadeh Derakhshan knows English (at least more than the rest of us do, more than volume one of *Essential English*) and she reads foreign magazines. She brings them to school and during recess she sits on the stairs outside and leafs through them. The entire schoolyard is filled with her presence. I see no one but her. The other students wandering about transform into pale shadows and the teachers lose their power and authority. She is different from everyone else, especially from me. I am clumsy and shy and no matter how hard I try to at least become a second-rate champion at some sport—ping-pong, running, jumping, or basketball—I don't get anywhere. In late afternoons, after our last class, we are allowed to stay in the schoolyard and practice sports. Of all the options, I have chosen disc throwing. Frail and scrawny and having only recently recovered from pneumonia, I will collapse if someone so much as blows on me, but I want to go up against an invisible opponent. I want to receive the gold medal so that I can show it to Azadeh Derakhshan. I want to be noticed. I want to state my presence. Despite all my efforts and hours of practice, the steel disc plops down to the ground right at my feet. I don't have the strength to throw it even half a meter away. I give up. Instead, I opt for jumping. I rank last. I choose swimming. I have shortness of breath and get heart palpitations. I catch pneumonia again and stay in bed for a month.

Oblivious to my sad struggles, Azadeh Derakhshan saunters around, head and shoulders above and thousands of meters ahead of everyone else. She smokes and talks politics. She reads leftist books and has her own particular beliefs. She says she will become a great writer. A few of her poems have been published in *Tehran-e Mossavar* newspaper and the teachers all look at her with respect.

We live in the same neighborhood. In Shemiran. We take the same bus and I secretly watch her. I look at her for so long that she notices and laughs. Her white teeth gleam. Her gaze passes over me indifferently and moves on to someplace far away, somewhere beyond Anoushiravan Dadgar High School and the Shemiran bus. She gets off one stop before me, but her proud look and confident smile stay with me until the next morning and all the mornings that follow.

Where is she traveling from? Why has she gotten fat? Fat and sad. The lines on her forehead, the wrinkles around her eyes, and the protruding blue veins on her hands are not temporary. They are the product of time and hidden pains, of the anger that ripples in her eyes and the anxiety that stirs in her hands.

She glances at me and again pulls herself aside, giving me more room. I'm waiting for a familiar look and a friendly hello, for an expression of surprise and joy. I wait. Azadeh Derakhshan, drowsy and distant, is deep in her own thoughts. No, she doesn't remember me, nor does she remember the ping-pong matches, the Shemiran bus, the teachers, the exams, our tricks and the times we cheated. I wonder . . . perhaps I, too, have changed as much as she has, maybe even more. I try to picture my reflection in her dazed eyes. A heavy weight presses down on my chest. I want to take off the mask of time and reveal the face I used to have.

We were supposed to have a fencing match in front of Queen Soraya. It was her birthday and several high schools had organized a sports event. Our program was the most interesting. We had rented fencing outfits and wore mesh masks and white leather gloves. There were four of us from the same class. The sports instructor from the Firouz Bahram boys' high school taught us the basic fencing moves and every afternoon we practiced in the schoolyard.

The sports stadium was packed. Queen Soraya, wearing dark glasses and a striped dress, was in a special stand with important people from the royal court. The cheers and screams of the high school girls were deafening. Queen Soraya wasn't smiling, she didn't like noise. I was thinking of Azadeh Derakhshan. Our turn came. We walked into the arena and our classmates cheered for us. We stood shoulder to shoulder. Heads up. Shoulders back. Confident. The Knights of the Round Table. We performed the special salute with our foils. Three times. Left, right, center. Then we started. At first we ran slowly, then faster and faster. The grass was soft under our feet. We had to stop and bow when we arrived in front of the Queen's stand. We had practiced it a hundred times and memorized every move. The gold medal was definitely going to be ours. Happy and proud, we were holding our foils up in front of our face. Our mesh masks were dirty and like a heavy veil they were limiting our vision. We were running toward the Queen's stand when suddenly all four of us stumbled and fell flat on our face. There was a thin wire stretched right across our path, a few centimeters off the ground. Whether it was there intentionally or accidentally, we never found out. Our flimsy mesh masks had squashed in and were pressing against our face, distorting our nose, lips, and eyes.

Queen Soraya laughed for the first time and her entourage was happy. We each received a bronze medal for making the Queen of Iran laugh. But Azadeh Derakhshan became the running and jumping champion. She received the gold medal from the Queen and restored our high school's honor.

I take shortcuts through my memories and arrive at the day when Azadeh Derakhshan and a girl from Nourbakhsh high school were having a ping-pong match. I was worried. Azadeh Derakhshan was in me, in my thoughts, in my fears; my young, skinny legs wanted to run alongside her, ahead of everyone else. What if she loses? Her loss will be my loss. The students—the Nourbakhsh students, who were our old rivals, and the Anoushiravan girls—were all standing around the gym. My heart was racing. Azadeh Derakhshan had the ball. She started the game. The score was 1—2 . . . 2—2 . . . 3—3 . . . it was a tie. They continued to score points equally until suddenly Azadeh Derakhshan fell behind. Her opponent's offensive smashes were deadly. Azadeh Derakhshan lost the first round. Sweat was streaming down her face. She was flushed and panting. Her nostrils were quivering. The screams and shouts, the cheers, the applause, the stomping, all echoed in my head. The ping-pong ball leapt back and forth. Azadeh Derakhshan was in the lead. She fell back again. 20—16. Azadeh was behind. 20—17. 20—18. 20—19. 20—20. Another tie. 20—20. Azadeh Derakhshan looked like a wolf. She had bitten her lip and there was blood in the corner of her mouth. She had to win. She was determined. She must. At any cost. She wanted to devour her opponent. Shred her into pieces. She showed no mercy. And then, something unexpected happened. Azadeh Derakhshan's opponent stopped playing. She was gasping for air. She staggered. Her face had turned blue. The fight was too nerve-racking for her. Azadeh Derakhshan was unaware. Even if she was aware, she didn't care. The hell with her opponent. There was only one thing on her mind. To win at any cost. The podium and the gold medal were hers.

For me, the match continued in my dreams, every night until dawn, chaotically, breathlessly, 18–18, 19–19, 20–20, a tie, it continued until the end of the school year, all through the summer, for years and years. In my mind, the match remained unfinished and once in a while an irrational desire to compete and win got hold of me.

The plane's treacherous jolts have started again. I must strike up a conversation with Azadeh Derakhshan. I'm nervous and uncomfortable. I fidget like a shy, pubescent girl. I have drifted back in time, into the old ambiguous anxieties of youth.

Azadeh Derakhshan has put on her reading glasses. She is flipping through her book.

I take the leap and ask, "Are you . . . ?" I pronounce her name slowly, with the shyness of an awkward schoolgirl.

Azadeh Derakhshan looks at me. She blinks. I introduce myself. I wait. My face feels hot and flushed. My name has a humble ring to it and it doesn't denote anyone in particular. She knots her eyebrows. There is a nervous look in her eyes, reticent and unsure. She glances at my face and looks me up and down. She is looking for someone else (someone younger?). And then, as if she has woken from a deep sleep, she breathes in, a sign of recognition spreads over her face and a kind of lively and youthful joy shines in her eyes. I repeat my name with greater confidence.

The half-forgotten names of the students, the teachers, the morning anthem, the events and games, the craziness, a horde of images, all compressed into hurried irrepressible words, gush from my lips, from her lips. It doesn't seem as if more than thirty years have passed since we last saw each other. At this very moment, Azadeh Derakhshan and I are in the past. Pahlavi Avenue, the old classrooms, and André sandwich shop are more real to us than this plane, than this man standing two feet away, than the flight attendant walking down the aisle. I know that in a few hours, as soon as we part ways, the past will fade away like an image on a screen, and if we coincidentally meet again, we will have nothing to say to each other. These emotional and exciting encounters are limited to one time only. They cannot be repeated and that is what makes them so precious.

I pick up the thread of a memory and start, and Azadeh Derakhshan races ahead of me and revives another recollection. We laugh. We are casual and comfortable. We are young. We don't talk about the ping-pong match. Not me, not her. All the better.

The cabin lights are turned off. The plane will soon land. We grow quiet. Quiet and sad. We have both returned to the present, to ten minutes past midnight at an altitude of ten thousand meters above Tehran, and to the anxiety of going through customs.

Azadeh Derakhshan is coming from America. It's her first trip back in fifteen years. She says she has two grown sons, one in Canada, the other in Texas. She is a nurse and has been working in a hospital all these years. She has worked hard and struggled. She wasn't with her mother when she died. She has returned to take back her house from a bunch of strangers who seized it in the heat of the revolution, to take back her husband who has taken a second wife, and to persuade her sons to come back to Iran. What great challenges await her. What disappointments.

I know her husband. It's a small world. The entire city knew that doctor so-and-so had married a younger woman—young enough to be his daughter. At a boring party, a nosy woman, one of those women who know about everything that goes on in the world, whispered in my ear, "That gentleman wearing the four-button jacket (gold-colored buttons) and white shoes, the one who is acting too young for his age, he is the doctor who has taken a second wife. The young woman over there is his new wife. His first wife is in America. Do you remember Azadeh Derakhshan? She was the ping-pong champion; a few years ahead of us in high school."

Azadeh Derakhshan, with the remnants of her wasted beauty, is sitting next to me. She doesn't talk about her husband. She talks about her mother's old cook who has taken possession of her mother's house and has no intention of moving out. She doesn't talk about the young woman who has taken possession of her husband. And she doesn't talk about herself either. She talks about her sons. About the older one who has a Vietnamese wife and who has changed his name (Akbar is now Ike). About the younger one who speaks Persian with an American accent and who has quarreled with his father and doesn't speak to him anymore. She talks about America, about the great loneliness in New York, the most crowded city in the world, about nursing and all the hard work she has done for the sake of her sons.

The landing gear is lowered and the captain's voice echoes in the cabin.

"Ladies and gentlemen, please remain seated until the aircraft has come to a complete stop." He emphasizes the word "seated."

The majority of the passengers are standing. Everyone is in a rush. Everyone wants to get ahead of everyone else.

Azadeh Derakhshan is nervous and excited and has a thousand worries. Her eyes dart back and forth. She has waited fifteen years for this moment.

"Things have changed, haven't they?" she asks. "A lot? The people? The street names?"

The passengers are standing in the aisle, pushing each other. The plane is still taxiing down the runway. Azadeh Derakhshan nervously looks out of the window. She is scared of showing her passport and the possibility of being interrogated.

We exchange telephone numbers. We make tentative plans. We say goodbye and part ways.

The passengers muscle their way ahead of each other. Those who are frequent travelers know the tricks. They know when to run, when to stop, where to take shortcuts, and how to get ahead while hauling all those bags. Climbing on board the bus that takes the passengers to the terminal requires know-how. Whoever gets on last gets off first and will be a good distance ahead of the others. Running, panting, he will get to the police and passport check booths before everyone else, he will pass the first two obstacles, he will triumphantly scramble up the stairs (two at a time), and he will be the first to pick up his luggage. "Just Me," fully focused on his goal, energy pumping through his veins, is the first person on line to go through customs' inspection. He is in a rush. He closes his suitcase, and pleased with his success hops into the first taxi and hurries home. He goes to bed early and wakes up at the crack of dawn. He arrives at work before all his colleagues, he gets ahead, and receives a promotion. He is the champion of the race of life and death. He retires before so-and-so and so-and-so. He rushes through the nights and the days, through the months and the years, and arrives at the end of the century before all those people he left behind, still waiting in the customs line. He will be first to cross the bridge to heaven.

Customs. Azadeh Derakhshan is ahead of me on line. She catches sight of me, but she doesn't acknowledge me. She is looking around, dazed and confused. Her headscarf is lopsided and she looks wretched. She recoils in fear every time a bearded man walks past her. I don't have too much luggage and I am not worried about getting through the inspection. My suitcase contains some clothes and personal items, a few gifts, some medicine, and French cheese for a special friend. In keeping with the regulations and based on logical reasoning, I should make it through without any trouble. I feel confident. I have the bearing of someone who is undaunted. Given that I don't have too many suitcases or any banned products, and given that I have committed no crime and no offense (as far as I know), I am cool and composed. And I am ignorant of the fact that standing in this pose (hands in coverall pockets and looking visibly indifferent) is a great infraction, and I have no clue that being unperturbed and looking detached (with a touch of unintended smugness) will work against me.

I have laid open my suitcase and with subtle gestures I am expressing my impatience. I am tired. I yawn. The customs agent seems decent and polite. He has a gentle face.

"Madam," he says, "we're all tired."

The passenger next to me wants to ingratiate himself. "Yes,

you're right," he says. "We're indebted to you. The country is in the hands of people like you. May you always succeed."

The agent goes about his business. He is used to such flatteries. He's had his fill of them. I think to myself, I'm lucky to have ended up with a kindhearted customs agent. But for some reason I feel he doesn't like me and he is not going to let me go easily. He's taking his time searching my suitcase. He's looking for an excuse. I try to be polite and humble. I smile. My smile and humility look fake and make matters worse. The gentle agent is carefully examining several boxes of medicine. He puts one of them aside.

As if talking to someone else, he casually mumbles, "This medication is banned."

No. I shouldn't get angry. I shouldn't argue. I shouldn't scream and shout. He is probably right. Some medicines have to be examined. But still, is anything in this country based on rules and regulations? Look, that woman just walked through with three huge suitcases.

Again, the agent says, "This medication has to be examined."

"Who has to examine it?"

"The officer in charge isn't here tonight. It has to be put in storage."

"You think people have nothing better to do?" I snap. "You think it's just that simple; go and come back tomorrow?"

"It has nothing to do with me. It's the law," he replies.

"Where is it written?"

"My dear sister, don't be obstinate or I will confiscate your entire suitcase."

The argument has gotten heated. One of us must defeat the other. The passenger next to me has a suitcase as big as a crate.

This is his fourth trip overseas this year. Regardless, he is holding his head down and wants to quietly sneak through. He even has a TV with him, in addition to a hundred pairs of children's socks and a hundred pairs of women's socks all stuffed in plastic bags. He is coming from Germany. He is a merchant and has to pay customs duty. But he begs and pleads. I'm your servant. I'm your obedient servant. Meek and humble. His stories are all tall tales, his promises are all lies. The customs agent speaks his language and knows his tricks. His position is clear. They argue. They haggle. A little discount here, a few tears and pleas there, and in the end, they reach a compromise. They are familiar with each other's world. The agent's behavior toward me is different. He thinks I'm conceited (I suppose I am) and that despite the revolution and all that has come to pass, I am still cocky and look down on the likes of him.

I will not give up. I will not give in.

"My good man," I say, "this is a vitamin and it is allowed."

I read the name on the box out loud. He doesn't respond.

I hold the box in front of his face and ask, "Can you read and write?"

I've been rude. Bad question. Alas.

The agent gives me a look, an angry look. His pride has been injured. He talks to the man next to me.

A tired passenger waiting his turn says, "Lady, what is it you don't understand? Go and come back tomorrow."

"It's written here: sodium chloride, amino acid, and potassium," I say.

"Lady!" the passenger shouts. "Give it up! Don't you understand Persian?"

A porter starts pestering me.

He whispers in my ear, "Pay me five and I'll pass your suitcase through."

I ignore him. I won't be bribed. By anyone. I'm right. Perhaps I'm not. In any case, I want to fight and to win.

I raise my voice. Futile posturing.

"Sister, stop shouting," the agent snaps. "This medication is banned."

"No it is not."

"Don't argue with me. I'm busy."

"I'm busy, too."

"Please move along, the other passengers are waiting."

A ping-pong ball bounces back and forth in my mind. 20–20. A tie. I must win. Azadeh Derakhshan bounces back and forth in my mind. It is she who gives the orders. Old voices ring in my ears. The students cheer. Eyes are glued on me.

"Come on, lady!" a woman gripes. "Give it up. It's almost dawn."

"Please don't interfere," I retort.

She loses her temper, raises her voice, and starts to shriek. An elderly, fatherly-looking man takes my side. The woman starts quarreling with him. The old man, the angry woman, the agent, and I take turns arguing.

The porter repeats his offer. "Pay me five and I'll pass your suitcase through."

"What do you want?" I shout. "Go away! Leave me alone. I won't pay you even two."

The customs agent says, "Go get permission from the chief."

Now, that sounds reasonable. At least I will be dealing with someone else.

"Where is the chief?"

The agent points behind him. I set off and the porter follows me. The chief's office is nearby. The door is ajar. I knock.

"Go in," the porter says. "Why are you knocking?"

No one answers my knock. A man walks out of the office and hurries away.

Again. Knock, knock, knock.

"Stop knocking," the porter says. "Just walk in. Can't you see there is no one there?"

He's right. There is no one in the office. A woman walks in holding a letter. I ask her where the chief is. She shakes her head. She's in a hurry and says, "Go ask the information desk."

"Where is the information desk?"

"There's a free phone at the end of the hallway," she says. "Go make a call."

"Whom should I call?"

"The domestic terminal."

"Let's go and make the call," the porter says. "I know how."

I turn to him and ask, "Call who?"

"The domestic terminal."

"Why the domestic terminal? What does this have to do with them?"

"I don't know."

"Are you nuts?"

The porter gets angry. The veins on his neck pop up.

"Why are you insulting me?" he says. "You are so nasty. Wasting my time. You're too stubborn."

The phone at the end of the hallway is free. A man pushes his way past me to get to it first. We both reach for the receiver.

"Excuse me," he says. "It's my turn."

He shoves me aside with his shoulder and starts dialing.

"Come on," the porter says. "Give me four and I'll pass your suitcase through."

I snap at him. He loses his temper, turns red in the face, and again the veins on his neck protrude.

"You are so foul-tempered," he grumbles. "Why are you shouting at me? It's not my fault. You think I'm the mayor? If you have the guts, go fight with him. Why are you picking on me?"

I go back to square one. The customs agent is busy. Again, more of the same.

"It's banned. You can't."

"It's not. I can."

Can't.

Can.

18—18. 20—20.

"Go file a complaint."

"I will."

"Leave me alone."

"I won't."

I shout. I'm short of breath.

"Is there gold in that box?" the porter says. "Just let them put it in storage. Come and pick it up tomorrow. The agent is only doing his job. Why do you want to embarrass him in front of everyone?"

"Huh?"

"Go home and get some sleep. You're making yourself sick. You're giving yourself a heart attack."

I see Azadeh Derakhshan in the distance. She looks sad and lost. Exhaustion, anxiety, and a deep sense of emptiness suddenly make me nauseous. The porter senses my sudden sadness. He sighs and shakes his head.

"We have bloody fights at home, too," he says. "The land-lord said we have to move out at the end of the month. I said, 'Where do you want me to go to?' My wife told me to file a complaint against him. She gives the orders. But the landlord was in cahoots with a bunch of junior street thugs. He came after me. Yelling and shouting. I hit him in the head with a hammer. The thugs got involved. I don't know what happened, but somehow my wife's skull got cracked. She has a profound sense of honor. You so much as make a comment and she'll slap you in the face."

The customs agent is tired. He stifles a yawn. He looks misera-ble and his mind is elsewhere. He has no patience left. It's late and most of the passengers have left. He is called away and another agent replaces him.

"Put the box of medicine in your handbag and let's go," the porter says. "Don't say a word."

The second agent is unaware of what has transpired. I toss the box of vitamins on the table and close my suitcase. It's a hollow loss and a hollow victory. A fight over nothing.

Still grumbling, the porter puts my suitcase on a trolley. He can't figure me out. It's almost dawn. The customs agents look drowsy. The flight from Damascus has just landed and hundreds of women clad in black chadors are scurrying up the stairs. Again the same supplications, the same tricks, the same double-deal-ings over a pair of socks, over a pittance.

"You raised all that havoc for what?" the porter says. "You've worn yourself out. All you had to do was pay me four thousand tumans, I would have taken care of everything, and you would have done me a good deed."

Perhaps.

"Why didn't you take the box of medicine?" he asks. "You just wanted to raise hell?

"It was a match."

He is confused. He looks at me for a second and then he asks for his money. I pay him. He haggles. He wants more.

"Taxi?"

"Yes."

I give the driver the address and I ask, "How much?" I want to determine the fare so that we don't get into an argument later.

"My treat," the driver says. "You're my guest."

"What is the fare?" I insist.

"Whatever you want to pay."

I am too tired to argue with him. I know this "you're my guest" ceremony. It is routine. In the end he will ask for more than the ride is worth.

I climb into the taxi, take my shoes off, and lean back. I can smell the fresh scent of the early morning and the warm aroma of a delicious breakfast. I can feel the pleasure of falling asleep in a warm, cozy bed.

The driver talks to a man standing next to the taxi (apparently a second passenger) and then he gets in behind the wheel.

"This gentleman will get off at the turn, then I'll drop you off," he says. "You will get to your destination. A little sooner, a little later, in the end we all get to our destination. Is it all right?"

I have no objections. The man takes the front passenger seat and we drive off.

Valiasr Avenue is rain-washed and clean. The same old sycamore trees full of new sparrows, the view of the old familiar mountains full of unfamiliar hikers. The other passenger says something to the driver. The driver nods and pulls over in front of a bakery. The man gets out. He buys a few freshly baked loaves of bread and returns. He offers the driver a large piece of bread and then offers me some. The smell of warm bread fills the car. I'm hungry and he doesn't need to insist. I eagerly take the bread and thank him from the bottom of my heart.

The early morning sun, lavish and warm, slithers over the man's hands, the rear seat, and the hem of my skirt, and then it climbs up and gently sits on the driver's shoulders. I feel a pleasant sensation creeping under my skin.

Half an hour later, the other passenger gets out, with only a small piece of bread left in his hand.

When we arrive, the sun is still in its full morning glory and the driver still doesn't want to accept any money. He ceremoniously rejects my offer and maintains that I should consider myself his guest. The same old rituals of courtesy. He carries my suitcase to the door. He gives me his telephone number and says, "Call me if you ever need anything. I'm always ready to serve."

He bashfully accepts the fare I offer him, closes the car door, nods to me, and drives away slowly.

The neighbor's dog is out on the street. It comes to welcome me and rubs its nose on my shoes. Behind this door (another gate to heaven), a safe and familiar world is waiting for me. I take a deep breath. The chaos of Iran Air Flight 766, its native generosity, its shrewd yet oppressed passengers, the disguised compassion and pointless aggressions, are all erased from my mind, as is Azadeh Derakhshan and the memory of that old unfinished game.

THE ENCOUNTER

I know going to Mr. M.'s party is a mistake. I feel it. Especially in these times of chaos and turmoil. Strict regulations are again in force. Again, headscarves have to be pulled down below the eyebrows. Again, we have to wear thick black socks and long, loose coveralls. Again, they are slashing women's bare legs with razors and shaving the heads of young boys with long hair. And yet, no one is frightened enough to conform and no one has been disciplined. Gathering together, chatting, eating and drinking, are requisites of survival.

Mr. M. is a former diplomat. He believes that our ancient heritage and the glory of the Persian monarchy have been buried in the dusty pages of history and that the Islamic regime will remain in power for years to come. And so, he lives his life. He eats well, drinks well, exercises, reads, he has a satellite dish and watches foreign television programs, and he goes to parties or hosts them. He knows the Revolutionary Guards at the committee branch in his neighborhood. He stuffs their pockets with cash and has no worries. And the Armenian middleman brings him the finest available wines and the best homemade vodka.

I am friends with his wife and they always invite me to their

parties. Of course, going to noisy weddings and social gatherings isn't free of danger. Everyone knows this and everyone has
come to terms with the risk. If the Revolutionary Guards raid the
party, you can often come to an understanding with them and
whitewash the entire incident with a cash payoff. But once in a
while, things don't work out this way.

I ARRIVE LATE. I hesitate at the door. It's a crowded party and
all sorts of people have been invited—from young girls and boys
to middle-aged women dressed in sleeveless, open-neck dresses,
retired generals, and the nouveau riche. There are also several
film directors, singers, musicians, and old-time writers.

I wish I hadn't come. The music is far too loud and the noise
can be heard three houses away. The danger is always that a jealous or fed-up neighbor might call the committee to come and
see what is going on at so-and-so's house. My instinct warns me
that something is going to happen tonight. I tell myself, Get
up, lady, say goodbye, and leave before it's too late. Anxiety over
what might happen has become second nature to us. Still, no
one makes a move, and I, like all the other optimists, tell myself
that perhaps nothing bad will happen and the evening will end
peacefully. There is no other option. Retreating is the beginning
of surrender and the acceptance of defeat.

We are at the dinner table when the Revolutionary Guards
burst in. Unexpected and unannounced. No one knows who
opened the door for them. The guests had been told to ring the
doorbell three times—two short rings followed by a long ring.
The secret code. No one heard the doorbell. Much later, we learn
that the Afghan servant was to blame. He was taking out the gar-
bage when the guards confronted him on the sidewalk. Questions

and answers (more questions than answers, because the young Afghan had gone dumb with fear).

"Who are the guests? How many are they?"

"Are the men and women together?"

"Are the women wearing hijab?"

"Is there alcohol?"

"Opium?"

"Music and dancing?"

The Afghan servant pleads innocence and ignorance. They beat him up and take the house keys from him. They shove him in a jeep to take him to the committee so that they can determine how to deal with him. It's obvious how they will deal with him. He has crossed the border into Iran illegally. He has to return to his own country. It doesn't matter that there is a war in Afghanistan, that he will be arrested at the border, and that he will most likely be put through the wringer.

I tell myself, I wish I hadn't come. What was I thinking? That I can survive any accident and incident unscathed? That I have a guardian angel watching over me? It's too late. There's no time for such thoughts. I have to think of a way out. Perhaps I can escape over the rooftop, or through a window in the basement, or by jumping down from the balcony. There are four Revolutionary Guards. They are standing around the dinner table, carefully monitoring everything. One of them has a video camera and he is quickly filming the empty bottles of alcohol. No one has fully grasped the gravity of their presence, until one of the women suddenly leaps up from her chair and starts to scream. Her dinner plate flips over and she drops her glass. The woman's shriek is the siren that suddenly wakes everyone up. Young girls and women without hijab, hoping to escape or to hide, jump up and create pandemonium. Our hostess has only now realized that the strangers are agents from the committee. She gets up, puts her glass down on the table, laughs hysterically, takes a few steps back, turns, and all of a sudden drops down and faints. Our host has turned pale, but he is smiling and trying to pretend nothing serious has happened. The women are now scrambling around looking for their headscarves. Some of them cover their hair with the white dinner napkins and others crawl under the table. A few run and hide behind the curtains.

Suddenly I feel cold and my heart is beating so fast that I'm afraid I will have a heart attack. I have planned a trip overseas and I'm scared they will confiscate my passport and ban me from leaving the country. The young man sitting next to me is calmly looking at the guards and watching the scene unfolding around him. He has noticed that I'm trembling and he quietly whispers, "Don't worry. They just want money. I was at a party last night and the exact same thing happened. We're used to it." But I'm not used to it. My stomach is in knots. Voices echo in my head and a silent scream is choking me.

Mr. M. pulls himself together. He swallows and says, "I have permission from the neighborhood committee. I don't know any of you. Who are you?"

"They're from a different neighborhood," the young man whispers in my ear. "This is turning out to be more serious."

I have heard that the Revolutionary Guards' neighborhood committees compete with each other, especially when there is money involved. They keep a watchful eye on each other and have spies who inform them about the glitzy parties.

Mr. M. asks the guards to go with him to another room to discuss the situation. He means to discuss money and the amount of

the payoff. But there's more in store for us. These men are fanat-
ical members of Hezbollah and they have no interest in pledges
and promises. They shove the host aside and yell for all the men
to go stand at one end of the dining room and for the women to
move to the opposite end. The one who seems to be their leader
calls the committee and reports the incident. They will send two
minibuses—one for the men and one for the women. The young
man next to me is still optimistic.

"It's all a show. Money will change hands with the committee.
This is all to hike up the amount."

Our host fetches the women's coveralls and headscarves. He
wants to call an influential acquaintance, a respected haji, a clever
lawyer, a specialist in such incidents. The guards don't allow it.
He offers them dinner. They turn him down. They say the food is
trash. Tainted. Impure. Eating it would be a sin. We don't know
what is going through their minds. We are not sure whether
the threats are real or just a ploy to increase the amount of the
transaction.

The minibuses arrive. There are two revolutionary Sisters to
escort the women. The guards go through the rooms searching
for an opium brazier. Opium paraphernalia are laid out in the
adjoining room. They film the brazier, the cushions strewn on the
floor, and the samovar. They put the bottles of alcohol in a plastic
bag and seal it. There are picture frames everywhere. They take
the photographs of women wearing low-cut dresses and no hijab
as evidence.

"This is a photo of my wife, and this other one is my daughter,"
our host explains.

They ignore him and carry on with their work.

The Sisters order the women to wipe off their lipstick, eye

shadow, and mascara. They have nail polish remover in their pockets, as well as a pair of small scissors to deal with long nails.

I can't believe it. I'm sure in the end they will take some money and let us go. Perhaps we should make a deal with the head of the committee. I still think this is just a show. I find it impossible that they would sentence us to a lashing. Impossible. But it has happened to many people. Our host is seething with anger and anxiety. Again, he invites their leader to another room, but the man refuses to go and our host has no choice but to increase his offer of money right there in front of everyone. He doubles the amount, but it's no use.

We women are herded into one of the minibuses and the men are piled into the other. The mothers among us are screaming and wailing and fretting for their children. One of them has an infant she breast-feeds. She has grabbed one of the Sisters and is pleading with her. The Sister is used to all this. She is unmoved.

"You should have stayed home with your kid or taken her to the mosque."

The young girls are fearless. They protest. "You'll see who the winner is in the end," they shout. "The future belongs to us. We'll show you!"

The wiser women intervene and explain to the young girls that a calm, polite tone is more effective. But nothing works, gentle or harsh. We have to see the head of the committee and to stand trial so that the religious judge can determine our punishment. No matter how, I must save myself. My only hope is that they will charge us a monetary fine commensurate with the number of lashes we are sentenced to receive. Thirty lashes would add up to a hundred fifty tumans, or more, depending on the judge we have to deal with. If he happens to be one of those diehard fanatics, we'll be done for. We will have a flogging, prison, as well as monetary fines to look forward to.

We arrive at the committee building and stand in line like common thieves and criminals. The men have arrived before us and we can hear them inside the compound. One of the girls lights a cigarette and takes a deep drag. A Sister walks up to her, slaps her hand, yanks the cigarette out of her mouth, and crushes it under her foot. The men are locked up together in a cell and we are not allowed to visit them. The women's temporary jail, where offenders are held until they are sentenced, is on a lower floor. The younger girls know the way and they take the lead. Clearly, it isn't their first time. At the bottom of the stairs an older lady swoons and collapses. She feels tightness in her chest and has difficulty breathing.

"She has had too much to drink," a foul-tempered Sister barks. "Shove a finger down her throat and make her throw up."

We take the ailing woman under the arms and drag her into the cell. There is a dim lightbulb hanging from the ceiling. There are a few other women in the cell—addicts and streetwalkers. They are sitting together on the damp floor. Terrified, our group huddles in a corner. After an hour of fidgeting on our feet, we can't take it any- more and plunk down on the floor. Two or three older women fall asleep right away. But the young girls stay awake and spend their time discussing new restaurants, newly released foreign films, and other forms of entertainment.

We are exhausted and hungry. Finally, the door opens and a Sister walks in. "You have fifteen minutes," she says. "You'll all line up, go to the bathroom, and come back. And don't make a sound."

"You mean one minute per person?" one of the young girls

snaps. "It's a joke! My dear lady, perhaps you think we are pissing champions."

Strangely, the Sister laughs instead of frowning. But she quickly swallows her laughter and raises her voice. "You should call me Sister. 'Dear lady' and the like belong to the old regime. And it's just as I said. Fifteen minutes. Move!"

The young girl won't give up. "You're not my sister. You're not my mother either. In fact, you're not one of us."

I forgo going to the bathroom. My legs have gone to sleep and I can't move. The others are in no better shape. The older women are rubbing their legs and stumbling to their feet. Two by two they go and come back. The ones at the end of the line are desperate and struggling to hold it in. We want water, but there isn't any. We have to wait. The hallway is dim and I can't clearly see the woman—or as they insist, the Sister. She is different from the others, she likes to joke and laugh. The streetwalkers are friends with her and treat her casually. Perhaps we can pay her off. She has her back to me and she is talking to the women who are coming back from the bathroom. My eyes are closed when the woman's laughter, like a sudden gust of wind, ruffles my dozing thoughts and wakes me up. I have heard this laughter before; I know who it belongs to. Just then, she turns and the faint light reveals her face. It's Delbar! My heart skips a beat and cold sweat seeps onto my skin. No, I'm not mistaken. It is she. The same plump lips, the same large bosom and sturdy body. Her eyes are puffy and time has stomped on her face with its steely shoes. But remnants of her former beauty are still visible through the mask of old age that has settled on her face like a swath of fine lace. From across distant years, her eyes are staring into my stunned and nervous eyes. I pull myself to the side. My headscarf is covering my forehead and eyebrows and I am hoping she hasn't recognized me. What should I do? Should I tell her who I am? She may help me. Help?! Delbar is my enemy and she will want to take revenge for the past. What is she doing here? How did she end up at the committee? Perhaps because of poverty and being out of work. When I first met her, she had no inclination toward religion and piety.

The committee, the jail, and that evening's party grow distant from my mind. Delbar has taken over my thoughts. I will never forget the last time I saw her. If you ask me where I was last week, I'd have to think about it, I'd have to search for names and images. But every detail of that particular day—the day I tore up Delbar's employment contract and shut the door on her—is vivid in my mind. It was a Friday evening, it was raining, and the Little Monkey (the name Delbar had given my son) was calling her and tugging at my skirt with his tiny hands. I had made up my mind to get Delbar out of my life, but she wouldn't leave. She screamed, argued, and threatened to kill herself. And then she started to cry, to beg, to plead. I wasn't faring any better than her, but I had to curb my emotions. With her hand on the door handle, she turned and looked at me with bitterness, rage, and hatred. "Someday, our paths will cross," she said. "And you will see who was right."

Today, after twenty-two years, our paths have crossed. The difference is that our positions are reversed. Over the years, I have often wondered whether I was justified in treating her the way I did. Or should I have given her a second chance? And now, I need to tell Delbar's story to someone, to myself, from the beginning, minute by minute, day by day, so that it all becomes clear to me. I have until morning, until I have to stand in front of her and look into her eyes.

IT WAS TWO or three years before the revolution. I don't remember the exact date. I was looking for a trustworthy nanny for my young son. The nursemaids of bygone days, the ones who stayed with you for a lifetime, had become a thing of the past. It was difficult to find an experienced helper and keep her forever, and the few who were still around, their salaries had tripled and their demands had increased tenfold. Servants were now calling themselves maids, housekeepers, and nurses, and they were all unreasonably arrogant and unruly. The younger ones who were literate preferred to work for companies or hospitals. I was at a loss as to what to do.

The evening newspapers were full of advertisements for house-maids, but most of my friends were wary of hiring a stranger. Who was she? Where was she from? She could be a thief or a woman of ill-repute. She could harm the child in a thousand ways, they cautioned me, and I knew they were right. Nevertheless, perhaps out of desperation, I turned to the classifieds. One particular ad caught my attention. It was for the White Angels Agency, which offered all sorts of assistants, from educated nurses to medical aides and housemaids. I called them. A man who sounded sleepy and had a nasal voice answered the phone. He let out a protracted yawn and repeatedly asked who I wanted to speak with. He was either hard of hearing or his telephone wasn't working properly. He asked me to redial and he hung up. I called again and this time someone else answered. He said I had to speak with the manager and asked me to hold. I waited a long time until a man with an awful cough came on the line. He, too, told me to hold for the

manager. I was about to scream and hang up when the manager
came to the phone and immediately started talking about money.
The price he quoted was too high. I would have to make a sub-
stantial up-front payment, and at the end of six months when the
contract expired, I would have to pay an even greater amount to
renew. These were clearly swindlers and I decided against working with them. A few days later, the manager, who had taken my
telephone number, called to share the good news that a wonderful maid had just joined their agency.

"Madam, you're in luck. This woman is exactly the type of
person you are looking for. She is dignified and sensible. She is
educated and can do everything you can imagine. Child care,
cooking, sewing—"

I cut him off and asked, "How old is she?"

"She's forty-two, give or take a couple of years, but what's
important is that she is healthy and strong and doesn't have the
airs younger women have. She's the one you want. You have to see
her for yourself."

I was sure he was laying it on thick and that much of what he
was saying were lies.

"Does she have a husband and children?"

"Fortunately, she has neither. Don't worry. She's all yours."

I didn't trust anything the man said. Still, I was curious and I
told him that I wanted to meet the woman and then I would take
my time and decide.

The offices of the White Angels Agency were on the third floor
of an old building in the city center, with two crowded rooms,
two desks and a few chairs, dirty walls and dusty curtains. Three
men were sitting at a desk drinking tea. One of them was the
manager—thin and tall, sallow skin, wearing an old suit and tie

and thick eyeglasses. A little farther away, a woman was leaning against the wall and flipping through a magazine. She glanced at me and went back to her reading. The manager was not expecting me. He gulped down his tea, stared at me, scratched his head, and started shuffling through the papers on his desk, searching for the appointment he had forgotten. I introduced myself and explained that I was there to meet the maid. I was hoping she wasn't the woman standing to the side. The so-called manager suddenly leapt up, hastily straightened his tie and buttoned his jacket, and after offering a few empty pleasantries, pointed to the woman and said that she was the one he had in mind for me. The woman tossed the magazine on a table, looked me up and down, and turned away. It was as if I were the one hoping to be hired. The manager saw the look on my face and started praising the nursemaid, the housemaid, the seamstress, the cook . . .

Anyone else would have turned around and walked out. Why didn't I? Why didn't I say, That woman, in that getup, is not right for me? She looked like anything but a housekeeper or a nursemaid. I was expecting a proper, dignified-looking woman. But instead, I was facing someone who looked irresponsible and sloppy. She took out the chewing gum she was chewing and tossed it in the trash can. She yawned and glanced at her watch. Then she picked up the telephone on the manager's desk and started to dial.

The manager smiled sheepishly, motioned to the maid, frowned, and grabbed the telephone receiver out of her hand. Then he turned to me and said, "This is the lady I told you about." He wanted to add, the dignified and sensible . . . but he stopped himself. He saw me staring at my future maid and left the judgment up to me. The woman looked angry. She was determined to make a telephone call and the manager's scorn had upset her. I thought she was a loose woman, a streetwalker. My gaze lingered on her tight-fitting dress with short sleeves and a low neckline. She wasn't wearing pantyhose and her shoes looked more like slippers. Her hair was short and she had dyed it a light color, half blond. What I liked the least in her appearance were the chipped remnants of red nail polish on her fingernails; this amplified her sloppiness. Housemaids usually wore long-sleeve dresses that resembled work uniforms and many wore a chador or a dark headscarf.

"Who did you work for before?" I asked.

She didn't feel like answering. She was searching for something in her pocket—a broken cigarette, which she snapped in two and put back in her pocket.

The manager answered for her. "She has worked for the rich and the elite. The best families. Most of them in the military. Generals, colonels, and lieutenant generals."

The woman laughed and exposed her white teeth. She had a firm body and healthy skin, and despite her large breasts and fleshy stomach, she looked strong and fit.

"Do you have a birth certificate?" I asked.

"Of course she does," the manager answered. "And even more important than a birth certificate, I will personally vouch for her."

The woman snickered and said, "No. I don't have one. I lost it. What you see is what you get. My hands are clean. I don't steal and I don't go after other women's husbands. And what's more, if you have the will to work, you will work, with or without a birth certificate. Most of them are fakes anyway. My name is Delbar, but it's something else on my birth certificate. I chose this name myself. I like it. Delbar."

The manager looked nervous. Once or twice he motioned to Delbar to keep quiet. Finally, he interrupted her and said, "Madam, you can rest assured. We'll write up a contract and sign it. We are a well-known and reputable agency. If in a few days you decide that you're dissatisfied with this lady, just call us. We will send you someone else within twenty-four hours. Give us a try."

"Where does she live? Does she have any relatives? A mother or a brother?" I asked.

"Of course. She didn't grow up under a bush."

Delbar laughed and said, "You sound like you're looking for a murderer. My dear lady, listen to your heart. I have no one. Give it some thought and make up your mind."

Delbar seemed neither hungry nor desperate for a job. She took a sugar cube from the sugar bowl on the desk and popped it in her mouth.

"You go your way, I'll go mine," she said.

Again, the manager cut her off. "I'm not trying to ingratiate myself, but believe me, she's an intelligent woman. Pay no attention to her appearance and the things she says. Try her. If you don't like her, fire her."

I was desperate to find someone. Delbar seemed sincere and frank and she didn't care to impress me. I signed the contract and the manager gave me a letter as some sort of a guaranty (which was worth nothing) and he took a check from me that was worth a lot. Delbar didn't have too many belongings. A small duffel bag and a plastic sack full of odds and ends. We took a taxi. When I gave the driver the address, Delbar whistled and shook her head.

"So, you live in the posh neighborhood. I know the area well."

I didn't respond. She was cheeky and I had to put her in her place from the very start.

"What are my duties?" she asked. "Housekeeping, cooking, taking care of children?"

"Child care and cleaning."

"I can't do two jobs at the same time. Taking care of a child will take up all my time. Either one or the other."

"Primarily, child care."

"How many children?"

"One. A two-year-old boy."

Delbar was deep in thought. "I wish it was a girl," she mumbled. "I've been married three times, but I don't have any children. I wish God had given me a daughter."

"Listen, Mrs. Delbar, I'll be frank with you," I said. "If you see that you don't like my son, I don't want you to stay for even a minute. You will leave immediately."

"I have never raised a hand to a child. I've gotten into scuffles with adults, but I leave people smaller than myself alone. Especially two-year-olds."

When we walked into the apartment, Delbar took a look around and said, "Isn't there a man in this house?" I didn't answer her. My little boy was standing up in his bed and he was screaming with joy at my return. The young girl who had come to take care of him nodded to Delbar, collected her pay, and left in a hurry.

I had a long, loose housemaid's uniform that was washed and ironed. I gave it to Delbar and asked her to take a shower and change before picking up my son. She went to the kitchen and changed into one of her own dresses and she tossed the uniform on a chair.

"This is a new dress," she said. "I just bought it. I don't wear other people's clothes."

She turned and looked into my eyes with a direct and sar-

castic expression and she made me understand from the very
start that I had no right to boss her around, that she would do
as she pleased, that she would dress any way she liked, and that
if I stepped over the line, she would walk out and slam the door
shut behind her.

I kept quiet and told myself that for the time being, it was best
that I not tangle with her, that later, I would show her who gives
the orders and would make her place and position quite clear.

My son had just started to talk and could repeat simple words.
He was calling me. I went to him; Delbar followed me. She took
a look at him and shook her head.

"Wow! What an ugly, funny-looking kid. Little Monkey."

Little Monkey became my son's name during the time Delbar
lived in my home. That's what we all called him. Little Monkey
was bald and had large eyes. His two front teeth were large and
made him look like a playful rabbit. He was a cheerful and pleasant child who liked people and didn't shy away from anyone. The
moment he laid eyes on Delbar, he started to jump up and down
and held his arms out to her. Delbar puffed out her cheeks and
crossed her eyes and Little Monkey laughed. He tried to mimic
her. He stuck his tongue out and leaned his head to one side.

"What a cheeky boy!" Delbar said as she tickled his belly. She
talked to him a little and stroked his head. Then she glanced at
her watch and all of a sudden she looked bored.

"I have to make a phone call."

"For now, mind the child while I go take care of a few things."

Delbar frowned, but said nothing. I was incapable of giving
orders to the hired help—it was my usual weakness.

"Go make your phone call," I said. "But don't take too long."
And I pointed to the telephone in the hallway.

I wanted to give an order and at the same time comply with her request. Delbar muttered something and went straight into my bedroom and closed the door. How did she know there was a telephone next to my bed? She had guessed and she had guessed right.

I didn't like anyone going into my bedroom without my permission; especially not a new maid. I called her. She didn't answer. I raised my voice. My son got scared and started to cry. I thought, No, this woman is not right for me. I have to find someone else. I went to my bedroom. Delbar was sitting there flipping through a magazine.

"There was no answer," she said. "I'll call again in an hour."

She tossed the magazine on the bedside table and walked out. I wanted to say, You are not allowed to go into my bedroom without my permission. I wanted to say, You are not allowed to touch my magazines. I wanted to say, Delbar, take your things and leave. I repeated these sentences in my head, but I said nothing. I didn't know how to discipline and reprimand, especially not the hired help. Instead of telling them off, I would grow quiet and sad. I would wait until later. Until the right time. Until events inevitably put me in the lead.

I took a week off from my work at the university and stayed at home. I wanted to see how Delbar treated my son. She never kissed him and never faked speaking affectionately to him. Yet Delbar wasn't mean. She didn't yell at my son or slap his hand. She took care of him, fed him, changed him, put him to sleep, and then she went to her room. She had a small radio and loved upbeat dance music. She went shopping and often took too long to return home. She had barely moved in when she made friends with the local butcher, grocer, baker, and the neighbor's manser-

vant. She was lively. She was the type of woman who would have
a boyfriend, drink, sing, and dance. She liked it when we took
my son out for a drive. Staying at home frustrated her, especially
since I liked to read and hated chitchatting and excessive noise.
The moment I suggested we go out, she would jump up, change
her shoes, and run out ahead of me. She would sit in the back seat
of the car, hold my son on her lap, and quietly sing. At home, she
would turn up the volume on the radio, take my son by the hands,
and teach him to sway to the beat of the music.

The first two months passed peacefully. Delbar had her own
habits and I let her be. I couldn't boss her around or criticize her.
She was independent and stubborn and didn't put much weight
in anything I said. I didn't know anything about her life and her
past and I preferred not to know. She had one day off each week
and on that same day my sunglasses and one of my dresses would
disappear. She didn't steal them. She always put them back after she
returned. I didn't confront her. One day, I found a big knife in the
pocket of one of my coats. It was hers. She had forgotten to take it
out. Another time, she came back from her day off with cuts on her
face and neck. She looked like she'd gotten into a brawl. She said
her home was in the southern parts of the city and she had to walk
through some dangerous ruins to get there. She had been attacked
a few times and that was why she carried a knife. But that day she
had forgotten her knife and couldn't defend herself. She had been
hit and she had hit back. I believed half of what she said and chalked
up the other half to storytelling. I told myself that her life outside
of my home was none of my business. We had learned to tolerate
each other and to leave each other alone.

Little Monkey always reached out for her. Before going to
sleep, he would clasp her hand and not let go. Delbar would laugh

and stroke his head and face. I didn't expect her to show deep
affection for my son. It was enough that she was pleasant and gentle
with him.

Delbar's true feelings for Little Monkey emerged one particular night. I had moved my son's bed to my room and put it at a
distance from my bed. He was with me and away from me at the
same time. Delbar slept in the room next door. Then there was
an outbreak of the flu and despite all the care I took, I caught it
too—chills, fever, coughing, and body aches. I was worried for
my son. I moved his bed to Delbar's room and asked her to keep
him away from me. She didn't complain, but I knew she didn't
like it. Eating well and sleeping well were most important to her.
She didn't like being called in the middle of the night and having her sleep disturbed. Still, she took Little Monkey and closed
the door to my bedroom. The following night, I woke up to the
sound of my son crying and whimpering. I was weak, my legs
were shaking, and I still had a high fever. I opened the door to
Delbar's room and saw her rocking Little Monkey in her arms. I
felt his forehead. He was hot and had difficulty breathing. It was
the first time he had gotten so sick. He was panting and looking
up at Delbar with tearful eyes. My thoughts were all over the
place. I was in a panic.

"We have to put his feet in cold water," Delbar said.

"No!" I shouted. "He'll catch pneumonia."

"When I was at Mrs. Mahdavi's house, her son developed a
fever of over a hundred degrees," she said. "They put him under
a cold shower and his fever came down."

I was running in circles and didn't know what I was looking for.
Every medication I took out of the medicine cabinet wasn't the
one I wanted. Or was it? My head was throbbing and I couldn't

read the labels on the bottles. I called a doctor I knew. I misdialed. A man answered the phone and yelled obscenities at me. He had every right. It was very late at night. I redialed. No one answered.

"Let's go to the hospital," I said. "Hurry up and get dressed."

I took my son from her. He couldn't hold his head up. It was a bad sign. It could have been meningitis. I was blind with fear. I bumped into a wall and cried out in pain.

Delbar was calm.

"Give Little Monkey to me," she said. And she pulled him out of my arms.

"Missus, calm down. Go to bed. Trust me."

I was shaking. I was in a daze. I had no willpower. Delbar's firm voice, like the voice of a short-tempered teacher chiding a stupid student, took away my power to object. Delbar took my son to the bathroom. I followed her like a windup doll. She stripped Little Monkey and was about to hold him under an ice cold shower when I suddenly started to scream. I was sure she had gone mad and wanted to kill my son. She didn't like him. She hated me. Her real name wasn't Delbar. She had no birth certificate. I thought of the knife she carried in her pocket and I imagined it being bloody. I was hallucinating. Delbar's face seemed to grow very large and then shrink again. I tried to take my son from her, but she shouted at me and pushed me out of the bathroom and locked the door. I pounded on the door. I ran out of the apartment and into the hallway to ask my neighbors for help. I put my finger on their doorbell and only then remembered that they were away. They had gone overseas. I went back to the bathroom door. I yelled, threatened, and begged, and finally I collapsed on the floor. I was in a worse condition than my son. I was burning with fever. Everything seemed strange and unfamiliar and this strangeness was blooming in my mind. Finally, the bathroom door opened. Delbar had wrapped the child in a towel.

"Bring his clothes," she said.

His clothes. Whose clothes?

She felt my forehead and went to the bedroom. I followed her. "Missus, you're sick," she said. "You're worse than this child. Go to bed. I'll stay up and watch over Little Monkey."

She brought me a glass of water and forced two fever reducers into my mouth. My son was breathing more easily. I didn't want him to sleep next to Delbar, but I had no energy to argue with her. I dropped down on my bed and fainted. I woke up at dawn. My fever had broken. I could hear Delbar talking to my son. I tiptoed to her room. The door was ajar. She was sitting on the floor with her back against the wall. Little Monkey was lying on a pillow on her outstretched legs and she was rocking him and singing a lullaby. This continued for several nights while I was recuperating. My son slept next to Delbar, and whenever he cried she would hold him tight against her chest and hum a song to him.

"Delbar," I said, "I am grateful. But he's feeling better and should go back to his own bed."

"No," she argued. "He is still coughing; especially during the night. He'll sleep right here with me."

A week went by and I decided to return my son to his own bed. He had recovered and wasn't coughing anymore. Delbar said nothing, but she was in a sour mood all day. In the middle of the night, she opened the door to my room and peeped in. I was awake and reading a book. She saw Little Monkey sleeping and she quietly closed the door. The next morning, I woke up early and saw that my son wasn't in his bed. My heart dropped. I leapt up and ran over to Delbar's room. To my shock, Little Monkey was in Delbar's bed, sleeping in her arms. No. No. I didn't like it. This was not part of the plan. I walked over to take my son, but with my arms stretched out and my legs firm on the floor, I froze. Little Monkey was sleeping with his head resting on Delbar's chest. He looked so peaceful and content that I didn't have the heart to wake him. And Delbar was in such a deep sleep that she neither felt my presence nor heard the door being slammed shut.

That was the start of Delbar's love for my son. She believed she had saved Little Monkey's life and now he belonged to her. At first, I was happy that Delbar had finally developed real affection for my son and that I could confidently leave him alone with her and go out. It was something I had not done in a long time. From that day on, each time I came back home, I found Delbar playing with Little Monkey. She would swing him around, make him laugh, put him on her back and crawl on all fours. Gradually, she started to curb my authority and acted as if I was the nanny and Little Monkey her child. She didn't follow my instructions about his meals. She put him to bed or kept him awake as she saw fit. One night I came back late from a party and saw that my son was still awake and Delbar was deep in conversation on the telephone. I got angry.

I frowned and asked, "Why is the child still up?"

She shrugged and said, "He's not tired. He shouldn't be forced to sleep. You can't put him in a hole like a mouse."

I should have been pleased with her affection for my son, but I wasn't. Whenever I tried to take him from her, he would scream and cling to her and she would laugh euphorically. I couldn't restrain my jealousy. Delbar was using my son's love for her to take over my house and my life. On her days off, I would sigh with relief, but my son was always restless and pined for her, fussing and refusing to eat. Delbar believed that God had punished her by depriving her of the ability to have a child, and she had suffered deeply. Now, God had sent her Little Monkey and had planted the child's love in her heart to make up for all those years of loneliness and yearning. It always upset me when she said such things. It frightened me and made me want to drive her out of our lives.

Day after day, week after week, Delbar's power increased. Obstinately, she took care of everything that had to do with my son and used every excuse to exclude me and keep me away from him. And yet, I couldn't complain. My son was happy and healthy and thriving in the glow of Delbar's affection. I had separated from my husband a year earlier and now my son rarely fussed because he missed his father, and he no longer cried when I wanted to go out. Instead, with his head resting on Delbar's shoulder, he would wave goodbye to me. He wanted her more than he wanted me. He would leap from my arms into hers and press his face against her chest. If I reached for him, he would slap my hand away and shout. Delbar would laugh. It was the laughter of victory, the laughter of utter satisfaction. Each time my son reached out for her, each time he jumped from my arms into hers, or refused to leave her embrace for mine, I got angry. Especially because Delbar would laugh and clutch my son tighter to her chest. He developed bad habits. On Delbar's days off, he wouldn't sleep. He wanted the scent and the warmth of his nanny's body. My big mistake was that I told Delbar. She was beside herself with joy.

"Then I won't take any days off," she said. "I don't have any children and a family of my own to go to. I always go to a friend's house. I would love to stay right here with my little boy."

My little boy!

"No. Your contract stipulates that each week you must have one day of rest," I insisted. "You have to go. You'll get bored if you stay here."

She ignored me. It was as if she had gone deaf. She took my son to her room and started to change his clothes. My heart was pounding. Why? What was I afraid of? All my life, ever since I was a child, I had been afraid of an invisible rival—someone who could steal a friend, a lover, a husband, a person who belonged to me. I wasn't willing to share and I didn't like three-person games. I didn't know how to fight and how to defend myself. I always retreated and sank into the painful darkness of my injured pride. But this time, it was different. My son's future was at stake. I wasn't going to hand him over to someone else.

"For now, go and do the ironing," I said. "We'll talk about it later."

"It's sunny outside. We'll go for a walk. Me and my little boy."

"No. I want to take him to my mother's house."

Delbar ignored me. She was putting my son's shoes on his feet and looking around for his hat.

"I'll come, too," she said.

"No. You'll stay home and see to the cleaning."

"I'll do whatever Little Monkey wants."

I thought, No, you'll do whatever I want. And I took my son by the hand and dragged him out of the apartment. I was sure he would start screaming. I was right. And he did so with his free arm reaching out for Delbar, who turned her back to us and went to the kitchen. My son yanked his hand out of my fist and ran after her. But halfway down the hallway, he tripped and fell down hard. His forehead was cut. Delbar rushed over and picked him up.

"My God! Missus, what in the world do you want from us?" she screamed.

From us? From her and my son? She had gone mad. She had no idea what she was saying. That day, I relented. I was in no mood for a fight, but I became even more troubled by her misplaced love for my son. Strange thoughts started running through my mind. I was afraid she would run away and take him with her. I was afraid I would come home one day and see that Delbar and my son had disappeared. Who was she? Where did she live? I knew nothing about her. During the past three months, no one had called for her, not on the phone and not in person. I called the Angels in White agency to get her exact home address and the telephone number of someone who knew her, a landlord, or a neighbor. A man answered the telephone. He said the agency had relocated. He was a housepainter. When did they move? Where did they move to? I became even more anxious.

One day I returned home and saw that Delbar had dressed my son in a girl's dress. She had tied a red ribbon in his hair and she had painted his cheeks and lips red. I was furious, but Delbar laughed and said, "He looks beautiful. I wish he were a girl. We would call her Delaram."

"Where did you get this dress?"

"I bought it. It's not like I stole it or killed someone for it."

I picked up my son and pulled the dress off of him and washed his face. He was screaming and asking for the dress. Delbar picked the dress up from the floor and gave it to him. She took him in her arms and kissed his face.

"This isn't right," I said. "Little Monkey is a boy and he will remain a boy."

"What's wrong with girls? I will turn him into a girl as beautiful as a flower."

She had an answer for everything I said. She changed into someone else. She started talking about her future with Little Monkey; not to me, but to herself and to Little Monkey. She made up fairy tales and lullabies, and there was no place for me in any of them.

One day I called Delbar from the office and told her that I had to work late into the evening. I asked her to give Little Monkey his dinner and not to wait for me. It was eight o'clock when I went home. The lights were out. I thought they were both sleeping. I opened my bedroom door and peeked in. Little Monkey's bed was empty. I thought she had again taken him to sleep in her bed and I angrily swung open the door to her room. The curtains were closed and my eyes weren't accustomed to the dark. I turned on the light. There was no sign of them. The first thought that crossed my mind was that she had kidnapped my son. No. It was impossible. I couldn't believe it. I told myself that they had gone out and would be back soon. But where? At that hour of the night? Perhaps they had gone to my mother's house, to my brother's, to a friend's, I don't know, perhaps a relative stopped by and took them out. But who? My ex-husband was traveling. I thought perhaps he had returned and taken them to his house. I picked up the telephone. What if they weren't there? I ran out to the street. I ran left, I ran right. I rang the neighbor's doorbell. Their maid was friends with Delbar.

"Is Delbar here?"

"No. Has something happened?"

"No. No. Have you seen her and my son?"

"No. I swear. Maybe she went shopping."

She was right. Shopping. Shopping for bread. For fruit. And she had taken Little Monkey with her. Thank God. The grocery store was on the next street. It closed at eight o'clock. Its metal gate was down. There were three people in front of the bakery. The baker stared at me. The same questions. The same negative answers. No one had seen Delbar. I ran home and called my mother. She was home. She didn't mention Delbar and my son. I didn't want to worry her and I said nothing about them being gone. I hung up the phone. My husband. My ex-husband. What difference did it make? He wasn't there. The police? What would I tell them? I was shaking. I thought I was having a heart attack when I heard the downstairs door open and close. Footsteps. Laughter. Voices. Delbar's voice. The sound of something falling. Little Monkey's voice. The sound of a car horn. The sound of happiness and the drip-drop of the bathroom faucet. The sound of my heart beating and of me breathing. She walked in ignoring the fact that it was almost nine o'clock and way past my son's bedtime, that I, this child's mother, was on the verge of a nervous breakdown with a thousand horrifying thoughts rushing through my mind, and ignoring the fact that she was not allowed to take my son out without my permission. The stupid lunatic. She said the weather was nice and the child was fussing, so she took him to Mellat Park. Little Monkey had had a good time and didn't want to come home. She wanted to take a taxi to come back, but she couldn't find one. They had walked. There was no reason to worry. Then, she took the upper hand. What's wrong? What's the matter? And she sulked and acted as if she had been wronged. She went to her room and closed the door. I told myself, Enough is enough. I have to get rid of her. I was afraid that the next time she would really kidnap my son or harm him in some way. I was looking for an excuse to fire her and an excuse presented itself. A few days later, one of the neighbors called and warned me to keep an eye on Delbar. She had seen Delbar take my son to the end of the road where a car had pulled up and they had gotten in. They had returned an hour later. I was enraged. I confronted Delbar. She tried to deny it but realized that it was no use. She confessed.

"I know this man. Do you think I would get into a stranger's car? If anyone so much as looks sideways at this child, I'll pluck out their eyes. Little Monkey had a good time. He's like a prisoner in this apartment. We went to Darband, by the river. The child has no father. He was clinging to Hossein Agha and wouldn't leave his arms."

Now, there was Hossein Agha to deal with. Someone who, according to Delbar, could play the part of Little Monkey's father. The scenario was complete. The more she talked, the worse I felt. She had to go and she had to go as soon as possible. She said she didn't want any money, that she didn't want any vacation, that she wouldn't set foot outside the apartment, that she would do all the housework. She fell to her knees. She said that the love of the child had seeped into her bones and that she would die without him.

She reached out and stroked my son's hair. She ran his small hand over her face and kissed his fingers. What could I do? Keep her? No. No. It was impossible. I was afraid of her. She was insane. Her love for my little boy was beyond logic and reason. I had made up my mind and Delbar knew that pleading with me was useless. She kept quiet and waited for my anger to subside. She assumed that in a few days I would forget all about the incident. But this time I did not.

She stayed until her day off. She didn't take the little salary I still owed her and she left behind her odds and ends so that she would have an excuse to come back. For a long time, I had no news of her. The day she came back I didn't recognize her. She was wearing a headscarf. She said she had gone to Mashad and prayed at the shrine of Imam Reza. She had vowed that if the love of the child were to leave her heart, she would live forever near his shrine. But the love of the child was still in her heart. I told her that we were going on a trip and that I had hired a new nanny. She looked down and said nothing. She turned pale. She couldn't believe that this was no longer her home. Her proud and arrogant eyes were for the first time filled with desperation.

"I don't want a salary. I don't want anything. Just let me stay," she begged.

"No." Uttering this small word wasn't easy.

"At least give me a photograph of the boy."

I agreed.

"Give me a pair of his socks and a set of his clothes, too."

I did.

She wanted to see my son. I said, No. She was standing there and wouldn't leave.

"He has finally gotten used to you not being here," I argued. "Just leave him alone."

But Little Monkey had heard her voice and was kicking the closed door. It was an awkward moment for me, for Delbar, and for the child who couldn't understand what was happening and knew nothing about the good and evil in life.

Delbar left.

She's gone, I told myself. I'm free. Anyone else would have done the same.

No. I wasn't free. My heart ached and I felt guilty. I couldn't come to terms with myself. My intelligent half was satisfied and whispered that I had done the right thing, that she could have caused us great harm, that she could have kidnapped my son and disappeared. My other half that shunned pettiness, fear, and caution, scolded me. Perhaps Delbar was right, perhaps she was telling the truth and she had really changed, or wanted to change, wanted to start a new life.

Little Monkey was crying and running from one room to another looking for Delbar. I took him in my arms and kissed him. It was no use. He was flailing his arms and legs and wouldn't quiet down. I sang to him and made faces—things Delbar would do. I tickled him, but he screamed and slapped my hand away. Candy, chocolate, banana? I meowed and barked, I neighed, I crowed like a rooster—sounds Delbar used to make that made Little Monkey laugh and laugh. He could tell that I was tired and fed up, that I didn't know how to play those games, and he kept calling Delbar. I screamed that Delbar wasn't there. I didn't know what to do with that weeping child who wanted his nanny. I picked him up and went to the window. I showed him the trees, the birds, and the cars that were driving by. And I caught sight of Delbar. She was standing at the corner, looking up at the window of Little Monkey's room. Then she turned and walked away with slow, heavy steps. I remembered the first day she came to my home. She was agile and healthy. She slept soundly and had a good appetite and plenty of energy. The day she left, she was a sad and bitter woman.

I would sometimes see her wandering around our building. She would stand at the corner, hoping to see Little Monkey. Each time I saw her, I felt depressed, I felt guilty, and I couldn't understand why. After all, hadn't I made the right decision?

When the revolution started, I lost track of her. My life was in turmoil and I forgot all about Delbar. Terrified of the arrests and executions, I wandered through the rooms in my apartment, certain that soon the Revolutionary Guards would come and arrest me for some unknown crime. Before the borders were closed off, I took my son and left the country. Paris was the city of my dreams. I decided to stay there for a year. I thought the political unrest in Iran was temporary and that life would return to the way it was. But soon, war broke out between Iran and Iraq and it dragged on for eight years. I stayed in Paris. My son was in school, he had settled into his new life and Iran had become foreign to him. Once a year we came for a visit; and this was one of those occasions.

IT IS A LONG NIGHT. I fall asleep for an instant and suddenly jolt awake. It takes a while for me to remember where I am and what has happened. Delbar comes and goes. She jokes with the young girls and consoles the older women. She has a reputation for being a fair and just Sister. I am cowering in a dark corner of the cell, but she has recognized me. I'm sure of it. When her eyes caught sight of me, for an instant her expression changed, she blushed, and her mouth remained open. But she quickly composed herself and turned away. My fate is in her hands. A painful angst is choking me. I can't talk. I imagine the lashes of the whip on my skin and I feel nauseous.

Early in the morning, they call us and we are taken upstairs. There is no sign of the men. Two new Sisters show up. They are dressed in black from head to toe and look like they're coming from a funeral. We learn that the men have been taken to a different location for sentencing. As for us women, it has been decided that some of us may be exempt from a lashing in exchange for a monetary fine. The young boys are in trouble. Their heads will be shaven and they will be publicly flogged in a city square. Their parents have been notified. They arrive in a frenzy. They have brought cash and all sorts of documents— deeds to their house and car. They offer to be whipped instead of their children. The head of the committee says paying a fine is not enough and that the boys must repent. They must put in writing that they will embrace Islam and will never again commit immoral acts contrary to divine laws. Two of the girls are seething with anger. They are like embers under ash, ready to leap back into flame. They are sentenced to one month in prison as well as a fine. My situation remains unclear. The wait-ing is what frustrates me the most.

The morning prayers are over and the guards have returned to their post. They call me.

Without looking at my face, the head of the committee says, "We have investigated you. You have a tarnished past and you are currently involved in an illicit affair with a married man. You live overseas and it's not clear why you travel back and forth. It is possible that you're a foreign spy."

Dangerous and false accusations. How can I prove that these are all lies? There is no court to appeal to. Delbar has finally done it. She has created a heavy case file for me.

I know I'm no match for these people. Still, I won't hang my head like a sheep and give in.

"According to civil, religious, and divine laws, I have the right to defend myself," I say. "All these accusations are false. I object. You have no proof."

Delbar is standing by the door. She pretends to be reading a sheet of paper, but I know that all her attention is focused on me. These are her words that are being spoken to me. Otherwise, how would they know anything about my past? How would the head of the committee know that I live overseas? This battle is between Delbar and me.

I raise my voice. "What wrong have I done? Is it a crime to go to a party?"

The guard standing at the door glares at me. The head of the committee turns red and angrily throws his pen down on the desk.

I don't know how I have suddenly become so daring and belligerent. Just a few hours ago I was dying of fright. Seeing Delbar has aroused the anger, jealousy, and rivalry I thought I had forgotten. I will not let her see me desperate and despondent, I will not allow her to humiliate me or pity me. She is waiting for me to beg and grovel and to throw myself at her feet.

Delbar is quiet, but there is an unnerving smile on her lips. Upstairs is where they flog the women.

"Are you pregnant?" a Sister asks.

I don't answer.

"Do you have heart or kidney problems?" she asks.

Delbar is responsible for delivering the lashes. Without looking at me, she turns and leads the way. My legs are shaking. Neither one of us acknowledges the other. There is a large chandelier hanging from the ceiling of the upstairs hallway and the walls are painted pink. It is obvious that this was once the home of a wealthy person—affluent, but lacking good taste. God knows what has become of him. In one corner, there is a walnut wood credenza with gilded embellishments (doubtless, it belongs to the former homeowner). A man opens a drawer and puts a few files in it. We walk into a large, empty room. Delbar doesn't look at me. I'm standing motionless in the middle of the room. Another Sister walks in, looks me over, and checks my nails. I'm not wearing nail polish.

"You have to perform ablution and pray," she says.

"I don't know how and I'm not going to pretend."

"You're not worth dirt," she sneers. And she walks out.

There is a wooden bed in a corner. They flog you with your clothes on. You have to take off your shoes and lie facedown. Another Sister walks in. She looks at my trembling lips and chalk white face.

She turns to Delbar and says, "This miserable woman is about to faint. She can't take thirty lashes."

I'm waiting for Delbar's response. She says nothing.

"Here, put this Quran under your arm," the Sister tells Delbar.

I've heard that some of the Sisters get very excited and flog the accused harder than is necessary. They lose control. They put a Quran under the flogging arm to stop themselves from raising it too high.

Fear, anger, hatred, and humiliation churn inside me. My mouth is dry and I'm short of breath.

"Lie down," the Sister says. "Think about God and ask Imam Ali for help."

Twenty years have passed, twenty thousand things have happened, the earth has revolved and the moon, the sun, and the galaxy have been hard at work for Delbar and I to come together again—I as a prisoner, she as a judge. I put myself in destiny's hands and lie facedown on the bed. The mattress is covered with a filthy sheet. It smells of sweat. The sweat of the person who lay here before me. She has left behind the scent of her hatred, pain, and anger. Delbar is idling around. What is she doing? I wish she would say something; at least say, I recognize you, I know who you are. I hear water being poured in a glass. I wish she would give me a sip, too. She wants to torment me. I know her. She's standing next to the bed. She runs her hand over my back. I shudder. She touches the back of my legs. I'm about to scream. I want her to do her job and get it over with. Anticipating torture is more painful than the torture itself. I spent most of the night on my feet and my body aches with fatigue. Where am I? Fantasy and reality have merged and I have lost track of time. Ouch! The first lash is delivered to the soles of my feet. It isn't hard. It's some sort of a test. A warning. The next lashes land on the metal edge of the bed. She is testing her whip. At the sound of each blow, I jolt and tremble. Delbar's hand is on my neck. She tugs at my earlobe and laughs. It's a game of cat and mouse. I turn my head left and right. I look up and see the dirty wall in front of me. Pictures of martyrs, a newspaper clipping, a framed photograph of the Supreme Leader, deep cracks, crumbled plaster, the light switch. My arms, hanging down from the sides of the bed, have gone numb. There is an unfamiliar smell, an unpleasant odor, the stench of the pair of army boots next to the bed. I hear a closet door being opened and closed. Someone coughs. There is another person in the room. She whispers to Delbar. I move my arms and rest my forehead on the palm of my hands. I'm restless. I breathe against the bedsheet and my stomach churns. Delbar, damn you, what are you doing? She's dragging this out. She is trifling with me. Her hand creeps over my ankle. A pause. Silence. She feels my calf muscle as if I'm cattle being sold. "Hurry up," I hiss under my breath. "Get on with it! You've waited twenty years for this. You said our paths would someday cross. Today our paths have crossed. Take your revenge."

I feel the touch of the whip on my back. My spine is waiting for excruciating pain. The muscles in my neck have tightened. I wait. Nothing happens. I can't tolerate this game. I have been sentenced to thirty lashes. I have to receive thirty lashes. Should I sit up? Scream? I'm scared of confronting Delbar. So far, everything has been veiled. Neither one of us has acknowledged the other. Perhaps it's best that we remain behind our masks. But for how long? I'll wait. I'll wait. I'll count to a hundred. Where are you? Silence.

I leap up and scream, "Do your job and get it over with!"

There is no one in the room. I'm confused. I look around. One minute, two minutes, ten minutes, an eternity passes. At last, the door opens and another Sister walks in.

"Get up and get dressed," she says.

"I am supposed to receive thirty lashes."

"Didn't you?"

I shake my head. She shrugs.

"It's none of my business. Sister Islami has done her job. Get up and go."

Sister Islami! She has picked a good name for herself.

"Why didn't she flog me?"

The Sister looks at me in surprise.

"Lady, get up and go. Don't argue. Do you want me to call someone to come and get you or will you take a taxi?"

It's over? I'm looking for my shoes. I'm numb. Am I dreaming? Nothing seems real, not even the Sister standing next to me. The pink walls, the dusty grand chandelier, the photograph of the bearded man wearing a turban, the whip on the table, the army boots next to the bed, the noise coming from the street, the blare of car horns, the siren of the ambulance stuck in traffic, the sound of two people fighting, and someone laughing, and a woman being flogged—all are unreal, fake.

I go out into the hallway. My eyes are searching for Delbar. The door to the room across the hall is open. I peek in. I climb down the stairs, slowly, one at a time. I feel like someone who has really been flogged. A man is standing at the foot of the stairs. He looks down to avoid looking at my face.

"Pull down your scarf," he says.

I open the door to a room. It's empty. The next door is locked.

"Who are you looking for?" the man asks.

"Where is the Sister who flogged me? Sister Islami."

He doesn't answer. A young Sister is sitting at a desk in the hallway. She motions to me and puts my wallet and my earrings in front of me on the desk.

"Count your money so you don't accuse us of taking any."

There is nothing missing. I put on my sunglasses. The Revolutionary Guard at the front door says, "Take off those Western sunglasses. They are forbidden."

I walk out. My son is waiting for me. He looks pale and frightened.

He takes me in his arms and holds me tight. There is a taxi waiting in the shade. Before getting in, I turn and look at the pink committee building with a feeling of curiosity and disgust. It is then that I see Delbar standing in the frame of a half-open window. She is staring at my son. The Little Monkey.

THE OTHER ONE

*D*espite suffering from diabetes, gout, and high blood pressure, at seventy-five and just when everyone thought he would not live much longer, Colonel Zamani became a father. Can you believe it? He kept his forty-four-year-old wife's pregnancy a secret until the day she gave birth. The child was the colonel's first offspring to survive nine months in the womb. His wife had miscarried twelve times. The colonel, who was a deeply religious man, believed that the child was a gift from God, and recalling the story of Abraham and his son, he had decided to name the baby Ismael. But the child turned out to be a girl and having a boy's name would have made her a laughingstock. Instead, he named her Naz Maryam, because it was a religious name and the little creature was as beautiful as a white flower. The colonel nicknamed her Sweet Almond (he loved pistachios and almonds), and in gratitude for this miracle, for the rest of his life he gave alms regularly and prayed several times a day; and twice he went on a pilgrimage to the shrine of Imam Reza. Over time, the colonel's profound happiness made him superstitious and a bit half-witted.

During childbirth, Naz Maryam's mother lost a lot of blood

and the doctors worried about her health. Soon she developed a cough and a fever and at night she sweated so much that they had to change her nightgown and bedsheets several times. The doctors determined that the colonel's wife had tuberculosis and they quickly took Naz Maryam away from her. They hired a nursemaid (whose daughter, Gohar, would stay with Naz Maryam until the end of her life), but in reality, it was the colonel who took care of the child. He put Naz Maryam to sleep in his own bed, he fed her—cow's milk in a large bottle, because Sweet Almond had a big appetite—and he changed her diaper, too.

When Naz Maryam was a bit older, they would take her to see her mother from behind a window. The woman on the other side of the glass was like a faint shadow. She would put her lips against the glass and kiss her daughter. Sometimes she would cry and Naz Maryam would get scared. The woman would reach out to caress her daughter's cheek, but she couldn't touch her. One day, the woman behind the glass disappeared and Naz Maryam never saw her again.

The colonel, with that tall figure and large, angular nose, with that thick mustache and knee-high leather boots, with all those stars and medals and pomp and circumstance, was like putty in his daughter's hand and he didn't dare challenge her commands. Naz Maryam would sit on his lap and only ate if he fed her. She would ride on his shoulders and order the horse to gallop around the room. She would blindfold the colonel and he would grope around the room looking for her. He would trip over chairs and run into tables and whatever was on them would fall and break.

When Sweet Almond was older, she still clung to her father and had no interest in children her own age. She would pull her classmates' hair and bite their cheeks. She hated school and studying.

No one dared wake her up early in the morning. She would bury her head under the pillow and scream, or she would cry so hard she would make the colonel cry, too. They hired tutors to work with her at home. If the tutor was a man, the colonel would get jealous. If it were a woman, Sweet Almond would get jealous. The colonel had no choice but to tutor her himself. He had forgotten math and geometry, so he secretly hired a teacher and prepared the lessons ahead of time. Once a week, he took Naz Maryam to the movies or to a café or restaurant, and once a month he took her to shops that sold fashionable Western clothes.

The colonel lived a long life, perhaps because he smoked opium, or more likely because of the miracle of his daughter's birth. His love for the girl nourished him; otherwise, given all his ailments, he should have died many years earlier.

Twice he took Sweet Almond overseas. When she was twelve, they went to Paris and the colonel showed her all the sights—from the Eiffel Tower, to Napoleon's tomb, to the Palace of Versailles and the Champs-Élysées. He bought her coats, hats, shoes, and dresses in every color, and he bought her a ballet costume, too. Their second trip was to London. But the weather suddenly turned cold and rainy and Sweet Almond caught a bad cold and ran a fever. The colonel was running around like a madman. He was so nervous that while leaving her room he hit his head against the edge of the door and his head swelled. He asked the hotel manager for help and he died a thousand deaths until a doctor arrived. Any other sick child would have taken her medication and stayed in bed. But Sweet Almond wasn't just any other child. She didn't like her cough syrup and she spat out her pills. The English doctor was at the end of his rope. Naz Maryam wanted to go back to Tehran, so they did. It was a difficult trip.

When the girl turned eighteen, Colonel Zamani was over ninety years old. He hosted a stately feast and stuffed himself with food and drink. Everyone was afraid he was going to die. But it wasn't his time. The next morning, he woke up earlier than usual, said half his prayers—he got tired and forgot the rest—he shaved, exercised, and showed up at the breakfast table all chipper and cheerful. The moment he saw Naz Maryam, he thought an angel had descended from the heavens and tears welled up in his eyes. Of course, for some time now, he had been quite sensitive and cried easily. Once, he even became so upset at the sight of a chicken sizzling in a frying pan that he turned down the flame.

Naz Maryam's beauty was known to one and all and she had dozens of persistent suitors. But the colonel always came up with some excuse to turn them away, and the young lady herself didn't fancy anyone. Hand in hand with the colonel, she went on outings and attended parties and couldn't tolerate any man other than her father. Her paternal aunts were angry and concerned. A thousand rumors were going around. They thought everything had to have its limits, even fatherly love. But all their advice and admonishments were to no avail. Everyone was worried about Naz Maryam. They couldn't understand why the girl kept away from young, handsome men and stuck to her ninety-year-old father. What would become of her when the colonel died?

The colonel was certain that he would live to be a hundred and twenty and that even if he were to die, he would somehow come back. But one night when he was ninety-five, he ate a wonderful dinner with his daughter, kissed her four times, went to sleep, and didn't wake up. And as long as Sweet Almond was alive, he never came back to call on her.

Sweet Almond screamed when she learned of her father's death.

She tore the living room curtains and broke all the crystal dishes. No one could calm her down. She walked around all day and talked to him. She beat her fists on Gohar's chest and clawed at the young maid's hair. One day she set her bed on fire, another time she turned on all the water faucets in the house. The living room was flooded and the fine carpets were ruined. She wore black for five years and wouldn't stop crying. Gradually her strength waned and she quieted down. She sat and stared at her father's photograph. She slept in his bed and talked to him. She wouldn't talk to anyone else and she wouldn't set foot outside the house. But eventually, she grew tired of being alone. Her nursemaid and her father's sisters had died and the woman behind the glass no longer kissed her. She was left with only her maternal aunt, who, despite her old age, could still be counted on.

Naz Maryam didn't really know this aunt. She had even forgotten her name. She went to her house a couple of times but she didn't stay long. She would toss the box of pastries she had brought on the table and leave in a hurry. She decided to live with Gohar in her father's house for the rest of her life. But what about money? Who was going to pay for her expenses? She hadn't thought about this. She hadn't thought about a lot of things and didn't know about her father's bankruptcy.

Soon the creditors started showing up. Bewildered and not knowing what to do, Naz Maryam simply stared at them. Who were they? Where did they come from? Her cousins came to her rescue. They told her the only way out was to sell the house and get married.

Get married? To whom? One of the cousins volunteered to help and invited one of Naz Maryam's suitors to her house. He was a middle-aged man and far too timid. All he did was stare at the floral pattern on the carpet. His lips didn't come together. He looked like there was a ball stuffed in his mouth. Naz Maryam walked in one door and walked out the other.

The second suitor turned out to be one of the creditors. He was blunt and straightforward and acted as if he had come to make a trade or conduct a transaction. He explained that he had a wife and four children, but he would buy a separate house for the young lady and he would take her with him on his trips abroad. Naz Maryam was shaking with rage, and when the suitor left, she slammed the door behind him. The man's finger got caught in the door and he cried out in pain. The man threatened that he would file a complaint against Naz Maryam and that he wouldn't leave her alone until he received what was owed to him.

The creditors weren't giving up. They sent notices to Naz Maryam and intimidated her. She had no option but to sell the house and no choice but to marry one of her suitors. It didn't matter which one; she hated them all. Of course, being married to Naz Maryam was not going to be easy. There were terms and conditions. The girl despised pregnancy and hated children, she was afraid of unfamiliar men, cats, dogs, and all birds. The future groom, whoever he was, had to sign an agreement: no dogs, no cats, no birds, no children. Understood? No children.

Engineer Safaa had returned from the West. He was handsome and well-educated and he was from a prominent family. He saw Naz Maryam and told himself, This girl belongs to me. He ignored people's warnings about the girl's strange behavior and sent his mother to visit Naz Maryam's cousin and to ask for the young lady's hand in marriage. Naz Maryam's initial answer was a definite no.

However, like all people in love who tend to be hasty and stupid, Engineer Safaa didn't give up. He sent letter after letter and gift after gift and he recruited Gohar as his accomplice. The two of them were so persistent that Naz Maryam got fed up and agreed—first to selling the house and then to getting married. Both decisions were painful for her.

Engineer Safaa was beside himself with joy. In black ink, he signed the agreement Naz Maryam had written. No dogs, no cats, no birds, no children. In his heart he laughed at his future wife's demands. He was so excited that he walked all the way home and tipped the neighborhood watchman a thousand tumans. He cuddled his cute cat that came to greet him and kissed her head ten times. Then he tossed a slab of meat with a bone in it to his Doberman and stretched out on his bed and thought he was the happiest man on earth.

Naz Maryam didn't want a wedding or a wedding dress. So much the better. Engineer Safaa was leaving on a short trip—a business trip to sign important contracts—and he was worried that she would change her mind and go back on her word. Therefore, he insisted that they perform their religious marriage ceremony before he left. He was so in love that he had forgotten all about the conditions regarding cats and dogs and birds and kids.

The ceremony was held at Naz Maryam's house with her cousins and Gohar in attendance. From the groom's family, only his mother was present. And without much fanfare, the bride went to the groom's house. On the first night of their marriage, she pretended she was sick. Or perhaps she really was sick—coughing, sneezing, and body aches. She turned away the excited engineer and postponed even a small kiss until after his trip. Engineer Safaa was desperate to consummate his marriage and his thigh and stomach muscles were painfully contracted, but he showed patience and survived the night by taking sleeping pills and biting the corner of his pillow. The next day, he left on his trip, brimming with love and desire and after blowing a thousand kisses to his wife from a distance.

In his absence, Naz Maryam threw his pampered cat out on the street and gave away his lovebird to the street sweeper. She was at a loss as to what to do with the massive dog. She didn't have the courage to go near it, so she called one of her father's friends who had a large garden estate in Karaj. A few men came and hurled the dog onto a pickup truck and took it away. The house was now safe and secure.

Engineer Safaa returned from his trip feeling sprightly and whistling happily. He brought Naz Maryam a large bouquet of flowers and fastened a pearl necklace he had previously bought for her around her neck. He sat on the edge of her bed and stared at her like someone who saves the tastiest bite of his meal for last and he savored the pleasure of anticipation with his entire being. And then he casually looked around for his cat.

Sweet Almond, while thanking him for the necklace, said, "I let the cat go. It went out on the street and didn't come back."

In his state of delirium and thinking that his wife was joking, the happy engineer laughed. He called the cat a few times, bent down and looked under the bed, and finally he realized that his cat had really disappeared. Miss Pussycat wasn't an average cat. She was very valuable and she was the young engineer's constant companion. At night, she slept next to him and purred.

Naz Maryam was composed and reminded her husband of the terms of marriage he had agreed to. Engineer Safaa didn't take it to heart and told himself that it wasn't important, that wherever his precious cat had gone, she would soon come back. For a few minutes he forgot about his cat's disappearance. He lit a cigarette and was again spellbound by his wife's beauty. He was holding her hand when the bark of the neighbor's dog reminded him of his dear Doberman.

"My dear," Naz Maryam said, "I sent the dog someplace very nice. Don't worry."

Of course, the cook and the gardener were happy that the dog was gone. They were not only afraid of the massive beast, but they considered dogs to be unclean and had to wash their hands ten times a day and constantly change their trousers. But for Engineer Safaa this was an unexpected blow and a dark cloud settled over his besotted heart. Again, he tried not to be upset and deferred bitter thoughts to a later time. He didn't want anything to ruin the bliss he was feeling at that moment. He wrapped his arms around his wife's waist and pulled her to himself. Naz Maryam reluctantly caressed her husband's cheek, wiggled her body, and got up saying she had to use the bathroom. "I'll be right back." And she disappeared.

Ten minutes, twenty minutes, twenty-five minutes. There was no sign of the bride. Engineer Safaa was aching with desire and fantasizing about making love to his beautiful wife. Soon he got worried. He went to the bathroom door and turned the handle. Naz Maryam had locked the door and wouldn't come out.

"My beauty, my darling, are you well?" he called out. "Answer me. I'm sick with worry."

Naz Maryam muttered something but didn't open the door.

Engineer Safaa was confused. He couldn't understand his dear wife's behavior. He was about to break down the door when Gohar showed up. She told Engineer Safaa that Naz Maryam was very innocent, that no man other than her father had ever touched her, and that it was best to give her two days to get over her fear.

"Fear of what?"

"Just two days," Gohar pleaded.

Two days? Engineer Safaa moaned, swallowed hard, and leaned his head against the bathroom door. He spoke tenderly to his wife and thought, My little bird is scared and she has every right to be scared. Two days is nothing.

But the problem wasn't resolved in two or three days. Each time Engineer Safaa approached his wife, the little bird would get scared and run away. The engineer's pleas were useless. This went on day and night and over and over again. The engineer was a civilized man, educated in the West. He didn't want to bully his wife. He thought this was some sort of game and laughed it off. He chalked up Naz Maryam's silliness to amorous games and coquetry. But after a while, he concluded that the problem was serious. He spoke with the family doctor. The doctor said he had to be patient. Patient! Engineer Safaa was tense and restless. He had lost his cat and dog and couldn't tolerate his wife's strange behavior. He appealed to a psychologist he was acquainted with. The doctor wasn't surprised. He explained that fear of lovemaking was a mental disorder and had to do with the patient's past and her relationship with her father.

How long could he wait? Psychotherapy could take years and its outcome was unclear. Engineer Safaa was losing his mind. Every night, he sat behind the locked door to Naz Maryam's bedroom and talked to her. He wanted to play the role of a psychologist. He asked her about her father and she refused to say a word. Engineer Safaa persevered. He read a couple of books on psychology and took notes. He asked Naz Maryam about her mother and her childhood. Naz Maryam cried and kicked the door. This approach didn't work either. Engineer Safaa turned to literature and poetry. He read a few pages from *Leyli and Majnoon* to her and recited poems by Lamartine. He begged and pleaded with her to open the door. All to no avail.

Six months passed. Engineer Safaa was biting his nails and seething inside. Gradually, he turned against his wife. He felt humiliated. His male pride had been injured. One night, after drinking a bottle of wine, he kicked open the door to his wife's bedroom and dove on top of her. Naz Maryam was struck with horror. She couldn't scream. She opened her mouth, but she couldn't make a sound. She beat Engineer Safaa with her fists, but she was no match for him. She bit his ear and poked his eye. It was no use. Her bites and punches only made him more excited. The ceiling turned round and round above her. Her dizziness continued until morning.

The next day, the little bird woke up with an awful backache. She felt like she had been pummeled. She had a bruise under her eye and her lips were swollen. She looked at herself in the mirror and screamed. She tore off her pearl necklace and hurled a perfume bottle at the mirror. Tearful and sulking, she packed her bags and went to her aunt. Auntie's house had two floors, but because of her leg pains, Auntie only used the ground floor. Naz Maryam settled in on the second floor. She had brought Gohar with her. She didn't offer her aunt a detailed explanation. She simply said that she didn't get along with her husband and she had nowhere else to go.

Auntie thought the couple had gotten into a fight and that they would soon reconcile. She asked Gohar what had happened. But Gohar's lips were sealed.

Everyone was certain that Engineer Safaa would go chasing after his wife or he would die of sorrow. Not so. The engineer neither chased after her nor died of sorrow. He shrugged and said, "The hell with her." At first, people were puzzled, but then they remembered that life is a sequence of ephemeral events and a succession of fleeting loves.

At the first opportunity, Engineer Safaa divorced Naz Maryam and went about searching for another wife. He told himself, What an idiot I was! Why didn't I think of saving myself sooner? I lost my pretty cat for nothing and I don't know what became of my dog.

Naz Maryam didn't know what to do with herself. Ever since her father's death, she had felt lost and insecure. She was anxious and afraid of life. Sleep was her escape to another world—to silence and oblivion. She hated daylight and stayed in bed until two in the afternoon. Gohar would tear the blanket off of her and force her to wake up. She would get up, wash, eat something, turn on the radio, walk aimlessly from room to room, call her cousin, flip through a magazine, and sit by the window for a while and watch the passersby. To kill time, she would tell her fortune with playing cards, and finally, sick with boredom, she would go back to bed and hide her head under the pillow.

Naz Maryam had sold her father's house and the creditors had taken almost everything she had. She lived a modest life with the little money she had left and she didn't bother with Auntie on the ground floor. Once a week her cousins and a few other women would come over to play cards. One day, while sitting at the table and holding her cards, she felt sick, turned pale, and rushed to the bathroom. Her cousins exchanged glances but said nothing. The following month, a worried Naz Maryam went to her gynecologist who determined that she was pregnant and congratulated her. Naz Maryam was devastated. She screamed so loud that the doctor leapt from his chair and his assistant came running into the room.

Weeping, staggering, cursing, Naz Maryam went home and threw herself down the stairs. Her head hit the wall and got swollen and she hurt her arm, but nothing else happened. She sat in a bathtub filled with very hot water, she lifted heavy weights, she drank a bottle of castor oil and vomited violently. In short, she did everything that could possibly cause a miscarriage, but she didn't miscarry. She went to see a couple of women who secretly performed abortions. They wanted more money than Naz Maryam had. She decided to sell her father's ring which she had kept as a memento. That same night, Gohar dreamt of the colonel and saw that he was very upset. She told Naz Maryam about her dream and it terrified her. She realized there was nothing she could do other than to accept her fate.

Naz Maryam felt nauseous from the moment she woke up in the morning and she cursed her husband every time she vomited. During her fourth month of pregnancy, the gynecologist joyfully told her that he could hear two hearts and that she was carrying twins. Twins! Naz Maryam leapt up and got sick on the doctor's desk. Distraught, she went home and decided to hang herself or slash her veins. Auntie and Gohar stopped her.

"You keep one of the twins and give the other one to me," Auntie said.

"You can have both of them!" Naz Maryam cried. "I'll call their scoundrel father and tell him to come and take his kids."

The scoundrel father was in America and no one had his address. There was nothing Naz Maryam could do. Auntie's suggestion was fair enough. She decided that without looking at the twins she would pick one and give the other one away. Then she begged Gohar, "Please take the other one. Give it to your mother or to your aunt. I'll pay its expenses."

"This is blasphemy," Gohar lamented. "It's a sin." And in her prayers she'd implored her Holiness Fatima to help Naz Maryam and to bring her back to her senses. She even vowed that she'd walk halfway to the sacred city of Qum. Then she got scared that she might not be able to live up to that promise and took it back.

THE PREGNANCY PROGRESSED with moans and groans and nausea and vomiting. Auntie and Gohar got busy cleaning the ground floor of the house. They painted, planted flowers in front of the windows, and bought baby clothes, towels, sheets, diapers, bottles, and then they sat and waited.

A week before Naz Maryam's due date, contractions started and she screamed and raised havoc in the house. She called out for her father and cursed Engineer Safaa. At the hospital, she exasperated the doctors and nurses. The happy mothers who were feeding their babies in nearby rooms were incensed by the constant shouting and they complained to the hospital director. Fortunately, the twins came quickly and relative calm was restored.

The nurses brought the children to show them to their mother. Naz Maryam half opened one eye and screamed at the sight of the first child and turned away. "Oh my God!" she said. "This one looks like a tarantula. I don't want to look at it. Take it away!" They brought the second child. Naz Maryam refused to open her eyes and shoved the child aside.

Auntie yelled at her and said that she should be ashamed of

herself, and Gohar burst into tears. Naz Maryam covered her face with her hands, but finally she took a quick, tearful peek at the second child. She turned away, but she didn't scream. This one was a chubby boy with a full head of hair. He was opening and closing his mouth, looking for his mother's breast. Naz Maryam opened her eyes a bit more and took a second look. She didn't gasp.

"Fine, you take the other one," she said.

I WAS "THE other one." I grew up in Auntie and Gohar's arms. I don't think there ever was a baby happier than me. Auntie constantly told me how much she loved me. She washed my feet and rubbed almond oil on my body. Gohar said I had a healthy appetite and ate without a fuss. At night, I would fall asleep next to Auntie or on Gohar's lap. Gohar would sing to me and stroke my hair. Once in a while, my mother would send down my brother's hand-me-downs, but she never came to see me.

Little by little, I grew up and no longer needed Gohar to tell me my life story. I could see and understand everything. I was small for my age. I had curly hair, big ears, and two large front teeth. Auntie would chuckle and say that I looked like a rabbit, that I was the cutest little boy in the world, that I looked funny. I guess I did. On the street, people would look at me and giggle and then they would affectionately pinch my cheeks.

Gohar spent the days upstairs, but at night she would come downstairs and stay with us. She was young and she knew how to dance. We would dance together and Auntie would clap for us. We had a bald cat that always sat outside on the windowsill and there was a stray dog that had made friends with us and with the bald cat. Auntie knew how to make little paper dolls. We would line them up on a tray and shake the tray to make them dance.

One day Gohar covered her eyes with a handkerchief and started chasing me, trying to catch me. Auntie joined our game and the three of us were running around the room. The radio was on at a high volume. Suddenly the door swung open and I saw my mother's angry face. I froze. Gohar grew quiet, too. Auntie was the only one who wasn't afraid of her.

"What is all this racket?" Mother screamed. "Are you crazy? The walls are shaking!" Then she turned to Gohar and snapped, "Shut that radio off and come upstairs."

She didn't look at me. She slammed the door and left. I had a big lump in my throat, but I didn't want to cry. Auntie quickly put on her shoes and said, "Take your bicycle and go play with the children outside."

My bicycle was old and too big for me. My feet didn't reach the pedals if I sat on the saddle, so I used to pedal while standing up on the stirrups. Auntie liked to stand in front of the door and watch us. The neighborhood kids liked her and always gathered around her. They knew her pockets were always full of candy.

That night, I didn't feel well. I didn't like the way my mother had screamed at Auntie. I wanted to go upstairs and see my brother.

"Forget about it, my dear," Gohar said. "Your brother is cranky. All he does is sit in front of the television and eat."

"Why doesn't he ever ask about me?" I asked.

Gohar wouldn't give me a straight answer. "Wait," she said. "When you start school, everything will work itself out."

"Gohar, where is my father?"

Auntie knew. "He's overseas," she said. "In a different city. He's married and has a child. A blue-eyed child."

A blue-eyed child! Mr. Aran had blue eyes, too. He was Auntie's friend and came to see us once a month. He was from Poland and he was fat. Very, very fat. Gohar knew Mr. Aran from years ago. She told me that when he was young he was in love with Auntie. But Auntie liked her cousin and married him. After a few years, her husband died and Auntie would put her head on Mr. Aran's chest and cry. But she wasn't willing to marry him and they stayed friends, like a brother and sister.

Mr. Aran would bring us chocolates and sweet concentrated milk and foreign cheese. Auntie would wear her best dress and the three of us would go out. Mr. Aran would take my hand, but his eyes were always on Auntie. I wished my brother would come with us, but Mother would never allow it. Sometimes I would see him at a window, looking out at the street. But the minute he caught sight of me he would move away. We were six years old and had to start going to school in the fall. I was happy and told Gohar that I would sit next to my brother in the classroom.

"Your brother is fat," Gohar said. "He's embarrassed and he won't leave his room. He says he doesn't want to go to school."

"Gohar, does my mother love my brother?"

"Yes. She would die for him. It's all God's doing. She didn't want any children and now she's obsessed with the boy."

"Even though he's fat?"

"Fat or thin doesn't matter. He's her child."

I was her child, too, and I couldn't understand why she didn't love me. Perhaps it was because of my two big front teeth. Auntie used to tell me that they would fall out and two small pretty teeth would grow in their place. I was waiting for my teeth to fall out. I didn't want my mother to see me looking like a rabbit.

Several times a day I would ask Gohar, "Is my brother really fat?"

Gohar would shake her head. She didn't approve of this sort of talk.

Mr. Aran was fat, too. One day he sat in Auntie's big easy chair with the leather armrests and he couldn't get up. His big butt was stuck and the chair would lift up with him. Gohar and Auntie kept pulling him and pushing him, but it was no use. We were dying of laughter. Mr. Aran said it wasn't important. "I'll hobble home with the chair and whenever I get tired I'll just sit down." In the end, the leather armrests broke and Mr. Aran fell flat on the floor.

Gohar brought down a set of my brother's clothes for me to wear on the first day of school. They were too big for me. The waist sagged around me. Auntie got angry.

"I'll buy new clothes for you," she said. "You don't need to wear your brother's hand-me-downs."

She planned for us to go shopping on Lalehzar Street with Mr. Aran. When Auntie fell asleep, I put on my brother's clothes and pranced around the room. My hands were lost in the sleeves and the pants dragged on the floor, but I felt like I was hugging my brother or that I had become like him. After all, we were twins and we used to play together in our mother's stomach. I lay down next to Auntie and I cried. The next day, Mr. Aran came. We took a taxi and went to Lalehzar Street and we ate cream puffs and lemonade. Auntie gave me her cream puff, too, and we bought one for Gohar and one for the bald cat as well. Mr. Aran was holding one of my hands and Auntie was holding the other one. Mr. Aran bought a pair of gray trousers and a blue shirt for me.

One day I was playing on the street when I saw my brother and mother coming. My brother was holding his head down and not looking at anyone. My mother saw me, but I think she didn't recognize me or pretended not to. I wanted to run over to them, but Gohar grabbed me from behind. I called my mother, but she went in the house and closed the door.

I sulked. No matter how much Auntie begged for me to eat, I refused. She went upstairs and knocked and knocked, but my mother wouldn't open the door. She came back downstairs and called Mr. Aran.

"Stop being so stubborn," Gohar said. "Have a bite to eat. Don't be a nuisance to Auntie."

No. I wouldn't eat. I sat in a corner and put my head down on my knees. I refused to speak. That night, Mr. Aran came to see us. He picked me up and tickled me. He made faces and did everything he could to make me laugh. It was no use.

"Look at what I brought for you," he said. "Look!"

I looked. It was a long stick with ten holes. Mr. Aran put one end of the stick in his mouth and blew in it. "They call this a reed flute," he said. "You can play beautiful music with it."

He started blowing in the stick and played a nice song. Auntie clapped and Gohar kissed my cheeks and danced.

Mr. Aran picked me up, gave me a hug, and sat me down on the table. I couldn't take my eyes off the reed flute. There was only one thought going through my mind: I had to play a beautiful song for my mother.

Mr. Aran started coming to the house three times a week to teach me to play the reed flute. He showed me what to do, which holes to cover with my fingers, when to lift my fingers, and how to blow into the reed flute. Little by little, I learned. I could play a simple song and each time I played it Gohar cried. Unlike her, Auntie would laugh and give me a piece of chocolate. I learned two other songs, too. One afternoon when Auntie was sleeping, I went upstairs and sat behind the door and played a song. No one opened the door. I was angry and heartbroken. I kicked the door three or four times and then I picked up the pot of geraniums sitting on the stairs and hurled it to the ground. No. I didn't want this mother. Gohar got to me just in time and stopped me from screaming. She dragged me downstairs and went into Auntie's room. Auntie wasn't feeling well. She was coughing.

That night Mr. Aran took Auntie and me to a place full of trees and he bought kebab for us. We bought a skewer of kebab for Gohar, too. We wrapped it in bread and took it home for her.

"Your brother wanted one of these reed flutes," Gohar said. "He insisted so much that your mother finally bought one for him. But he doesn't know how to play it."

Two days later, she came and said that Mother had hired a music teacher for him. From then on, each time I played my reed flute, my brother would answer from upstairs. That's how our friendship began. They left us alone and we were happy with our reed flutes.

The first day of school was approaching and I had prepared myself to talk to my brother. That day Mr. Aran came to walk me to school. Auntie wasn't feeling well and stayed at home. Gohar had gone upstairs to get my brother ready. My hand was in Mr. Aran's hand and my heart was beating fast. I was both happy and scared. Every two steps, I turned and looked behind to see if my brother was coming or not. There was no one there. I thought he had perhaps left earlier than me. I was walking slowly and on tiptoes to make sure my shoes didn't get dirty. The children were standing in line in the schoolyard. Mr. Aran had to leave. I didn't want to let go of his hand. All the children my age were crying. The school principal yelled at them to be quiet and they cried even harder. I was looking around searching for my brother. We went to class. They had me sit in the front row because I was smaller than everyone else. I took my notebook, pencil, and reed flute out of my schoolbag and put them on the desk.

The lady teacher saw my reed flute and said, "What is that? Put it back in your bag."

I didn't.

"Put it in your bag!" she shouted.

I did.

During recess I started to play my reed flute. I was waiting for my brother to answer me. I was sure no matter where he was he would hear it. The children gathered around me and clapped, but my brother didn't answer. He wasn't there.

Despite being sick and coughing, Auntie came to pick me up from school. She was in a bad mood. I was sure something had happened to my brother. But no matter how many times I asked her, she said nothing. When we got home, I took out my reed flute and played. My brother wasn't there either.

Gohar told me my father had returned and he had taken my brother to stay with him for a few days. He had asked to see me, too, and said he'd come back.

Every day in school, I waited for my father and brother to come. When the school bell rang, I would run and stand by the door and peek out to see my father. I had no idea what he looked like.

One day when I came home from school, I saw Auntie standing in the hallway. I could hear people arguing and crying upstairs. I dropped my schoolbag and ran up the stairs. The door was open. I walked in. My mother was standing next to the dining room table crying. My brother was there; whole and healthy. I was relieved. There was a man there. He had a black mustache and he was wearing eyeglasses.

Gohar rushed over and whispered, "Go up to your father and say hello."

My heart skipped a beat. I started to hiccup. My brother was looking at the floor and not saying anything.

My father was kind. "So you are the other one?" he said.

It seemed he liked me. I couldn't figure out why my mother was crying.

"Do you want to come to America with me?" father asked.

I froze. "No, sir. I want to stay with Auntie."

My mother gave me a nasty look, as if she wanted to beat me.

"Auntie is old," she screamed. "She'll die in a year and you'll be all alone. Any other kid would jump at the chance to go to America."

I grabbed Gohar's hand. I was shaking. "I want to stay right here with my auntie," I said. And I dashed out and ran downstairs.

Gohar followed me. She looked pale. "He wants to take one of you to America," she explained.

I could hear my mother arguing. "Take the other one," she begged. "Let this one stay here with me."

I was clinging to Auntie. I was terrified they would give me to my father. I wanted to run away and go to my friend's house next door, or hide under the bed or behind the curtain.

Auntie grabbed my hand tight and said, "Don't be afraid, my dear. I won't let them take you away from me. You can be sure."

Gohar kept running upstairs and running back downstairs. Then she said it was done. "The gentleman has put your brother's coat on him and he's taking him away. And the missus is sprawled out on her bed, weeping."

I climbed up on a chair and looked out the window. My mother had run out to the street, but it was too late. My father and brother were in the car. I didn't know why that boy wasn't saying anything or fighting. It was as if he was asleep.

WITH MY BROTHER gone, my mother was all alone. Gohar said she slept until noon and then sat at the dining room table telling her fortune with playing cards. I wanted to go upstairs, but Auntie had forbidden it. She said I had to wait until my mother sent for me. Sometimes my mother would go out and I would watch her from the corner of the door. She staggered like a confused person. I went to school, came home, and did my homework, but my ears were listening for sounds coming from upstairs. I felt sorry for my mother because she ate dinner all alone. Why didn't she come and join us? Why was she angry with Auntie? Mr. Aran had enrolled me in a music class and once a week he would come and take me there. I now played a proper flute.

Even though we had always been apart, I missed my brother. There wasn't a day that I didn't think about him. I didn't know where he was and what he was doing. Gohar said he sent letters from America and Mother took them all to bed and read them over and over again. She slept with the letters tucked under her pillow or spread out on her blanket. Mother said the letters had my brother's smell.

One day I saw my mother on the street. Her eyes were puffy and red. She walked past me. It was as if she didn't recognize me. It wasn't her fault. It had been three years since my brother left and I had suddenly grown taller. A lot had changed. The bald cat had been run over by a car, Gohar didn't have the patience she used to have, and Auntie was coughing again. She would lie in bed and close her eyes and I would sit with my back to her and my head buried in books. But I felt her love even then.

I was in the last year of high school when demonstrations against the Shah started. Gohar was terrified. She closed all the windows and wouldn't set foot outside the house. School was disrupted, too, and I was out on the streets, just like everyone else in the city. Gohar would try to stop me, but Auntie didn't object. She didn't want to lock me in the house. The household shopping was now my responsibility and Auntie always gave half of it to Gohar to take upstairs for my mother.

The Shah left. Khomeini came. The arrests and imprisonments started. And then war broke out with Iraq and we had to turn off the lights and cover the windows with sheets of newspaper. We lived in darkness. I would go upstairs and stand behind the door, wandering what my mother was doing all alone. Often I would hear her walking aimlessly around or hear her talking to herself. Gohar had told me about her dreadful marriage to my father whom she didn't love and about the loss of her father whom she worshiped. I was already a young man and felt it was my duty to protect her.

She still had her card game gatherings. Four women would come, play cards, eat dinner, and afraid of the nightly bombardments, they would stay the night. One night the city sirens went off, warning people that an air raid was imminent and that everyone should immediately seek shelter. My mother and her guests came down to the basement and sat around a table. They had brought their playing cards with them. Gohar lit a few candles. I was sitting next to Auntie and couldn't tear my eyes away from my mother's sad face. She looked like a lost child and her small hands trembled as she held her cards. Thanks to Auntie who had bathed me in a pool of love, I had had a happy childhood and did not harbor any ill feelings toward my mother. I heard one of her guests quietly ask, "Is this the other one?" And she discreetly pointed at me. My mother didn't answer, but she looked at me from the corner of her eyes. Then she nodded and I thought she smiled. Or maybe I imagined it. I took a box of pastries out from under the bed and offered some to the guests and especially to my mother, who thanked me but didn't take any. My hands were shaking. The guests each took three or four pieces and ate them quickly.

I had grown tall and my teeth were small and straight. I wasn't ugly. Gohar used to say I was as handsome as the moon, but I never believed her. My mother kept peeking at me from behind her cards. Perhaps because I looked like my brother. But she didn't speak to me. We kept lighting one candle after another until suddenly the blast of an explosion made us all jump. Auntie screamed my name and Gohar ran and hid in the closet. My mother and two of the women dove under the table and I saw another woman quickly slip a joker in her sleeve before crawling under the bed. It took an hour for the sirens to stop blaring. The women came out from under the bed and the table and again sat down to play, but first they searched the fat lady's pockets and sleeves and found the joker. The fat lady sulked. Morning came and we all got up and left. I was desperately praying for another bombardment so that my mother would take shelter in the basement again.

By now, Auntie was constantly coughing and couldn't sleep at night. We took her to the hospital. She had fluid in her lungs. Mr. Aran had grown older and heavier. He had difficulty walking, but he came to visit Auntie every day and brought her sweet lemons. Auntie was not going to recover. My mother had been told and she came to visit her regularly. One day I went to the hospital after school and saw my mother standing behind the door to Auntie's room. Her head was down and she wouldn't look at me. Mr. Aran was there, too. He was crying. I realized Auntie had died. I don't know why I didn't cry. Maybe it was because I didn't want to cry in front of my mother or because my sadness was so deep that it wouldn't let me cry. I was numb. For the first time ever, my mother spoke to me with concern in her eyes. As she left, she said, "Come have dinner upstairs. Don't stay downstairs."

I didn't go. I locked the door and didn't even let Gohar come in. I lay down on Auntie's bed and cried myself to sleep.

For the next three months, Gohar brought me food from upstairs. I went to school every day and went straight back home. I was the best student in class, but I was unhappy. I would put Auntie's paper dolls on a tray and shake the tray to make them dance.

One day Gohar came downstairs and said that my mother had fallen and broken her leg. I rushed upstairs. She was lying on her bed, moaning. Her eyes were brimming with tears. She was too embarrassed to look at me. I wanted to kiss her face and her broken leg that was in a cast. I picked her up. She was as light as a child. I sat her down on a chair at the dining room table and Gohar brought her breakfast.

"Sit down," she said. "You have to eat, too." I had already eaten, but I suddenly felt hungry again. It was the first time I was eating with my mother. I started to talk. Fast. As if I was being chased. My mother listened. I told her about school, my classes, my teachers, about the latest books I had read. Gohar had told me that my mother's eyes had grown weak and she couldn't read anymore.

"Would you read to me?" she asked.

I brought the books I was reading and I put them next to her bed. But I continued to live downstairs until the day my mother insisted I live with her. I didn't want to move into my brother's room. There was a smaller room at the end of the hallway. Gohar tidied it up for me and I brought my books and belongings. I felt I had been reborn and this time my mother had chosen me.

Living upstairs wasn't easy. I had walked into a new world, a world that had only existed in my dreams. It was someplace on the other side of reality, someplace outside of my reach. I didn't know my mother. I observed her from a distance and I searched for a sliver of similarity between us. I couldn't find it. I had had a different image of her in my mind. She was like the shadow of a different woman, a woman who existed in my fantasies. She had the hands of a girl. Delicate, with small, slim fingers. I loved her eyes. Large, sad eyes. Sleepy eyes. Her hair was short. She had cut it herself. It was patchy and uneven. She smoked. One cigarette after the other. She coughed and I was afraid she would catch tuberculosis and die. I wanted to take away her cigarettes, but I didn't dare. I was still "the other one" and I wasn't allowed to interfere in her life.

The first few weeks, she didn't talk much and rarely looked at me. She was like a lonely bird in a cage. I decided to buy a lovebird for her, but Gohar reminded me that she was afraid of cats, dogs, and birds. She didn't watch television. She was always thinking about my brother and was blind to my presence. Gradually, she started to talk. She had dreamt of her father. She cried. She brought her father's photographs and showed them to me. She spread them out on the dining room table like a deck of cards and moved them around as if she was telling a fortune. She stared at them for a long time, frowning, smiling. She was drowned in her memories. Then she gathered up the photographs and put them aside and she brought photographs of my brother and spread them out. She lovingly ran her fingers over them and talked about him. I had not seen this brother and didn't know him. But somewhere in our mind, in our heart, in our dreams, we were connected. After all, we were twins and had been together for nine entire months with our arms and legs rubbing, touching. I looked at photographs of him at different ages and re-created his life in my mind.

Mr. Aran was only half-alive. Once or twice a week I would invite him to dinner and I would play the flute for him. I saw to my mother's affairs, took her on outings, and made sure she took her medication. We would play cards together and occasionally laugh. Little by little, she had grown accustomed to me and would worry if I was late returning home. One day, Gohar announced that she wanted to go back to her village. My mother panicked. What would she do without her? I put her mind at ease. I took over the shopping, cleaning, and cooking. At night, I would wait for her to fall asleep and then I would sit and study. I was in my second year of university. Once a week, a woman came to help my mother bathe. I was happy. The only thing that troubled me was being far from my brother—from the other one.

WEEKS AND MONTHS flew by. I was so busy with my studies and taking care of Mother that I often forgot what month and what day of the week it was. My mother galvanized my life and it was only when I looked at her gray hair and the fine wrinkles on her face that I sensed the passage of time. I could see how quickly she had aged and lost her memory and the souvenirs of her life.

She often mistook me for my brother and was happy that he had returned. Then, for a long time, she would forget him, too. The doctor who visited her was alarmed. Mother was suffering from acute Alzheimer's.

I would read my brother's letters to her. She would listen, but I wasn't sure she understood. I read the letters over and over again and I tried to imagine his life, his face, his voice. He was on his university's soccer team and he had won first prize in a ski competition.

I tried not to think about Auntie and the bald cat and the past. I was young and my future was ahead of me. I had only one thought in mind—to go to America to be with my brother. I would take Mother with me. Occasionally, my father would send us some U.S. dollars and I would put the money in the bank so that I could pay for our trip.

It was early summer when I received a short letter from my father. He wrote that my brother had died in a car accident. When? Where? No explanation. The letter wasn't even dated. I told no one. I went for long walks at night and tried to console myself. I stood behind the trees and quietly cried. I was happy that my mother was no longer alert. Her loss of memory was a blessing. She often held me tight in her arms and I didn't know which one of us she was thinking of. Perhaps me. And then she would forget me, too.

IT WAS MY twenty-fifth birthday. I bought a small strawberry cake from the local bakery and I invited Mr. Aran to join us. Gohar was there, too. She had come from her village to stay with us for a few days. My mother was in another world and no longer in touch with reality. Mr. Aran had lost his hearing and was now completely deaf.

I changed my mother's clothes and combed her hair. I wiped her hands with a wet towel and put scented cream on her face and neck. She looked beautiful. I kissed her face and her hands.

I lit the candles. Mr. Aran clapped. Mother stared at the candles. She tried to say something and opened and closed her lips, but she didn't make a sound. I blew out the candles. Mr. Aran cheered and Gohar, perhaps thinking of my brother, sighed. I put a large slice of cake on a plate for Gohar and a smaller slice for my mother. Mr. Aran had diabetes and only picked at a tiny piece with the tip of his fork. Gohar ate with her hands and then fell asleep right where she was sitting. Mother pushed away her plate.

It was a quiet and sedate birthday party. Sad and silent like a funeral. Until Mother suddenly woke up, raised her head, and smiled. She had long forgotten how to smile. She threw the sheets off her frail legs. It was rare for her to want to walk. I took her under the arm and helped her stand. She nodded toward the window and we took a few steps closer to it.

She was trembling. She pointed up at the sky and said, "Look. Look."

I looked up. The stars were shining brighter than usual. They seemed so close that you could jump up and touch them.

She said, "Can you hear it?"

"What?"

"Listen. Someone is playing the flute somewhere far away."

"Where?"

"Behind the stars."

Mr. Aran was deaf, but he heard it, too. Gohar was sleeping. She had heard it in her sleep.

Again, my mother asked, "Can you hear it?"

Mr. Aran said, "I hear it."

Gohar muttered, "Me, too."

Mother was leaning out of the window as if wishing to fly. She kept staring at the sky and humming a song in an unknown language. I couldn't understand a word of it.

THE POMEGRANATE LADY

AND HER SONS

Mehrabad Airport, Tehran. Air France, Flight 726

J hate this life of constant wandering, these eternal comings and goings, these middle-of-the-night flights, dragging along my suitcase, going through customs, and the final torture, the humiliating body search. "Take off your shoes, open your handbag, let's see inside your pockets, your mouth, your ears, your nostrils, your heart, your mind, your soul." I'm exhausted. I feel homesick—can you believe it? Already homesick. And yet I want to run, get away, escape. I will leave and never come back, I tell myself. No. I will stay right here, in my beloved Tehran, with all its good and bad, and I will never leave. Nonsense. I'm confused. All I want is to close my eyes and sleep, to glide into that enchanted land of oblivion and to disappear.

Leave-taking. Silently, quickly, with a lump in my throat and an inexplicable anxiety that I try to hide from those who have come to see me off.

The so-called "Sisters Entrance"—women only. My appearance is not acceptable. My headscarf has slipped back and the lowermost button on my long coverall is undone. Fine. "You're right, Sister." I make the necessary adjustments. The porter carrying my suitcase and duffel bag is in a hurry. He wants to get paid. He is looking for another customer.

"You have to come with me as far as customs," I tell him.

I had made this a condition from the start, but he keeps repeating himself. He wants to go. He puts my suitcase on the X-ray machine's conveyor belt and motions to another passenger.

Don't lose your cool, lady, I tell myself. Let it go. That's the way things are. Give him his money and let him go.

A glass wall separates those inside from the others outside. Those who stay and the others who leave. Both groups look sad and forlorn. Their unspoken words and meaningful looks pass through the thick glass and settle on our faces like a layer of gray dust.

The innards of my suitcase are carefully X-rayed. Some suspicious and fearsome item—I have no idea what—is discovered.

An accusing finger points to the image of my suitcase on the computer monitor.

"A murder weapon."

"What murder weapon? In my suitcase?"

The customs inspector consults with another agent. They both lean forward and stare at the mysterious image on the screen.

The people who have come to see their friends and relatives off are craning their necks. Those around me are speaking in hushed tones. Muted questions float in their eyes. In one second, I have metamorphosed into a dangerous being. I am guilty and my conviction is certain.

A terrorist?

Perhaps. Anything is possible.

The murder weapon is a gold-colored battle-ax I bought for

my son from a junk shop in Isfahan. It isn't worth a penny and you can't kill anyone with it, especially not the flight captain.

My suitcase is moved to the side. It has to be carefully inspected. The other passengers stare at me and my suitcase with suspicion and even fear.

"It's just a funny old battle-ax," I explain. "It's not the real thing. It's part of the paraphernalia dervishes carry. It caught my eye and I bought it. And it's packed in my suitcase. What could I possibly do with it?"

They have turned a deaf ear to me. The battle-ax—the murder weapon—is carefully removed from my suitcase. People watch. The customs inspector says it's old, it's an antique, it's valuable, it's part of our nation's cultural heritage.

Nonsense!

I have the sales receipt. It's barely worth five thousand tumans. Its surface is decorated with Arabic words, probably a verse from the Quran.

"Mr. Parrot has to examine and appraise it."

Mr. Parrot is paged. A few people laugh and someone, mimicking a parrot, keeps repeating the same word. A hand grabs my arm.

"Dear lady . . ."

It is an old woman. She's mumbling something. She wants something, but I don't understand her. I'm in a hurry. I have to find out what the decision is about the murder weapon.

"I don't want the battle-ax," I say. "Keep it and let me go."

But my fate is in Mr. Parrot's hands. I have to wait. It's my own mistake and I have to pay for it.

The old woman taps me on the shoulder. "Dear lady, I'd give my life for you. I'm late. I'm afraid I'll be left behind."

She is a villager, confused and panicked. She begs me to complete the customs declaration form for her.

"Dear lady," she says, "my eyes are weak and I can't read or write. My sons said, 'Mom, just get on the plane and come.' I didn't know it would be so difficult. I fainted twice in the passport office. I almost died."

"Look, I'm busy," I say. "Ask someone else to help you."

"Who? Everyone is in a hurry."

I point to a well-dressed young man.

"I already asked him. He grew up abroad and he can't write in Persian. I'm afraid my sons have forgotten to read and write Persian, too. What if they've forgotten their mother tongue? May God have mercy on me!"

Mr. Parrot is again paged over the loudspeakers. The old lady won't give up. She keeps going in circles and doesn't know what to do.

"Dear lady, where is the Swedish airplane?" she asks.

I leaf through her passport. Most of the pages are blank. It's her first trip overseas. Her first name is Anar-Banu (Pomegranate Lady) and her last name is Chenari. I quickly fill out her customs declaration form. She was born in 1917. She is eighty-three years old. She is on the same flight as me. To Paris, and from there to Sweden.

"I haven't seen my sons in ten years," she says. "My heart goes pit-a-pat for them. I told them, 'My darlings, I'd give my life for you, but why did you move to the other end of the world? What was wrong with our own Yazd?' But they wanted to go and they wouldn't change their mind. My late husband used to say the madness of youth has affected their brain."

Mr. Parrot has arrived and he is looking for me. He is short and thin, the size of a ten-year-old boy, but he has a large, aging nose and he's wearing thick eyeglasses. Without uttering a word, he examines the battle-ax. He holds it up to the lamp.

"This battle-ax is old."

I shake my head. Anar-Banu cranes her neck to get a closer look. She reaches out and runs her fingers over the battle-ax's blade.

"Dear lady," she says, "couldn't you find anything else to take with you? This thing belongs to dervishes."

"How old is old?" I ask.

Mr. Parrot doesn't approve of my persistence. He's in a hurry. "The ax head is antique," he says. "But the handle is new."

Regardless, it is a dangerous weapon. It can be used to behead the captain and the crew and all the security agents, and it can be used to take the passengers hostage and to divert the plane to Africa.

"You can have this Achamenid battle-ax," I snap. "Take it!"

They won't take it. The old woman won't budge from my side. Mr. Parrot wants to leave. He is tired. He yawns.

I take the battle-ax and walk back to the airport lounge so that I can give it to my friend who has come to see me off. There is no sign of him. The people standing behind the glass wall laugh and clap for me. I squirm in embarrassment.

A group of forty or fifty people, young and old, with a brood of children wielding bouquets of wilted gladioli, are waiting for the arrival of passengers from India. It is mayhem.

A child steps on my toes and runs off gleefully waving his withered bouquet.

I offer the battle-ax to a porter standing by the door. Out of breath and in a foul mood, I hurry back inside and see the old lady still standing there, anxiously looking around and not knowing where to go. She sees me and beams with joy. She waves and quickly makes her way over to me.

"Where were you, dear lady? I thought you'd gone ahead without me."

She follows me. Her bag is heavy and she is panting. Sweat is streaming down her cheeks. She takes a checkered handkerchief out of her pocket and dries her face.

The handkerchief is half the size of a tablecloth.

"Soheila Khanom is a schoolteacher in our village," she says. "She knows the names of all the cities in the world. She says in Sweden water freezes even in the summer. The temperature drops to minus 150 degrees. Cattle and sheep freeze to death even as they stand. I put on all the wool clothes I have, one on top of the other. Now I'm dying of heat."

The flight is delayed by one hour. Perhaps two. It's not clear. The people seeing off friends and relatives stand waiting behind the glass wall with cheerless patience. Those inside watch the others outside.

The date and time of the flight was determined long in advance, but there is no guarantee that its departure will become a reality. It is plagued by a thousand maybes, doubts, and fears. Dark thoughts swirl around in my head. What if my name is on the list of those banned from leaving the country? What if I never see my loved ones again? What if so-and-so and so-and-so die while I'm away?

Anar-Banu Chenari follows me like a shadow and talks incessantly. Her anxiety is so overwhelming that it pours out from her roving gaze and trembling hands.

"Lucky those who have obedient children. My two sons had their heads in the clouds ever since they were children. They were always restless. They hated our village and the villagers. All they wanted to do was to move to the big city. To Tehran. To some other city. Where? They didn't know. When we were young the only place we knew was Yazd. For us, Yazd was the beginning and the end of the world."

The beginning and the end of the world!

"Lady, you're lucky you found your niche in the world," I say.

She's thinking of her sons. She has forgotten where she is and the long road that lies ahead for her. Her eyes are full of dreams—dreams of the Yazd she has left behind and the strange city that awaits her.

"I sent them a letter," she says. "You see, I can't read or write. I told Soheila Khanom what I was thinking and she wrote the letter. I asked them, 'Tell me, are you happy and healthy there at the other end of the world?' They wrote back, 'Mom, we are all alone here, far away from our family. This horrid cold has frozen our bones. Some nights we weep out loud. We want to go to America.' Soheila Khanom said, 'America is evil.' My husband nearly had a heart attack. He said, 'My sons have turned into nomads. They've lost their roots. Wherever they go they will be strangers, aliens.'"

"Hurry up," I say. "You have to show your bag for inspection."

Anar-Banu's bag is crammed with odds and ends—a few boxes of pastries, two or three lengths of taffeta from Yazd, several plastic bowls, and a number of plastic bags filled with pomegranates and rice.

"The pomegranates are from our own orchard," she explains.

We are done here. Another obstacle is behind us. We pick up

our bags and move on. Anar-Banu follows me. At the check-in counter, I give the agent Anar-Banu's ticket together with my own. Our seats are assigned. We go upstairs. I hold my passport ready. For no good reason, perhaps out of sheer habit, I feel pangs of anxiety stabbing at my heart. I am expecting trouble. My heart is racing. I'm afraid there may be something missing, or something extra, in my passport—a missing stamp or the presence of some special mark—that may give the authorities reason to prevent me from leaving. Why? I don't know. Anything is possible.

My fears are unfounded. All goes well.

The body search is not as bad as it used to be. It's less stringent. Anar-Banu is ticklish. She giggles and squirms. She is wearing two gold bangles on each wrist and an agate ring on her finger. She shows them to the Sister conducting the body search. She is offering too much information. She looks around nervously and then she looks at me. She is hiding a pair of ruby earrings, which are not of any great value, in her pocket. She is afraid she might be caught and accused of smuggling jewelry. And she is caught. She is trembling.

"I'm taking these for my daughter-in-law," she stammers. "Soheila Khanom gave them to me. May God strike me blind if I'm lying. My daughter-in-law is European. She has converted to Islam. She says her prayers regularly." And she starts to plead with the Sister.

They return the earrings to her and let her go.

"My older son married a European girl," she says. "She's from some village in Sweden. I told him, 'Son, come back to your home-town. The girls in Yazd are as beautiful as the best of them. We don't speak Swedish. How are we supposed to talk to your wife?'"

We reach the waiting lounge. Anar-Banu sinks into the chair

next to me and dozes off. She mumbles under her breath. Her chin has sunk into her chest and her legs are flung wide open. She is probably dreaming of her sons, those boys with their heads in the clouds, in search of better lives in icy wastelands. She slumps forward and slides off the chair. I leap up. The passenger sitting on her other side also jumps to her rescue. She is confused and doesn't remember where she is. A young boy bursts into laughter and a woman shakes her head sadly.

"Dear lady!" Anar-Banu cries. There is a lump in her throat. I straighten her headscarf. She sits up properly and holds her head up high. She tries to laugh, or at least to smile. She is trying hard to keep her composure, but her eyes are brimming with sleep and her old body is ready to collapse.

The passengers are called to board the plane. The long and disorderly line makes exiting the lounge difficult. Anar-Banu is in a hurry and pushes her way through the crowd. At the foot of the stairs leading up to the airplane door, she stops. Stunned and frightened, she stares up at the huge airplane wings. She can hardly move. She climbs two steps and stops again. She is blocking the way. A flight attendant comes to her aid. She holds Anar-Banu under the arm and pulls her up, step by step, all the way to the top.

Anar-Banu's seat is next to mine. She beams with joy. She sits down and shoves her bag down under her feet.

"O sons of mine!" she says. "What am I going to do with you? I wish I could stop loving you so that I wouldn't have to roam around the world."

She takes off her shoes. She groans. She is wearing thick black stockings and she is hot. Her face is covered with beads of sweat.

"Thank God I'm sitting next to you," she says. "Soheila Kha-nom said, 'Mama Pomegranate, if you're lucky, you'll be sitting next to a caring person, someone like your own daughter.' It's a pity I don't have a daughter. Mothers and daughters are closer. She would have never left me to go to Sweden. What about you? Do you have any children?"

I turn away and bury my face in my pillow. I have to sleep.

Mama Pomegranate's soft, plump arm gently presses against me. Her warm and tired body fills her seat and spills over to occupy half of mine. There is a faint smell of hunger on her breath, but her body has a pleasant scent. I pull the edge of the blanket over my eyes and stare at the sleep that is hovering behind my eyelids.

"Dear lady, are you going to Sweden, too?"

I shake my head.

"I'm afraid I might miss my stop."

I don't answer.

"Dear lady, please tell me when we get to Sweden."

"Try to sleep, Anar-Banu. Close your eyes and go to sleep."

A flight attendant is checking to see if the passengers have fastened their seatbelts. I have fastened mine. Anar-Banu has no notion of the routines of air travel. She is confused and fidgets in her seat. She nudges me with her elbow.

"Dear lady, I don't speak any foreign language," she says.

The flight attendant wants to fasten her seatbelt for her, but one end of the belt is stuck under her. I force my hand under Anar-Banu's hot and tired body. It tickles her and she twists and turns and giggles.

"Please lift yourself up a little," I say. And I grab the end of the belt and try to pull it out. It doesn't budge. I pull harder, but it's no use. She is heavy and sitting on the belt and on my hand and has no intention of moving. The flight attendant slides her hand under Anar-Banu from the other side. Again, it tickles her. She laughs, bounces up and down, and lands in a heap. She falls sideways on top of me and the seatbelt slides out from under her.

"Oh dear lady! That was fun," she says. "God, how I laughed! I wish my sons could see me now."

She giggles and takes my hand in her coarse, warm hands.

She has a kind and pleasant face and there is a glint in her dark eyes. She says, "Dear lady, please let me know when we get to Sweden. I'm scared I might miss my stop."

I explain that an airplane is not like a bus. It doesn't make ten stops. It takes off from Tehran and lands in Charles de Gaulle Airport in Paris. There, she has to get off and change planes.

She becomes even more confused and stares at me wide-eyed. She doesn't understand. Sweden is her destination; she has memorized this.

"Dear lady," she says, "I've been traveling for three days. From Yazd I took the bus to Tehran. On the way, the bus broke down. It burst a tire. The driver lost control and the bus swerved and hit an old man and his donkey. The poor old man lost his life. To make a long story short, we had to spend the night by the road-side, in the desert. The flies and mosquitoes feasted on me all night long. I almost died. I thought I would never make it. I have a thousand and one ailments. I'm over eighty years old, but the joy of soon seeing my two sons gives me strength. This bag here is full of rice and pomegranates. And I've brought along a few bottles of pomegranate molasses. Excellent quality! It's from our own village. That's why they call me Mama Pomegranate."

She laughs out loud, digs into her bag, and pulls out two large red pomegranates.

"Please, have one."

I shake my head. She starts to squeeze a pomegranate to soften it so that I can pierce its skin and drink its juice. I stare at the fruit. It looks like it's ready to burst.

"No, no, I don't want any!" I say. "Please stop squeezing it." And I pull myself away from her. My Islamic coverall is white.

"Don't worry, dear lady," she says. "This is not just any pomegranate. It's the pomegranate of love." And with her strong fingers she presses down on the still-unsoftened parts of the fruit.

"I was raised under a pomegranate tree," she says. "I had no father and no mother. I drank pomegranate juice instead of mother's milk. I would pull down a branch and squeeze a pomegranate and suck out its juice. I thought it was my mother's breast. People would say, 'Anarak (Little Pomegranate), this tree is your mother. It is the tree of love.' And they would point to the sycamore tree (Chenarak) next to it and say, 'This is your father.' And that is how I found a mother and a father. One day I went to get my identity card and the man in the office said, 'What's your name?' I said, 'Anarak.' He said, 'What's your father's name?' I said, 'Chenarak (Little Sycamore).' He said, 'Get lost. Were you born from a tree?' I said, 'Yes.'"

She has a gentle voice and playful eyes. Her face looks like a succulent pomegranate, ready to be squeezed—red cheeks and full lips. She is a charming, lively old woman. She constantly fidgets in her seat and swings her small, fleshy feet. They don't reach the cabin floor.

I'm no longer sleepy.

One hour into the flight, they serve breakfast. Mama Pomegranate is famished and wolfs down her bread and jam.

"Dear lady," she says, "aren't you hungry? Why aren't you eating?"

With my permission, she puts the remainder of my breakfast in front of her and makes smacking noises as she eats.

"Do you have any children?" she asks.

I nod.

"Do they live with you?"

"Yes."

"Lucky you. A child is the essence of life. I haven't seen my sons in twelve years. I never imagined that my children, the offspring of Mama Pomegranate, would end up in Europe one day. My older boy wrote, 'Mom, I say my prayers every day and I fight for my country.' I wrote back and asked, 'Son, who are you fighting?' He wrote, 'I am fighting the enemies of my religion and of my country.'

"My younger boy is different. He writes once a year and he tries to sweet-talk me. He writes, 'Mom, come here and we'll go dancing.' The scoundrel, he lies! But he cheers me up with his lies. The other one only thinks of fighting. He just wants to cut people's heads off. I asked him, 'What are you? A butcher? A killer?' He said, 'One day I'll finally kill Colonel Zamani.' My poor husband slapped himself on the head and said, 'The idiot! Colonel Zamani is a Muslim. He has a wife and children. It would be a sin.' But my son kept writing, 'I'll kill so-and-so and so-and-so, too.' But he lies. Big lies.

"He has been married twice, to European women. His first wife looked like a cat. Just a sack of bones. My husband spat at the photo of his daughter-in-law, tore it up, and threw it in the toilet. And then we received a photo of our younger son. He had dyed his hair blond. He looked gorgeous, just like a girl. He wrote, 'Mom, I play Western music and sing at weddings.'

"My husband said, 'We've been disgraced. He plucks his eyebrows and wears makeup. He is not my son. My sons are dead.' He mourned and moaned and groaned so much that finally he died.

"I said to myself, Life is hell without my husband and my sons. And I went and lay down under the pomegranate tree and waited for the Angel of Death to come and take me. Suddenly there was a commotion and I heard the villagers calling me. The mailman had come. I can still hear the sound of his bicycle bells. What a loud cling-clang. The children were sitting on the garden wall clapping. The village elder also came. He said, 'Mama Pomegranate, guess what! You have a letter from Europe.' And then he took the letter, opened it, and saved the envelope and the stamps for himself. 'This is an official document, and it must be archived.'

"The letter was from my younger son. He wrote, 'Mom, come over here right away. I'm dying to see you. I'm afraid you, too, might die.' His words made me feel a hundred years younger. I jumped up and said, 'My darling, I'd give my life for you. So what if you look like a woman. You are still the apple of my eye. But where's Sweden?' I asked around.

"No one in our village knew where Sweden was. The village elder said, 'Don't go. You'll die before you get there.' I said, 'I will go even if I have to walk all the way there.' People said, 'You will have to cross the Seven Seas.' I said, 'I'll cross the Seven Seas. God is with me. My boys are waiting for me.'

"My older son is the angry, hot-tempered type. All he does is talk about revenge. He is politically active. During the Shah's regime he went to prison twice. But he didn't learn his lesson. He kept on saying they must all be hanged, they must pay with their lives. I told him, 'My son, they are God's creatures, just like you and me.' He said, 'No. This is blasphemy. Only we are God's creatures. They are all enemies of our faith and our country.' One day a few Revolutionary Guards came to our village looking for him. He was scared to death and trembling like a chicken. He forgot his big words and his threats and asked Colonel Zamani for help. The dear colonel hid him in his cellar for forty days and kept him fed, until one day he ran away to the mountains and became a homeless wanderer.

"For three years, we had no news of him. We thought he was dead. We mourned for him. We told everyone he had been martyred. People came and offered their condolences and felicitations. We sold the very carpets we sat on and gave the money to the mosque to celebrate his martyrdom. Then one day, thank God, news came that he was in Sweden. At first we thought Sweden was someplace in Iran, a village up north, in the Caspian region. Then we found out it was at the edge of the world.

"Around that time, the younger boy caught the bug, too. I pleaded with him, 'Don't go. Stay with us.' I begged him, but it was no use. He said, 'I want to go away, to another country.' Young men are as stubborn as mules. They do what they want and refuse to listen to anyone. He left. He was stuck in Turkey for several years until his brother arranged for him to go to Sweden, too.

"Dear lady, I've talked too much and given you a headache. I didn't let you sleep. I just wanted you to know what children do to you. For the past ten years, asleep or awake, I've talked to my sons in my thoughts. I was afraid I would get amnesia and forget them. My husband used to say, 'Amnesia would be a blessing from God. I wish we could stop loving them. I wish we could lie down and die.' But I swore I would not die until I saw my sons again.

Every time I said my prayers, I called their names out loud. I kept it up until they heard me and sent me an airplane ticket.

"I traveled from Yazd to Tehran. I stayed with Soheila Khanom's brother, the engineer. He helped me and drove me to the airport. People said there are no eggplants in Sweden, so I brought a few kilos with me. I wish you were coming to Sweden, too. Tonight, I'm going to cook eggplant stew for the boys. And then *fesenjān*, with chicken and pomegranate molasses. Every night, I will cook a different Iranian dish for these unkind sons of mine until they finally become homesick for Yazd. Where in God's name is Sweden anyway? Soheila Khanom said in Sweden water freezes right in your mouth and tears turn into shards of glass and people go blind. I said to myself, Oh God, I hope my sons haven't gone blind. Who knows what they've been eating all this time. My husband said, 'They eat pork. That's why they now look like women.'

"My older son is a big man. He hasn't plucked his eyebrows. But he has frowned so much and he has wanted to take revenge on this and that person for so long that he has become squinty-eyed. As soon as I get to Sweden, I'm going to hug my younger son and hold him tight against my chest. I'm going to sleep at the foot of his bed and lay my head on his feet. When he was a child he always walked barefoot. His feet smelled of grass and there were nettle blisters all over his body. Now I am sure he washes his hands and feet with European soap and smells like foreign people.

"My older son smelled like an adult from the moment he was born. He had a grownup's sweaty scent. My husband said, 'This boy is wicked. I can tell from his smell.' I said, 'It's God's will and wisdom. Not everyone has to smell like a rose. We all have our own scent. Cats and dogs don't smell nice, but there is no mischief in them. Chickens stink, but they are poor innocent creatures.' My husband said, 'This boy has a rotten brain. The foul smell isn't from his feet, it's from his head.' What can I say? To me, he smells like rose water. Well, I love him; I can't help it. They told Majnoon that his beloved Leyli looks like a jackal. He said, 'Oh that I could give my life for her jackal's face.' This is how love works.

"My younger son is gentle. He is going to play European music for me and I'm going to dance for him. If only you could be there to see me. He wrote, 'Mom, you're an excellent cook. We'll open up an Iranian restaurant and call it The Pomegranate Lady and Her Sons. We'll get rich. We will.'"

The plane is caught in turbulence and it jerks up and down. Mama Pomegranate likes the sudden soars and drops. She claps her hands and swings her legs.

Doesn't she know that we are hovering between heaven and earth? That if the plane crashes, we will all end up in a thousand pieces? That our lives are hanging by a thread?

"Dear lady," she says, "where can I go to answer the call of nature?"

I don't answer. My body is numb and my heart is pounding. Time has become one interminable moment. My feet are yearning painfully for terra firma.

Mama Pomegranate is desperate. She unbuckles her seatbelt and half rises. The flight attendant motions to her to sit down. Mama Pomegranate squeezes her fat thighs together.

"Sit down," I say. "Wait. You're going to fall."

She doesn't listen to me. She's in a hurry and heads off. Her shoes are still under her seat. She stumbles.

The passenger sitting behind us rushes to her aid. He is a patient young man. He grabs her by the arm and steers her forward. The plane hits an air pocket and a woman screams. Mama

Pomegranate clings to the young man with one hand, grabs onto the shoulder of a man sitting next to the aisle with the other, and she laughs. The French flight attendant has given up on the Iranian passengers and stops trying to restore order.

My eyes close. Mama Pomegranate's sons float behind my eyelids. They are cold, shivering. I call out to them. "Boys, is this the place you were searching for?" They don't answer. A layer of snow has settled on their black hair. They are leaving for another city, a city across the seas and mountains. A warm, familiar city. "Wait!" I cry. "I'm coming with you." A whistle blows. Passengers are hanging from the train's doors and out its windows. Mama Pomegranate is there, too. "Where are you all going?" she asks. No one knows.

The plane's sudden jolts wake me up. I hear Mama Pomegranate in the distance. She is pounding on the toilet door.

"Dear lady, help! Dear lady!"

The flight attendant is tired and fed up. She doesn't budge. A passenger gets up and pushes the toilet door open for Mama Pomegranate. She has washed her hands and face and water is dripping from the end of her scarf.

"What a small space," she says. "May God spare us. You'll have to excuse me, but when it comes to toilets, nothing beats our own."

The plane is leveling out. There is less turbulence. I can breathe more easily, but my body is limp and my hands are numb. I pull the blanket over my face. I won't open my eyes until the plane has come to a stop.

The plane's wheels hit the ground with a thud and Mama Pomegranate jumps up in her seat. She sees the other passengers busy gathering their belongings and quickly unbuckles her seatbelt.

"Dear lady, have we arrived?"

"Yes."

"Are we in Sweden?"

"No."

"Then where are we?"

"Paris."

The passengers are in a rush, already standing in the aisle pushing each other forward.

"Is Sweden the next stop?"

For the umpteenth time I explain that she has to get off and change planes. "Oh my God!" she exclaims. "I don't know how. I can't read or write. I don't understand their language."

"Show them your ticket," I tell her. "They will guide you."

"Show who my ticket?"

"Show it to the Air France people."

"I'm not getting off. I won't. What if I'm left behind? I might get lost."

"Come," I say. "I'll show you."

"Dear lady," she pleads, "I'd give my life for you. Come with me as far as Sweden."

Tears well up in her eyes. She lowers her head and starts to mumble to herself.

"Get up, Pomegranate Lady. Don't be scared. You won't get lost. I'll find someone to help you; someone better than me." She hesitates, but there is nothing she can do.

"Trust in God," she says. "Perhaps my sons are waiting for me right here."

"Perhaps."

Her feet are swollen and she can't put her shoes back on. She tucks them under her arm and gets up. She groans. Her knees are stiff.

"If it wasn't for the sake of my boys, I would have never left home," she says. "Our own Yazd is heaven. What a pity. The revolution is for city people. It has nothing to do with us. Mashdi Akbar's son went to the city and became a Revolutionary Guard. He's not a bad boy. I told my sons to stay at home and help me in my old age, but they wouldn't listen."

The cabin crew is standing in line at the exit door. Mama Pomegranate says something to the French flight attendant. She tries to kiss her on the cheeks, but she is too short. The flight attendant laughs and shakes her hand instead.

A long corridor stretches ahead of us.

"Is Sweden very far from here?" she asks.

I take her bag. It's too heavy for me. I hand it back to her.

"Look here," I say. "Now you have to go that way and I have to go this way." I point to two airline employees and add, "Show your ticket to those two ladies and ask them to help you."

She looks at me perplexed. She wasn't expecting such an abrupt parting. She grabs hold of my coat.

"Mama Pomegranate, I wish you a safe journey," I say. "Save a plateful of your eggplant stew and steamed rice for me."

"How am I going to make myself understood? I don't speak their language."

"Just show them your ticket."

"What should I tell them?"

"Just say Sweden."

She stares at her ticket and repeats, "Sweden, Sweden."

"Dear lady!" she calls after me.

I keep walking. I don't look back. The flight was long and exhausting. I'm happy to be walking on solid ground. The Iranian passengers are all running and trying to get ahead of each other.

Mama Pomegranate is still in the back of my mind. Did she go or didn't she?

Most of the passengers have reached the passport control section ahead of me. There is a long line. The line to the left is for European citizens. The line to the right is for foreigners—Arabs, Iranians, Africans, Asians, and so on. Someone taps me on the shoulder. It's a man I don't know.

"Excuse me," he says. "The old lady who was sitting next to you is still back there. She's sitting on the floor. She can't walk. She's asking for you."

"I'm in a hurry. Isn't there anyone else who can help her?"

"She's asking for you. She doesn't speak French or English. She's afraid of strangers."

Oh God. I go back and look toward the end of the corridor. Mama Pomegranate is right where I left her. All alone, she's sitting on the floor, clutching her bag to her chest. People are rushing past her. She sees me and screams with joy. Her face lights up. She crawls toward me on all fours.

"Dear lady, forgive me. I'd give my life for you. My legs are frozen stiff. I can't walk. I said, 'Sweden, Sweden,' to several people, but no one gave a damn."

A woman in a wheelchair passes by. Mama Pomegranate looks at her with envy.

"Dear lady, find me one of those chairs."

"Okay, okay. You sit tight; I'll be right back."

I quibble with the Air France people. I beg. It's no use. All the wheelchairs have been reserved in advance. I have to file a request and wait several days.

"But this woman is from a village in Iran," I explain (a pointless explanation), "and her legs are frozen stiff. She can't walk."

They sympathize, but there are rules and regulations that must be observed. We should have requested a wheelchair ahead of time. There is nothing they can do.

But what am I to do? Abandon her? No, I can't. I see a baggage trolley. A trolley with open front and sides. It's easy for someone to ride on it. I run. Mama Pomegranate is sitting in the middle of the corridor with her legs spread wide open and her shoes in her hands. People walk past her indifferently. I put her bag on the trolley.

"Get up, Mama Pomegranate," I tell her. "Come and sit on the trolley."

Shocked, she looks at me and says, "Oh no, dear lady!" And she starts to giggle.

"Stop 'ladying' me! Come on, up you get."

"O Imam Ali, help me."

Reluctantly, she agrees. She's embarrassed and looks at the people around us.

"You want me to sit on this trolley?" she asks.

"Yes, on your feet now. I have things to do. I'm late."

She gets flustered. She blushes and tears well up in her eyes.

"It's embarrassing," she says. "People will laugh at me."

"Dear Mama, nobody knows you here. And in the West, nothing is embarrassing. Get a move on."

Her legs are sore. I help her. She groans. She struggles to stand, falls, half rises, and finally, with her hands pressing down on her knees and her back to the trolley, she manages to lift herself up.

"Now, sit down," I say, and push down on her shoulders.

She mutters an "Oh dear lady" and sits down. She is heavy. The trolley rolls sideways and crashes into the wall. The passersby laugh. Mama Pomegranate covers her face with the loose end of her scarf.

Steering the trolley, with all that weight on it, isn't easy. It swings and rolls from side to side. With her heels digging into the floor, Mama Pomegranate helps us move forward. A man comes over to help. We both hold on to the trolley's handle and push Mama Pomegranate forward.

"O sons of mine," she says, "if only you could see the state I'm in."

I take her ticket and look at it. Gothenburg. My knowledge of geography is rather limited. I gather Gothenburg is a city in Sweden. Where in Sweden? I don't know. But that is where the sons are waiting for their mother. I ask airport personnel for directions. She has to go to Terminal B. In other words, to the other end of the airport. It's a good ten minutes away, by bus.

Mama Pomegranate looks up and listens. Her eyes are glued to my face. The bus stop is quite far.

I'm still holding her ticket. I read it carefully. The Paris-Gothenburg flight is in an hour. There isn't much time left. Using every ounce of my energy, I push the trolley forward with Mama Pomegranate sitting on it like a big bundle of bedclothes. We reach the end of the hallway and turn. There is an escalator in front of us. Wondering what to do, I stop.

Mama Pomegranate is startled. Her eyes grow wide.

"Oh dear lady, the stairs are moving. I'm staying put. Let's find another way. Let's go that way; there are proper stairs, like our own. I won't go this way. I'll fall and die."

"Oh stop fussing and keep quiet. Otherwise, I'll leave you right here and go."

I'm exhausted and I've run out of patience.

"Mama, what in the world are you going to Sweden for?" I snap. "You will be miserable. You will die of sorrow." I'm angry and I don't know who to blame.

"I will carry your bag," I say. "Now get off the trolley. Come on."
I take her arm and help her. She groans. She can't straighten her knees. She gets off the trolley and leans against the wall. I grab her bag and go down the escalator. She watches me from her perch. She is holding on to the wall and staring at me and the moving escalator with horror. Once or twice she musters the courage to take a few steps forward. She lifts one leg up and then shakes her head and recoils. I'm sure she will tumble down headfirst.

"Mama Pomegranate," I say. "Just sit down on the first step and come down sitting."

"Oh dear lady! Oh my God! What am I to do? I can't do this. My sons said Sweden was just on the other side of the city gates. They said getting there was easier than going to Mashad. They said, 'Just get on a plane and you'll be here in no time.'"

I'm trying to think of a solution when I see two tall men trying to get on the escalator, but Mama Pomegranate is blocking their way. They say something to her that she doesn't understand and they say something to me in a language that I don't understand. Then they gently push Mama Pomegranate to one side, but they still can't get through. They exchange a few words with each other, point to me, and before I can explain, they grab Mama Pomegranate under the arms and lift her up. She screams and laughs and oohs and aahs. She is tickled. She wiggles around and drops her shoes. They are black, with small metallic bows on them. She swings her short, chubby legs in the air and clings to the two men. Holding her up isn't easy. For a moment, I'm afraid the three of them will tumble headfirst down the escalator. I close my eyes. But they arrive safely and the men, laughing, deposit the old lady next to me. I fetch her shoes which are now on the floor at the bottom of the escalator. It takes Mama Pomegranate a while to catch her breath. Sweat is streaming down her face. Her headscarf is awry and a lock of her hair, half-gray and half-henna red, has escaped from under it.

"The village elder said, 'Mama Pomegranate, you will have to cross seven mountains and seven seas,'" she says. "But he didn't know that I would have to ride on a trolley and get piggybacks from strange men."

The trolley is still at the top of the escalator. We hobble toward the exit. A porter is standing idly by, watching us. I call him over. In exchange for a fee, he agrees to take Mama Pomegranate as far as the bus stop and to help her onto her bus. I explain, "Terminal B." He knows.

"Pomegranate Lady, we have to part ways," I tell her. "This gentleman will take you to the bus and he will tell the driver where to let you off. Don't worry, they are good people."

"What about you?" she asks.

"I have to be on my way."

"Dear lady!"

"Go. Godspeed."

Her eyes fill with tears. She takes my hand and kisses me three or four times on the cheeks. She opens her bag and takes out a pomegranate and offers it to me.

The pomegranate of love.

"I wish you were coming to Sweden," she says. "We would all be together. You could taste my cooking. My sons are both really lovely. You wouldn't believe how good and kind they are. I swear to the Holy City of Mecca, I'm telling the truth." She wants to point toward Mecca, but she doesn't know which direction it is.

"Perhaps another time," I say.

"There won't be another time. For me, today is the day."

The porter is waiting for her. He is a friendly-looking African man. Mama Pomegranate stares at him for a moment. Then she hands him her bag, puts her arm around his, and walks away with slow, measured steps; just like an ant. Finally, she turns around and looks at me with the kindest eyes in the world.

I'm holding her pomegranate.

I have to find my luggage. An hour has passed and my fellow passengers have all left. My suitcases have been put in storage. Exhaustion and hunger have made me agitated.

The Air France agent calls someone on the telephone and then he tells me that I have to wait a few minutes. A few minutes turn into half an hour. An hour. An eternity. I sit and wait.

I think of the Pomegranate Lady. I tell myself that she has already arrived in Gothenburg and is busy cooking. Her sons will buy her new clothes and they will replace her big, thick head-scarf with a delicate chiffon one. They will take her out to see the sights, the city square, the movies, the seashore, the zoo.

Tonight, after ten years, she will lay her head on her older son's smelly feet and she will sleep blissfully. More blissfully than ever before.

IT'S WEDNESDAY AFTERNOON. I've been back for three days. I have unpacked my suitcases and I'm putting aside my Islamic coverall to take to the dry cleaners. I empty its pockets. Two hundred-tuman bills, a pack of chewing gum, a folded piece of paper, a bank receipt, and an airline ticket.

An airline ticket?

Tehran-Paris-Gothenburg. Sunday, September 29.

Sunday, September 29.

Paris-Gothenburg.

Anar-Banu Chenari.

Gothenburg.

Sunday, September 29.

I am dumbfounded, flabbergasted. It's not possible. The Pomegranate Lady left. I saw her get on the airport bus with my own eyes.

I put the ticket facedown on the table. I don't want to look at it. I don't even want to think about it. My mouth tastes bitter. An excruciating pain churns in my stomach. My eyes are glued to the damned ticket.

"Lady with your head in the clouds, look to make sure you have everything," I told her.

She looked and she clasped her bag to her chest. She was holding her passport.

But her ticket? I had her ticket. I must have put it in my pocket, idiot that I am. Such a scatterbrain. I must find her. But how? Where?

Oh, I wish I had not helped her. I wish I had not run into her. I wish she had met somebody else.

Oh, I don't know. It's my fault. It's her sons' fault. It's that damned mailman's fault who delivered her son's letter. I will go to Sweden. I will go to Gothenburg. I will go to Yazd. I will find her.

"I just want to see my sons," she said. "I want to hold them and kiss them a hundred times. And then I can lay my head down and die happy."

I call Air France. The line is busy. I dial again, and again, and again. The same busy signal. Then the call goes through, but no one answers. There's music playing, and then a pre-recorded tape tells me, "Please hold, someone will take your call shortly." Shortly means a lifetime. An eternity. I feel as if my heart is being wrenched out of my chest. I hang up.

I call the airport. This time someone answers. I ask for the list of passengers on the Paris-Gothenburg flight that departed at 1:00 p.m. on September 29. Silence. The world's longest silence. Ten minutes. Have I been cut off?

"Hello! *Helloooo!*" I shout.

There is someone on the line. They don't have the list, and even if they did, they couldn't give me any information. I beg and plead. I explain that an old Iranian lady named Anar-Banu Chenari is missing.

"I have her ticket. She was traveling from Tehran to Gothenburg, Sweden. Hello?"

The connection keeps breaking up. Now someone else is on the phone. I start explaining all over again. There is no one by that name on the passenger list.

I call the Embassy of the Islamic Republic in Paris. They promise to help. They will make inquiries, but their administration offices are closed for three days. I call the embassy in Stockholm. "No," they say. "No such lady has contacted us." I call a friend in Stockholm and beg her to find out if two young men by the name of Chenari or Anari live in Gothenburg. Two young men from Yazd—one is a singer with long, bleached-blond hair and the other one has dark eyes and dark hair and he is hot-tempered and angry.

And I wait. Perhaps the Pomegranate Lady will try to find my telephone number through the Paris phone directory. But how? In what language?

Friday, Saturday, Sunday, Monday, Tuesday.

A week.

A month.

And then.

Her pomegranate is sitting on my bedside table. The pomegranate of love, remember? I have asked myself a thousand times, Where is she? What is she doing? I can think of a thousand things, good and bad. Today is one of those bright, happy days; one of those rare days when invisible birds chirp behind the window, the cranky neighbor walks by whistling happily, and the concierge has gotten up on the right side of bed and greets the old mailman with a smile. I take the bird's chirping and the unexpected blue sky as a good omen and I tell myself that the Pomegranate Lady is now sitting cozily by her sons. She has cooked *fesenjān* with chicken and pomegranate molasses and she is well rested after her long journey.

I tell myself that one day, one good and happy day, I will return and I will buy a house with a small garden that faces the sun and has a view of the mountains. I will plant the seeds of the good lady's pomegranate and I will divide its fruit among the people in the neighborhood. Those who taste the pomegranate of love will know that they are brothers and sisters. Whenever their eyes meet, their hearts will fill with joy and their soul will find peace. And it will all be because of a hundred-year-old pomegranate lady who is sleeping so peacefully under her pomegranate tree that no one has the heart to wake her up. Her younger son has composed a beautiful song for her; lovesick pomegranate-sellers hum it all the time. The older son has two dark-eyed, chubby daughters who look like their grandmother and he has forgotten all about revenge. The European bride is happy. Every night, before going to sleep, she repeats the word *aash* (soup) under her breath like a miracle prayer and she sleeps soundly.

I'm sure wherever she is, asleep or awake, the Pomegranate Lady is thinking about her long journey, about fastening that seat belt, about getting tickled, about riding on the luggage trolley and being hoisted by two strangers, about losing her airline ticket, and about me.

Sometimes I see her in my dreams and hear her voice from far away.

"Dear lady, I received a letter from my sons. They feel all alone and abandoned in America, too. Again, they're thinking of moving to someplace else. Where to this time?"

"Pomegranate Lady," I say, "don't worry. There are many people like them. They feel they are strangers no matter where they go. They are always restless. One day your sons will come back. They will be happy. They will lie down in the shade of the pomegranate trees and doze off. And once again, they will be bitten by the bug and off they will go, over the mountains and across the deserts. Well, going away and coming back is another way to live."

"What is wrong with our own Yazd?" she says.

"Pomegranate Lady, go to sleep and let me catch my forty winks."

She murmurs under her breath. I can no longer hear her. Her image slowly fades away in the hazy realm of sleep.

—originally translated in collaboration with Karim Emami

ACKNOWLEDGMENTS

I am deeply indebted to my editor Alane Salierno Mason for her tremendous kindness and enthusiasm. This book would not have been possible without her support. Sincere thanks are due to my translator Sara Khalili for her competence and punctuality. My deep gratitude goes to Mahnaz Afkhami for her friendship and genuine willingness to promote my work, to Azar Nafisi for her invaluable trust in my writings and our mutual love for Nabokov, to Y. Z. Kami for being the first reader and critic of my stories, and to my son Farhad and my daughter Leyli for making my life meaningful.

"Encounter," "The Pomegranate Lady and Her Sons," and "The Neighbor" originally appeared in different translation in *Words Without Borders.* "Unfinished Game" appeared in *Words Without Borders: The World Through the Eyes of Writers: An Anthology.* "Gentleman Thief"" appeared in different translation in *Boston Review.* "In Another Place" appeared in *Strange Times, My Dear: The PEN Anthology of Contemporary Iranian Literature.* "The Great Lady of My Soul" appeared in *Tablet and Pen: Literary Landscapes from the Modern Middle East*, ed. Reza Aslan.

GOLI TARAGHI (b. 1939 in Tehran) has been honored as a Chevalier des Arts et des Lettres in France and won the Bita Prize for Literature and Freedon given by Stanford University in 2009. She earned an undergraduate degree in philosophy in the United States and returned to Tehran to study and work in international relations and, later, to teach philosophy. Most of her work has been published in France and, though frequently censored in Iran, circulates widely there and internationally. Her stories have been included in various anthologies, including Reza Aslan's *Tablet & Pen: Literary Landscapes from the Modern Middle East* (Norton, 2011); *Words without Borders: The World through the Eyes of Writers* (Anchor: 2007); and Nahid Mozaffari's *Strange Times, My Dear: The PEN Anthology of Contemporary Iranian Literature* (Arcade, 2005). She lives in Paris.

SARA KHALILI's translations include *Censoring an Iranian Love Story* by Shahriar Mandanipour, *The Book of Fate* by Parinoush Saniee, and *Kissing the Sword: A Prison Memoir* by Shahrnush Parsipur. She has also translated several volumes of poetry by Forough Farrokhzad, Simin Behbahani, Siavash Kasraii, and Fereydoon Moshiri. She lives in New York.